Adventures
IN
South America

Adventures

IN

South America

BY
JEANETTE WINDLE

MULTNOMAH YOUTH
SISTERS, OREGON

ADVENTURES IN SOUTH AMERICA

published by Multnomah Youth
a part of the Questar publishing family

© 1994 by Jeanette Windle
International Standard Book Number: 0-88070-647-3

Cover illustration by David Slonim

Printed in the United States of America

For information:
QUESTAR PUBLISHERS, INC.
POST OFFICE BOX 1720
SISTERS, OREGON 97759

94 95 96 97 98 99 00 01 02 — 10 9 8 7 6 5 4 3 2 1

BOOK ONE

Cave of the Inca Re

BOOK TWO

Jungle Hideout

BOOK THREE

Captured in Colombia

TO MELODY HOBBS,

my first and most loyal fan.

BOOK ONE

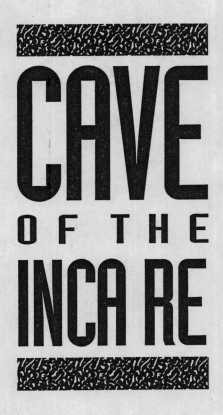

CAVE
OF THE
INCA RE

A Desperate Decision

Glistening white in the silver light of a full moon, the massive stone walls of the ancient Indian city loomed ahead of the running children. Shouts of anger behind them told the pair that their escape had been discovered. Feeling like their lungs would burst, the two panting children ran along the outer wall of the main temple complex.

Pulling his sister to a halt at the foot of a narrow stone staircase, Justin peered around the crumbling blocks of stone carved by Inca craftsmen centuries ago. He jumped back as he caught sight of two shadowy figures running along the high wire fence that encircled the complex.

The clang of a metal-tipped boot echoed across the rough ground as one of the figures, a bulky outline against the shimmering dust of the stars, stumbled and fell against a dark boulder. Cursing, he jumped to his feet. A moment later, a bright finger of light from an electric lantern probed the darkness behind the children.

"Come on, Jenny!" Justin hissed. He pushed his sister up the narrow steps that opened onto a vast courtyard. Dodging among the giant stone figures—tokens of long-past conquered nations—that dotted the open courtyard, the two children made their way toward the main entrance.

Suddenly both children startled with fear as a strangely high, thin voice echoed, seemingly inches away. Then they relaxed as they remembered the stone "loudspeaker" across the court where Inca priests had addressed the crowds that once filled this temple. Hidden behind a featureless granite figure, the children looked up anxiously at the wide-open grass strip that lay between them and safety.

A wispy cloud skittered across the face of the pale-gold ball above them. Taking advantage of the sudden shadow, Justin grabbed his sister's hand and yanked her across the open ground, and then through a wide, crumbled opening that had once been a door.

It was not a *real* door; it was just two weathered granite blocks on either side of a wide opening. A third stone block balanced on top of the other two to form a square entryway. Here, feather-caped warriors glistening with gold ornaments had guarded the temple hundreds of years ago.

A sudden cold beam of light told them their pursuers were again close behind. Holding hands, the two children sprinted for open fields beyond the courtyard, but Jenny stumbled and fell, her sudden cry alerting the men behind them. They froze for a moment, hoping no one had heard Jenny's cry. But seconds later they heard running feet.

Justin pulled Jenny to her feet. Reluctantly turning away from the open fields, the two children jumped over a shallow ditch the short rainy season had dug in the sandy soil. A solitary, evenly shaped hill lay before them. When they reached the base of the mound, no one was in sight. "I think we can slow down now," Justin wheezed.

But just as he spoke, a large, bulky figure rose from behind a jumbled pile of stone blocks only yards away. The white-gold rays of the full moon showed a cruel face smiling triumphantly.

"We've got you now," their massive pursuer gloated hoarsely. Justin glanced back toward the ruins. A short, skinny man walked unhurriedly toward the pair cowering against the hillside.

Justin tapped his sister on the shoulder. "Come on!" he whispered. Taking their would-be captors by surprise, the two children turned and quickly climbed the steep side of the mound. The two men went after them with hoarse, angry shouts, but the children had the head start they needed.

Above them, a large opening in the face of the hill had been sealed shut with cement bricks. Heavy boulders had been piled against the bricks as added insurance against intruders, but at one side a dark, ragged-looking area above the heaped-up boulders showed where a few bricks had crumbled away. Justin scrambled toward that spot.

Realizing where he was going, Jenny hesitated. "We can't go in there! We'll be killed!"

Justin was already squeezing through the small opening. "Yes, we can. God will protect us. Besides, there's nowhere else to go!"

He pulled his sister through the narrow hole, and the two of them backed into the darkness as a long arm reached in and groped for them. The men swore loudly. The opening was too small for either of them. They kicked against the bricks, but the solid wall resisted their kicking and pounding.

Jenny and Justin leaned against the stone wall of the cave, their chests on fire from the violent exercise. They hugged their thin jackets close to ward off the intense cold, and Justin remembered that this plateau sat at thirteen thousand feet—well over two miles above sea level. When they had climbed down from the airplane only a few days ago, they had gasped for breath after simply walking across the airport.

It was now quiet outside. The cave was pitch black, except for the faint moon-glow that shone through the opening. Anything could be hiding in that blackness, they knew. His arm around Jenny, Justin shut his eyes and tried to think.

How in the world did we get into this mess? he wondered desperately.

CHAPTER ONE

An Unexpected Visitor

A sudden bang echoed through the one-story, cream-colored house as the kitchen door slammed hard. Mrs. Parker glanced up from the head of lettuce she was washing, frowning at the noise. "Justin Parker!"

The tall, husky thirteen-year-old flushed to the roots of his short-cropped red hair, and turned to shut the door again—more quietly this time. He knew his mother's strict rule against slamming doors. He paused a moment to breathe in the sweet, spicy fragrance coming from the oven, then threw a well-worn bat and baseball glove into the corner by the door. Tossing an equally well-used baseball up and down in one hand, he joined his mother at the sink.

"Mom!" he growled, his eyes stormy with annoyance, "you've got to keep Jenny out of my hair!"

Mrs. Parker moved to a wide work island in the center of the kitchen. Before she could answer, the door slammed again. A slim girl rushed into the kitchen. She too carried a baseball glove. Tossing it after her brother's, she leaned on the counter and pushed back heavy, dark curls that were slightly damp from running. Her golden eyes flashed fire.

"Mom, you've got to stop Justin from being so mean to me!"

Reaching for a small knife, Mrs. Parker, an older version of Jenny, calmly began slicing a tomato into a large wooden salad bowl. She didn't seem at all surprised at the storm.

"Why, I thought you two were the best of friends today. What happened?"

Before Jenny could open her mouth, Justin complained, "It's Jenny, Mom! You've got to keep her away when I'm playing ball with the boys. It's embarrassing! None of the other guys' sisters tag along!"

Jenny lifted an unapologetic chin and said huffily, "You know I can play better than any of them!"

There was truth in her words. Only a few minutes younger than Justin, his twin sister, Jenny, was as tall as he and a forward on her seventh-grade basketball team. She loved sports as much as she did books. Though in looks so much like her easygoing mother, Jenny seemed to move through life at a gallop.

At the moment, her height ran to long, slim arms and legs, but Jenny didn't have the awkwardness of many lanky girls. As she had said, she could beat most of the boys in the neighborhood in a foot-race or a baseball game.

Justin provided a good balance to the up-and-down moods of his sister. Calm and even-tempered most of the time, a stubborn streak kept him from being pushed around. His steady, hazel eyes noticed everything that went on around him, and he liked to think things through before talking.

Jenny, on the other hand, let everyone know exactly what she was thinking. "Justin used to like playing ball with me," she continued, now in a sadder tone.

"That was different!" Justin replied with exasperation. "The guys don't like girls hanging around during a ball

game! I get teased about having Jenny along. You understand, don't you, Mom?"

Mrs. Parker sighed and laid her chopping knife beside
the wooden salad bowl. Putting an arm around her angry
daughter's shoulders, she said, "Jenny, there are times when
boys like to play on their own without girls. You wouldn't
like Justin tagging along all the time when you're playing
with your girl friends, would you?"

"But that's the problem, Mom!" Sudden tears brimmed
in Jenny's golden-brown eyes. "I don't *have* any girl friends
now that school is out. There aren't any girls my age in the
neighborhood—just boys! The only time I see my friends is in
Sunday school. I get so bored playing by myself all the time
while Justin is out having fun with the boys. It's not fair! Why
should they mind me playing?"

Mrs. Parker cracked the door of the oven and inspected
its contents, then lifted two pies onto the counter.

"Jenny, I'm sorry you don't have any friends close by, but
you need to be more understanding of your brother. Let him
spend some time alone with his friends. As for you, Justin,
try to be more patient with your sister. It's hard for her this
summer."

Her stern eye caught theirs, and they reluctantly nodded
their heads. Glancing at his sister, a grin hovered on the corner of Justin's mouth. Being twins, Justin and Jenny had
always been the best of friends.

"I have to admit, she really is the best catcher in the
neighborhood, Mom." The grin spread across his freckled
face. "You should have seen her! She grabbed a pop fly ball
and got Danny Olson out just as he slid into home plate. I
guess that's why the guys were so mad. If she'd miss occasionally, they'd think she was okay."

An answering smile banished the tears from Jenny's eyes.

"I'm sorry I teased you so much," she told her brother sincerely.

"Yeah, well, I'm sorry I yelled," Justin growled back. Apologies embarrassed him. "I don't mind you playing with us, but…the guys don't see it that way. Hey, the game's probably over by now anyway. Want to play catch until supper?"

Harmony restored, Justin gave his mother a hard hug, then collected his baseball equipment. Jenny added a quick kiss, then picked up her glove from the corner. Leaning over her mother's shoulder, she sniffed and inspected the two pies, oozing dark-red through slits in the top crust.

"Ummm, cherry pie! What's the special occasion, Mom?"

"Oh, didn't I mention it?" her mother answered. "We're having company for supper."

"Company? Who is it, Mom?"

Mrs. Parker swatted Justin's fingers with a pot holder as he reached for a dangling edge of golden crust. "I thought I'd keep that a secret for now," she said with a straight face.

"Aw, Mom!" the twins groaned in unison. "Come on, tell us!" Jenny added.

Their mother gave an exaggerated sigh. She knew she would have no peace until she told them, but she enjoyed teasing her two lively children once in a while. "Okay, I'll give you one hint. Your father just left for SeaTac airport."

"Uncle Pete!" the two chorused.

Seeing the smile that crept into her mother's eyes in spite of her attempts to look innocent, Jenny threw her arms around her mom. "We're right, aren't we?" she asked. Mrs. Parker nodded. "Yippee!"

Pete Parker, their father's brother, was Justin and Jenny's favorite uncle. A widower with no children, he was an executive of a large oil company, Triton Oil. He spent much of his time jetting around the world, troubleshooting for the company in different countries. Whenever he had free time, often at an hour's notice, he would fly into Seattle where his brother Ron worked as a computer analyst for Boeing.

The children were used to Uncle Pete's sudden appearances, and had a large collection of "treasures" he had brought them from all corners of the world. Like the twins' parents, Uncle Pete was a dedicated Christian. His special interest was missions, and he often visited missionaries in different countries while he was there on business. Jenny and Justin loved the stories he told of the strange and wonderful things that happened when these missionaries told people about Jesus.

Mrs. Parker smiled at her children's exuberance. "Okay, kids, you got what you wanted. Now get on out of here and give me some peace and quiet! Jenny, I need to have you back here in half an hour to set the table. Justin, it's your turn to do dishes.

"And put away your junk when you're done with it," she called out the screen door to their rapidly retreating backs. "I don't want to find it all over the yard!"

Justin had just scrambled over the fence to recover a missed ball when he heard the distinct rumble of his father's station wagon.

"Come on, Jenny. They're here!" he shouted, vaulting back over the fence. He tossed the ball and glove onto the front steps, but remembering his mother's plea, he picked them up again. Together they quickly stored the baseball equipment in its proper place in the garage.

By the time they had finished, their father had already pulled their dark-green station wagon into the garage and was stepping out of the driver's seat. Jenny threw herself into her tall, lanky father's arms. Upon meeting Mr. Parker, it was obvious to people how Justin came to have red hair and hazel eyes!

Ron Parker enthusiastically lifted his daughter from the

floor and whirled her around. If Justin had inherited his coloring, it was Jenny who shared his outgoing personality.

"Hey, don't I get a hug, too?" Like his brother, Uncle Pete was tall and red-headed, but he was much broader. A full red beard made him look like a youthful Santa Claus. Slapping his well-rounded front, he liked to blame his size on the hospitality he couldn't refuse in the many countries he visited.

After greeting his nephew and niece, Uncle Pete reached into the back seat and pulled out the one small suitcase that was all he ever carried. "Something smells mighty good in your mother's kitchen," he declared. "Let's go eat, kids. I'm starved!"

▼▼▼

Gathered around the dining table, the family shared all that had happened since Uncle Pete's last visit three months earlier. Uncle Pete held out his plate for a second piece of cherry pie and leaned back in his chair.

"Helen, I haven't eaten so well since the last time I was here," he boomed.

The twins had been reasonably quiet during supper while the adults visited. Now they moved restlessly in their chairs. Jenny, who never hesitated to ask questions, burst out, "Do you have any new stories, Uncle Pete?"

"Yeah, where did you go this trip?" Justin added eagerly.

Uncle Pete's eyes twinkled at the impatient pair as he settled more comfortably into his chair. "As a matter of fact, I haven't been anywhere special since my last visit."

His red beard split in a smile at their disappointed look. "But I do have one little story that might interest you. What can you two tell me about the Incas?"

"Weren't they an ancient empire in South America?" Justin responded thoughtfully.

"Yeah, they built lots of stone cities. There was a picture

in our history book last year of that secret stone city up in the mountains," Jenny added.

"Very good! You're both right. The city you're talking about, Jenny, is Machu-Pichu in Peru. In fact, a thousand years ago the Inca had one of the most advanced civilizations in the world. They governed from a high plateau in the Andes mountains around Lake Titicaca, the highest navigable lake in the world. Their empire spread over most of Bolivia, Ecuador, and Peru."

Uncle Pete stopped for a bite of cherry pie. Waving his fork, he continued: "The Inca were most famous for their stone cities and roads—all carved out by hand. Even today's technology can't beat their stone work, and a lot of their roads are still being used.

"But the Inca wasn't the first empire in South America. They took over from another great civilization—one that lasted three thousand years. Tiawanaku, the ruins of that civilization, still lies across Lake Titicaca, in the country of Bolivia."

He looked keenly at his nephew and niece. "Can you tell me what finally happened to the Inca?"

"Didn't Pizarro and just a couple of hundred Spanish soldiers defeat them?" asked Justin. "As I remember, they tricked them and captured their king, and the whole nation just gave up. It seems pretty cowardly to give in to two hundred men!"

"Well, that's what your history books may tell you, but it isn't the whole story. The Inca had a very advanced civilization but also a very cruel one. They conquered hundreds of smaller tribes around them and practiced human sacrifice with their enemies. Everyone but the Inca overlords were turned into slaves.

"When the Spanish arrived, these slave tribes rose up to fight beside them, hoping to win freedom from the Inca. So Pizarro didn't only have two hundred soldiers, he also had thousands of Indian rebels fighting with him. And he had cannon and gun powder, something the Inca had never seen."

"So what happened to the Inca after that?" Justin inquired.

"Their descendants are still there and so are the ruins of their empire. Imagine yourselves, kids, in the capital of Bolivia—the cold winds whistling through the stone walls of Tiawanaku...reed boats dancing across the waves of Lake Titicaca to ruined palaces of ancient Inca princes..."

Mrs. Parker, glancing in amusement at her spellbound children, interrupted, "I take it you are visiting Bolivia soon?"

"You guessed it! Triton Oil has several offices in the country, and I'll be checking out a bit of trouble at the head office in La Paz. I have some friends in the city, the Evanses. They are a young missionary couple who work with the Quechua Indians, Bolivia's biggest ethnic group. The Quechua are direct descendants of the ancient Inca.

"My business in La Paz should only take a few hours, but I have some vacation time built up. I've been writing my friends in La Paz, and they've talked me into staying in Bolivia a couple of weeks for a real vacation."

"Boy, don't I wish I could go!" Justin exclaimed enviously. "I'm going to have a job just like yours someday, Uncle Pete, so I can see the world the way you do."

Jenny sighed. "It sounds so exciting. You'll take lots of pictures, won't you, Uncle Pete, especially of the Inca ruins? I'd love to see what they look like."

Uncle Pete grinned, looking suddenly like Justin when he was planning some mischief. "Well, as a matter of fact..." He glanced across the table at his brother, who mirrored his grin.

"Actually, I thought maybe you'd like to take your own pictures."

Jenny and Justin froze in their seats. "Do you mean?" they burst out in unison.

Uncle Pete looked apologetically at Mrs. Parker. "I hadn't meant to say anything until I had a chance to talk to you, Helen. Ron wrote that you wouldn't be able to take a family vacation this summer—with that big project Boeing is working on. With the kids out of school, I thought maybe they'd like to come along with me."

Mrs. Parker frowned, and Justin held his breath. He knew his mother didn't like surprises—and the two Parker men had a habit of springing surprises on her.

"I talked the idea over with Ron on the way here from the airport. He said he'd leave it up to you. It would be an educational experience for the children, and I'd really enjoy their company…"

"You don't know what kind of trouble these two can think up!" she protested. "Besides, they're too young to be traveling alone."

"They wouldn't be alone! I'd keep a good eye on them," Uncle Pete promised.

"I don't know…" Mrs. Parker said, still frowning. "This is a little sudden. I'll have to talk it over with Ron." She made the mistake of looking up into a circle of pleading eyes, and her expression softened.

"Well, I don't suppose anything can happen to them with you along, Pete." Justin slowly let out his breath as his mother continued, "This *is* quite an opportunity. If you kids will promise to be careful and do everything your uncle tells you…"

She never got a chance to finish her sentence because Jenny was out of her chair and dancing around the table. Even Justin was quivering with excitement.

"Thanks, Mom! You won't be sorry!" Justin said. Jenny exuberantly hugged first her mother, then Uncle Pete, and finally her father. Whirling around the room, she chanted, "We're going to Bolivia! We're going to Bolivia!"

"Well, kids," Uncle Pete said in an amused tone, "I take it you're willing to come?" Their shining eyes alone would have been answer enough.

"Okay, Jenny, let's sit down," Uncle Pete commanded. As he pulled out a small notebook from his breast pocket, the twins were reminded that their favorite uncle was also a very capable business executive.

"We will be leaving three weeks from Saturday. In that time we'll need to get your passports, contact the nearest Bolivian consulate, and make travel reservations."

He fastened a stern eye on both children. "I'm allowing you only one suitcase apiece. You'll need warm clothing as well as a few lighter outfits. Bolivia lies south of the equator and, if you remember your geography, it's in the middle of winter right now. It isn't as cold as our northern winters, but it can get pretty chilly—especially since the buildings are unheated.

"Now I'm sure you've had all your vaccinations, but you'll need a few extra shots for traveling—yellow fever, typhoid, malaria…"

Jenny poked Justin in the ribs and whispered, "Did you hear that? Yuck! I can't stand shots!"

But Justin was listening with only half an ear. He was seeing visions of ancient golden cities; of haughty Indian warriors marching across a vast, brown plateau, bronze-tipped spears glittering under a deep-blue sky; of thousands of half-naked slaves hauling on giant blocks of granite, groaning under the cruel whip of their Inca overseer.

I'm not dreaming! he thought to himself in awe. *I'm really going. You, Justin Parker, are actually going to see the land of the mighty Incas!*

CHAPTER TWO

Land of the Incas

His nose pressed to the round window of the Boeing 727, Justin watched the barren landscape roll away beneath him. They had been traveling since early morning and were now nearing their destination.

Only an occasional hint of green showed in the valleys nestled far below between rugged, dusty peaks. Here and there Justin could pick out a few crude houses, the same mud-brown as the land around them. The peaks of the Andes mountains didn't seem as high as he expected, until he remembered that even the valleys were 10,000 feet or more above sea level.

Above him a light blinked, commanding in Spanish, "Abroche tu cinturòn." Below it, another light spelled out, "Fasten your seat belt."

As he snapped his seat belt shut, the plane began to shake. His ears popped as they started to lose altitude. Jenny, sitting in the seat next to Justin's, slipped her hand into his. Neither had flown before and, though Justin would never admit it to his twin sister, he was glad to see that she looked as nervous as he felt.

As the plane circled, Jenny gasped in delight. "Look, Justin! Isn't it beautiful?"

A snowcapped mountain, stained rose and orange by the late afternoon sun, filled the horizon. Its majestic peak rose high above the smaller peaks that surrounded a vast plateau.

"That's Mount Illimani," Justin informed his sister. "Uncle Pete says it's over twenty-thousand feet high. They actually *ski* up there. Can you believe it? I wonder how they even breathe."

Justin pulled the airline travel guide out of the deep pocket on the back of the seat in front of him, and opened it to the page marked "Bolivia." Three columns down each page showed the words in English, German, and Spanish.

His eyes were caught by a picture of a warmly dressed Indian struggling up the side of a snowy mountain, using a thick rod to help guide a herd of heavily loaded llamas. He read the accompanying paragraphs:

"The 'altiplano,' or high plateau of the Andes, home of the original Inca empire, ranges from 9,000 to 16,000 feet in elevation. The international airport of La Paz, capital of Bolivia, sits at 13,500 feet above sea level. The low oxygen level at this altitude, and the lack of wind resistance, has made necessary for the landing of jets a runway four miles long.

"The charming colonial capital of La Paz ranges from 8,500 to 13,500 feet in elevation. You may find yourself suffering from shortness of breath during your stay. Walk slowly, carry little, and take it easy during the first few days of your visit."

How can a city be from eight thousand to thirteen thousand feet high? he wondered. *It must go straight uphill!*

At that moment the plane banked for a landing, and Justin discovered just how this was possible. Below, a thin gray line stretched across a flat, tan desert, ending in a group of low, isolated buildings. A control tower on one side identified these as the airport.

Beyond the high, flat plateau, the ground broke away in a sudden drop of several thousand feet. In an immense, jagged bowl, carved out of the mountains themselves, nestled the modern skyscrapers and colonial buildings of La Paz. Mud shacks clung to the steep sides of the chasm, and dusty roads, zigzagging across the face of the cliffs, climbed from the city center to the flat plateau above.

As the plane dipped into the valley, Justin clutched his armrests tightly; it seemed to him that they would fly right into the side of the gigantic crater! But the plane lifted at the last moment and circled around, lining up with the runway. Moments later they were taxiing to a stop.

Uncle Pete leaned over the seat behind them. "Put your jackets on, kids. It'll be cold."

The plane stopped half a kilometer from the airport buildings. Straggling behind the other passengers, Jenny and Justin pulled their jackets tighter as the bitter wind of the 'altiplano' hit them. They were breathing hard before they covered half the distance. Justin's shoulder bag felt as though it carried rocks, and he wished he'd followed his sister's lead and handed it over to one of the porters who met the plane.

From behind a wire fence, an excited crowd waved at the incoming passengers. Towering over the dark heads around him, a young man with blond hair waved frantically.

"There's Bob Evans, my missionary friend," Uncle Pete told the children, waving back. Moments later, they were shaking Mr. Evans' hand.

"Stay close to me," the young missionary told them. "We'll need to collect your luggage and clear customs."

As Mr. Evans led the Parkers toward the luggage area, Justin paused to watch soldiers in olive-green leisurely pace their rounds, machine guns slung casually across their backs.

Porters were already unloading the baggage, and Justin helped Uncle Pete pick their luggage off the conveyor belt. As Justin swung his own suitcase down, a large, hairy arm reached past him to grab at a duffel bag. Glancing sideways, Justin raised his eyes, then tilted his head far back to stare at the man looming beside him.

Obviously a foreigner in this country, his massive head was shaved bald except for a wide strip of dark hair that ran from just above his eyebrows to the nape of his neck. Even for his great height, the man was so wide that he might have looked fat were it not for the rock-hard muscles that bulged under the rolled-up sleeves of his jacket. Without looking down, he tossed the duffel bag over his shoulder and moved away.

Mr. Evans helped the Parkers carry their suitcases over to a series of long counters. Here, uniformed officials dug through each piece of luggage. A large German shepherd, its trainer holding tightly to its collar, sniffed at each bag. Uncle Pete lifted their own suitcases onto one of the counters.

Never shy with strangers, Jenny tugged on Mr. Evans' sleeve. "Why are they looking through our bags? And what's that dog doing?"

Smiling down at her, Mr. Evans answered pleasantly, "They're searching for *contraband*. There are always a few who try smuggling something illegal in or out! The German shepherd is a trained narcotics dogs. He can smell out cocaine or marijuana."

The dog, at that moment sniffing at a khaki-green knapsack at the next table, whined eagerly. Two soldiers closed in behind a bearded foreigner who began protesting in loud German. Justin, observing the scene with curiosity, noticed that the man who had been standing beside him at the luggage checkout was next in line.

As the customs official ripped open the knapsack with a

razor-sharp knife, Justin saw the heavy giant look around nervously, then edge past the counter, his duffel bag still over his shoulder. The customs official glanced up and snapped out an order. A short, thin man in a new, poorly fitting suit pulled at the big man's elbow.

"What do you think you're doing? We don't have anything to hide!" Justin heard him hiss in distinctly American English. The big man shrugged his massive shoulders and dropped the duffel bag on the counter.

Justin turned back to open his own suitcase. Their bags were quickly checked, and fifteen minutes later they were climbing into a red, double-cab pickup.

"Actually," Mr. Evans explained as he started the engine, "We don't have too much trouble with customs coming into Bolivia. Now, *leaving* is another story. They'll check every inch of your suitcases, inside and out."

"Why's that?" asked Justin from the back seat.

"Well, there isn't much contraband coming in. Most smuggling is going the other way. That German they picked up was probably on a through flight home from down in the lowlands. Drugs is the major item since Bolivia is a big producer of cocaine, but Indian artifacts and other valuables are also popular contraband."

▼▼▼

The pickup was now swinging down the broad, modern highway that led to the city center. Mr. Evans glanced at Uncle Pete. "You're sure you don't want us to put you up? You know you're welcome. We don't have many bedrooms, but we've got lots of floor space and sleeping bags."

"We'll do fine in a hotel," Uncle Pete answered. "As I mentioned in my letter, I have some business to take care of, and I plan to do some sightseeing with the kids. We'll be in and out a lot. I know you and your wife are busy, and I don't want to disrupt your whole schedule."

"Well, Pete, Peggy is expecting you for supper tonight at least. In the meantime, why don't we get you checked into a hotel."

The pickup was moving into the city now, and Mr. Evans swung away from the main avenue. The children stared at tin or straw-roofed shacks huddled tight against stately, whitewashed mansions whose red-tiled roofs peeked out at passersby over the shards of broken glass that guarded their high walls.

As Mr. Evans stopped for a red light, a bent, elderly man, thin rags clutched tightly against the brisk wind, hobbled up to the truck. "*Limosna, Limosna,*" he whined, holding out a twisted claw of a hand.

Jenny shuddered as Mr. Evans took his foot off the brake. "Who is that man?" she asked. "What does he want?"

"Just a local beggar," Mr. Evans answered as he dropped a coin out the window.

As he drove on, he continued, "Bolivia is a very poor country. There are a few very rich people, most of them the descendants of the Spanish conquerors. But most Bolivians are Indian or part Indian and live very humbly."

With a grin, he added, "Any more questions?"

Justin and Jenny shook their heads and turned their attention to the strange new sights around them. They were driving through the business section now. The narrow streets were choked with people and vehicles, and Mr. Evans slowed the truck to a crawl. Colonial-style buildings lined the streets in a solid wall, broken here and there by a modern skyscraper.

On all sides, wooden stands filled with goods crowded the sidewalks, and walking vendors shouted their wares. Justin counted shoes, matches, radios, watches, plastic tubs, cotton candy, and a horde of other goods before Mr. Evans pulled into a quiet side street.

Mr. Evans turned to Uncle Pete as he pulled up in front of a long, flat-roofed, two-story building. "You mentioned in your letter that you didn't want to stay in a tourist hotel—that you wanted to practice your Spanish." A sign swinging from a second story balcony announced, "Hotel Las Amèricas."

"This isn't as fancy as the Holiday Inn or the Presidential Hotel, but you'll see more of the real Bolivia here. And you shouldn't run into any other tourists. The clerks may know a bit of English—they study it in school here—but I'm afraid you'll have to get by mainly in Spanish."

"We'll be fine," Uncle Pete answered heartily. "I've picked up a bit of Spanish in my travels. We're looking forward to exploring on our own, aren't we, kids?"

Justin and Jenny nodded doubtfully. Their own Spanish consisted of two words: "hola" (hello) and "adios" (good-bye).

As Mr. Evans and Uncle Pete lifted the suitcases from the back of the truck, a boy darted around the corner of the building. Thin and wiry, his straight dark hair flopped over alert black eyes. His hand-woven sweater and faded blue jeans were ragged, but he shone with cleanliness. He held his hand out for Uncle Pete's luggage.

"I carry bags, no?" he inquired in strongly accented English. "Only fifty centavos."

Mr. Evans looked closely at the boy and grinned. "Why, it's Pedro! What are you doing here, Pedro?"

"Hola, Don Roberto," the boy replied with a grin. "I did not recognize your new red truck. I am working in this fine hotel now. I make much money when I carry bags for the 'turistas' and take them around the city. You like me to help your kind visitors?"

Mr. Evans turned to the Parkers. "Pedro's mother helps my wife with the cleaning now and then. He's a good boy, and responsible. You could do worse than to hire him for a guide."

Justin instantly decided that he liked this boy with the cheeky grin and twinkle in his eyes. "Yes, can't he come with us, Uncle Pete? It would be fun to have someone to talk to.

"How did you learn English, anyway?" he asked the boy.

"My mother work for many important Americanos," Pedro boasted. "I listen and learn good Inglish."

"Mrs. Gutierrez, Pedro's mother, was a maid at the American embassy for many years," Mr. Evans added. "Pedro grew up around *gringos*."

"But how can you have a job already?" Jenny exclaimed. "You're just a little boy. I'll bet you're not even as old as I am!"

Pedro patted his chest with a thin, brown hand. "I have twelve years," he told her proudly. "I am a man already. I have worked many years."

Mr. Evans explained. "Here, many children work as soon as they are old enough to run errands. Children of poor families have to help earn money for food."

"Just like I have a paper route at home," said Justin. "Only I get to keep the money I earn."

"It's not as bad as it sounds," Mr. Evans continued. "Most children go to school and only work part-time. You're on winter vacation now, aren't you, Pedro?"

"Sì, I can work all day for these fine visitors." He looked hopefully at Uncle Pete.

Uncle Pete laughed and handed the boy a suitcase. "All right, you're hired. But I'll expect you here at the hotel first thing every morning."

"I be there," Pedro answered eagerly. "I show you Lake Titicaca and Inca ruins and—"

Mr. Evans held up his hand. "All right, all right. Let's get these bags inside. You can give your guide talk another time."

At the simple wooden desk in the wide, tiled entryway, Mr. Evans requested two rooms, speaking in clear Spanish. Uncle Pete looked puzzled at the clerk's answering flow of words. "I guess we *do* need a guide," he joked.

The clerk took two keys from the row of wooden boxes behind him and walked around the desk, motioning for them to follow. Pedro eagerly grabbed one of the suitcases and bounded up the stairs behind the clerk.

Mr. Evans was frowning. "I'm afraid even this is turning into a tourist hotel. There are two *other* Americans staying here..."

"Don't be concerned," Uncle Pete reassured him. "Someone from home doesn't sound so bad right now!"

Their rooms were on the second floor and opened onto a long balcony that overlooked a large central courtyard. Shrubs in giant clay pots, the only decoration, drooped unhappily in the winter weather. To Justin's disappointment, the rooms could have been from any motel back home.

"How does a plate of spaghetti sound?" Mr. Evans asked as they deposited the suitcases inside the door of one room.

Justin suddenly realized how long it had been since lunch. He quickly joined his sister in the back seat of the pickup. Mr. Evans waved to Pedro as he started the engine. "We'll see you first thing in the morning."

He leaned out of the window and added, "By the way, my wife has missed you at Bible Club. Why haven't you been coming?"

The dark-haired boy looked scornful. "I am not interested in children's teaching. You tell me of a God who is kind and merciful and soft. That is not the way life is. One must be strong!"

He stepped back from the vehicle. "I do not need your God! My people have own gods. They are strong and powerful, and have served us many years."

"God loves all men, but He is also a God of power," Mr. Evans insisted. "He made the world and everything in it. Your mother has come to believe this. Won't you believe too?"

"Your teaching is for women," Pedro answered politely but with conviction. "How can a God who forgives His enemies be strong? Enemies are to be destroyed. No, the old gods are stronger. I will work for your friends, Don Roberto, but I do not wish to hear of your God!"

Mr. Evans didn't argue further but moved sadly away from the curb.

▼▼▼

An hour later, at the Evans' simple brick home, the two families crowded around the dining table. Mrs. Evans held a ten-month-old baby in her lap. Another one hammered a spoon against his high chair. The twins were the reason she hadn't met them at the airport.

Justin was still thinking over Pedro's words. Turning to Mrs. Evans at the foot of the table, he asked, "What did Pedro mean by the 'old gods'? Doesn't he believe in one God?"

She thought for a moment before answering. "Pedro is a Quechua Indian. He is descended directly from the Incas, who ruled here long ago. When the Spanish conquerors arrived, they brought their priests as well. The Indians were ordered to become Christian or die.

"Most converted, supposedly, but they continued to worship in their old ways, mixing them with the teachings the Spanish brought. The Indians still pour out offerings of wine to Pachamama, or Mother Earth, whom they now also call Mother Mary. Sacrifices of baby llamas or goats are still made to Inti, the sun god, who they believe is also Saint Peter. Witch doctors still hold power in the country villages, and even in the cities."

Scooping up a spoonful of mashed carrot, she continued,

"Pedro's father followed the old ways. He died two years ago, and Mrs. Gutierrez accepted Jesus as her Savior last year. But Pedro is set against following Jesus."

"Maybe we could invite him to church with us," Jenny suggested eagerly. "Tomorrow is Sunday. I'd love to see a Bolivian church."

"Good idea," Mr. Evans approved. "We'll be visiting a Quechua church tomorrow, about a three-hour drive from here. I was hoping you'd want to come with us."

The Parkers agreed to join the Evanses the next day, then Uncle Pete announced they had better be getting back to the hotel. "It's been a long day, and someone needs to get to bed!" He grinned at Jenny, who was almost nodding with sleepiness.

▼▼▼

The hotel seemed empty when Mr. Evans dropped them off. Even the desk clerk was gone. "I want you two ready for bed right away," Uncle Pete told the children firmly. "I've got some phone calls to make at the pay phone downstairs. I'll be back in a few minutes."

Justin hurried into the sweat suit he used as pajamas. He was brushing his teeth when Jenny banged open the door of the room he shared with Uncle Pete. "I'm not sleepy anymore!" she announced, plopping down on a bed.

"Me either!" Justin agreed. "Let's sit out on the balcony awhile."

Justin was leaning over the balcony railing, showing Jenny which group of brilliant stars overhead was the Southern Cross, when the door of the next room slammed open. The children jumped back in surprise as a tall, very broad man walked out.

"If we don't get that delivery soon, I'm going to get mad," he growled to someone behind him, running a massive hand over his partially shaved head. "I'm beginning to think your friends are putting us on!"

A small, thin man followed at the other's heels, tugging on a dark suit jacket. "Give them time, Skinner!" he answered crisply, in a peculiarly high, thin voice. "You know how hard it is to come up with a load like that!"

Justin turned around as the two men stepped into the circle of light cast by the open door of their room. "Hey!" he exclaimed in a low voice to his sister. "I saw those two guys at the airport!"

The big man suddenly noticed Justin and Jenny. "Great, just what we need. I thought you said this hotel was empty, Short!"

"Be quiet, you idiot!" the smaller man hissed. "They probably speak English. Who cares, anyhow? They're just kids!"

"Kids have parents!"

Justin was tired of being talked about as though he were deaf. He moved toward his room, but Jenny had already stepped into the circle of light. She held out a hand to the smaller man with her usual friendly smile. "Hi! You must be the other Americans the clerk told us about. I'm Jenny Parker."

"Beat it, kid!" the thin man called Short snapped, ignoring her outstretched hand.

"Yeah!" agreed the giant man called Skinner as he leaned down so close that Jenny could smell his putrid breath. His heavy jowls quivered as he scowled at the two children. "We don't like kids, see? And we *really* don't like kids getting in our way. So you two just keep away from us, got it? We don't want to see you again."

The two men turned and marched off into the night. Justin met his sister's gaze in wide-eyed astonishment. What had they done wrong this time?

CHAPTER THREE

A Church and a Witch Doctor

The bang of a drawer slamming shut woke Justin the next morning. It was still dark, and he couldn't quite make out the hands of his watch. Switching on a bedside lamp, he saw that it was only six a.m. As he swung his feet to the cold tile floor, soft snoring from the next bed told him that Uncle Pete was still asleep.

Justin heard a faint rumble of voices and realized the noise that had awakened him had come from the other side of the wall—the room where the two American men were staying. Padding across the floor in bare feet, he quietly opened the door and slipped out onto the balcony.

The stars were fading against the pale sky of early dawn, and his breath hung white in the cold air. Shivering, he started to swing the door shut, but at that instant the door to the next room slammed open.

The big man named Skinner stomped out, followed closely by the smaller man. Remembering their reaction the night before, Justin stepped back into the doorway, but the two men didn't even glance his way as they hurried by, talking in low voices.

"Those diggers want another raise," the big man grumbled, running his hand across his shaved head.

"They're already getting twice the normal wage!" the smaller man answered sharply.

"They're greedy, that's what!" the big man added.

Justin stepped out to stare after them as they started down the stairs. The deep grumble of the giant Skinner drifted back, "You think those kids will give us any trouble, Short?"

"Of course not!" a high, tenor voice snapped back. "They're just tourists."

Justin slipped back into his room. *They must be archeologists*, he decided. He grinned. Neither of that pair looked much like his idea of an archeologist!

Uncle Pete was now up. Justin could hear his off-key whistle coming from the bathroom. Pulling on a heavy turtleneck and a pair of jeans, Justin hurried next door to his sister's room. He gave a quick ta-tat, ta-tat on the door, a special rap the two had invented years before to let the other know who was knocking.

A moment later, Jenny flung the door open and said crossly, "Isn't it kind of early to be up?"

"It's almost seven o'clock!" Justin answered. "Didn't you hear Mr. Evans say he'd be here to get us at eight?"

He took a closer look at his sister. "Hey, are you feeling okay? You look awful!"

Jenny was pale, and dark circles lined her eyes. She pushed back her tousled curls with one hand and wearily rubbed her forehead.

"I've got a nasty headache, that's all!" she replied. "Nothing a little more sleep wouldn't help!"

"Sorry! You want me to tell Uncle Pete you can't go with us?"

"No, I might as well get up..." Jenny rubbed her forehead again and eyed her brother's casual clothes with distaste.

"You aren't wearing those to church, are you?"

"Sure! Mr. Evans said not to dress fancy. We might be sitting on the floor!"

Grabbing some clothes, Jenny hurried into the bathroom. She came out a few minutes later dressed much like her brother, and running a comb through wet curls.

"Weren't those men unfriendly last night?" she commented, frowning at herself in a small wall mirror. "I wonder why they're staying here. Mr. Evans says tourists never come here."

"Maybe they're here for the same reason *we* are," Justin answered dryly.

"Oh, come on! Don't you think there was something funny about them? Maybe they're criminals hiding out or something!"

"Don't be silly!" Justin knew better than to take his sister's vivid imagination seriously. "They're—"

He was interrupted by a knock at the door. Uncle Pete walked in, carrying a folding card table. He was followed by a stout lady carrying a large metal tray. She cried out in horror at the sight of Jenny's colorless face. Rattling off a long sentence in Spanish, she dropped the tray on the bed and hurried off.

"That was our landlady," Uncle Pete informed them as he set up the card table. "She says Jenny is suffering from altitude sickness."

Uncle Pete studied his niece's pale face. "You certainly *don't* look well. Our landlady has gone for some local remedy. If that doesn't work, we'll hunt up some aspirin."

Uncle Pete picked up the tray and motioned Justin and Jenny to sit on the nearest bed. He unloaded a plate of what looked like some sort of turnovers.

"They don't eat much breakfast in Bolivia, but the landlady came up with these. They're called *salteñas*, and are a popular breakfast dish. That white stuff is goat cheese."

Uncle Pete was asking the blessing on their meal when the landlady bustled in, carrying a small teapot. She gestured at Jenny, then at the teapot.

"Te de coca para la niña," she beamed, pouring out a cup of pale green liquid and handing it to Jenny. Gesturing toward Uncle Pete and Justin, she poured out two more cups. Placing the teapot on the table, she bustled away.

"I think she said, 'coca tea for the little girl,' " Uncle Pete translated, picking up his own cup. Jenny sipped the green tea, grimacing at its bitter taste.

"It tastes awful, but it seems to work," she said cautiously after a moment. "What is it?"

"From what I've read," Uncle Pete answered, "it's a tea made from the leaves of the coca plant."

"You mean the stuff *cocaine* is made from?" Justin asked.

Uncle Pete grinned at his shocked expression. "Justin, you forget that the coca leaf is used in many medicines. The refined powder we call cocaine is removed from the coca leaf and is a deadly narcotic. But the mild tea made by steeping the leaves is considered the best treatment for altitude sickness there is."

He handed Justin his own cup. "Go ahead and drink it, Justin. It also *prevents* altitude sickness, and we'll be climbing even higher today."

Justin drank the vile-tasting liquid and had to admit that the tight pressure at the back of his head quickly ebbed away. With a renewed appetite, he bit cautiously into a 'salteña.' The strange-looking turnover was filled with a very spicy stew of beef, potato, pea, hard-boiled eggs, and raisins. To his surprise, it was delicious—even if not his idea of a breakfast treat.

Rustling the pages of a local newspaper, Uncle Pete asked, "Seen any sign of our fellow Americans?"

"We sure did!" Jenny answered, reaching for a second salteña. Now that her headache was gone, she was recovering her normal high spirits. "They weren't very friendly, either!"

"Hmmph," Uncle Pete grunted, more interested in deciphering the Spanish headlines than in his elusive fellow guests.

A sharp knock sounded at the door. Jenny, jumping to answer it, exclaimed with pleasure, "Pedro! You're here early! Just in time to go with us to church."

"Church! You mean *'iglesia'*?" The dark-haired boy frowned angrily. "I will not go to any *'iglesia'*! This is a trick of Don Roberto, is it not? To make me hear of his God!"

Uncle Pete stepped forward. "No, Pedro, Mr. Evans has played no trick. We always go to church on Sunday. It is God's holy day when His people come together to worship Him. You're welcome to come with us, but you certainly don't have to if you'd rather not."

Pedro backed out the door. "I do not go to any *evangèlico* church. I will come back tomorrow if you need a guide."

Jenny followed Pedro to the door, her gold-brown eyes pleading. "Please come with us, Pedro! We won't have anyone to talk to if you don't come. You could tell us what everyone is saying. Please?"

"Yeah, please come!" Justin added.

Pedro looked from one to the other. "All right, I come this once," he agreed finally. "But no more tricks."

Soon, the red pickup was bumping its way up one of the narrow, dusty roads Justin had seen from the air. He held on tightly as the pickup jolted over deep ruts. There were no guard rails, and Justin caught his breath at sudden drop-offs of several hundred feet.

Unconcerned, Mr. Evans whipped around narrow U-turns and zipped past oncoming traffic with only inches to spare, while carrying on non-stop conversation. He glanced out the back window to where Uncle Pete and Pedro, hair tossed back by the wind, held on tightly.

Cuddling the twin she carried on her lap, Jenny asked, "What is an 'evangèlico' church? Why is Pedro so angry about coming?"

Mr. Evans glanced at her in his rearview mirror. "Bolivians call any church that isn't the state church 'evangèlico.' It really means a church where the gospel or 'evangelio' of Jesus Christ is preached."

Justin thought about this as he stared out the window. A year ago at Bible camp, both he and Jenny had accepted Jesus Christ to be their Savior. He remembered the happiness he felt that day. *It would be wonderful if Pedro could come to know Jesus as his Savior, too.*

He forgot about the other boy in his fascination with the scenes flashing past the window. They were up on the "altiplano" now, and the brown, flat plateau stretched away in every direction. Snowy mountain peaks, dominated by Mount Ilimani, circled the horizon. They bumped through a village where Indian women squatted in front of their one-room homes, spinning thread on wooden spindles.

"Are these people all Quechua?" Jenny asked, watching the women with interest.

Mr. Evans glanced into his rearview mirror. "No, these villages are Aymara. Most of the country people right around La Paz are Aymara. You have to travel a couple of hours out, as we are doing, to reach the Quechua villages."

Confused, Justin asked, "You mean these people aren't descended from the Inca like Pedro is?"

Mr. Evans smiled. "No, the Aymara are descended from the civilization that built the ancient city of Tiawanaku. We'll

take you there tomorrow. The Aymara are very proud of having been here even before the Inca."

Justin watched two men kneading a trough full of mud
and straw into large, square blocks. Rows of the adobe bricks
dried in the sun beside them. Beyond the village, dug-up
plots of land, now barren under the winter chill, showed
where the villagers worked to earn a meager existence.

Mr. Evans slammed on the brakes as a herd of sheep and
llamas—the pack animals of the Andes—wandered across
the road. A small shepherd boy, piping a haunting minor
tune on a wooden flute, prodded them along with a sharpened stick. Justin took the opportunity to join Pedro and his
uncle in the back. He looked curiously at the Indian boy.

"Have you been up here before?" Justin asked. "Can you
speak the Quechua language?"

"I speak Quechua and Aymara," Pedro answered proudly. "I am not one of those city boys who boast that they speak
only Spanish. They are ashamed of their Indian blood! My
grandfather was great man among the Quechua."

Before Justin could ask about Pedro's grandfather the
truck started up again, and the whistling of the wind cut off
any further conversation until they reached their destination.

Except for a tin roof, the building looked no different
than the few other houses scattered nearby. It was much bigger, but built of the same mud bricks.

"Is *this* a church?" Jenny whispered to Justin.

"Of course, can't you see the sign?" Justin whispered
back.

A weathered board nailed over the wide wooden door
read, "Iglesia Evangèlica Dios Es Amor."

"What does that mean?" Jenny asked Pedro.

Pedro shrugged uncomfortably. "It is the name of the
church—'God Is Love.' It is a stupid name!"

"But God *does* love us," Jenny protested.

"The gods I know don't love. They are strong and have great power to destroy their enemies. My grandfather—"

Pedro's words were cut off as Mr. Evans motioned the children to enter the church. The inside was dimly lit by two small windows cut in the thick adobe walls. To Justin and Jenny it seemed much too small to be a church, but the room was packed wall to wall with people.

The Parker twins had never seen the Quechua people up close before, and stared around the room in fascination. The Indian women wore hand-embroidered blouses and brightly colored skirts layered on top of each other until the top skirt stood out like a bell. Many of the women carried a dark-faced baby tied to their back in a thick, homespun blanket. Bows of bright-colored yarn decorated their long, dark braids, and intricate silver earrings dangled to their shoulders.

The dark, homespun pants and shirts of the Indian men were covered against the cold by heavy ponchos, which looked to the children like a blanket with a hole cut in the center. Most curious were their head coverings. Made of leather, they were designed after the helmets of the Spanish *conquistadors*—conquerors—embroidered with strange, colorful designs. Earflaps hung down on each side of the dark, solemn faces.

Pedro tugged Justin's arm. "Do not stare!" he ordered. "It is very rude!"

Jenny and Justin hurriedly lowered their eyes. A young woman in the back row, openly nursing a tiny baby, smiled shyly and scooted over, making room for them on a bench along the side wall. Justin smiled a thank you and sat down, Pedro and Jenny squeezing in on either side of him. The bench was cool beneath them, and Jenny made a face as she held out dirty fingers to Justin.

"It's made of mud!"

Justin rubbed a finger against the seat and grinned. The

benches had been built up from the floor out of more mud bricks. No wonder Mr. Evans had suggested jeans.

A young man dressed in Western clothes, but with the high cheekbones and round, dark face of the Quechua, stepped to the front of the room, strumming a battered guitar. A boy followed him, plucking a high, tinny tune on a small instrument. Somewhat like a miniature guitar, it had ten strings and its gray back was covered with short hair.

"What *is* that?" Jenny asked in a whisper, pointing at the strange instrument.

"It is a *'charango,'* " Pedro answered. "The back is made from the shell of an armadillo. Do you know what this animal is?"

When they both nodded, Pedro continued, "Sometimes they are made of wood. My people make beautiful music with them."

Justin had his doubts about that as the whole congregation stood up and began singing a mournful chorus in a minor key. But the dark faces beamed with joy as they clapped their hands vigorously to the unusual melody.

Looking around, Justin noticed the many bare feet and ragged clothing for the first time. *How can they be so happy when they are so poor?* he wondered. Suddenly the song leader broke into a tune Justin recognized. The words were strange, but he had sung the song often at home in Sunday school.

"I've got a mansion just over the hilltops," he sang along in English. This was why they were so happy, he realized! They had little now, but all the joys of heaven were waiting for them someday.

The singing continued for what seemed hours. At last, Mr. Evans stood up and opened his Bible. There was no Sunday school, but Mrs. Evans invited the small children outside for a Bible story. Smiling, she handed Justin and Jenny each one of the babies.

Mr. Evans' voice rose and fell as he flipped to different pages of his Bible. The baby Justin held whimpered, and Justin bounced him up and down. Jenny didn't seem to be having any problem.

He tried to understand the strange-sounding words, but his attention soon wandered. *It must be interesting*, he decided, looking around at the absorbed faces.

He poked Pedro in the side with his elbow. "What's he saying?" he whispered.

Pedro listened for a moment. "He is teaching about Jesus," he whispered back. "He tells how Jesus loves men and came to the world to die. He tells how He has great power to forgive..."

Pedro stiffened. "That is enough! You listen yourself. I am not interested." He leaned back against the wall and shut his eyes for the rest of the sermon.

▼▼▼

After the long service, a church family invited them over to their one-room home for dinner. The visitors ate on a long table outdoors.

Justin had almost finished his plateful of boiled rice, potatoes, and chicken doused with a spicy hot sauce, when he noticed that their hosts weren't eating. The woman of the house bent over the outdoor fire, stirring the contents of several large iron pots, while the rest of the family stood and watched their visitors.

"Why aren't they eating?" he asked Mr. Evans.

"It's their custom," Mr. Evans answered quietly. "They give the best they have to their guests. They'll eat what is left after we leave."

His appetite gone, Justin pushed back his plate. "I wish I hadn't eaten so much!"

Mr. Evans laughed. "Don't worry. They would be offended if you didn't eat. They want to do what they can for those who bring the news of Jesus to them."

Somewhat humbled, Justin joined Pedro and Jenny in the back of Mr. Evans' truck. Uncle Pete had chosen to ride inside this time.

"I'm glad we came," he told his sister soberly.

"Me too!" Jenny answered. Red was already staining the snows of Mount Ilimani as the truck jolted slowly away from the simple brick house. Jenny began to sing, as she often did on her way home from church. Justin joined in.

"There is power, power, wonder working power..." the two children shouted to the wind as they rolled along. Justin broke off as he noticed Pedro's frown.

"What's the matter? Don't you like our singing?"

"I do not like your song!" Pedro muttered. "You sing that this Jesus is powerful. What power does He have? At Bible club I have heard of how this Jesus loves and is kind to all men. That is weakness, not strength!"

"Jesus can forgive sins," Jenny answered.

"That is nothing. Any priest can do that," Pedro sneered. "My grandfather—"

"What *about* your grandfather?" Justin demanded. "What's so great about him?"

"My grandfather was a *'curandero,'* a witch doctor. He had true power. He could kill with a curse. My father told me of how he dried up the crops of his enemies. He even healed a man who stepped on a *'chullpa.'* "

"What's a *chullpa*?" the children chorused.

"You do not know what the chullpa is?"

Pedro's thin shoulders hunched as he cast a careful look around at the darkening hills. In a voice so low the children had to strain to hear, he said, "When you go out on the hills on a night of full moon you may see fire of green or red burning on the ground. But if you should come close, there is nothing there but a rise in the ground. It is a chullpa."

"It's probably nothing but phosphorescence," Justin said loudly. "You know, stuff that glows in the dark..."

"It is *not* what you say," Pedro answered angrily. "The chullpa is a tomb where some great Inca of long ago lies buried with his treasure. If you see a green fire, there is silver. If the fire is red, there is gold."

"Doesn't anyone try to dig up the treasure?" Jenny asked.

"Some tombs in the ruins have been dug up," Pedro admitted reluctantly. "But the fire on the ground is where the Inca have put a powerful curse on their tomb. To step on such a chullpa brings great sickness and even death. None of my people would go near the places of the chullpa."

Justin laughed. "That's just superstition!"

Pedro shivered. "Do not laugh! My aunt stepped on a chullpa one night many years ago. She has never walked again. She has a great sore on her foot that never heals."

He looked defiantly at their skeptical faces. "It is true! You ask Don Roberto. But my grandfather had power even over the chullpa. He could go to the tombs in safety and take away their curse. He served the old gods, and they gave him that power."

Justin and Jenny looked at each other doubtfully. Justin answered defensively, "God is more powerful than any witch doctor! He took the sin out of my heart and gave me eternal life. That's more than your grandfather could do."

"So you tell me," Pedro retorted. "I have seen the power of the old gods with my own eyes, but what have I seen your God do?"

His black eyes flashed scornfully. "You show me the power of your God! Let me see your God defeat the gods of my grandfather. *Then* I will believe in your Jesus and worship your God!"

CHAPTER FOUR

Curse of the Incas

Over a breakfast of fresh rolls and cheese the next morning, Justin and Jenny told Uncle Pete the whole story of Pedro's grandfather and the *chullpa*.

"Do you think he was telling the truth, Uncle Pete?" asked Jenny. "I mean, a witch doctor for a grandfather? That's weird!"

Justin swallowed a large bite of bread and added, "I always thought that kind of stuff was just in fairy tales or back in Bible days."

Uncle Pete was still trying to decipher the Spanish headlines of the day's local paper. At their questions, he folded his newspaper and fixed his keen gaze on them.

"Kids, I've been in many parts of the world. I've heard *and* seen some strange things—some fake, but others definitely true. Satan has a lot of power, and he can give strange powers to those who serve him."

Leaning back in his chair, he continued. "The ancient Inca worshiped idols and demons, and where Satan was worshiped, his influence may remain in control."

He smiled at their anxious faces. "I find it very interesting, however, that in all my travels I have never heard of a witch doctor or his curses having power over a person who has put his trust in Jesus. Satan is powerful, but God is far *more* powerful. He will protect His children against the power of the enemy. Does that answer your questions, kids?"

Justin and Jenny nodded soberly. Uncle Pete stood up and tossed his paper onto the bed. "Speaking of Incas," he said with a twinkle in his green eyes, "Bob Evans has arranged a visit to Tiawanaku today."

To their excited exclamations, he added, "He'll be here in half an hour, so let's get this mess cleaned up."

The twins quickly picked up the remainders of breakfast. Justin carried the breakfast tray down to the hotel kitchen, while Jenny straightened beds. Their rooms tidy again, they went outside and leaned over the balcony, watching the empty courtyard below for signs of Pedro and Mr. Evans.

"I wonder if those two Americans checked out. I haven't heard or seen them since that first night," Jenny commented.

"I'm sure they're still around," Justin answered. "They're probably working."

"Working at what?" Jenny asked curiously. She didn't wait for an answer but turned to wave at Pedro, who was coming up the stairs. A horn honked loudly outside.

"That's our ride," Uncle Pete called. "Let's go!"

"Don't forget the camera!" Jenny reminded Justin as she locked the door of her room. When they had found out about their trip to South America, the twins had pooled their savings to buy a small camera. Justin locked his own door now, the camera swinging from his neck by a black strap.

"Now you look like a *real* tourist!" Jenny joked. The two children hurried down the stairs as the horn honked again. Uncle Pete and Pedro had already climbed inside the red truck.

Justin and Jenny crowded into the back seat of the cab beside Pedro. A pile of straw hats lay on the seat. Mr. Evans explained, "The sun's rays are especially strong at this altitude, even in the winter, and can cause a nasty burn in a short time. You'll need a hat any time you're out in the sun for an extended time."

As Mr. Evans threaded his way through the narrow streets, Justin and Jenny tried on several hats until each found one that fit well enough. Uncle Pete had already picked out a hat, and Pedro was wearing his own battered black bowler.

"Won't the girls at school be jealous when I tell them about this!" Jenny was bouncing up and down with excitement. "Real Inca ruins!"

Mr. Evans glanced back. "Well, yes and no. The Incas certainly lived *near* Tiawanaku for hundreds of years, but they didn't build it. Tiawanaku was built almost two thousand years B.C. At one time, Tiawanaku ruled most of South America. The city stretched as far as the eye could see, and many of the walls and buildings were covered with gold and silver."

"Gold and silver!" Jenny squealed. "Is any still there? Maybe we can find some treasure!"

Mr. Evans smiled. "No, the gold is long gone. When the Spanish came, they stripped the gold and silver from everything they could find. They also destroyed many priceless artifacts. Over the years, most of the tombs and ruins have been looted and much of Bolivia's Indian heritage lost."

Pedro spoke up, frowning. "Sì, the gringos have stolen much of our treasure!"

"Bolivians have done quite a bit of looting too, Pedro," Mr. Evans answered dryly. "However, there is probably a bit of Inca treasure still buried here and there, maybe even around Tiawanaku. Until recently, the Bolivian government hasn't even allowed archeologists to excavate the ruins. Some excavations have been opened in recent years, but most

Bolivians leave the ruins alone, believing the ancient burial grounds are cursed."

Pedro nodded triumphantly at Justin and Jenny. Jenny wrinkled her nose at him as she asked, "Do you think we might find something today?"

"I'm afraid you'd have to turn over anything you found, Jenny. By law, all Indian artifacts belong to the Bolivian government."

"Didn't you say a lot of finds are still smuggled out?" Uncle Pete asked.

"That's right! A poor Indian who digs up a piece of pottery or gold in his field often can't see why he should turn it over to the government when some tourist will pay what to him is a fortune for it. But it's the big-time smugglers, generally Americans or Europeans, who make fortunes selling Indian artifacts to foreign collectors."

They were now up on the "altiplano," the road a narrow, dusty ribbon dividing the flat wasteland. A solitary juniper tree and the scattered sagebrush-like plants that covered the altiplano provided the only touches of dusty green. Justin and Jenny clung to their seats as the pickup jolted over deep ruts.

After an hour of steady driving, Mr. Evans pulled off into an open field beside the road, an area that had been cleared to serve as a parking lot. A small whitewashed building stood at the edge of the road. There was just one other vehicle there—a long, black touring car.

"No wonder this place is almost empty," Jenny muttered to Justin. "You practically need four-wheel drive to get out here!"

"This is where we'll buy our tickets," Mr. Evans announced, pointing at the small concrete building. Uncle Pete insisted on buying the tickets, and a smiling, dark-eyed young lady handed over five pieces of white paper stamped, "Entrada—Five Pesos."

"You kids stay with Pedro now," Uncle Pete ordered. "Don't get out of sight of the main buildings."

Jenny ran eagerly across the road. Justin and Pedro followed more slowly. A wire fence divided the ruins from the road, and the children handed their tickets to the unarmed guard who stood at the wide gate. There were no other guards, and the wire fence looked easy enough to climb over, in spite of several strands of barbwire at the top.

"No wonder there's smugglers," Justin pointed out to Jenny. "You could steal anything you want in there!"

Pedro led the way across the sparse, dry grass. Justin stopped in surprise as what looked like a giant stone swimming pool opened up at his feet.

"Come on!" Pedro called, waving to them from the top of a set of stairs. The three clambered down the stone steps. They were ten feet below the ground here and could see nothing but aging stone around them, and a cloudless blue sky stretching overhead.

"Wow, what is this place?" Justin exclaimed, walking over to inspect a massive squat figure that stood in the center of the immense, below-ground-level courtyard. A solemn granite face stared straight ahead, ignoring the humans at its feet as it had for centuries.

"This is the *Templo Semisubteraneo*," Pedro answered in his best guide's voice. "That means the 'semi-underground temple.' Those are called monoliths." He gestured at the various-sized granite figures that dotted the temple floor. "There once were many more, but some have been taken away."

Jenny reached out and stroked the smooth, cool stone of the wall. She jumped backward with a shriek as a dark face leered at her, wicked eyes twinkling with mischief. Justin was at her side in an instant.

"What's wrong?"

Jenny laughed shakily. "Nothing. I just thought that was alive!"

Justin saw that what had startled her was a stone head, carved from rock. The wicked twinkle dissolved into sunlight glinting on flecks of metal in the granite eyes. More of the carved heads stretched around the walls in every direction, each with a different face and style of carving. Justin lifted the camera to his eye and carefully snapped several shots of the carvings.

"These are the 'Framed Heads,' " Pedro explained. "Each head and monolith stands for a nation the Tiawanaku defeated in war. They were great warriors. They cut off the heads of their enemies and hung them from their belts to show their bravery."

"They don't sound like the kind of people I'd want for a best friend," Jenny muttered. "Let's get out of here. Those heads give me the creeps!"

"We will go," Pedro announced. "But first you must look here." He guided them to a spot at the far side of the temple.

"Now look up," he commanded. This time it was Justin who stepped back in surprise. A large, square doorway opened up above them. Silhouetted in the doorway was a giant figure that appeared to be floating in the blue sky.

"Wow," exclaimed Justin when he could speak. "How did they get it up there?"

Pedro looked very pleased with himself. "It is not really up in the air at all," he explained smugly. "I will show you."

He led the way out of the subterranean temple. Ahead of them, another set of stairs climbed to the crumbling walls of another temple—this one above ground. A towering block of whole granite stood on each side of the entryway with a third giant block laid across the other two to form a door. Justin and Jenny recognized this as the doorway they had seen floating in the air.

"But where's the statue?" Jenny looked around, puzzled.

"You cannot see it from here," Pedro informed them. "It is on the other side of the Temple of Kalasasaya. Only from below may you see the Mother of All standing in the Doorway of Life."

"Mother of All! Doorway of Life!" Jenny muttered. "That's crazy!"

"How did they get those blocks out here without trucks?" Justin interrupted as Pedro's dark face clouded over. "Each one must weigh tons!"

"Ten tons each," Pedro answered proudly. "No one has ever discovered the secrets of the Tiawanaku. Some of the stones in this temple weigh more than 160 tons. Here, the great gods of the Tiawanaku were worshiped."

"I don't see how they got that big rock up there!" Jenny declared, staring up at the carefully balanced slab that formed the top of the doorway.

"It's just a matter of leverage and..." Justin stooped to pick up a small, light-colored piece of rock. It made a faint white line when he rubbed it against the stone step.

"Here, I'll show you how they did it." Justin, who planned to be an engineer someday, made a few quick marks on the step.

But Jenny had turned away. One hand shielding her eyes, she asked, "Hey, aren't those the two Americans staying at our hotel?"

Disgusted, Justin stood up, shoving the small stone into his jacket pocket. Following the direction of her gaze, he instantly recognized the two men—one short and thin, the other tall and broad—who walked rapidly toward the temple. At the sound of Jenny's voice they stopped. The short man pointed and said something to his companion in an angry voice.

"Now, don't you think that's odd?" Jenny demanded. "Why are they so determined to avoid us?"

"Oh, who cares!" Justin answered in an annoyed voice. "They're archeologists. They're probably here working!"

"How do you know that?" Jenny demanded. Justin repeated the conversation he had overheard the day before.

"Well, it wouldn't hurt them to be a little more friendly!" Jenny insisted stubbornly.

Jenny turned to follow Pedro into the Temple Kalasasaya, but Justin paused to shoot one last photo of the ruins spread out behind him. He had forgotten the two Americans, but as he focused, they moved into view. He could see their faces clearly as he shot the picture.

It was the last shot on the roll, and he was rewinding the film when he heard an angry shout from below. He looked down to see the big man named Skinner running up the steps toward him.

"Give me that camera!" he growled roughly, and grabbed it from Justin's hand. Opening the back, he yanked out the film.

"Give that back!" Justin yelled, snatching the camera back. In answer, the big man shoved the roll of film into his pocket.

"Hey, you can't do that!" Justin protested angrily. "I'm going to call the guard!"

The smaller man named Short was instantly at their side. "What are you doing, Skinner?" he demanded sharply in his high, thin voice. "We don't want any trouble here!"

The big man subsided and stepped back, scowling, but he didn't return the film. Turning to Justin, Short said soothingly, "I'm sorry about this. My friend here has this thing about having his picture taken."

He shoved a five dollar bill into Justin's hand. "Here! This should cover the damage." With a sharp order to his large friend, he turned and walked quickly down the stairs.

Justin burned with anger as he stared after the two men. It wasn't so much the film. He had spare rolls, and the five dollars more than covered the cost of the lost film. But there were irreplaceable pictures on that roll!

What a fuss over one picture! he fumed. He considered calling for Uncle Pete or the guard, but the two men were already out of sight. He turned to join Pedro and Jenny inside the temple.

Inside, Justin saw another vast courtyard dotted with granite statues. In a straight line with the entrance stood the monolith they had seen from below ground. Using exact mathematics, the city's builders had placed the thirty-foot-high monolith in a direct line with both gates so as to be seen from the underground temple and from no other angle.

"This is Pacha Mama," Pedro was telling Jenny. "The names means 'Mother Earth'—she who gives life." Jenny and Justin stared up at the massive figure who held some sort of cup in each hand.

A long stone wall divided the area to Justin's left. He was fascinated with the elaborate stonework, and he pushed his anger to the back of his mind as he studied the stones.

"They fit together so perfectly!" he exclaimed. "Just imagine cutting that many huge stones without any machines!" Pedro shrugged his thin shoulders and looked bored. None of this was new or exciting to him.

Justin shut his eyes, ignoring the grass creeping through cracks, and the weathered walls. In his mind he saw the great city full of life—the golden buildings on fire with the blaze of the sun; warriors pushing through the crowd, their grisly trophies of war hanging from leather belts; an Indian noble in a litter staring haughtily at the common people, his gold chest-piece and armbands glittering with emeralds and turquoise.

How exciting it would have been to live back then! Justin thought. Then he remembered the bloody battles and human sacrifice, and decided the twentieth century really wasn't so bad.

"Justin, are you going to nap all day?" a low, spooky voice inquired, seemingly at his shoulder. Startled, he whirled around, but neither Jenny nor Pedro was in sight. A moment later Jenny peered around one end of the low stone wall.

"Over here," she called, looking pleased with herself. When Justin joined her, she showed him a hollowed-out cone in the stone wall. When Justin whistled into the opening, his voice reverberated across the courtyard.

"Wow!" he exclaimed. "Their own loudspeaker system!"

Pedro nodded. "Yes, the priests spoke to the people from here. They thought it was the voice of a god."

They were leaving the temple area when a man in Indian homespun clothing crept up to Justin. He looked much like the villagers Justin had seen the day before. *"Tesoro! Treasure!"* he whispered. Before Justin could move away, he swung open his ragged coat and showed Justin a small stone figure that looked like the much smaller twin of the Pacha Mama monolith at the back of the courtyard. The six-inch figure was encrusted with earth and looked as ancient as the hills.

"Only forty pesos!" the man whispered, glancing around furtively. "A great treasure!"

Jenny, too, had pressed close to look at the miniature monolith when Pedro suddenly pushed his way in. He spoke a few sharp words to the Aymara villager, and the man walked away reluctantly.

"It is not worth a peso!" Pedro explained with a grin.

"The villagers carve the Pacha Mamas from stone, then bury them a few weeks. The tourists pay well for the 'great treasure.'"

"But that's cheating!" Jenny cried hotly. "We should report it to the guard!"

Pedro shrugged. "The tourists know it is illegal to buy artifacts. It is only their fault if they are cheated."

They were now at the temple entrance. Skipping down the steps, Jenny suddenly called out, "Look! There are those guys again!"

Justin's eyes followed Jenny's pointed finger. The two Americans had rounded the corner of the temple and were walking rapidly toward the children.

Justin scowled. "Let's get out of here. I don't want anything more to do with them!"

"I don't think they can see us here anyway," she answered. "See? They're going toward that hill."

Sure enough, the men had walked by without glancing their way. Beyond the ruins was a hill perhaps a hundred feet high and several hundred feet long. Its sides and flat top were too even to be natural.

"I think it is time to go," Pedro said loudly. "Your uncle will be looking for you." Jenny and Justin stared at him in surprise.

"I'm not ready to go," Jenny answered sharply. "Isn't that a cave or something up there? It looks interesting. Let's go see." She started in the direction of the two men.

"No, do not go!" Pedro called, running after her. Justin followed on his heels. Pedro caught Jenny by the arm and pulled her to a stop. The mound was only fifty yards away now; the opening Jenny had seen was a third of the way up the steep hillside. They could now see that a brick wall had been built a short way into the cave, blocking the opening. Large boulders were piled up against the bricks.

"I guess we can't get in!" Jenny grumbled with disappointment.

"You do not want to go there!" Pedro answered urgently. "It is a very bad place!"

The two Americans, only a few yards ahead, halted at the sight of the trio. "It's those pesky kids again," the shorter man grunted.

Jenny pulled away from Pedro. "What's the matter? Why shouldn't I go there, Pedro? Look! A piece of the wall has crumbled away… I'll bet we could get in."

Catching sight of Justin, the massive Skinner scowled and edged away, but the shorter man stopped, obviously eavesdropping on the children's discussion.

Pedro looked around nervously and lowered his voice. "It is the 'Cueva de la Inca Re,'—the Tomb of the Inca Re. They say a great Inca king was buried there long ago. He put a very powerful curse of death on the man who disturbs his resting place. They say there are tunnels leading deep into the ground and much treasure, but no one will go near to search for it."

Justin groaned. "Oh, come on, Pedro! Not another horror story!"

"It is true!" Pedro insisted. "Everyone knows that it is a very bad place. In past times men tried to steal the treasure, but none who entered the Cueva ever came out again. You see that brick wall? So many were lost to the curse that our government sealed the door. Now no one may disturb the burial place again."

At his words, the big American turned back and gave an ugly laugh. "Hey, kid," he growled, grabbing Pedro by the shoulders. "Are you saying there's treasure in there, and you people are letting it rot because of some stupid superstition?"

Pedro stood his ground unafraid, meeting Skinner's eyes

squarely. "Once, before the cave was sealed, another American came to Tiawanaku," he answered scornfully.

"Oh, yeah?" Skinner growled. "So what happened?"

"He too laughed at the curse of the Cueva," Pedro continued. "He said there must be some strange gas inside that killed people. He put on a suit with air like an astronaut, and said he would bring out the treasure of the Inca. He went inside the cave."

The big man thrust his heavy, ugly face close to Pedro's. "Well, kid, tell us! Did he get out with anything?"

"He was lost for several days, but at last he made his way out of the Cueva," Pedro answered soberly.

His audience waited expectantly. His black eyes bright with triumph, Pedro broke into a malicious grin at the sudden greed on the two Americans' faces.

"No, he had no treasure with him. When his friends found him, he knew nothing of what he had done or where he had been. He was 'loco.' He had become what you gringos call completely insane!"

An Overheard Plot

The short, thin American tugged on his companion's sleeve. "Let's get out of here, Skinner!" he commanded in his curiously high voice. "This kid's giving me the creeps."

Skinner laughed uneasily as he backed away from Pedro. "Okay, Short. We've wasted enough time already. These natives always have a few stories like that for the tourists. You can't believe a word they say!"

The two turned and marched off along the base of the mound. Pedro stared after them angrily. Justin turned to his sister.

"I agree with them; let's get out of here. I don't think Uncle Pete would want us exploring out here."

Jenny shrugged and started walking back toward the main temple complex. "Okay. I just lost my appetite for exploring anyway." She grimaced. "You couldn't *pay* me to go near that place again!"

Justin glanced back at the Cueva de la Inca. The blocked opening dark against the hillside, it now seemed menacing and eerie. Unaccountable goose bumps rose on Justin's arms, and he hurried after the others, thrusting the strange mound out of his mind.

The trio found Uncle Pete and Mr. Evans in the Templo Semisubteraneo, inspecting the row of carved heads. The sun shone brightly directly overhead, and the twins were grateful for the shade the straw hats provided. By now, two tourist buses had arrived on the scene. Cameras clicked and voices exclaimed in a dozen different languages.

Uncle Pete glanced at his watch. "Twelve o'clock on the dot!" he boomed. "Let's see about scraping up some lunch."

Mrs. Evans had packed them a picnic lunch of sandwiches and fresh fruit, but Jenny and Justin were attracted to the appetizing odors coming from the little wooden food stands that lined the road outside the barbwire fence. A withered old lady, her hand-woven shawl pulled tight, fanned the coals under a homemade barbecue. Chunks of meat, potato, and onion threaded on long, hand-whittled sticks sizzled deliciously over the flame.

She turned the shish-kebobs to brown the other side, and Justin and Jenny watched in fascination as her long braids bobbed inches from the glowing coals. Jenny sighed in relief when the old lady sat back without catching on fire.

Next to her, a serious-looking Indian woman, rocking a toddler on her lap, shyly offered a basket of tamales wrapped in corn husks. An old-fashioned ice cream cart bounced by. It had been converted into a grill for hamburgers and plump highland sausages.

"Please, can't we try something here?" Justin and Jenny begged Uncle Pete. "We can get sandwiches back home."

"Well, go ahead," Uncle Pete agreed finally. "But don't blame me if you come down with a case of dysentery."

By pointing and using their few words of Spanish, the twins managed to pick out a pair of shish-kebobs. Jenny chose a juicy sausage wrapped in a bun, and Justin decided to try the hamburgers. From a soda vender, they also picked out a bottle of soda pop for each person in the party.

Justin carefully counted out the Bolivian pesos Uncle Pete had given him, then settled down on the grass with his booty. Pedro had decided to stick with the "American" sandwiches. He grinned as Justin bit deeply into his hamburger and choked.

"It's hot!" he exclaimed, grabbing at his bottle of cola. "What's in it?" Lifting up the corner of the thick, heavy bun, he discovered that Bolivian hamburgers included a fried egg, french fries, and a liberal amount of hot sauce. He tried a smaller bite, and decided it was really quite good.

Lunch over, Uncle Pete looked at his watch again. "Well, are you kids ready to head back? I'm sure Bob—Mr. Evans, that is—has things to do."

"Oh, don't worry about me," Mr. Evans said, hurriedly swallowing the last of his egg sandwich. "I've got all afternoon."

"Oh, please, can't we stay a bit longer, Uncle Pete?" pleaded Jenny. "We'll never get another chance to come here…"

Justin suddenly remembered his lost roll of film. "Yeah, and I've got to take more pictures!" he muttered glumly.

Uncle Pete stretched out on the grass, his arms behind his head. "I don't know where you kids get your energy. Okay, you've got two hours. Be at the car by three o'clock. I'm going to take a bit of a nap." He waved them off, then tilted his hat against the sun.

The three children spent the next half-hour wandering through the main buildings again, Justin quickly filling up another roll of film. Jenny perched on the edge of a low stone wall, gazing restlessly around the ruins.

"I want to see something new!" she complained. "We've already been through all this. What's across the road there?

Look at all those broken-down walls in the field. And those houses over there are so cute. Let's explore."

"There is nothing to see," Pedro answered sharply. "It is a village like any other village. And those ruins in the field have not been excavated yet."

"Well, I want to see what's over there. Are you coming, Justin?"

"I guess so. You're coming too, aren't you, Pedro?"

Pedro sat down and leaned against the outer wall of the Temple Kalasasaya. "If you wish to go, go! There is nothing to see, and it is too hot to walk more. I will stay and have a siesta."

He slid further down, folding his arms behind his head. Justin and Jenny left him stretched full length on the ground, his black bowler tilted to cover his face. Stepping over a strand of barbwire, they hurried toward the field they had glimpsed.

Broken granite boulders were scattered throughout the sparse grass. Some were massive, but most protruded only a few inches out of the ground. Hordes of black grasshoppers scattered in all directions with every step they took.

Justin kicked against something solid in the grass. Bending down, he tugged at an object half-buried in the packed earth. Pulling it free, he found that he was holding a broken shard of pottery. It was caked with dirt, but when Justin knocked the piece against a stone wall, he discovered faint red and black markings under the earth.

"You know we aren't supposed to take stuff!" Jenny reminded him as he thrust the piece of pottery into his jacket pocket. His fingers felt the small stone he had put there earlier, and he pulled it out.

"I know!" he answered, absently shoving the stone back into his pocket. "I'll give it to the man at the gate. Who knows, maybe he'll say we can keep it. It can't be worth any-thing!"

They walked around the field again. "Pedro was right," Justin declared. "There's nothing to see here!"

"Let's explore the village," Jenny suggested. "After all, they're *real live Incas*."

Beyond the unexcavated ruins, the ground dipped to form a shallow valley. A cluster of adobe homes huddled on the banks of a narrow creek. The sandy flats sloping up from the nearly dried-up stream bed showed it would widen into a respectable river with the arrival of the annual rains.

Outside the nearest hut, three small, ragged children danced in a circle, holding hands and playing the Quechua equivalent of "ring around the rosies." As Justin and Jenny walked by, they stopped their game, staring at the two strangers with solemn, dark eyes. Jenny smiled at them, and Justin called, "Hello!" Startled, the children scurried into the safety of the hut.

Behind the hut, the twins watched the woman of the home lift small, flat loaves of bread out of an igloo-shaped clay oven with a giant-size wooden spatula. She, too, just stared in response to their smiles, and hurried away around the side of the hut.

Down at the stream edge, other women beat clothes against flat, well-worn boulders. Jenny was interested to see girls half her age scrubbing vigorously beside their mothers. Clean clothes, spread over low, thorny bushes along the banks, bleached white in the brilliant sun.

From down in the shallow valley, the two could not see the ruins of Tiawanaku. The sun had moved well to their right before Justin remembered to check his watch.

"Oh, no—it's twenty to three already! We'd better get back now, Jenny. Uncle Pete's not going to be very happy if we're late."

They were far down the river bed now, and quickly clambered up the slope of the shallow valley. When they stood once more on the high plateau, they gazed around in dismay. The ancient city of Tiawanaku was nowhere in sight. Low, rolling hills spread out in front of them.

"Come on!" Justin commanded, setting off toward the nearest rise. "It must be just over that hill there."

"Don't you think we should go back the way we came?" Jenny asked.

"We'd never get back in time that way!" Justin answered. "You know how Uncle Pete is about being late!"

Justin led the way up one low knoll, then down the other side. He continued confidently up the next rise, but when he reached the top, he saw nothing ahead but more rolling hills. Even the stream was now out of sight. He continued on for a few moments more, then stopped, looking around uncertainly.

"What's the matter?" Jenny demanded impatiently. "You didn't get us lost, did you?"

"Give a guy time to think!" Justin snapped. Then he admitted reluctantly, "Well, I'm not too sure which way we should be going. All these hills look alike!"

"No problem," Jenny said, her brown eyes glowing with a sudden idea. "We'll ask directions at that house over there." She waved toward a metallic sparkle to their left, just visible over the next rise. A closer look showed the glimmer to be a peaked tin roof.

"Sure," answered Justin scornfully. "And how do you plan to ask? With sign language?" He hated asking directions or admitting he was lost.

"Exactly! Just wait and see! Come on, or we'll be late."

Jenny began running toward the lonely house, and Justin trotted reluctantly behind. They stopped at the edge of the grassless yard. One lone tree, its wide branches giving evidence of water close by, swayed gently in the slight breeze, providing welcome shade to the baked earth.

This family must be well-off, for Bolivians, Justin thought, noticing a Honda motorcycle standing against one adobe wall—not to mention the tin roof in place of the usual thatch. A shiny new shovel leaned against the front door. Latin-style country western music blasted from the one small window.

"Hello," Jenny called. The only answer was a menacing growl. Around the corner of the house rushed a scrawny black mongrel. Every rib stood out with the effort of his wild barking. It paused when it saw the two strangers.

"Nice doggy, nice doggy," Jenny called out nervously, holding out a hand to make friends. The dog's response was to bare his yellowed fangs again in an ugly snarl. It moved forward slowly, growling continuously, and the twins backed up until they reached the shade of the big tree. Justin leaned down to pick up a dry branch beside the tree trunk. The dog lunged forward, barking wildly.

"Get up in the tree, Jenny," Justin told his sister in a low voice. He struck threateningly at the dog, who backed up a few feet. Jenny, pale with fear, climbed for the nearest branch that would hold her. Dropping his stick, Justin scrambled up behind her. No sooner had his feet cleared the ground than the black mongrel lunged. Jaws snapping viciously, it threw itself high into the air, its fangs brushing the bottoms of Justin's sneakers.

"*Vète!*" A stone was hurled through the air, striking the black dog in the ribs. The dog dropped to its belly, whining. There was a loud snap of fingers, and the dog slunk around the side of the hut.

Still clinging to the branch, Justin and Jenny gave a joint sigh of relief and looked around for their rescuer. A tall man in Western clothes leaned against the doorjamb of the hut. A bowler hat crushed his dark, kinky curls, and he carried what the twins recognized as an expensive radio/double-cassette player, which still blasted out music. As he stepped into the sunlight, he slipped on a pair of sunglasses.

Jenny giggled. "Does he think he's a movie star?"

Waving his hands expressively, the man poured out a flow of smooth Spanish; Jenny and Justin didn't understand a word. The children slid down the tree trunk as the man walked over to meet them.

Wiping a dirty hand against dusty jeans, Jenny held it out in greeting. "Thank you for saving us!" she said. Assuming from his blank expression that he didn't understand, she waved her arm toward the hills and asked hopefully, "Tiawanaku? Please!"

In the shade of the big tree, the stranger took off his sunglasses. His dark-brown eyes crinkled with amusement. "You wish to go to Tiawanaku?" he asked politely.

"Oh, you know English! Great!" Jenny exclaimed. "Yes, we're lost. We have to get back right away."

"My name is Pepe. I study one year in U.S.A.," the curly-haired man told them proudly. "My English is pretty good, no? I help you get home."

Justin interrupted, "Uh, sir, is that your dog? I mean, could you keep hold of him till we get away?"

A wide grin split the tanned face. "You might say he go with house. You need not be afraid. You must go in that direc—"

As he raised his arm to point, he suddenly froze, his smiling expression slowly changing to shocked fear. Recovering himself, he grabbed the surprised twins by the arm and pushed them toward the corner of the building.

"Go! *Vète! Fuera de aquì*," he shouted, lapsing into Spanish. Jenny held back. "But … the directions."

The man didn't answer. His face was set with anger and fear. He whistled loudly. Justin grabbed Jenny's arm and broke into a run as a loud yapping broke out behind them. Glancing back as they ran, he saw the black mongrel loping along after them.

The dog followed them for a few hundred yards. Then, with one last growl, he turned back to his guard duties. Justin and Jenny ran until they collapsed onto the grass behind a patch of bushy, sagebrush-like "tola," clutching their aching sides. Justin was sure they were out of sight here, but he raised his head cautiously so that only his eyes showed above the scratchy bushes that shielded them.

"So that's what they are!" he exclaimed. "Boy, am I ever stupid!"

"What *who* are?" Jenny gasped, still out of breath.

"I'll show you!" Justin answered grimly. "Look!"

Jenny inched up beside him, staring back the way they had come. Entering the barren yard they had just left were two figures she recognized—one tall and broad, the other short and wiry. They both carried knapsacks over their shoulders.

Walking right behind them, two Aymara men carried an assortment of shovels and pickaxes. The strange man named Pepe, black dog at his side, hurried to meet the two Americans, his hands in the air as he talked energetically. Justin strained to hear his words, but he was out of earshot.

"That's funny!" Jenny exclaimed. "What are *they* doing here? And why did that man shove us out of there? We weren't hurting anything!"

"I've got a good idea," Justin told her gloomily. "Remember how you thought those guys might be criminals? Well, I'm beginning to think you were right. That man was afraid of those two. He was afraid of them finding us there."

"But you said they were archeologists!" Jenny protested. "See? They're carrying digging tools."

"Archeologists aren't the only ones who dig. I'll bet those

guys are smugglers, digging up Inca artifacts like Mr. Evans told us. No wonder that Skinner didn't want his picture taken!"

"What picture?" Jenny asked curiously.

Justin explained quickly. Jenny still looked puzzled. "But none of us would have recognized his picture anyway! And no one else would ever have seen it!"

Justin grinned. "Maybe he didn't think of that. I get the impression he isn't very smart!"

"Look!" Jenny pointed. "They're leaving again!"

Sure enough, the two Americans were walking away from the house now. The three Bolivians followed behind, carrying their tools, the black dog still at Pepe's side.

"Come on!" Justin commanded urgently, jumping to his feet. "We've got to see what they're up to!"

"We can't follow them! We're already late!" Jenny protested. "You know how mad they got when they saw us before. And Uncle Pete's going to be mad too, if we don't get back soon. We weren't supposed to come this far."

"He'll understand when we tell him what happened," Justin assured her a little doubtfully. "If these guys are up to something, it's our responsibility to find out and tell the police. Besides, maybe they'll lead us back to the ruins. Now, are you coming, or am I going alone?"

"Oh, I guess!" Jenny agreed reluctantly, standing up slowly and brushing bits of debris from her clothes.

"Hurry up!" Justin urged impatiently. "They're getting away!"

By now, the five men had disappeared around a bend in the terrain beyond the tin-roofed house. Justin trotted in the direction they had gone, Jenny close behind. By the time they were out of breath again, they could hear muffled voices.

Justin pulled his sister to a halt and pointed. Not far ahead, the five men still walked rapidly without looking back. Keeping out of sight but still within earshot, the two children now followed more slowly.

They were climbing a low ridge the men had just disappeared behind when Justin realized the muffled voices had grown louder. He placed a finger to his lips, motioning toward the side of the ridge. Jenny nodded that she understood, and they both crept up the ridge as quietly as they could, slipping occasionally on the loose shale.

They had reached the end of the uneven land that ran along the river bed, and the top of the ridge gave a clear view of the plateau stretching for miles off to their left. The twins were relieved to see the ruined temples of Tiawanaku only a half mile away. Voices rang out clearly from the other side of the ridge.

Lying flat on his stomach, Justin inched toward the voices. Taking cover behind a small boulder that perched on the very edge of the ridge, he lay quietly, watching the scene below. He felt Jenny inch up beside him, and she too froze to a mouse-like quiet.

In a shallow gully below them lay a mound perhaps ten feet high and a hundred feet long. Like the Cueva de la Inca, its sides were too regular to be a natural hill. The two Aymara men were already digging deep into the baked ground while Short and their curly-haired friend sifted through a pile of loose soil. It was evident from the turned-up piles of earth that the excavation had been going on for some time.

Skinner was pulling a strange-looking object from his knapsack. Justin recognized the object immediately. The summer before, his father had taken him gold prospecting in the Montana Rockies. "A metal detector," he muttered.

"Maybe they really are archeologists," Jenny whispered in Justin's ear.

"They wouldn't be so sneaky if they had permission to dig," Justin whispered back.

As the children watched intently, Skinner began running the metal detector over the surface of the mound. "Haven't found anything yet!" he called loudly after a few minutes. "Maybe there's nothing here. We shouldn't have listened to those villagers' wild tales."

"Just keep moving!" Short snapped back. "This spot isn't that important anyway. We've got that Island of the Sun delivery coming in tomorrow. If Pepe here comes through on that, we'll have a pretty good haul this trip."

"Yeah, *if* he comes through! I wouldn't trust him too far."

Justin put his mouth to Jenny's ear. "We'd better get out of here. Uncle Pete will know what to do about these guys. Let's go!"

Still flat on his stomach, he crawled back from the edge until he could sit up without being seen from below. He touched Jenny's ankle and motioned for her to follow. Jenny rose to her hands and knees, but as she started her backward crawl, her hand knocked away a fist-sized rock. She grabbed for it, but the rock rolled toward the edge, gaining speed.

Before she could move, the rock tumbled over the edge of the ridge, followed by a small avalanche of pebbles. They heard a crash below and an angry shout. Then a gravelly voice bellowed, "Hey! There's someone up there! Get 'em before he gets away!"

Gold in the Dark

"**C**ome on! We've got to get out of here! Fast!"

Justin jumped to his feet and grabbed his sister's hand. No longer trying to be quiet, the two children scrambled down the rough slope, slipping and sliding through the loose shale.

They paused momentarily at the bottom. Then Justin, remembering the glimpse of Tiawanaku from the top of the ridge, pointed left, and they ran as fast as their tired legs could carry them along the shallow ravine at the bottom of the ridge. They could now hear the shrill barking of the black dog.

Rounding one last rise, the twins suddenly broke into the open. The ruined walls of Tiawanaku loomed only a few hundred yards away. But the ground between them and the safety of the ruins was flat, offering only a few stunted bushes for cover, and the men behind them would be upon them in seconds.

Justin hesitated, looking around frantically. The baked earth of the high plain absorbed little water, even during the rainy season, and the runoff had carved shallow, winding ditches across the face of the plateau. The limited cover these ditches offered was the twins' only hope of escape.

Already, the mongrel's barking sounded much closer. The two children sprinted toward the nearest ditch. They jumped into it just as the barking dog broke into the open. The narrow crevice was just deep enough to hide them if they lay flat.

Hardly breathing, Justin lay motionless, expecting the dog to be on them any minute. But a sharp voice yelled an order, and the barking stopped.

Jenny moved beside him. "Did they see us?" she whispered breathlessly.

Justin shook his head nervously. "I don't know!"

"Well, I'm not going to lie here and wait for them to catch us!" Jenny answered firmly. She raised her head until her eyes barely showed over the edge of the ditch, her brown curls blending into the dusty background.

"They're there, all right!" she said a moment later, dropping back down. "They're standing on top of the rise, looking this way. But I don't think they saw us."

Justin didn't dare lift *his* head to see. His bright red hair would be a dead giveaway. The two children lay motionless for a full five minutes, then Jenny slowly lifted her head again.

"They're leaving!" she whispered triumphantly. She started to sit up, but Justin pulled her back down.

"Give them time to get out of sight!"

Justin kept an eye on his watch. Not until another five minutes had passed did he motion for Jenny to take another look. She raised her head again, then jumped to her feet.

"They're gone! Let's go!"

Justin too raised his head. The low rise ahead of them was now empty, and he could see no sign of the strange Americans or their helpers. He too jumped to his feet.

"We've got to tell Uncle Pete about this right away," he said, breaking into a run again. Jenny groaned, but began running as well, her long legs easily keeping up with her brother.

As they neared the ruins, they saw Pedro standing at the top of the broad temple steps, his hand shading his eyes as he searched the horizon. Catching sight of them, he waved and ran to meet them. Breathless, the twins dropped to the ground and waited for Pedro.

Pedro's dark face was anxious. "Where have you been gone to? Three o'clock has gone long ago. We search for you everywhere! Your uncle is very worried."

He took in their rumpled appearance. "What has happened to you?"

"We're really sorry we're late," Justin apologized. "But just wait till you hear what we've been doing." He quickly filled Pedro in on the adventures of the last couple of hours.

"I'm sure they're stealing Inca artifacts," Justin finished. "Once we tell Uncle Pete, he'll tell the police and have them arrested. That will be the end of their little game!"

Pedro frowned. "I do not think you understand our country. The police will do nothing to these men. They will not believe your story. You have no ... no 'evidencia'—what is the word?"

"Evidence," Jenny supplied.

"Yes, you have no evidence. There is no law that says a man may not dig in a field. The policia will not bother Americanos for that."

"But we saw the mound!" Jenny protested.

"There are many mounds in the altiplano. And they will be gone long before you can tell anyone. No, you will not catch these men."

Justin frowned thoughtfully. "What if they actually caught them with Inca gold? Would they arrest them then?"

"Oh, yes. Stealing my country's treasures is a great crime. But you would have to be very sure. The police do not like to make trouble with the American embassy."

"Well, I have an idea," Justin said. He stood up, brushing off the tan-colored dust that covered his clothes. "Come on, we'd better go apologize to Uncle Pete and Mr. Evans."

The two men were too relieved over Jenny and Justin's safe return to scold much. The twins explained that they had gotten lost and told in detail of their hair-raising adventure with the black dog. They left out their run-in with the smugglers, though Justin did mention they had seen the other two Americans.

At the gate, Justin remembered the piece of pottery he had found and handed it to the guard. The guard examined the grimy piece carefully, then handed it back with a flourish and a smiling flow of Spanish words.

"He says that it is worth nothing," Pedro translated. "You may keep it as a reminder of our country."

Justin carefully wrapped the ancient fragment of pottery in his handkerchief and thrust it back into his pocket.

As they drove toward La Paz, Justin listened with only half an ear to Jenny's excited chatter and Uncle Pete's deep answers. They were dipping down into the valley when Justin suddenly asked, "Uncle Pete, do you think we could visit the Island of the Sun tomorrow?"

"You mean on Lake Titicaca? Where did you hear of the Island of the Sun, Justin?"

"Oh, I heard somebody mention it," he answered vaguely. He added hopefully, "I'm sure it would be educational. Please, couldn't we go there tomorrow?"

Uncle Pete laughed. "Yes, of course we can. I hadn't planned on leaving La Paz without visiting Lake Titicaca. Pedro can help me rent a car and we'll drive up in time to have lunch at the lake."

Once back at the hotel, Justin and Jenny returned their straw hats to the pile on the back seat. Noticing this, Mr. Evans urged, "You'll need those for your trip tomorrow. You might as well keep them as long as you're here in La Paz."

Bent over a map early the next morning, Pedro and Uncle Pete were making plans. "We'll drive to Copacabana for lunch, then rent a boat to tour the lake," Uncle Pete decided at last.

"And the Island of the Sun?" Justin asked anxiously.

"We'll be sure not to miss that," Uncle Pete promised.

Uncle Pete swung the rented car around the curves to the plain above as expertly as Mr. Evans had. Pedro sat beside him, giving directions and pointing out objects of interest to the twins in the back seat. Jenny exclaimed over each new sight, but Justin slumped over, quiet and preoccupied.

"What's the matter?" Jenny asked curiously.

Justin looked up. "I was wondering if those guys will really be on the Island of the Sun today. Wouldn't it be great if we could catch them in the act?"

Pedro had turned around to face them. "I think it is very stupid! If those men are what you say, then they are not good men. They may be very dangerous. I think it better if you leave them alone."

"Well, we can at least keep an eye out for them," Justin said, determination in his voice. "We might discover something the police would listen to."

"Okay," Jenny agreed. "We probably won't even see them, but we'll keep an eye out. But that's all! If we find out anything, we'll tell Uncle Pete. In the meantime, can't we try to have a fun time?"

"What are you kids muttering about?" demanded Uncle Pete.

"Oh, uh ... nothing important," Justin answered hastily.

He sat up and tried to pay attention to the scenery. Soon

he had forgotten the smugglers and was enjoying himself. The road curved, and suddenly Lake Titicaca stretched before them as far as they could see. Circling the horizon, snow-capped mountains peeked at their reflection in the calm, greenish blue water.

"Why, it's as big as an ocean!" Jenny exclaimed.

"It is very big and the highest in the world!" Pedro informed them loftily. "Peru is on the other side of the lake. We even have a navy here to watch against Peru."

▼▼▼

Copacabana was a sleepy waterside town seemingly transported directly from colonial Spain. Here the green of trees and flowers, fed by the fresh waters of Lake Titicaca, contrasted with the tans and beiges of the altiplano. At Pedro's instruction, Uncle Pete stopped the car two miles from town, and the group scrambled up a steep path to a grassy meadow several hundred feet above the road.

Pedro led them to an enormous flat boulder, its gray surface streaked with pale-green lichens. Hacked out of the rock, a series of stone seats faced each other. On the highest part of the boulder, one seat ruled alone over the rest.

"The Tribunal of the Inca," Pedro announced, pointing to the highest seat. "It is said that here a great Inca would sit, judging the quarrels and crimes of my people."

Justin and Jenny had to try out the ancient seats before they left. Hurrying down the path to the car, Justin groaned and clutched his stomach.

"Isn't it about lunch time, Uncle Pete? I'm starving."

"Let's get going then," Uncle Pete ordered. "How about some seafood on the waterfront?"

As Justin opened the back car door, he heard the roar of a powerful engine coming up the road behind them. The twins piled into the back seat as a long, sleek touring car rushed by, leaving them choking in a cloud of dust.

"Well, well!" Justin exclaimed triumphantly, staring after the black car. "If it isn't Skinner and Short!"

"*And* our good friend Pepe," Jenny added.

The black car was lost to sight by the time Uncle Pete started the engine. As they turned into the cobblestone streets of Copacabana, the children gazed down each side street, searching for the black car. Easing the rental car down a steep, narrow street, Uncle Pete pulled up at the waterfront under a sign that announced, "Restaurant La Cabaña."

"Hey, guys—*look!*" Justin pointed across the street to the lake front. A row of wooden piers extended out over the water. Moored alongside the piers, small boats bobbed gently up and down. Pedro and Jenny followed Justin's finger to the wharf, where a black car identical to the one that had passed them sat parked beside the water.

"Come on!" Justin jumped out of the car and hurried toward the wharf. Pedro and Jenny followed more slowly, leaving the astonished Uncle Pete staring after them. As Justin ran out onto the nearest pier, he saw a small motorboat with three familiar men in it moving away, toward the green sprinkle of islands in the distance.

The little boat made waves which wet Justin's sneakers as he stood on the end of the pier. He watched the boat disappear around a bend in the shoreline. Thrusting his hands angrily into his pockets, he waited for Pedro and his sister to catch up. "Well, that's that!" he growled.

"What are you kids up to?" Uncle Pete demanded as the three children joined him outside the restaurant.

"We thought we saw someone we knew," Jenny explained quickly.

Uncle Pete raised his eyebrows but dropped the subject. Justin's spirits lifted as he tackled a plate of fresh rainbow trout. It was hard to remember his disappointment when sunshine sparkled through the big picture windows, and tiny wooden sailboats danced on the waves below.

"Can I ride in one of those?" Jenny asked as they gathered on the wharf after lunch. They were choosing a boat for their excursion to the Island of the Sun. Gliding up to the pier was a curious craft. Woven from bundles of reeds, it looked like an Eskimo kayak and was large enough to hold just one person.

"Oh, no you don't...," Uncle Pete announced firmly.

"I know what those are," Justin told her. "They're balsa boats, aren't they, Uncle Pete? Made out of reeds that grow in the lake. I read about them in the travel guide."

"That's right, Justin," Uncle Pete answered. "But I think we'll travel in something a bit more up-to-date—like *that* one." He chose a small sailboat with an auxiliary motor, and dropped some bills into the smiling owner's hand.

The twins held on tightly to the sides as the sailboat skittered across the waves. Ahead, a small emerald-colored island floated under a cloudless blue sky. In spite of winter temperatures, lush vegetation tumbled down terraced fields still in use after centuries.

The boat docked at the bottom of a wide stone staircase that rose from the water's edge to disappear in a tangle of shrubs far above. Grass forced itself through cracks in the rock, but the staircase was as solid as when slave laborers had built it for Inca emperors a thousand years before.

"Why is this called the Island of the Sun?" Jenny asked Pedro as they climbed the stairs.

"From this island the Sun first rose to shed his light," Pedro told her seriously. "This is the birthplace of the Inca. Here the sun god, Viracocha, creator of all, placed the first Inca, Manco Kapac, and his woman, Mama Ocllo, to bring civilized life to the tribes that lived then on the earth. It is the most sacred of all places to my people."

Justin and Jenny exchanged doubtful glances, but didn't argue. At the peak of the island, Pedro guided them through an ancient Inca palace. After making them promise not to leave Pedro, Uncle Pete had stayed behind with the boat owner as guide to explore the island at a slower pace. Justin put Short and Skinner out of his mind. They would be long gone by now.

"You really believe all this stuff, don't you?" Jenny inquired after hearing still another Inca legend.

"You do not believe me?" Pedro asked angrily. "Come, I will show you!" Taking Jenny by the arm, he hurried them down a brushy trail until they stood at the water's edge again. Turning them to face the cliff, he indicated a rock formation far above.

"That is the Sacred Rock, the rock where all things began." In the curiously shaped rock were two long, shallow openings, one above the other.

"You see there ... and there. In the Great Flood that destroyed the world, the Sun and the Moon took refuge there in the sacred rock. All but they were drowned. When the Flood finished, they came out and made life again on the earth. Come!"

Almost running, he hurried them along the waterfront. In the hard limestone that covered the beach were shallow depressions about a yard long, shaped vaguely like giant human footprints.

"See!" Pedro said triumphantly. "There are the footprints of the Sun. The stone was still soft when he rose from the Sacred Rock after the Flood, and his steps were sealed in the stone forever."

"They look like natural rock formations to me," Justin answered skeptically. "So does your 'Sacred Rock'!"

"If you will not believe me, I will tell you no more," Pedro grunted.

"Don't be mad," Jenny pleaded. "You won't believe what we tell you about Jesus, and we don't believe in your sun gods. But we still like hearing your stories, don't we, Justin? Please!"

Responding to Jenny's coaxing, Pedro led them to a mass of ruined buildings just a hundred yards south of the Sacred Rock. A square, manmade opening led down into a maze of underground tunnels, but Pedro led them through a series of crumbling rooms to an open courtyard. In the middle of the courtyard was a square altar made of a single block of stone, big enough to hold an ox—or a man.

"Here in La Chinkana, sacrifices were made to the Sun," Pedro informed them. "Llamas, sheep, and the most beautiful of the young maidens of my people were given to the Sun for his pleasure."

Jenny shuddered. "How horrible!"

"How can you worship gods who were so cruel?" Justin asked. "They were evil!"

Pedro looked troubled. "The gods are not like men. They do not have to be good. They need only be strong."

"Jesus is good *and* strong," Jenny insisted. But Pedro only shook his head.

"We promised Uncle Pete we'd be back at the landing at four," Justin said as they came back out into the open. "We'd better not be late again. We've only got an hour before we need to start back."

"Can't we see the underground tunnels?" Jenny asked, turning to Pedro.

"How are you supposed to *see* in there?" Justin demanded.

"No one must come to the Island of the Sun without seeing the Laberinto de La Chinkana," Pedro answered. He reached into his pocket and pulled out a pair of candle stubs and a box of matches. "See? I always am ready."

Outside the opening to the labyrinth, Pedro lit the candle stubs and handed one to Justin. "You must stay close to me. I know the turns needed to come out again. If you do not stay close, you will be lost in the tunnels."

Water dripped from the low roof and walls of the tunnels. The only light was the dim circles of the candles, and black shadows danced on the damp walls just beyond their reach. The smallest sound echoed down the black halls, and the children instinctively lowered their voices to a whisper.

The tunnel twisted right and left, crossing many smaller side passages, until the twins were thoroughly confused. Jenny had just announced she had seen enough when a glow of light appeared only a dozen yards away, down a side tunnel to their right. Instinctively, Justin reached over and knocked Pedro's candle from his hand, blowing out his own in the same instant.

"What did you do *that* for?" Jenny muttered with annoyance into the dark.

"Shhh!" Signaling for Pedro and Jenny to follow, Justin hurried after the light before it could turn into another tunnel. As they crept closer to the light that weaved through the darkness, Jenny and Pedro saw what Justin had immediately recognized. The small American, Short, hurried in front of them, carrying a powerful flashlight. At his heels were the massive Skinner and their Latin friend, Pepe.

"They haven't gone after all," Justin whispered. "I'll bet they're on their way to that 'delivery' right now. Come on!"

The three children moved as quietly as they could as they followed the men through the maze of tunnels. The slightest sound echoed, but the heavy footsteps of the three men in front of them concealed their own footsteps. The men suddenly stopped at a junction of three tunnels, and the children's own footsteps pattered on several paces before they could come to a halt.

Short pulled what looked like a map from his pocket, but Skinner stared back down the tunnel, the flashlight Short held reflecting a puzzled look on his broad face. The three children pressed back against the wall of the tunnel.

"Did you hear something?" he growled.

Intent on the map he was studying, Short shook his head impatiently. Justin held his breath as Skinner continued staring back down the tunnel for a long moment, trying to pierce the thick darkness that hid the children. Justin's foot began itching, and he felt an almost uncontrollable urge to sneeze.

"I know I heard something!" the big man said at last. "I'm going to check it out!"

"There are always sounds in places like this!" Short snapped. "We don't have time to waste!"

He folded his map, and he and Pepe strode off down the left tunnel, Skinner trailing reluctantly behind. Skinner kept glancing back over his shoulder, but the three children were careful to keep out of sight.

They stopped as the three men descended a short stairway into a wide underground room. There were no other openings into the chamber. In the center of the room, a single candle glowed.

Crouching in the shadows at the top of the stairs, the three children watched as a strange man with the dark, round face and traditional clothing of the Quechua stepped into the candlelight. He carried a small wooden crate.

Pepe greeted the stranger and took the crate. Placing it on the floor, he pulled a screwdriver out of his pocket and proceeded to pry up the lid.

Skinner grunted in approval as he reached into the chest and lifted an object to the light. Then Justin heard his sister gasp softly, and he bit his own lip to stifle a shout. For in the flashlight beam, the object in Skinner's hand shone with the distinct yellow glitter of gold!

CHAPTER SEVEN

Escape
by Boat

P edro tugged on Justin's sleeve. "Let us go!" he whispered sharply. "We must leave this place now!"

"Just a minute," Justin whispered back. "I want to see what they're doing." The Indian who had delivered the crate backed into the corner, the flickering candlelight outlining his dark face. Short and his two companions bent over the box, carefully examining its contents.

Lifting a long gold chain to the electric light, Short grunted with satisfaction. He motioned irritably to Skinner, who pulled out his wallet. The delivery man came forward eagerly as Skinner counted out a wad of green bills and thrust them into his hand. Short dropped the chain back into the crate and carefully replaced the lid. Pepe picked up the screwdriver. With the blunt end, he pounded the first nail back into place.

"You are crazy to stay here!" Pedro hissed against Justin's ear. "They will be leaving soon. We will be in great trouble if they find us here. They are very bad men! You may stay here, but I go now!"

"I'm going too," Jenny added firmly. "This is spooky!"

"All right," Justin agreed reluctantly. The three crouching children carefully got to their feet without making a sound. They tiptoed quietly back into the pitch-black of the tunnel, the glow of the flashlight rapidly disappearing behind them.

Only when they had turned two corners, groping their way with one hand on the cold, damp stone of the tunnel wall, did Pedro pull out his box of matches and light the one candle stub they had left.

"We must go quickly!" he said harshly. "You are two very stupid gringos! You think this is some game to be played, a great adventure to tell your friends when you go back to your country and your nice, safe home."

The dim glow of the candle reflected the worried anger on his face. "You do not think that there may be real trouble. I have seen this kind of men before. They will kill those who get in their way—and here there is much money to be had. Do not think your kind God will protect you while you play with serpents!"

Pedro set off at a trot, shielding the candle with one hand. He turned right, left, then right again with the ease of someone who had traveled these halls often. Chastened by his words, Justin and Jenny followed meekly. Within minutes they were blinking as their eyes adjusted again to the bright afternoon sun.

Pedro didn't stop at the entrance, but urged them up the hill until they were well hidden by dense shrubs that grew over and around the old stone walls. Justin stopped as Pedro indicated the path that would take them back to the boat landing.

"Just a minute, Pedro. I guess you're right," he said humbly. "I *have* been stupid. I *have* been thinking of this as a great adventure. I never really thought there'd be any danger. I guess it's time we told Uncle Pete and let him handle it."

A triumphant grin split his freckled face as he added,

"But we *did* get what we came for, didn't we? We know they really are smugglers, and we've caught them red-handed."

He frowned suddenly. "Now, we just need some proof for the police. We'll have to stay long enough to see where they go next."

Pedro was shaking his head vigorously, his expression still dark with anger. Justin urged, "Come on, Pedro, you don't want them to get away with this, do you? I mean, it's part of that 'Inca heritage' you're so proud of."

"Justin's right!" Jenny interrupted suddenly. "We can't just let them steal all that stuff."

Justin grinned at his sister, then continued, "We'll watch from up here until they come out—just to make sure they've got the stuff with them. Maybe we can see where they store it. The police will have to believe us if we show them where the stuff is hidden. What danger can there possibly be in that?"

After a moment of thought, Pedro nodded reluctantly. "Okay. We watch from here to see where they go. But we watch only. Then we go back to the boat and tell your uncle what has happened."

Pushing through the bushes, Pedro led the twins to a relatively flat spot above the opening to the labyrinth. Taking cover under the thick underbrush, he stretched out on the rough ground and motioned for Justin and Jenny to join him.

They had found cover in the middle of a briar patch, Justin discovered as he stretched out beside Pedro. He was lying on top of a stickery bramble, and as he shifted position, thorns caught at his hair and clothing. He half-rose to find a more comfortable spot, but Pedro grabbed his arm.

The four men were now emerging from the underground passageway. They moved directly below the children's hiding place so that they were hidden by the overhang of the cliff. The three children could hear the rumble of low voices, but the sounds were too quiet for them to catch more than scattered words of the conversation.

After what seemed a very long wait, the children saw the Indian man move out from beneath the overhang and disappear into the ruins they had explored earlier. The other three men hurried down the path toward the lake. Pepe and Skinner carried the wooden crate, staggering a little under its weight, while Short walked behind them, keeping a sharp eye on the cargo.

"They've got it with them!" Justin muttered triumphantly. Then he added anxiously, "They're climbing down to the beach! They'll get away!"

"Do not worry," Pedro told him. "They cannot get away there unless they swim. There is no landing and no boats."

Pepe and Skinner set down the heavy crate, and the three men moved to the water's edge.

"Don't be so sure!" Justin answered. "Look! What's Skinner got in his hand?"

Skinner had pulled a large whistle out of a pocket. He blew a piercing blast. A few moments later, the motorboat the children had seen carry the men away from the wharf in Copacabana chugged into view. The pilot brought the boat in close to shore. Cutting the engine, he dropped anchor a few yards offshore.

Skinner and Pepe again picked up an end of the crate, and the three men splashed their way toward the boat. Carefully hoisting the crate aboard, they clambered into boat. The pilot was already gunning the engine, and a moment later, the smugglers and their stolen treasure were lost to view.

"Great!" Justin yelled, his clenched fist striking the ground in frustration. He winced and pulled a thorn from his hand as he added with disgust, "They must have had that boat waiting there the whole time!"

Somehow he'd had the idea that the men would hide their treasure somewhere on the island. He had imagined himself discovering the spot and leading the police victoriously to the treasure.

"We'll never find out what they do with it now!" he said gloomily as he stood up. "And without the gold, the police still won't believe us."

After a pause, he added, "We need more information... Look, guys, I know we agreed to get Uncle Pete's help with this mess, but I don't think we can tell him about what we've seen just yet. We need a little more time to think. Agreed?"

Jenny slowly nodded her head. Pedro absently nodded his assent too, as he stared across the beach where waves made by the motorboat still slapped at the shore. His black eyes flashed. "How can men of my own people betray the treasures of our past this way!"

"Well, I suppose some of your people will do anything for money, just like some Americans," Jenny answered.

The three children forced their way back through the briars, stopping to untangle their clothing from the thorns. When they were back on the main path, Justin blew a twig off his watch.

"It's a quarter to four! We'd better get back to the boat landing or Uncle Pete will never let us out alone again."

He started down the path at a run, Pedro and Jenny close behind. Arriving back at the ruined palace, the three hurried down the ancient staircase, two steps at a time. They reached the bottom, panting and out of breath, just as Uncle Pete and his guide walked up to the landing.

"Right on time," was his only comment.

▼▼▼

The boat ride back over the dancing blue-green waves was just as beautiful as before, but somehow Justin and Jenny were no longer in the mood for sightseeing. Stepping out at the dock, they walked slowly back to the rental car. All three children piled into the back seat. The twins both rested back against the vinyl seat, not even looking at the spectacular scenery flashing by. Pedro stared moodily out the window.

They had just turned into the outskirts of La Paz when Justin sat up straight, sudden excitement chasing the gloom from his face.

"Jenny," he demanded in a voice too low for anyone else to hear, "if you were those guys, where would you take that stuff next?"

Jenny was tired of the whole affair. "I don't know!" she answered crossly. "Anywhere, I guess."

"Not just anywhere. You see, we know something about them no one else does. *We know where they're staying!*"

"You mean, their hotel room?" Jenny asked. "Don't be crazy! They'd never go back there—not when they know we're on to them."

"But that's the whole point! They *don't* know we're on to them. They didn't see us at the digging site, and I'm sure Pepe hasn't said anything about meeting us ... not after the way he hurried us out of there. They can't possibly know we were watching them on the island. As far as they know, we're just dumb tourists."

His eyebrows knit together as he thought. "Now, if we could just get a look inside their room..."

"You promised to let Uncle Pete handle it," Jenny protested.

"We will. But it'd make more sense for us to take a peek at their room first. Then he'd have something to tell the police."

Pedro continued to stare out the window, and Justin didn't think he had overheard their whispered conversation. He was sure the other boy wouldn't approve. When they arrived back at their hotel, Uncle Pete dropped them off at the front door.

"I need to take the car back, then I have a short business appointment. Restaurants don't open around here until about eight o'clock. I should be back by then, and we'll get something to eat. Mr. Evans mentioned a good pizza place around the corner. If you kids want something to do, maybe you'd like to walk down to the market with Pedro. You've never seen anything like the open-air market here."

"No, thanks, Uncle Pete," Justin answered politely. "Uh... I think we'll just stay here at the hotel and rest. Right, Jenny? It's been a long day, and we're really tired. Pedro is probably tired too. It'd be nice if he could have the rest of the day off."

Uncle Pete raised his eyebrows, obviously surprised to hear his energetic relatives admitting fatigue. "Fine, I'll meet you back here then," he agreed. "I suppose you're not quite used to the altitude yet. Just don't go wandering off alone!"

Pedro stared at them suspiciously, as though wondering what the two were up to. "I be here first thing tomorrow," he said at last. "You not make any trouble, okay?"

When Uncle Pete and Pedro were gone, Justin and Jenny hurried into the wide lobby. As usual, the clerk was gone. Justin suspected that he spent most of his time taking a siesta in the back room. He checked the boxes.

"They're not here yet. Their key is still in the box." Reaching over the counter, he pulled down the key to his room. "Come on. We'll sit quietly in my room. That way we'll be able to hear them when they come in, and they won't know we're here. Once they get here, we'll find out if they still have the treasure."

"*If* they get here," Jenny muttered. "Anyway, they'll check just like we did. When they see your key is missing from the box, they'll know we're back."

"You're right." Opening the small gate that led behind the counter, Justin groped around on a knee-high shelf.

"I saw him put it here yesterday. Ah ha, here it is!" He held up an extra room key and slipped it into the empty box.

Upstairs, Justin and Jenny stretched out quietly on Justin's bed, Jenny still unhappy at what she considered a complete waste of time. Whenever she opened her mouth to give her opinion of the whole idea, Justin whispered "Shhh!" So they waited in silence in the slowly darkening room.

They had almost fallen asleep when they heard heavy footsteps on the stairs and the rattle of a key. The door of the next room slammed shut. A deep voice growled something they couldn't make out, and a higher one answered. Justin sat up and jumped off the bed.

"It's them! Come on."

Jenny grabbed at the back of Justin's jacket. "Are you crazy?" she hissed. "You can't just barge in on them! Pedro's right. We could get hurt doing this!"

Justin flushed. "Sorry!" he mumbled apologetically. "I guess we'd better wait until they've gone."

He sat back down. The minutes stretched like years as the room next door settled into quiet. Only an occasional murmur of voices told the two children that someone was still there. The sun's late afternoon rays lengthened and dimmed, and finally disappeared altogether. But they didn't dare turn on the light.

The twins had just decided the smugglers had settled in for the night when they heard the door open and several pair of heavy footsteps stomp out onto the balcony. The door slammed shut again, and there was the barely audible sound of a key turning in the lock. Justin and Jenny waited without moving until all was quiet on the balcony once more. Then Justin moved quietly to the window and lifted the curtain to peer out.

"I don't see anyone! Let's go."

He reached under the bed and pulled a small disposable flashlight out of his suitcase. His camera still hung around his neck, and he checked it for film. Motioning to his sister, he opened the door a crack. Jenny peered over his shoulder. The balcony was empty. Slipping out onto the balcony, they checked the courtyard below. No one was in sight. Jenny tried the knob of the next room.

"It's locked!" she said shortly. "Now what are we going to do?"

Justin produced the key to their room. "Watch!"

He slipped the key into the lock and jiggled it back and forth. When he heard a faint click, he turned the key. Justin grinned triumphantly as he swung the door inward.

"I mistook this door for mine our first day here," he explained. "That's when I found out these keys will open any door in the hotel with a little work."

The twins slipped through the open door, then Justin locked it behind them. Not until then did he flick the switch of his flashlight. He inhaled sharply at the sight that met his eyes.

In the center of the room stood a small, round table. On the table, still in the wooden crate, a treasure trove of riches glittered under the thin beam of the flashlight. Spellbound, the two children stepped closer. Justin moved his flashlight back and forth over the contents of the crate.

Golden bracelets and necklaces set with strange green stones, glinted up at them. Tiny silver statues of llamas and condors—the sacred bird of the Incas—lay against menacing figures that reminded Justin of the strange faces in the Underground Temple of Tiawanaku.

Jenny reached out slowly and picked up a figure that reminded her of the monolith she had seen of Pacha Mama. It fit snugly into the palm of her hand, and she ran a finger over the cool smoothness of the gold.

Placed carefully on top was the most wonderful piece of all: a six-inch balsa boat of pure gold, an exact miniature copy of those they had seen that afternoon. An Inca prince stood in the center of the boat, his arms folded across his chest. His proud features were perfectly formed. A feathered cloak worked in exquisite detail was flung over his shoulder. In the bow of the boat, a naked rower held his paddle high as he waited through the centuries for his master's orders.

"He's beautiful!" Jenny whispered in awe.

Justin handed the flashlight to Jenny and raised his camera to his eye. The brilliance of the flash lit the room as he took two shots of the golden treasure. Jenny turned the flashlight on the tiny figure of Pacha Mama for a closer look. So engrossed were they that neither heard the click of a key in the lock.

Suddenly, the door slammed open and the light snapped on. Startled, Justin shoved his camera into his jacket pocket as Skinner lunged into the room, his broad face ugly with anger.

"It's those kids!" Short and Pepe crowded into the room after him as Skinner quickly checked through the open crate of treasure. Instinctively, Jenny shut her hand tightly over the small gold figure she held.

The angry giant took a step toward the two children. "What do you think you're doing here?" he shouted.

Justin and Jenny stepped backward, but Skinner kept advancing on the frightened children until they were backed tight against the wall. Jenny pressed close to Justin as Skinner's heavy fists clenched and unclenched with rage.

"Answer me!" he bellowed threateningly.

Justin's hands were trembling, but his voice was almost steady as he answered, "Uh, we were coming by ... and we saw your souvenirs… They were so beautiful … we just had to take a closer look at them."

The two children crept along the wall toward the door. "Look, I'm awfully sorry we bothered your stuff," Justin added politely. "We just wanted to look. We'll leave you alone now. My uncle's waiting for us."

Short walked up to the children. He was smiling, but Justin shuddered as he got closer. "So you just happened by, did you? You just happened to open a locked door. For some reason, you didn't bother to turn on the light."

He looked at the flashlight in Jenny's shaking fingers. "You just happened to be carrying that, eh? And what else do you have?"

The smile suddenly disappeared as he grabbed Jenny's wrist and twisted it. The tiny figure of Pacha Mama fell to the floor.

"I'm afraid you two aren't going anywhere!" he continued as softly as a rattlesnake sliding across a rock. "You've got some explaining to do. Pepe, the door!"

Pepe reached behind him and the lock clicked. As the three men advanced toward them, Justin and Jenny stared at each other in dismay. They were trapped, and they could see no way out!

CHAPTER EIGHT

Trapped by Smugglers

"Let's see how much you know," Short said, still speaking softly.

He gave Skinner a quick nod. An unpleasant grin of enjoyment spread across the big man's face. Jenny was still clutching the flashlight, and she quickly shoved it into her jeans pocket just as Skinner grabbed both twins by the back of the neck and half-dragged them across the room.

Justin and Jenny twisted and turned, but Skinner's broad, meaty hands were iron-strong. Chuckling at their attempts to break loose, the big man shoved the two children onto a bed and loomed over them. Grabbing Justin by a handful of red curls, he shoved his face so close that Justin almost choked at the sour odor of his breath.

"You tell me what you two are doing here or I'm going to get real mean!" he demanded roughly.

Jenny jumped up from the bed. "You leave him alone!"

Skinner's thick lips spread into a nasty grin as he turned his attention to the girl. "Well, well! Is Mommy afraid her baby will get hurt?"

Releasing Justin, he shoved Jenny so hard that she fell

back across the bed. Then he turned his attention back to Justin, yanking his head back until Justin was sure his hair was coming out by the roots.

"If you don't want anyone hurt, you'd better start talking. I'll bet you two were our little spies yesterday out at the diggings, weren't you?" His grin grew wider with satisfaction as he read the answer in Justin's startled face.

"Okay, who else knows about this?" he growled, his voice deep and threatening. "Did you tell your uncle about your little treasure hunt?"

Skinner sounded so much like a "bad guy" in some old cowboy movie that Justin suddenly lost his fear. A slow anger began to burn within him as he stared unblinkingly up at the big man.

"Uncle Pete doesn't know anything about this!" he answered defiantly. "You'd better let us go right now! Someone's going to be looking for us pretty soon, and you're going to be in a lot of trouble if you don't let us go!"

Skinner let go of Justin's hair, shaking his head slowly as he thought about the boy's words. His broad, ugly face suddenly looked worried and unhappy.

"You really didn't tell anyone about us?" he asked uncertainly, running a hand through the strip of hair that crossed his shaved head.

"Of course we didn't!" he answered. "We were just looking around ... the way kids do."

Justin rubbed the back of his neck, wincing as he felt the marks of Skinner's fingers. *This guy really isn't very smart*, he thought.

Skinner hunched his massive shoulders and scratched his chin, thinking hard. "Well, I guess you can go ... if you promise you won't tell anyone!"

"Are you out of your mind?" Short paced across the

room and elbowed Skinner aside. "Let me handle this, you idiot!"

He cuffed Justin across the side of the head. "You think you're really smart, don't you, kid? We warned you about snooping around. Now you know more than is good for you, so I'm afraid you'll have to stay right here."

Jenny jumped to her feet again. "You'd better let us go!" she challenged bravely, but with a shakiness in her voice. "Uncle Pete is looking for us by now. You can't get away with keeping us here."

Short's narrow, weasel-like face held no expression, but something about the cold, pale-blue eyes made Justin swallow in sudden fear. Here, Justin suddenly realized, was the boss of the smuggling operation.

"You lie!" Short said flatly. "We've already checked through the building, and you two are the only ones here. In any case... Skinner, get downstairs and keep a lookout for anyone coming in. See if you can handle that, at least, without blowing it!"

He motioned to Pepe. "You! Get these two tied up and lock them in the bathroom. Gag 'em too." He handed Pepe a roll of thin nylon rope.

Pepe, his brown eyes faintly apologetic, pushed the two children into the bathroom. Pulling Justin's arms behind his back, he tied them tightly, then stretched the long length of rope over to tie Jenny's hands. There was little room to sit on the tiny bathroom floor, so he shoved the twins into the curtainless shower stall and pushed them to the floor.

"I am sorry," he told them in a low voice as he wound the rope around their ankles. "Did I not tell you to get away? Why did you come back?"

"I guess ... I guess we were just playing a game," Justin answered slowly, remembering Pedro's accusation. He looked thoughtfully at Pepe. "You seem nice. You aren't really going to help them get away with this, are you?"

"Please let us go!" Jenny pleaded.

Pepe shook his head sadly. "I am sorry. I wish I could help, but they will kill me if I allow your escape."

Avoiding their eyes, he reached for one of the bed sheets and tore off two strips of cloth. Gagging them securely, he left the room without looking back, swinging the door closed behind him.

When he had gone, Justin quietly tested the strength of his bonds. Pepe had left the light off, and the gags prevented the twins from talking. Justin tugged at the ropes until his wrists ached, but Pepe had tied them securely. He finally quit trying, realizing that they couldn't get by the men in the other room even if they did get loose.

Leaning back against the shower stall, he shut his eyes wearily and tried to concentrate on a plan of escape. Occasionally he caught the murmur of voices in the other room, but the men spoke too quietly for him to make out words. Beside him, Jenny lay on her side motionless, and Justin thought she must be asleep.

Justin couldn't tell how much time had passed before he opened his eyes again. He only knew that his hands and feet had lost all feeling. The rest of his body ached enough to make up for them, though. He glanced around the darkness, then sat up with a start as he caught a glimpse of Pepe leaning over an open suitcase.

He stared, confused, then he realized what had happened. When Pepe swung the door shut earlier, the latch hadn't caught. Now the door had opened slightly. In a full-length mirror on the bathroom wall Justin now had a clear view of part of the other room, including the locked door.

He watched Pepe's reflection snap a suitcase shut and place it beside the door. Then Short moved into his field of vision, carrying another suitcase. On the table, the chest of stolen treasure still winked at him, but as he watched, Pepe replaced the lid and picked up a hammer. The smugglers were obviously moving out.

A key rattled in the lock, and Skinner stomped in. "There ain't no one down there!" he growled. "Are you guys about ready to go? I've got the car ready and waiting."

Just then, Justin heard quick footsteps along the balcony, and a sharp knock sounded at the door. The three men froze. "Sure there's no one down there!" Short snapped. "Skinner, can't you do anything right?"

The big man shrugged helplessly as another knock was heard and a loud voice called out. Justin straightened up with a jerk, and Jenny struggled to a sitting position as they recognized the voice that spoke. Uncle Pete had found them at last!

Striding over to the door, Short opened it just enough to peer out. Justin kept his eyes glued to the faint reflection, grinning with delight under the gag as Uncle Pete's deep voice boomed, "Have you seen anything of a girl and a boy— thirteen-year-old twins?"

Standing in the doorway to prevent Uncle Pete from seeing into the room, Short answered, "As a matter of fact, we did see a couple of kids. American, right?"

He turned to Skinner. "You remember those kids we passed down the street, don't you? A redheaded boy and a girl. I noticed them because they were chattering away in English."

"Yeah," Skinner's gravelly voice added. "Toward the market, that's where they were heading."

Oh, no! He's going to believe them! Justin thought desperately. *I've got to make some noise!*

Raising his heels as far into the air as he could, he let them bang to the floor. The resulting thump echoed in the tiny bathroom, and he repeated it. Jenny too, catching on to what Justin was trying to do, thumped her heels against the wall.

"What's going on in there?" Uncle Pete demanded. Justin caught sight of a full red beard as Uncle Pete pushed through the doorway. Justin went limp with relief. *He'll find us after all,* he thought.

Then he saw Short nod to Pepe. Pepe picked up the hammer and began pounding in nails on the crate lid. Short opened the door wide and said loudly, "Oh, that's just Pepe, finishing up some packing. We have a late plane to catch tonight. Now, if you're through looking around..."

Justin and Jenny doubled their efforts, but Pepe's hammering drowned out the faint sound. Uncle Pete's exasperated words rang out over the noise. "Well, if they show up here before you leave, please let them know their uncle is looking for them. And tell them to stay put here at the hotel!"

"We'll give 'em the message, mister," Short promised, beaming with fatherly kindness as he ushered Uncle Pete out the door. "Don't you worry any. Kids are like that, always running off. They'll turn up safe and sound."

The twins heard Uncle Pete thank them. As he watched the door slam shut behind his uncle, Justin groaned inwardly. If only they had told Uncle Pete about this mess before! Now no one knew where they were, and their last chance of rescue was gone.

The bathroom door opened and Short stepped in. He slapped them both, hard. "That'll teach you not to make noise!"

His ears ringing from the blow, Justin glared at Short over his gag. Short leaned down with a knife and slashed the ropes at their ankles. "You've got some walking to do," he informed the two children, yanking them to their feet. But their legs, now completely numb, wouldn't hold them, and they collapsed again to the floor.

Impatiently, Short slashed the ropes on their wrists as well. "You've got five minutes to rub some life into those legs. Now move!"

He left the bathroom. Angry tears welled up in Jenny's brown eyes as she rubbed at her legs with almost useless hands. Justin reached over and patted her awkwardly, his eyes above the gag trying to convey his sympathy. Jenny nodded back and brushed the tears away, and both children turned back to rubbing. Painful prickles soon replaced the numbness as feeling returned to their limbs.

A few minutes later Pepe entered and helped them into the other room. Justin looked around. Dressers and closets stood open and empty. The packed suitcases were piled neatly beside the door. The wooden crate, its lid now nailed back on, still lay on the table. Short stood beside it, counting out bills from an open wallet.

Skinner lifted a pair of suitcases. "I'll go load up. Where do we go next, Short?"

"We've got that last load to pick up at Tiawanaku. We'll have to drag the kids along for now. For sure, we can't come back here again. We'll be out of the country by tomorrow anyway."

"Yeah, and I suppose we'll have to find a truck now and head south for the Argentine border," Skinner growled. "After we had your buddy's private plane all arranged!"

Satisfied with the contents of his wallet, Short shoved it back into his pocket and replied sharply, "We'll be on that plane tomorrow just like we planned."

"But, Short, they know who we are now. And they'll be watching every airport in the country once we turn the kids loose."

"*Who* knows who we are?" Short answered smoothly. "You heard these kids say they didn't tell anyone else. They are the only witnesses against us—the only ones between us and freedom. You aren't planning on letting two kids get in our way, are you, Skinner?"

Justin grew cold with terror as the two men turned and looked at them, Skinner with sudden cruel pleasure, Short with the flat, unwinking stare of a rattlesnake preparing to strike.

Turning away, Short commanded, "Pepe, get the kids something to eat and drink before we go. The coffee's all ready over there. And hurry up. We've got to get out of here before their uncle shows up again."

Picking up a pair of suitcases, he headed out the door. Skinner followed, leaving the two children alone with Pepe. The kinky-haired Spaniard looked strangely pale under his dark tan as he fumbled with their gags, and his hands trembled so much that he finally had to resort to a knife to cut the knots.

Justin spit out the grimy rag. His mouth was so dry he could hardly swallow. "Please!" he croaked. "A drink of water!"

Pepe shook his head and brought them each a piece of bread and a cup of black coffee. They gulped the hot coffee eagerly, but he snatched the cups away after one swallow and handed them the bread.

"No more!" he whispered. "It is bad coffee! Now remember, no matter what, pretend you are asleep!"

Before he could say more, Short and Skinner re-entered the room. Glancing nervously in their direction, Pepe carried the cups into the bathroom, and the children heard the sound of running water.

Justin managed only a few bites of bread before he began feeling strangely dizzy. Beside him, Jenny dropped her bread to the floor. "I feel awful!" she whispered.

Shaking his head to clear it, Justin helped his sister to a bed. As he collapsed down beside her, he saw Short watching them with satisfaction. Justin thrust his hands into his jacket pockets to keep them from shaking. One hand encountered the camera he had shoved in there earlier, but the other touched something sharp. It was the piece of pottery he had found in the ruins the day before.

He glanced around quickly. Short and Skinner were now bent over what looked like a road map, arguing in low voices. Hardly aware of what he was doing, he pulled the clay shard from his pocket and thrust it under the mattress.

Pepe hurried back into the room. Yanking Justin and Jenny to their feet, he grabbed both children by an arm and hurried them to the stairs. Justin was finding it difficult to concentrate on where he was going. His head spun, and each step dragged as though he were walking in quicksand. He vaguely sensed Jenny stumbling along beside him.

As he tumbled into the back of the long, black car, he managed to mutter, "It was the coffee! They drugged the coffee!" But no one heard him, and he and Jenny were already sound asleep.

CHAPTER NINE

Cave of the Inca Re

Justin awoke to the bumping of a moving car. *Where am I?* he wondered. *What am I doing in this car?* As he lay quietly, a voice echoed in his mind, "Remember, pretend you are asleep!"

The events of the past few hours came rushing back. *The coffee*, he remembered. Pepe had given them coffee, and they had fallen asleep. Justin guessed the coffee had been meant to put them out for many hours. But Pepe had allowed them only a swallow, just enough to fool the children's captors.

Good old Pepe, Justin thought gratefully.

Was Jenny awake too? He reached out in the dark and squeezed her hand. She squeezed back, but she too lay as though she were asleep.

The car pulled to a stop and the three men climbed out. One leaned through the open window and shone a bright light into the back seat, but Justin and Jenny kept their eyes shut and breathed lightly, as though sleeping. The light moved away, and Short's high voice directed, "They're still out! Let's get the stuff and get out of here!"

Justin lay still until the sound of the retreating footsteps died away, then he cautiously lifted his head to the window. A full moon shone on tumble-down stone walls. He touched his sister on the shoulder. "We're at Tiawanaku. Let's go! This is our only chance to escape!"

Justin started to open the car door but stopped. "No, wait ... they'll see the dome light." Seeing the window down, he scrambled over the seat and climbed out, sliding quietly to the ground. Jenny did the same. On hands and knees, they carefully crawled around to the other side of the car. The cold night air of the thirteen-thousand-feet-high plain blew away the last of their drug-induced sleep.

Raising his head slowly, Justin peered across the hood of the car into the night. There was no sign of their captors. Nor was there sign of any living soul. The guards and local Indians who peddled merchandise and fake artifacts to tourists had returned to their villages for the night.

Crouching now beside the car, Justin patted his jacket and discovered his camera was still there. The smugglers hadn't taken the time to search them. He turned to Jenny. "Do you still have the flashlight?"

Jenny pulled the small flashlight from a jeans pocket. "Yes, it's right here."

Justin stopped her before she could switch it on. "Not now! They might see the light. We don't need it anyway."

He pointed toward the full moon that floated serenely above them. The flat plain, touched with silver by the moonlight, stretched around them for miles, offering little opportunity to hide.

"We'll have to try the ruins," Justin whispered. "It's the only place that isn't in the open."

They began running up the slight incline toward the safe walls of Tiawanaku. There was no way to escape the bright, revealing light of the moon. As they reached the wire fence that cut the ruins off from the road, Justin glanced back. His heart sank as he saw a massive shadow move from behind the small concrete building where they had bought tickets the day before. An angry shout told the twins they had been seen.

Justin pushed frantically on the gate that opened into the ruins before he noticed the heavy iron padlock. "We'll have to climb over!" Jenny whispered loudly. But Justin was already scrambling up the heavy mesh of the gate. The strands of barbwire that ran along the top of the fence were missing here. At the top, he reached down a hand for Jenny.

The two children climbed over the gate, dropped to the ground, and ran. Seconds later they heard a heavy body slam against the wire fence only a hundred yards behind them. As a flashlight beam pierced the night, searching for they twins, they continued to run, chests heaving from the scant oxygen of the high plateau.

When they reached the outer wall of the main temple complex, Jenny collapsed against the rough granite, struggling to catch her breath. "I'm so ... tired!" she panted. "I can't ... run anymore!"

"You've got to!" Justin whispered fiercely. "They're coming!"

Following his pointing finger, Jenny recognized the heavy bulk of Skinner and the slighter shadow of Short. The sharp report of a gun burst the silence, and a moment later the gate swung open.

"They shot off the lock!" Justin hissed. "We've got to get out of here!" He grabbed Jenny's hand again, and the two began to run along the high stone wall. They paused at the foot of a narrow staircase that led up into the main temple complex, but as they caught the flicker of a light at the far end of the wall, they turned and ran up the stone steps.

Ghostly black silhouettes dotted the moonlit grass carpet of the vast temple courtyard. Pointing at the far side of the courtyard, Justin whispered, "If we can climb down that wall and get into those ruins over there, they'll never find us."

But before they had a chance to move, they saw a beam of light float up the steps they had just climbed. Justin quickly pulled his sister behind one of the stone monoliths. Peering around the crumbling block of granite, he waited. He breathed a sigh of relief as the light moved behind the low stone wall that ran half the length of the courtyard.

Suddenly he froze as Short's high, thin voice echoed, seemingly inches away. Jenny tensed beside him. The twins hardly dared breathe as Short grumbled loudly, "Where did those stupid kids go? You should have known they'd be waking up soon!"

"It's your own fault!" Skinner's deeper voice whined. "You said those drops would knock them out for hours."

Justin's eyes roamed the darkness behind them. Careful not to make a sound, he again peered around the granite figure. He was puzzled not to see any sign of the two smugglers, but Short's high tones rang out once more. "Never mind! If they get back to the police, we've both had it. I'll check in here. You go around the other side."

Justin suddenly relaxed as he remembered the age-old loudspeaker set into the stone not far from the staircase they had just climbed. The two smugglers must be standing directly behind the stone loudspeaker at the far end of the low wall that divided the courtyard.

Jenny echoed his thoughts in a whisper. "They're behind the wall. They can't see us!"

"But we can't get back to the wall and down into the ruins," Justin whispered back. "They'd catch us for sure. We'll have to go down the front steps."

The beam of light suddenly moved from behind the stone wall. "Come on!" Justin whispered urgently. Staying in the safety of the shadows, the two children slipped from the shelter of one giant monolith to the next, always moving toward the main temple entrance. Once, Justin almost cried out as a round, unearthly face loomed above them. He pulled Jenny to a stop before he recognized Pacha Mama, the "Mother Earth" that Pedro had pointed out the day before.

The Pacha Mama was the last of the granite monoliths between them and the entrance, and Justin suddenly realized that a wide expanse of open ground lay ahead of them. As he paused uncertainly, a cloud drifted over the moon. Taking advantage of the sudden shadow, the two children made a dash for the wide gateway of the temple and hurried down the broad steps.

The Semisubterranean Temple spread out before them like a submerged swimming pool. As they trotted across the ancient paving stones, the moon broke out again from behind its covering. Its ghostly light outlined the strange carved faces that lined the underground walls, their sightless eyes watching over the vast ruins of the city as they had for centuries.

"We'll have to go that way," he whispered, pointing across the pool to the open fields they had explored the day before. "There aren't many hiding places, but there are houses across the field. We can get help there."

"Those houses are only mud huts!" Jenny objected. "Besides, those Indians won't understand anything we say. And we saw some of those men helping Short and Skinner. How do we know they won't turn us over to them?"

"Do you have a better idea? We can't stay here! If we can get into the hills where they were digging, there's lots of places to hide."

They had almost reached the open fields when Jenny caught her foot in a tangled plant and fell forward, the breath knocked out of her in a loud gasp of pain. The twins froze for a moment, hoping no one had heard Jenny's cry. But seconds later they heard running feet.

"They're over your way!" Short's high voice shouted. It sounded very near. "Get them!"

Justin glanced back. A beam of light bobbed to their left, cutting them off from the open fields. Grabbing Jenny's hand, Justin turned toward the long, evenly shaped mound that loomed close ahead. Jenny pulled on her brother's arm. "Not that way! You're going toward the cave!"

"We've ... got no ... choice!" Justin panted out, running faster. "We'll have to go ... over the top!" But as the two children reached the mound, they slid to a stop in dismay. Stepping out from behind the massive building blocks that grave robbers had left piled at the foot of the mound, Skinner turned up the corners of his thick lips in gloating satisfaction.

The big man chuckled hoarsely as he walked forward, his great bulk blocking their escape. Behind them, Short played his flashlight over their motionless figures. There was only one way open. "Come on," Justin whispered. Before the two men could move, Justin and Jenny were scrambling straight up the steep hillside toward the Cueva de la Inca Re.

Justin had planned to climb to the top of the mound and try to lose the smugglers in the tumbled granite blocks on the other side, but as they reached the piled-up boulders that blocked the entrance of the cave, he pulled Jenny to a stop.

"In there!" he hissed, motioning toward the ragged opening, dark against the hillside.

Jenny stared at him in horror. "We can't go in there! We'll be killed! Don't you remember what Pedro said?"

Justin glanced back down the hillside. The two smugglers were only steps behind. "Yes, we can," he answered urgently, squeezing through the tight break in the brick wall. "God will protect us. Besides, there's nowhere else to go!"

Jenny tumbled in behind him, and he pulled her down beside him just as Skinner thrust his head through the opening. The two children backed away as the big man tried to force his way in. He swore viciously as his bulky shoulders jammed in the opening.

"Get out of the way, idiot, and let *me* in!" Short ordered coldly. Skinner moved away with a loud tear of ripping cloth. Justin held his breath as Short peered in, until he saw that the crumbled opening was too tight even for the smaller man. Outside, curses filled the air as Skinner pounded against the bricks with his bare fists.

"Don't be stupid!" the two children heard Short hiss. "We'll never reach them that way!"

Ignoring them, Justin put an arm around his sister, who was now shaking with cold and fear. Pressing his other hand to his aching side, he leaned his head back against the wall. Jenny groped for his hand.

"I'm so scared!" she sobbed.

"Let's pray," Justin whispered back, his own lips trembling. "Only God can help us now!"

As the two children bowed their heads in the darkness, Justin thought back over the events of the past few days and wondered, *How in the world did we get into this mess?*

CHAPTER TEN

Lost in the Labyrinth

The cursing and banging outside had died away. It was very quiet inside the cave, very dark, and very, very cold. Though the sun warmed it during the day, the "altiplano" dipped below freezing at night. A stray gust of wind whistled through the small opening in the wall, biting into their thin jackets. Backing away from the draft, Justin thought with longing of his heavy down coat back at the hotel.

Jenny huddled against him, still shivering. "Do you think they'll come back? Maybe we should get out of here while we have a chance."

"We're safer in here than out there right now," Justin said bluntly.

Jenny was silent for a moment. "Justin, do you believe that story of Pedro's ... about the curse of the Inca? Do you think something will happen to us for coming in here?"

"I don't know whether I believe it or not, but it doesn't matter," he answered. "Remember what Uncle Pete said—the power of God is stronger than any curse. He will protect us!"

"I ... I know. But I'm still afraid."

A sudden crash broke the silence of the cave. "Okay,

kids," bellowed Skinner's hoarse voice. "You come out of there or we're coming in after you. And if we have to come in, it'll be the worse for you!"

The two children scrambled to their feet. They froze as another crash sent a shower of broken bricks scattering across the cave. The thin beam of moonlight widened as a section of the wall caved in.

"They've got pickaxes!" Justin exclaimed. "Come on! We can't let them catch us!"

The full moon poured through the wider opening, turning the darkness into gray shadow. The twins could now make out the dim outline of their surroundings. They were in an immense vaulted chamber. The vast room was empty of furnishings, but deep shadows here and there offered promise of shelter.

The moon's silver turned to gold as a hairy, muscular arm lifted a flashlight through the opening. In its light the children saw that the shadows around the chamber were caused by archways of various sizes. Strange carvings filled the spaces in-between.

"They're coming in!" Justin whispered urgently. "We've got to hide!"

The twins ran across the stone blocks that paved the floor, and ducked into a small archway that was about three feet wide. They pressed backward into the darkness but had only taken two steps when they felt a wall at their backs. Justin groped for another opening, but only discovered more carvings.

Further blows of the pickax reverberated like thunder in the cave. A final crash toppled a whole section of the brick wall, then they heard a scrambling as the smugglers climbed through the gap.

"Nothing in here!" they heard Skinner grumble in disappointment as a beam of light drifted across their hiding place.

"We're here for the kids, not treasure!" Short shouted.

"They've got to be hidden somewhere. Search every one of those openings until you find them!"

The two children inched forward and peered out cautiously. The smugglers were on the far side of the room, Skinner's flashlight probing each archway. There was no sign of Pepe. Justin wondered if he had seized the chance to make his own escape.

The powerful beam slowly circled in their direction. "We've got to get out of here!" Justin whispered urgently. "We'll be trapped!"

"Let's try a bigger archway!" Jenny whispered back. "They may go further in."

Slipping away, Justin and Jenny crept through the shadows until they found the next opening. This arch was as wide as a doorway and reached far overhead. Holding hands, they stepped through the archway. This time their groping hands felt only empty space ahead, and rough stone walls to each side. They were in some sort of passageway.

Creeping along the wall until they were beyond the reach of the smugglers' light, the two children stopped and waited breathlessly as a light played across the archway, paused momentarily, then passed on.

"Those kids aren't anywhere!" they heard Skinner shout. "They must have gotten back out!"

"They've passed us!" Justin whispered with relief. "Now we just have to wait till they leave."

But a moment later, the light beam moved back across the opening. This time it stopped, probing the darkness deeply. Then, to their shock, the twins watched the circle of light enter the tunnel.

"No, those kids are still in here!" Short's high, expressionless words echoed off the stone walls. "Let's take a look down here."

The twins inched backward as Short and Skinner moved

quickly along the passageway. The approaching light illuminated other tunnels leading off on both sides of the passageway. Justin and Jenny ducked into the nearest opening just as the circle of light swept over them.

"Something moved down there!" Skinner rumbled.

"We know you're there, kids!" Short shouted. "You might as well give up!"

"What do we do now?" Jenny whispered in panic.

"We'll have to go further in," Justin answered. "Come on!"

"But we'll get lost!" Jenny protested. "We'd never find our way out of all these tunnels."

Justin thought frantically. The heavy footsteps of the two men were approaching rapidly and would soon reach their new hiding place.

"I've got it!" he whispered. Reaching into his jacket pocket, he pulled out the small stone he had used as chalk in the ruins the day before.

"We'll mark our way with this," he told his sister, rubbing the light-colored stone against the darker stone of the tunnel wall. The edge crumbled away slightly, but it left a clear mark beside the tunnel entrance.

"Once we lose them, we'll trace our way back with the flashlight. You've still got it, don't you?"

As she nodded, he broke into a run, pulling Jenny after him—just as the footsteps paused outside their hiding place. His free hand located another opening to his left, and he ducked inside.

Jenny hung back. "But won't they just see the marks and follow us?"

"Do you have a better idea?" Justin snapped back. "Besides, how would they know they're *our* marks?"

He scratched a mark beside the archway, his makeshift chalk crumbling even further as he did so.

"Maybe they won't look in here!" he told her as they backed into the darkness.

But it wasn't long before they again heard approaching footsteps. The twins hurried down this new tunnel as the beam of light entered their hiding place. They noticed that the passageway slanted downhill. Soon they were almost running as the incline grew steeper. The glow of the light behind them kept them from stumbling, and the heavy footsteps of the smugglers drowned out the sound of their own running feet.

The tunnel ended in a junction, and the two children lunged into the left passageway, Justin pausing to mark the tunnel they had just left. Then they grabbed hands again and ran blindly into the inky blackness ahead.

Jenny's outstretched arm found the next opening. Once inside, they could no longer see or hear any sign of their pursuers, and they dropped to the tunnel floor to rest. *There's something familiar about this place,* Justin thought as he leaned back against the stone wall.

Then he remembered the labyrinth they had explored with Pedro only that afternoon. Perhaps the same Inca architect had designed this similar maze of tunnels. But where those walls had oozed dampness, this place was as dry as the desert above. The air was still and heavy, and no longer as cold this far from the main entrance.

"Doesn't this remind you of the Island of the Sun?" Jenny asked, echoing his thoughts.

Before Justin could answer, he caught sight of a dim glow against the entrance of the passageway where they rested.

"Aren't they ever going to leave us alone?" he whispered savagely, jumping up and pulling Jenny to her feet. They began to run again, ducking into side tunnels and changing direction every few minutes. Yet the beam of light and the echoing footsteps followed them stubbornly.

The passageways continued to slope downward, and Justin guessed they must be well underground by now. At each turn he paused to mark on the wall, the white scrapes faintly visible in the weak beam of the flashlight far behind them. The twins grew to hate that light with a passion as the deadly game of hide and seek went on.

They had changed direction so often that Justin knew they could never find their way back to the surface on their own. But by now his makeshift piece of chalk was almost crumbled away. They would have to stop soon or risk losing their way in the endless maze of tunnels.

The twins had turned into yet another passageway when Jenny dropped to the tunnel floor, unable to go further. She bent over, wheezing. "I can't ... breathe!" she gasped. "I'm suffocating! Oh, Justin ... do you think it's ... the curse?"

Justin was breathing hard, too, but he answered firmly, "Of course not! The air's just stuffy, that's all! We're way underground here."

He glanced back. They were again free of the pursuing light—maybe this time for good. He slid down wearily beside his sister. Within a few minutes, they were both breathing normally again.

"I guess you were right," Jenny admitted.

Justin reached out in the dark to take her hand. "God won't let the curse hurt us, Jenny!" Just then a familiar glow moved into view, and the two children struggled to their feet once more.

"I wish God would do something about the smugglers!" Jenny muttered as they stumbled on.

By now they were too tired to move fast, and the persistent beam slowly gained on them. Its increasing light revealed that this passageway was much wider and higher than the others. To the twins' dismay, there were no longer any openings leading off to the sides.

The children came to a sudden stop as they ran into something solid. Taking a step back, they both screamed out of sheer terror! Hardly visible in the blackness, a face from a nightmare mocked cruelly at their fear. Strange horns twisted out from black temples, extending the width of the passageway. The fanged mouth opened wide enough to swallow them both.

For one long moment they stood there, petrified. Then a deep voice called, "There they are!"

The powerful beam passed over the children and lit up the demonic face. "It's just a statue!" Justin said shakily as he saw that the black depths of the open mouth formed yet another entryway.

He looked back. Short and Skinner were now running toward the twins, who stood unmoving in the glare of the flashlight. There was only one way open to them. Turning, the twins dove straight into the yawning blackness of the stone demon's open mouth.

Justin sensed instantly that this was not another tunnel. The sounds of their entry echoed against far walls as though they were in some great cathedral. They barely had time to step to one side of the entryway before the smugglers came after them, Skinner swearing as he banged his head against the low entrance. Then they caught their breath in awe as the heart of the great mound lit up for the first time in countless years.

The two smugglers did not even turn to look for Justin and Jenny, trapped in full view against the stone wall. Their attention was totally fixed on the treasures that lay before them.

"Hey, Short—look at all this!" Skinner exclaimed greedily, lifting the flashlight high. "That Spanish brat was right! We'll be set up for life!"

For a brief instant Justin and Jenny glimpsed a stone platform in the center of a high, vast chamber carved out of solid rock. The tightly bound figure of a man stretched out upon it, his withered features still preserved in the cold desert air of the high plain. His shrunken form glittered with silver and gold.

From perches high up on the stone walls, smaller gold versions of the stone demon that guarded the entrance glared down at the intruders, their jeweled eyes gleaming with a cold green light. Behind the funeral platform, the same strange figure that adorned the Gateway of the Sun shone down from an entryway identical to the one behind them. Stone chests heaped with the treasures of a lost civilization offered cold comfort to the long-dead ruler who would never again touch their shining splendor.

Justin and Jenny saw all this in a flash with their dazed eyes, then ... *the light went out!*

"Skinner, what's going on?" demanded a high voice out of the darkness.

"I don't know! This blasted thing just quit on me!"

"How could it go out? That flashlight was new!"

"I don't like this!" Skinner grunted nervously.

"Don't be a fool!" Short snapped. "So the batteries burnt out. You brought an extra pair, didn't you?"

"Yeah, I forgot!" Skinner sounded relieved. Justin and Jenny heard a faint clinking as the big man replaced the batteries, then a deep, frightened voice growled, "Short, these ones don't work either! I really don't like this!"

"Hey, you aren't worried about that kid's story of the curse, are you?" Short asked...but his own voice was strained.

"I don't know, but this place spooks me! I'm getting out of here!"

"And leave all this gold behind? We'll be rich, Skinner!"

"Yeah," growled the big man, more calmly. "I guess you're right."

There was a pause, then Skinner added, "What about the kids? Are we just going to let them get away?"

"Forget the kids! They'll never find their way out!" Short sneered. "Now grab some of that gold, and let's get going!"

Squeezed into the curved edges of the statue's backside, Justin and Jenny listened to the two men stumbling around in the darkness of the cavern. There was a muffled curse as someone banged a shin against something sharp.

The twins felt the warmth of a big body stumble by only inches away. Hoarse with fright, Skinner called, "Hey, Short—I can't find the gold! Or the entrance either!"

There was a crash, then Skinner cried out again, the words now muffled by distance. "Short, where are you? You've got to help me!"

Short's high voice answered faintly from somewhere far off. Frightened shouts echoed back and forth, each cry sounding farther and farther away. Then silence descended once more over the ancient tomb.

When the last cry had faded into the distance, Justin straightened up with relief. "Okay, let's get out of here!"

He waited a moment, then added impatiently, "Well? Aren't you going to turn on the flashlight!"

"I can't get it to turn on!" Jenny answered desperately.

"What do you mean?" Justin demanded. He reached into the darkness and took the small flashlight from Jenny's unresisting grasp. He flicked the switch again and again, but nothing happened. He shook the flashlight. Something rattled loosely inside.

"It must have broken when I fell!" Jenny was crying softly. "Now we'll never get out! We'll be lost forever—just like all those other people who came in here!"

Sick with despair, Justin tossed the flashlight aside and

slid to the floor. Without the pursuing glow of the smugglers' light, the darkness was absolute. It was a heavy, smothering blackness, so thick that Justin instinctively reached out as if to pull it away. But he couldn't even see the movement of his hand inches away from his face.

Jenny slid down beside him, and the two stared into the dark. Justin didn't know how long he sat there, arms wrapped around his knees, as his mind frantically rejected one idea after another.

"There's nothing we can do," he said at last. "We'll never find our way out alone."

Jenny sat up straight. She was no longer crying. "Yes, there is something we can do!" she answered firmly. "We can pray!"

Justin's despair lifted a little. "You're right, Jenny! We should have done that first."

He bowed his head. "Dear God, we're in real trouble! We'll never find our way out if You don't help us. Please show us what to do next."

"Please, God," Jenny echoed beside him. "We want to go home!"

The blackness around them didn't seem quite so heavy as they lifted their heads. *No matter what happens*, Justin thought, shoving his hands into his jacket pockets, *we aren't alone*.

One hand felt a hard object, and he jumped to his feet in sudden excitement. "My camera!"

He pulled the small camera from his pocket. "The flash will give us light!" he cried joyfully.

"But your batteries won't last the whole way back," Jenny responded.

"They won't have to," Justin answered confidently. "Just hold on to me tight!"

Jenny took a firm grip on the back of Justin's jacket. Justin felt for the rough edges of the carved entrance, then led the way through the stone mouth.

"There weren't any side tunnels here," he explained, "so we won't need any light."

Justin kept a hand firmly against one wall as they started back up the steep incline. It seemed a long time before his searching fingers felt emptiness. He stopped. "I don't remember which way we turned here. We'll have to use the flash."

He lifted the camera above his head. "Okay, here goes! Jenny, you watch for that mark."

He pressed the button, and a brilliant white light filled the tunnel, dazzling their eyes, then died away.

"Well, where's the mark?" Justin demanded.

"I didn't see it!" Jenny answered mournfully. "There wasn't time!"

Justin sighed. "We'll have to try again. I'll be looking too."

He pressed the button again. This time Jenny cried out excitedly. "There it is! We have to go left!"

As they turned up the left tunnel, Jenny suddenly commented, "You know, I'm not even afraid anymore."

"Me either," Justin answered.

That peace and confidence stayed with them as they pressed onward. Each time they came to an opening, Justin pressed the flash. Often the flash revealed no mark, and the two children continued on past the opening. Other times, they discovered the little white marks that were their lifeline and turned in a new direction.

Several times the twins were sure they had lost their way, but always they came at last upon another of the telltale marks. The passageways continued to slope gradually upward, telling them they were heading in the right direction. Not once did they hear a sound besides their own soft footsteps. The smugglers seemed to be lost for good in the depths of the maze.

By now they had lost all sense of time. It could have been hours or even days since they had entered the Cueva de la Inca Re. Occasionally they stopped for a brief rest, then pressed on, repeatedly placing one foot in front of the other until they were in a daze of exhaustion.

It was much later when Jenny pulled Justin to a halt after turning yet another corner. "Didn't the flash seem a lot dimmer that time?" she asked anxiously.

"I know!" Justin answered grimly. "The batteries are giving out!"

They turned twice more. As they stopped at still another junction, Justin raised the camera again and pressed the button, but this time there was no answering flash. He held the camera to his ear. There wasn't even the faint whirring of the charging flash.

CHAPTER ELEVEN

An Unexpected Reward

"It's no use!" he said at last. "The flash is dead." But somehow, even now, he wasn't afraid.

Jenny tugged on his jacket. "It doesn't matter!" she
cried excitedly. "Look!"

Justin scanned the blackness. Then he saw what
Jenny had seen—a faint gray glow far to their left.

"The entrance!" he exclaimed. "That must be the
archway we came through!"

Their exhaustion forgotten, the two children broke into a
run. Moments later, they burst through the stone archway
near the entrance of the cave. All was as they had left it. The
silver of the full moon still shone through the ruins of the
shattered brick wall, turning the stone chamber into a place of
quiet beauty.

But not for long. Before the twins had time to move,
sirens filled the air, and the roar of a powerful engine
screeched to a halt. The sound of running feet pounded
below the battered wall.

Then a flashlight was thrust through the broken brick
and the most welcome voice in the world called, "Justin!
Jenny! Are you in there?"

"Uncle Pete!" The twins were through the archway and running in an instant. Quickly climbing over the pile of shattered brick, they threw themselves into Uncle Pete's arms. The sirens were silent now, but headlights from several vehicles lit the scene. And below, at the base of the mound, men in green uniforms hurried back and forth.

"Oh, Uncle Pete," Jenny choked out, her arms around his neck in a stranglehold, "I thought you'd never find us!"

His strong arms holding both children close, Uncle Pete cleared his throat several times before he could speak. "I was beginning to wonder myself. When I came back to the hotel and found you gone..."

His deep voice broke, and he hugged Justin and Jenny tighter, then let them go. "Come on! Let's get out of here."

Justin and Jenny scrambled down the hillside, Uncle Pete close behind. When they were once more on level ground, he hugged them again. "Okay, kids, what happened? Are you both okay? I know about the smugglers, so just tell me what happened tonight."

The twins' words tumbled over each other as they poured out their story. Already, the terror of the last hours was ebbing away.

"And the flash gave out just as we found the entrance!" Jenny finished dramatically.

"By the way, Uncle Pete, how did you ever find us?" Justin interrupted suddenly.

"I didn't," Uncle Pete answered with a smile. "It was Pedro here."

He turned around and pulled the Quechua boy forward. Jenny and Justin had been so taken up with seeing their uncle again that they hadn't even noticed their friend standing patiently in the shadows.

Pedro's usually calm face was twisted with emotion, and the twins were surprised to see tears in the black eyes. "I thought you were all dead. I cannot believe that you have come out alive from the Cueva de la Inca Re, but my eyes tell me it is so. I ... I am so glad you are safe."

Justin reached out and gripped the other boy's hand. Jenny threw her arms around Pedro's neck and gave him a kiss on the cheek.

"You found us! Pedro, you're wonderful!" she exclaimed. A blush colored Pedro's high cheekbones, but his cheeky grin broke through the tears, and he hugged her back.

"You never said how you found us," Justin reminded impatiently.

Uncle Pete leaned back and crossed his long legs. "Well, it's like this. When I got back to the hotel and found you gone, I checked with our American neighbors..."

"Yeah, we know! We heard you," Jenny interrupted. "We were locked in the bathroom."

"I know that now," Uncle Pete continued. "Anyway, I wasn't too happy about you taking off like that. In fact, if I'd caught you then, I'd have disciplined you good—thirteen years old or not. I checked around the market, but you weren't there, of course.

"Then I thought Pedro might know where you'd gone. I called Mr. Evans, and we drove up to the room he and his mother rent across town. He said he had no idea where you were. He was very worried when he heard you were missing. That's when he told us about your run-in with the smugglers."

He fastened a stern eye on them. "Why didn't you tell me about this before, kids?"

Squaring his shoulders, Justin stepped forward. "I'm afraid that was my fault, Uncle Pete. I thought you'd laugh at us..."

Justin attempted to apologize, but Uncle Pete ruffled his

hair and said, "You're forgiven, Justin. But next time, please trust me.

"Anyway, we knew enough then to search their hotel room. We found the gag and rope they tied you up with on the bathroom floor. Then Pedro found... Well, I'll let him tell the rest."

Pedro pulled a small, sharp object from his pocket. Justin looked at it in surprise. He had forgotten about the piece of pottery. "We look all over the room. Then I find this under the mattress. That is a very smart thing to do. I remember you showing it to the guard, and I remember the digging you told me of. I think, *they are telling us that the men take them to Tiawanaku*."

Uncle Pete continued the narrative. "So we headed straight over to the embassy and got them out of bed. They called out the local police force—actually, their version of the National Guard. With you missing and the embassy behind us, they had to act."

He waved his arm toward the vehicles and activity surrounding them. "It took several hours to get things rolling. All the time I was afraid we'd be too late!"

For the first time since they had crawled out of the mound, Justin looked over his surroundings. A police car with red and blue flashing lights sat a few yards away. Beside it stood an open army jeep and a canvas-topped transport truck, painted in camouflage-green. Armed soldiers stood at attention on either side of the entrance to the tomb.

Jenny looked puzzled. "But why didn't we hear you coming? We didn't hear a thing until you got here."

"No, the colonel didn't want to warn the smugglers, so he left the siren off until Pedro here spotted the broken wall and guessed you were in the cave."

"Señor!" A tall man in a flashy, gold-braided uniform walked up to the group. Medals decorated his chest, and he walked with the bearing of a professional soldier. Justin guessed he must be the colonel. Mr. Evans and a short, over-weight young man followed him.

"Colonel Daniel Ramirez," Uncle Pete introduced. "And Mr. Appleby, an aide from the embassy ... and Mr. Evans, of course."

The colonel bowed slightly. "I am pleased to see that you are safe," he said to the twins in perfect but slightly accented English. "We have found the vehicle of your kidnappers and the articles they stole. My men are now investigating the site of their excavation. Now, Mr. Parker, I would like to speak awhile with these children."

Under the colonel's skillful questioning, Justin and Jenny gave a full account of the events of the last few days—all but that brief glimpse of the ancient tomb. By mutual agreement, they had decided the treasure of the Inca Re was safer left where it was.

When they finished, the colonel gestured toward the cave. "And you say these men are still in there?"

"As far as we know," Justin answered him.

"Are you sending soldiers in after them?" Jenny asked. Justin grinned to himself. His sister was obviously her nor-mal, inquisitive self again.

The colonel made the sign of a cross in the air. His hawk-like features were grim as he answered, "My men will not enter that evil place. I would not enter myself."

He studied the twins intently. "I still do not understand how it is that you have survived there alone."

"We weren't alone," Justin answered thoughtfully. "God was there with us." The colonel just nodded his head. He seemed to share Pedro's awe at seeing them alive.

"How will you catch the smugglers, then?" Justin inquired after a moment's silence.

"You need not preoccupy yourself," the colonel

answered dryly. "My men will guard the entrance. If the Americanos come out, we will have them. If they do not ... I think we need not worry ourselves about them again."

Jenny yawned, and the colonel's stern expression softened into a smile. He glanced at his watch. " *'El aurora,'* the *dawn* as you Americans say it, is not far away. Señor Parker, I do not think we need you any more tonight. You may take these two brave children home. But do not leave the city. I will need to speak with you further."

Jenny shuddered. "I don't think I could get to sleep in that hotel room—not without having nightmares. I'll think of those horrible men every time I see that place!"

Mr. Evans patted her shoulder. "Don't you worry. You aren't going back to the hotel. There are police all over the place anyway. You're coming to my place—that is, if you don't mind a sleeping bag."

"Oh, thank you, Mr. Evans. Thank you too, uh ... Colonel," Jenny said, holding her hand out to the colonel. Justin also thanked the colonel, and the tall officer strolled away, barking orders to his men.

"Isn't there someone else we need to thank, kids?" Uncle Pete asked, putting an arm around their shoulders. "Why don't we bow our heads before we go, and thank God for His protection."

For once Pedro had no scornful comment to make. He had listened with wide, unbelieving eyes as Justin and Jenny told of their adventures in the cave. Since then he had been strangely silent. Now he bowed his head with Mr. Evans and the Parkers as Uncle Pete prayed a short prayer of thanks.

▼▼▼

The sun was directly overhead when the twins awoke on the hard, tiled floor of the babies' bedroom. The Evans babies had been carried into their parents' room several hours earlier. Justin was rubbing the sleep from his eyes when Mrs. Evans bustled in. Her round face twinkled with excitement.

"I'm glad to see you're finally awake!" she said with a smile. "You have visitors coming in half an hour."

She laid a pile of clothing on the babies' changing table. "Your uncle brought your things over from the hotel. I ironed a change of clothes for each of you. I hope they'll do. There's a pot of stew simmering on the back of the stove when you're ready."

The two children scrambled out of their sleeping bags. They'd slept in the clothes they wore the day before. Jenny pushed her curls back from her face. "Who's coming to see us? The police?"

Mrs. Evans' eyes sparkled. "Colonel Ramirez will be here and, believe it or not, the mayor of La Paz. I never thought I'd see the mayor in my home!"

She turned to leave the room. "Oh, by the way, you have another guest waiting downstairs for you now."

Justin and Jenny hurried into their fresh clothes and were downstairs five minutes later. Pedro was waiting for them when they entered the dining room. Mrs. Evans bustled in and set a steaming pot on the table.

"Here are bowls and silverware, so help yourselves. There's a pitcher of milk, too. I'll be in the kitchen if you need anything. I'm mixing a coffee cake for the mayor."

She left, and Justin turned to Pedro. Then he stopped, puzzled. There was something different about Pedro today, and he suddenly realized the defiance that usually showed even through Pedro's cheeky grin was gone.

"Pedro, what's happened?" he asked as he sat down.

Beaming with happiness, Pedro answered shyly, "I wanted to tell you that I have asked Jesus to come in and save my heart. Last night I asked Him."

"Pedro, that's wonderful!" the twins exclaimed together.

"I am sorry now that I laughed when you tell me about God," Pedro continued slowly. "I did know in my heart that the old gods were not good—that they were evil and cruel.

"But I would not believe your words. I wanted no part of a God of weakness. When I saw you come out of the Cueva de la Inca Re, and saw that the curse of the old gods had no power to touch you, then I believed. I knew that your loving God was truly strong to protect you, and I asked Him to be my God, too."

Pedro was interrupted as Uncle Pete strolled into the dining room. "Hi, kids. Are you ready? Your visitors have just arrived. Come on, now. You too, Pedro."

Jenny and Justin looked hungrily at the untouched pot of stew, but they obediently followed Uncle Pete into the spacious living room. Two men stood looking out the window. Justin recognized Colonel Ramirez at once. Beside him stood a short, slim, middle-aged man in a dark dress suit. Colonel Ramirez introduced him as the mayor of La Paz.

Justin was disappointed to find that the mayor of Bolivia's capital city looked as ordinary as his friends' fathers back home, but Jenny was delighted when the mayor bowed over her hand in a most dignified way, and said in English, "I am enchanted to meet you, señorita." The twins later learned that many wealthy Bolivians spoke some English.

The mayor then shook hands with Justin. "You have done our country a great service, and I wish to thank you sincerely. Without your help, more of our great heritage would have been lost."

He turned to Pedro. "You, Pedro Gutierrez, are a true son of your country."

Pedro was speechless before one of the greatest men of his country, but he grinned proudly at Justin and Jenny.

The mayor held out a hand to the colonel, who handed him a small packet wrapped in silk cloth. "And now," he continued, "I would like to present each of you with a token of appreciation from our government."

Opening the packet, he presented each of the three children with a fine chain, from which hung a silver medal. Etched upon the medal was the national seal of Bolivia. A llama and a bundle of wheat were silhouetted against the towering Andes mountains in the center of the medal, with the Bolivian flag on each side, and a condor spreading his wings over the whole.

The mayor turned to Uncle Pete. "You must be very proud of these 'sobrinos' of yours."

Embarrassed, the twins shifted their feet uneasily. The mayor's sharp eyes noticed their discomfort, and he waved his arm at the sofa. "Come, let us all sit down. Colonel Ramirez has much to say before we must go."

As they sat down, Mrs. Evans, beaming with pleasure, carried in a tea tray and the promised coffee cake. She allowed herself to be introduced to the mayor, who rose and bowed over her hand.

As she finished serving, Colonel Ramirez said abruptly, "We must go soon, so let us now come to business. I will tell you what we have come to know since last night."

"Did you catch Skinner and Short? Are they still alive?" Jenny asked eagerly.

The colonel frowned at the interruption. "Yes, we did catch the two Americano thieves."

A strange expression crossed his face. "It was a very strange thing. My men say that they stumbled out of the Cueva not two hours ago. My men would not go near them at first, being afraid of the curse. But the two thieves did not try to escape. They just sat on the ground, staring at nothing.

"When my men finally arrested the men and brought them to headquarters, it was found that they remembered nothing—not about the cave, nor the smuggling, not even their names. The police medical officer declares that they are like children."

Justin and Jenny met Pedro's black eyes in a significant shudder.

The colonel continued, "Even now the entrance to the Cueva de la Inca Re is being bricked shut again. We had to pay double wages before anyone would approach the Cueva. Word has spread about the American smugglers, and the people are more than ever afraid of the curse of the Inca."

He eyed Justin and Jenny intently as he finished, "I am not superstitious myself, but ... I, too, will stay away."

The mayor set down his empty plate and added, "We have sealed off the smugglers' house and their excavation. The excavation will be of great interest to our archeologists. In the house we have found further evidence of the smuggling operation. However, there has been no sign of the third man, Pepe. Concerning the Americanos, it is doubtful now whether they will ever stand for trial."

Justin was pleased that Pepe had escaped. Pepe was a smuggler and a thief, but he and Jenny might not be alive now if it weren't for his help.

Colonel Ramirez and the mayor rose to their feet. "Now, if you will excuse us, there is much yet to do."

They shook hands all around again, then walked to the front door. At the door, the mayor turned to Justin and Jenny. "I have forgotten one thing. Please excuse me. There is a finder's reward for antiquities surrendered to our government. You two have earned this fee. Arrangements will be made before you go."

The twins looked at each other. They didn't need to say anything before nodding to each other in agreement. Justin spoke up, "Señor Mayor, we don't want the reward. The treasure would never have been found if it wasn't for Pedro. We would like the reward to go to him."

"You are sure about this? For such a great treasure it is a large sum of money."

Over Pedro's protests, Justin and Jenny insisted that was what they wanted. The mayor nodded abruptly. "If this is what you wish, it shall be done." Then the colonel and the mayor were gone.

Hours later the Parkers and the Evanses gathered around the supper table. Pedro was there too, crowded between Justin and Jenny. The twins had to tell their story again from the beginning for Mrs. Evans.

Now that they were safe, the terror of the night before had vanished from their minds and only the excitement of their adventure remained. Mrs. Evans exclaimed with horror at their tale as she shoveled mashed banana into her twin babies' open mouths.

When Jenny and Justin had run out of words, Pedro and Uncle Pete told their side of the story. Mr. and Mrs. Evans were delighted when Pedro then told of how he had asked Jesus to be his Savior. The long and noisy meal finally at an end, Uncle Pete leaned back in his chair and announced, "I bought plane tickets this afternoon—for tomorrow."

His bombshell stopped the conversation in mid-sentence. With everyone's eyes on him, Uncle Pete continued, "We've had a wonderful visit, thanks to you, Bob and Sally—not to mention a lot of excitement we could have done without. But I'm afraid it's time to bring our visit to an end."

He looked down at Justin and Jenny. "When I found you two missing, I told myself that if ... I mean, *when* I found you, I'd put you two on the first plane home."

The twins looked at each other in dismay and opened their mouths to protest. Uncle Pete held up his hand for silence. His green eyes twinkled as he added, "That's what I decided *yesterday*. But now you're back safe ... and—well, I changed my mind.

"I checked in at our company office this morning. While I was there, I received a call from the head office in New York. We have an oil exploration unit in the Bolivian lowlands that seems to be having a bit of trouble. I agreed to look into the problem. What do you say, kids, to a trip to the jungle?"

The twins' eyes shone with excitement. Over Jenny's excited squeals, Justin exclaimed, "Jungle! You mean a *real* jungle, like in Tarzan? Where they have monkeys, and dugout canoes, and ... and giant snakes?"

Justin leaned back in his chair, a satisfied grin on his freckled face. The adventure of the Inca treasure might be over, but he had a feeling plenty more adventures lay ahead.

BOOK TWO

JUNGLE HIDEOUT

Danger Everywhere

ts outstretched wings riding a rising current of air, the vulture watched hopefully. Its keen gaze narrowed as the tropical sun burned away the last wisp of cloud hiding the small running figure far below.

Without slowing his headlong speed, Justin brushed the sweat from his eyes with a sunburned arm that was scratched and sore from the sharp edges of man-high grasses. A long cut, ripped across one cheek by a poorly dodged bramble, stung from the salt of both sweat and tears. Wincing as a ragged tear in his jeans rubbed against a grazed knee, Justin paused to yank his T-shirt free from the stubborn grasp of a thorn bush.

His tongue was dry and swollen, and a growing pain in his side made him drag at his steps; but he ignored these minor discomforts. The urgency of his errand pushed him on toward the safety of the encampment whose metal roofs floated above the brush far to his right. He wondered briefly what might be happening to Jenny right now.

Justin broke from the cover of the brush into a once-cleared field of knee-high grasses. Like a grazing herd of pre-historic beasts, oil pumps of black-painted metal dotted the landscape. Too late, he dove for cover at the sight of a tall figure who scanned the horizon only thirty feet away. Justin groaned inwardly as the other's searching eyes widened in triumph.

Justin lurched to his feet and raced away, dodging between the oil derricks. He ran more easily, now that his precious package no longer tugged at his waist. The dangerous shelter of the jungle loomed just a few yards ahead. It was his one chance of escape—if he could only outdistance the powerful runner behind him.

A shout rang out from the edge of the jungle far to his left, and Justin felt a surge of hope as he saw the hazy outline of a man motioning in his direction. But an answering shout came from behind him, and hope turned to horror as Justin recognized the man who sprinted along the jungle edge to cut him off.

With a last, desperate burst of speed, Justin crashed into the dense cover of the jungle only yards ahead of his two pursuers. Instantly he froze, forgetting the danger behind him. Like a single frame from an old silent movie, every detail of the scene before him impressed itself upon his memory.

Unfamiliar trees formed a canopy here that shut out the relentless glare of the tropical sun. Vines as big around as Justin's arm roped the trees together in an almost impenetrable tangle. Countless varieties of orchids dripped from branches and spilled down tree trunks to splash drops of color across the watery-green gloom.

A gigantic downed tree of some exotic red wood lay across his path, the charred trunk giving evidence of the lightning storm that had caused its fall. A shaft of sunshine explored the opening the tree had left in the dense canopy, and danced across the tiny clearing. At the center of the setting was the great animal, crouched unmoving on padded feet. The light that glinted across its back was no brighter than the dappled pelt.

In the background, an orchestra of jungle sounds played an accompaniment to the dreamlike scene. A "guacamaya," the great rainbow-colored parrot of the tropics, called loudly overhead to its mate. A troop of chattering brown monkeys gossiped among the branches. A bright-green tree frog, its touch carrying a deadly poison, whistled through the air to land with a splat on a tree trunk above Justin's head. And underlying the jungle music was the rhythmic, almost purring rumble of the great beast—which now eyed the motionless boy with growing interest.

The loud snap of a branch broke the spell of the frozen moment. The low purr rose to an angry roar. A short tail lashed the ground in fury as powerful muscles bunched under the sleek skin. Justin's hands felt the sticky sap of the tree trunk at his back. Breathing deeply to control his fear, he glanced around, but he saw no hope of escape. Whispering a desperate prayer, he shut his eyes, just as the great gold-and-black animal launched itself into the air.

CHAPTER ONE

An Unusual Bus Ride

Justin Parker scowled down at the half-closed suitcase on the bedroom floor. Tucking in the escaping sleeve of a silky pink blouse, he forced the stuffed case together. Gripping the bulging sides between his legs, the tall, husky thirteen-year-old snapped the clasps shut before the contents could escape again.

Running his fingers through red-gold hair that would have curled if he hadn't kept it so short, he glanced around at the one empty suitcase and the chaos that still covered the floor.

"Where did all this junk come from, anyway?" he demanded. "I know it all fit in here before!"

Pushing dark curls back from a flushed face, Justin's twin sister, Jenny, shoved a heap of winter clothing into a duffel bag before answering, "Who was it that insisted on buying all those souvenirs this morning? That llama-skin rug took up half the suitcase!"

Justin's blue-green eyes twinkled as he protested, *"You* were the one who had to buy alpaca sweaters for everyone and his dog!"

Golden eyes flashing fire, Jenny jumped to her feet.

Hands on hips, she exploded, "Uncle Pete said we could get some presents for Mom and Dad and the rest of the family! Besides, he gave me a duffel bag so I wouldn't take up any extra room in the suitcase..."

Seeing the wide grin on her brother's freckled face, she realized she was being teased. With an exasperated frown, she grabbed a pillow and threw it at him.

Justin and Jenny Parker were as different in character as they were in appearance. Though Justin was usually calm and even-tempered, friends soon recognized a certain stubborn set of his jaw. Hazel eyes took in everything around him, and a scientific aptitude led him to investigate anything unusual.

Jenny was as outgoing and talkative as her brother was steady, but a strong streak of common sense balanced her excitable temperament. In spite of their differences, they were the best of friends—most of the time!

"Hey! Careful with the camera!" Kicking the pillow aside, Justin picked their small camera up off the floor. Slinging the camera strap around his neck, Justin leaned down to pick up a large, colored envelope that had been lying underneath.

"What's that?" Jenny reached for the envelope. Justin batted her hand away and slowly studied the writing on the front. Turning the envelope over and over, he carefully examined every inch until Jenny nearly danced with impatience.

"Don't be mean, Justin!" she pleaded. "Open it!"

With a teasing grin, Justin relented, slit the top of the envelope with his penknife, and pulled out a stack of photos.

"Our pictures!" Jenny squealed. Looking over his shoulder, she exclaimed, "Look, there's Lake Titicaca and the balsa boats. And there's Tiawanaku ... and the Gate to the Sun with Pedro and me standing in front. And ... and there's the cave!"

She shuddered at a picture of what looked like a high, manmade mound. A dark opening in the hillside promised entrance, but a closer look revealed that the opening had been bricked shut.

Justin and Jenny Parker had arrived in La Paz, the capital city of Bolivia, less than a week before. Their uncle—whose job required that he fly all over the world troubleshooting for Triton Oil, an international oil company—had invited the twins to spend their summer vacation with him. He planned to combine some business with holiday sightseeing.

During their few days in La Paz, the two children had stumbled onto a gang of criminals who smuggled ancient Inca artifacts out of the country. Taken captive by the smugglers, Justin and Jenny had escaped among the ruins. Only the power of God had rescued them from the cave and brought about the capture of the smugglers.

Justin quickly stuffed the pictures back into their envelope as the door swung open. A tall man obviously related to Justin walked in. A red-headed Santa Claus, Pete Parker liked to blame his size on the hospitality he couldn't refuse in the countries he visited all over the world. Now he raised reddish-brown eyebrows at the mess on the floor.

"Aren't you two done packing? We leave for the airport in just two hours. Mrs. Evans has lunch waiting downstairs." The Evanses were the young missionary couple who had made the three Parkers welcome during their stay in La Paz.

"We're almost ready, Uncle Pete," the twins said together, hurriedly shoving the rest of their belongings into the remaining suitcase.

"Did you remember to keep your summer clothes separate? It may be winter up here in the mountains, but it's always hot in the Beni." Since Bolivia was south of the equator, seasons were reversed. The Parker twins had left behind summer in their home city of Seattle, to find themselves in the middle of the cold season here. Now finished with his business in La Paz, Uncle Pete had been asked to check out a shutdown in an oil camp in the Beni, Bolivia's tropical jungle area.

▼▼▼

Several hours later, in the spacious airport lobby of the Bolivian lowland city of Santa Cruz, Jenny plopped down on top of her suitcase. "Can you believe it was winter just an hour ago?" she panted, pulling off her jacket.

Justin wiped his face with an already damp handkerchief and tugged unhappily at the high-necked sweater he'd put on that morning. "Uncle Pete says it's even hotter in the Beni!"

Jenny groaned. Just then Uncle Pete, a frown knitting his eyebrows, hurried over from the information desk. "Sorry, kids! It looks like our flight to the Beni got bumped. It'll be three days before the next flight. I guess we'd better find a hotel."

This time it was Justin who groaned. "Oh, Uncle Pete! Isn't there some other way we could go?"

Uncle Pete looked doubtful. "Well, there is the bus. But it's an eighteen-hour trip."

"I like bus travel!" Justin declared cheerfully. "Let's go for it!"

"Yeah, we took the bus to California last summer," Jenny agreed. "It was fun!"

"If you think you can handle it, that'll suit me fine! I'll telegraph the oil camp of our change of plans." His blue-green eyes crinkled in fun as Uncle Pete added, "But I'm warning you! This won't be like any bus ride you've ever had!"

▼▼▼

The sun was setting by the time a battered taxi let them off at the bus terminal on the far side of Santa Cruz. "This doesn't look so bad!" Justin declared as they watched their suitcases disappear under the heaped-up luggage on top of a bus much like a city bus back home. "Of course there isn't a bathroom, but I think it'll be lots of fun!"

Justin wondered about Uncle Pete's quick chuckle. Glancing up, he caught a look of mischief he'd seen before— when his dad had smuggled salt into Mom's sugar bowl last April Fool's Day.

"What does he know that we don't?" Justin whispered to Jenny as they threaded their way to seats in the back. Uncle Pete squeezed in beside a farmer several rows ahead of them. By the time they had settled in, the rest of the seats were filled up, but passengers continued to crowd onto the bus.

"Where do they think they're going to sit?" Jenny asked curiously.

She soon found out as a heavy woman dropped a large bundle into the narrow aisle beside the twins. Collapsing on top of the bundle, she pulled her thin cotton dress down over fat knees. Her plump, sweaty arm pressed against Justin as she tried to make herself comfortable in the too-narrow space.

As Justin edged away, a squawk startled both children. Peering over the high back of their seat, they saw several chickens, their feet tied together, resting on a teenage girl's lap.

The sun had now disappeared behind the city, and Justin reached up to flick on the overhead light. It didn't work. Standing up, he looked along the length of the bus. Every square inch of the aisle was now packed with standing or sitting passengers. Small children crowded in with those passengers fortunate enough to find seats.

A loud snuffle at Justin's feet whirled him around. Jenny hurriedly lifted her feet up as she exclaimed, "Hey, it's a baby pig!"

"*Disculpa* (excuse me)," a timid voice said, interrupting their amazed stare. A small, dark-haired boy dragged the piglet out from under the seat. With an apologetic smile, he disappeared down the aisle.

"It's going to be a long night at this rate!" Justin growled as the last of the light disappeared. "I guess we might as well get some sleep."

He soon discovered that this wasn't to be easy. As they left behind the paved streets of the city, ear-deafening rock music blasted from two ancient speakers at the front of the bus. The twins clung to their seats as the road became a pair of bone-rattling ruts.

Justin tried the recliner button on the arm rest, but that didn't work either. Finally, the twins wadded up their jackets as pillows and leaned against each other to rest as best they could.

Justin was in an uneasy sleep when a sudden jolt threw him to the floor. Picking himself up, he realized that the bus had stopped and was tilted dangerously. A glance at his luminous watch face told him it was two A.M.

Jenny rubbed her eyes sleepily. "What's wrong?" she asked anxiously.

Justin peered out the window. An earlier rain had churned a low spot in the dirt road into a sloppy mud hole. By the rising moon, he could see that the bus tires were buried to the hubcaps in mud.

"I think we're stuck!" he answered. "Come on!"

By now the bus was in an uproar as passengers grabbed their belongings and pushed their way toward the door. Justin and Jenny carefully picked their way down the now sharply slanting aisle to the open door, and jumped across to a grassy area. The tires on this side rested on the solid road edge, causing the bus to list heavily to one side.

Men were already lifting down the heavy luggage from

the top of the bus, while others tried to dig out the embedded tires. The bus driver called out orders over the crying of young children. Uncle Pete rolled up his pant legs and took a turn with a shovel, while the twins joined the women and older children in searching for stones and heavy pieces of wood to shove under the bus tires.

An hour later, the bus finally lumbered free of the clinging mud. Dirty and exhausted, the twins made their way back to their seats, only to find the heavy woman replaced by the small boy and his pig. The piglet's squeals ended their attempts to sleep.

Noon was long gone when the bus finally jolted into Trinidad, capital of the Beni, and pulled up in front of a small, red-brick terminal. Uncle Pete caught Jenny as she stumbled stiffly off the bus. Rubbing his hunched back, Justin hobbled down the steps. "Boy, what a night!"

A grin split the red beard. "Didn't you say it would be fun?"

"Well, it wasn't exactly *fun*," Justin answered, as he loosened dried mud from his pant legs. Remembering one of his dad's favorite expressions, he added, "But it certainly was an educational experience!"

Jenny dropped her handbag and fanned her face with a magazine. "You were right about one thing, Uncle Pete. This *is* even hotter than Santa Cruz!"

Porters were already lifting luggage down from the top of the bus, and a crowd of welcoming relatives and candy vendors pressed around the passengers. Uncle Pete looked around. "I don't see any Americans. Someone from the oil camp should be here to pick us up."

Justin had lifted the last of their suitcases from the pile of luggage when he noticed a slim, very blond young man half-running across the terminal. Pleasant sunburned features looked meant for a smile, but at the moment the man looked worried. His frown went away when he caught sight of the Parkers, and he waved over the crowd of dark heads.

The young man looked flustered as he pushed his way through to the Parkers. Pushing his hair back from his eyes, he apologized, "Sorry I'm late. We haven't made a mail run for over a week, and I just picked up your telegram, as well as the telegram from headquarters. I was afraid I'd missed you. Just as well, I guess—the bus was late, as usual."

Still breathless, he thrust out a hand. "I forgot to introduce myself. Alan Green at your service. I oversee the Triton oil camp here. You must be Pete Parker."

"Yes. Thanks for picking us up." Shaking the young man's hand, Uncle Pete introduced the twins, then added, "I'm sorry you had such short notice. I imagine the telegram from headquarters mentioned their concern about the shutdown of oil production at the camp."

Under his sunburn, Mr. Green flushed with sudden annoyance. "Yes, of course. We sent in a full report about the temporary shutdown," he emphasized. "But we sure didn't expect an on-site investigation. As our report stated, we have things well under control."

"That may be," Uncle Pete answered pleasantly, "but as I was already in the country, the head office asked me to check out the problem personally. I hope our unexpected arrival is no inconvenience."

"Well, actually things are a bit difficult..." Mr. Green looked even more flustered than before. "I mean, we weren't expecting visitors... Things are very..."

As he trailed off, Jenny whispered loudly to Justin, "He acts just like you do when Mom pulls a surprise room check!"

Justin grinned but stepped on her foot warningly as Mr. Green glanced back at the two children. Uncle Pete picked up a suitcase in each hand. "The kids and I are prepared to rough it," he said reassuringly. But his tone was firm as he added, "Why don't we continue this discussion on our way?"

Still looking unhappy, the camp administrator picked up the two remaining bags and led the way to an open, four-wheel-drive jeep. Justin noticed the insignia of Triton Oil painted on both doors. Once the luggage was settled in the back of the jeep, Mr. Green turned to Uncle Pete. "I'll be making a brief stop in town. It's a two-hour drive out to camp. I need to pick up some supplies, and you'll probably want a bite to eat before we head out."

As they left the terminal, they turned onto a wide, cobblestone street bordered by one-story houses of adobe brick. Fresh coats of whitewash shimmered in the sun. There was little traffic in the streets. Both pedestrians and cattle ambled down the center of the road, seemingly unaware as cars whizzed by.

"Is this really the capital city, Mr. Green?" Jenny asked doubtfully, as they dodged a small cart pulled by two sturdy oxen. "It seems so small!"

The camp administrator's expression brightened as he glanced back at Jenny's eager face. He pulled up beside a small central plaza before answering. "Yes, Trinidad is the capital of the Beni. It isn't very big, but then the Beni doesn't have a lot of people. It's a lot like the old American West. You'll find a lot more cattle, snakes, and monkeys around here than you will people ... not to mention every kind of bug you can imagine."

Justin's freckled face lit up. "Wow! It sounds like my kind of country, Mr. Green."

The young man smiled slightly. "I like it too. And you can call me Alan, okay?"

He opened the driver's door of the jeep and stepped out. "This is where we get out. The open-air market is a block down that way." He gestured down a narrow side street.

"You have about an hour for sightseeing—unless you'd rather come with me to the market."

Jenny was already at his side. "I'll go with you. I've never seen a real open-air market."

"Yeah, I'm coming too!" Justin agreed.

The three Parkers followed Alan down the dusty alley. Overhanging balconies blocked much of the light. The twins blinked as the gloom opened into a blaze of color. Plastic awnings of red, green, and blue shaded piles of every kind of goods. Black-haired women in bright cotton dresses lazily swished insects away from their produce. A roar of buyers bargained over the price of ripe bananas or fresh corn.

On Alan's heels, the Parkers threaded through the narrow footpaths between stands. Jenny stared with fascination at the baskets of tropical fruit: green and orange papayas, bright-yellow mangoes speckled with brown, pineapples, pale stalks of sugar cane peeled and ready to chew.

Uncle Pete moved away to examine a pile of supposedly genuine Swiss watches, while Alan bargained for fresh produce. Justin fingered a round, green object the size of a cantaloupe piled among other exotic fruits. "What's this called?"

Alan shrugged. "That's just an avocado."

Justin looked closely. "Boy, you sure don't see them this big back home!"

"Hey, take a look at these!" Jenny called.

At the next stand a young Indian woman nursed a toddler while she fanned small hills of every imaginable spice: black and red pepper, cumin, bay leaves, oregano, garlic, paprika, turmeric. A basket piled high with diamond-shaped green leaves caught Justin's attention. They didn't look like any herb he had ever seen. He raised his camera to snap a picture of the strange leaf when a tap on his shoulder whirled him around.

In front of him stood an old man. Deep wrinkles crisscrossed his gaunt face, but the oily strands that hung below a threadbare hat were still black. One cheek bulged. Wiping a claw-like hand across his mouth, he spat sideways, spraying Justin's sneakers with a stream of green.

With a frown, Justin stepped back, wiping his sneakers against a patch of grass. Hitching up well-patched pants belted with a piece of rope, the old man grabbed Justin's arm and pointed to the basket of green leaves.

"What does he want?" Justin asked, glancing frantically around for Alan.

He shrugged his shoulders helplessly as the old man continued to babble. But Alan suddenly stepped between the children and the old man, a frown on his face as he answered emphatically in Spanish. The only word Justin recognized was "No!"

"The poor old man! I think he just wants something to eat!"

At the sound of Jenny's voice, the old man held out a thin hand in her direction. He eagerly grabbed a handful of green leaves from the basket and motioned toward them. Jenny already had her coin purse open when Alan shook his head sharply.

"You don't want any of that!" he informed her curtly.

"Why not?" Justin asked curiously. "What is that stuff, anyway?"

Alan's short laugh held no humor as he gently removed the leaves from the old man's hand and replaced them with a handful of bananas. "You still don't know what this is? You really are *gringos* (foreigners)!"

Eyeing the bananas with scorn, the beggar shuffled away. Alan tossed the diamond-shaped leaves back into the basket. "That, kids, is coca leaf! That old man is a coca chewer."

As Justin and Jenny looked at each other in bewilderment, he added impatiently, "Don't you understand? It's from this leaf that cocaine—Bolivia's 'white gold'—is made!"

Surprise at the Oil Camp

"**M**r. Green—I mean, uh ... Alan—what is that coca stuff, anyway?" asked Jenny. "I mean ... if it's so bad for you, isn't it illegal or something?"

They were bumping along a dusty track cut through thick brush. Deep ruts showed where the rains had washed out the one-lane road. Palm trees dotted unfenced grasslands where cattle grazed, and bottle trees looked like giant brown vases topped with a cluster of leafy branches, instead of flowers. Occasionally they passed a bamboo shack with a roof of palm leaves.

The young oil worker hunched over the steering wheel, his expression still tense and worried. He didn't seem to have heard her question, so Jenny repeated it. Glancing up into the rearview mirror, Alan answered, "Actually, it's perfectly legal to grow and sell coca in Bolivia."

Surprised, Jenny demanded, "But didn't you say it's bad for you? I mean, look at that old man!"

Alan drove around a deep pothole, then said seriously, "Yes, coca is bad for you. Chewing the leaf keeps you from feeling hunger or cold or tiredness—that's why so many poor people chew it. But when it wears off, you're just that much more tired and hungry. After awhile it destroys your ability to think and work; you end up like that old man."

Justin joined in. "Why do they keep chewing it, then?"

Alan shrugged. "Why do Americans keep smoking when they know it's bad for them? It's hard to change things when these people have been growing and chewing coca for hundreds of years. Anyway, now Bolivia has a problem that's a lot bigger than coca."

He swerved suddenly to avoid a herd of long-horned steers that burst into the road. "Sorry!" Looking back, he continued, "How much do you kids know about cocaine?"

Justin hesitated a moment. "Isn't it a drug? A policeman came to school and told us about cocaine. It gets smuggled into the U.S. Lots of kids take it and get addicted, so they can't *stop* taking it."

"Yeah, and if someone offers it to you, you just say NO!" Jenny added forcefully.

A sudden grin transformed Alan's face. "You've got *that* right! The problem is, some kids *don't* say no."

"That's correct!" Uncle Pete added. "Cocaine is concentrated from the coca and is a thousand times more powerful. Some kids try it just to be 'cool,' or because some so-called friend talks them into it. It gives them a good feeling for a little while, but eventually they discover they're not more popular or cool—just *addicted*. It isn't long until they can't live without cocaine."

Alan added sadly, "Addicts will do anything—steal or even kill—to get money to buy cocaine. That's why it's called 'white gold'—because it's worth as much as gold to the people who buy and sell it. I saw too many of my high school friends ruin their lives with drugs. That's why…"

Alan glanced at Uncle Pete. The worried look was again on his face. But Justin and Jenny had turned their attention to the scenery. They were now moving out of the grasslands.

Here the brush gave way to towering trees. Vines as thick as a man's wrist twisted around branches and hung down into the jeep.

Overhead chattered whole colonies of brightly colored birds. Justin caught sight of a red, green, and black parrot fluttering from branch to branch. He was disappointed, though, not to see any of the exotic jungle animals he had read about and seen in zoos.

He leaned forward to ask, but Jenny took the words out of his mouth. "Where are all the monkeys and tigers—and those giant snakes?" she demanded.

Alan shook his head. "Too much of this area has been cleared for cattle. If you want to see real wildlife, you'll have to get your uncle to take you into the uncleared jungle."

Jenny leaned over the seat and hugged Uncle Pete around the neck. "Oh, Uncle Pete, would you?"

"Hey, this is a work trip, remember?" His eyes twinkled at the sight of their crestfallen faces. "But we'll try to get in one trip to the jungle."

Just then Alan slammed on the brakes as a strange animal burst into the road. The size of a pig, its long body was covered with short brown hair. Its red eyes glared down a pointed snout as it crashed into the brush and disappeared.

"Wow!" Justin exclaimed. "What was that?"

"That," Alan said as he shifted back into gear, "was a *hoche*, a kind of wild boar. It's actually of the rodent family—"

Jenny gave a horrified gasp. "Rodents! You mean it's a giant rat?"

Alan chuckled. "That's right! But it makes good eating ... just like homegrown pork."

Jenny shuddered, but Justin sat back with a grin of pleasure. He had finally left civilization behind.

An hour later, the trees opened up into a thick brush land. A barbwire fence ran alongside the road, broken by a padlocked gate. On the other side of the gate, several acres of brush had been cleared.

"The oil camp," Alan announced as he unlocked the gate and drove the jeep through.

The twins looked around curiously. Several small bungalows with red-tile roofs lined one side of the driveway, each with an identical verandah running around it. On the other side, two larger, whitewashed buildings appeared to be offices of some sort. Beyond the buildings, they glimpsed several oil pumps, their black heads rising above the uncut brush.

As Justin jumped out of the jeep, the loud whine of an approaching aircraft caught his attention. Shielding his eyes with one hand, he stared up as a small helicopter dropped over their heads and disappeared into the uncut brush behind the buildings.

"So Dr. Latour and Rodrigo are finally back," Alan commented. He turned to Uncle Pete.

"Dr. Latour is our chief geologist and the only other American in the camp at the moment. His assistant, Rodrigo, is the camp chemist. They've both been out all week on an oil exploration survey."

He gestured toward the unmoving oil pumps the twins had noticed and added gloomily, "In fact, except for the camp cook, they're the only others here at all, now that the oil pumps have been shut down."

He looked at Uncle Pete anxiously. "You said you knew about that."

"That's why I'm here," Uncle Pete answered pleasantly. "As I mentioned, my orders are to investigate the shutdown of production and make a recommendation as to the future of this camp. But we'll discuss that later."

Lifting out their luggage, the three Parkers followed Alan

toward the nearest bungalow. Stepping onto the verandah, Alan threw open a screened door.

"These are our sleeping quarters," he told them. "This one will be yours during your stay."

He motioned to an open door in one wall that revealed another small room. "Jenny can use that for her bedroom."

Justin set down the duffel bag he carried and looked around the simple building. The floor was of rough cement, and camp beds lined the far wall. A simple closet had been made out of packing crates with a curtain over the front. What interested Justin most were the muslin nets that hung from the ceiling, making of each bed a private tent.

"Those are mosquito nets," Alan answered his unspoken question. "Be sure to tuck them in around your bed at night. The mosquitoes around here carry malaria."

From the wide, screened window on the back wall, he pointed out a tiny wood structure about a hundred yards beyond the bungalow. "We don't have indoor plumbing, but we keep the outhouse clean. Just make sure you take your flashlight along at night, and keep the door shut against bugs and snakes."

He headed for the door, then paused. "Oh, and don't forget to shake out your shoes and clothes when you get dressed in the morning. They're favorite hiding places for scorpions."

Jenny edged closer to Justin and whispered. "I'm not so sure I'm going to like this place."

Alan was already on the verandah. "Now if you'll follow me, I'll give you a tour of camp."

As they walked leisurely around the oil camp, Alan showed the Parkers his own quarters—larger than their own, and with a kitchen added on to one side. The camp cook, wrapped in a large white apron, came to the kitchen door and greeted them in smiling Spanish.

"Our dining room," Alan commented, motioning toward several tables scattered around the verandah.

The block-shaped administration building was like any office the world over, but beyond the office was another long, low building that was protected by metal bars over the windows. Its heavy wooden shutters and metal door were shut tight.

"What's in there?" Jenny asked with her usual curiosity.

"That's the lab," Alan explained. "It's where we process soil samples, among other things."

Justin was always interested in anything scientific. He asked eagerly, "Do you mind if I look around?"

At Alan's nod, Justin hurried across the gravel driveway and up the cement steps. But as he reached for the metal latch, an angry voice shouted, "Get away from there, kid!"

Stumbling backward in surprise, Justin stared up at the man who had appeared around the side of the cinder-block building. Tall and broad, with silvering dark hair, he could pass for Spanish descent. But the man's speech was pure American. His good-looking features were flushed with anger, until he noticed the two adults who stepped up behind Justin.

"What's the problem, Gerard?" Alan asked quietly.

Changing expression, the strange man answered, "I beg your pardon. I thought someone was breaking into the lab, that's all. There's a lot of dangerous chemicals lying around in there."

He looked at the Parkers. "Who are your visitors, Green?"

"This is Pete Parker and his nephew and niece, Justin and Jenny," Alan introduced. He added, "Mr. Parker is here from the head office—to investigate the camp."

A glint of anger showed in the cool, gray eyes. "So they

think we need investigating, do they? Why wasn't I told about this visit?"

"I didn't know myself until this morning," Alan answered. "In fact, I almost missed picking them up."

Alan smiled down at Justin and Jenny. "These two would like to see the lab. You don't mind, do you?"

Dr. Latour hesitated noticeably, then swung open the heavy metal door. "Of course not. Let me show you around."

Tiled counters, littered with the usual beakers, microscopes, bottles, and other apparatus of a science lab, ran around three walls of the long room. A short, slim man stood at one counter, long black hair flopping into his eyes as he scribbled in a small ledger. At the sound of footsteps, he shoved the ledger into a drawer.

Dr. Latour waved toward the other man. "Rodrigo Ventuades."

Turning around, the Bolivian chemist took in the group of visitors. His dark face beaming pleasure, he threw his hands into the air. "But how good it is to have guests. And a lady, too!"

"Rodrigo, the Parkers are staying a few days. They'd like a *brief* look at the lab," he stressed, "before they tour the rest of the camp."

Looking around, Justin noticed a ham radio pushed into one corner.

Alan noticed it too. "When did you get your own radio, Gerard? What's wrong with the one in the office?"

Justin studied the set admiringly. "Wow, I'll bet it could reach anywhere in the world!"

Looking displeased, Dr. Latour answered Alan. "It's more convenient having one here."

Rodrigo hurriedly stepped forward. Taking Jenny's hand, he bowed and said, "You are very welcome here. I only regret that I cannot accompany you on your tour of this site. We have just returned from a long trip, and there is much to do."

"Then get back to work!" the geologist ordered curtly as Jenny giggled. Turning to the others, he added abruptly, "We have this week's surveys to process, so if you'll please excuse us..."

Alan led the Parkers away from the lab. "Sorry about that! Gerard isn't the friendliest man."

"I'll say he isn't!" Justin muttered to Jenny.

Alan continued, "He's a brilliant geologist, though. We're fortunate to have him here. They say he can actually smell out oil."

"Did he discover *this* field?" Uncle Pete asked.

"No, this site was discovered by an earlier team. After the camp was set up, Dr. Latour came in to take charge of exploration and development. He's only been with Triton a few months, but he's lived in Bolivia for years. He has a lot of friends in high places here. He even won a medal from the Bolivian government—the 'Condor of the Andes,' their highest honor—for his work in uncovering new oil fields. Not that he's had much luck here!" he added gloomily.

"What about Rodrigo?" Jenny asked curiously. "He sure speaks good English."

"Dr. Latour brought him along when he came. He lived in Miami for a few years. They take care of the scientific side of things. I just keep camp life running smoothly."

He grinned down at the two children. "Not very exciting, huh?"

But he had just lost the attention of his audience. "What in the world is that?" the twins exclaimed together.

Rounding the corner of the lab, they had come out on the edge of the uncut brush that bordered the camp. The twins stared in astonishment at what looked like a full-scale military encampment dropped into the brush. Though several hundred yards away, it was still inside the barbwire fence that bordered Triton property.

Army tents sat beside a prefabricated, dome-shaped aluminum hut. The grass had been clipped short around the hut, and two men in khaki-colored uniforms stood at attention on either side of the entrance. A half-dozen American army jeeps and one large transport truck lined one side of the encampment.

Justin's eyes opened wider as he noticed a real combat helicopter resting in a clearing beside the large hut. The long rotor blades glinted in the setting sun.

"What, exactly, is going on here, Alan?" Uncle Pete asked sternly. "I wasn't told about any military operation on Triton property. I doubt if headquarters knows either or they would have informed me."

"I ... I know, sir! I was going to let them know." Alan looked very unhappy. "It's just a DEA camp."

"A DEA camp? You mean the Drug Enforcement Agency?" Uncle Pete raised his eyebrows in amazement. "What is it doing here?"

"It ... it's like this," Alan explained hastily. "I usually go up to Santa Cruz when I have time off. You kind of get to know the other Americans—you know, at embassy parties and all. That's how I met Major Turner. He's with the DEA. I got to know him pretty well—stayed with him a couple of times—and I ... I told him he was welcome to stay here if he ever came to the Beni.

"I meant on his time off, but last week he called me up on the radio and told me the Bolivian government had finally given him permission to run an operation down here. He asked if my offer was still open..."

Alan flushed red to the roots of his ash-blond hair. "There wasn't time to go through the red tape at headquarters, and I didn't think anyone would mind... I mean, everything was shut up here anyway ... so I said fine!"

He waved toward the encampment. "They came down two days ago. I didn't know there'd be so many of them. Then I found out you were coming..."

Looking as unhappy as when he had met them at the bus station, he added gloomily, "Major Turner isn't going to be very happy about this. I told him he wouldn't have to worry about visitors. I guess I'm in trouble all the way around!"

The twins waited anxiously as Uncle Pete studied the encampment. They already liked the young camp administrator. After a long moment, Uncle Pete said thoughtfully, "I don't see any problem with them using the property. You did exceed your authority, and you'd better ask first next time, but I'll let the head office know I okayed it."

As Alan broke into a relieved smile, Justin asked, "Could we go see the helicopter?"

Alan nodded. "I guess I'd better let Major Turner know you're here. Come on."

The party of five threaded their way single-file along a narrow path trampled through the brush. When they reached the edge of the other camp, they found themselves surrounded by armed men in the uniform of the Bolivian army.

"*Son amigos* (they are friends)," a voice called from the hut. The soldiers relaxed their weapons as a short, stocky man in civilian clothing stepped outside. A gray crewcut set off his tan.

"That's Major Turner," Alan explained quickly as the DEA officer walked over.

He looked at Alan sharply. "I understood there'd be no visitors."

He listened with a frown as Alan tried to explain.

"Well, it can't be helped now!" Major Turner interrupted, cutting off Alan's apologies. Keen gray eyes studied the group for a long moment, then he held out a hand to Uncle Pete.

"Major Doug Turner at your service. We're trying to keep casual visitors out of the area, but I don't think you'll create a problem as long as you let us know when you leave. I trust you won't mind if we check out your credentials." At Uncle Pete's nod of agreement, he waved the group toward the hut.

High screens divided the interior of the aluminum building into several work areas. The central section was jammed with office equipment, computer stations, and other instruments the children couldn't identify. A tall young man barely out of his teens bent over what Justin guessed to be a radar screen, a headset topping his close-cropped, dark curls.

Major Turner pulled out some folding chairs and bellowed, "Mike, we've got company! Turn around and be sociable."

The young man turned in his office chair. Black eyes widened as he saw the visitors, and he yanked off the earphones. Long, dark fingers flew over a keyboard, and the screen before him blinked off.

"Sit down! Sit down!" The major still wasn't smiling, but he seemed a little more friendly. "Mike, why don't you bring some coffee."

As the younger man disappeared behind a screen, he added, "Mike Winters is my assistant, and the best pilot in the whole narcotics—illegal drugs—division. Now, what were your names again?"

As Uncle Pete introduced the group, Justin looked around at the fascinating equipment that filled the hut. The young pilot, Mike, brought coffee, then sat again in front of the radar screen. Justin wished he'd turn it back on, but the pilot just sat staring ahead—his broad, dark features unhappy—as Major Turner and Uncle Pete talked. Justin eyed him curiously, then turned his attention back to the conversation.

"What exactly is your mission here?" Uncle Pete asked. "Or are you allowed to say?"

"Oh, it's no secret—not after it's been splashed across every newspaper in the country. The DEA is here on the invitation of the Bolivian government to work with their anti-narcotics corps, UMOPAR."

Glancing down at the listening children, he added, "That's the Bolivian police department that deals with drugs-related crimes. The U.S. government provides the equipment, and the UMOPAR supplies the men."

The major leaned back in his chair. "We're actually down here now to teach the UMOPAR men our methods in fighting the drug trade. But if we can actually catch some drug traffickers, all the better. The Beni is a main source of cocaine shipments—billions of dollars worth.

"We were informed that there's a major cocaine smuggling ring in this area, but we haven't found any signs of it. The problem is that there are a thousand hiding places out there in the jungle. We aren't giving up, though!"

Justin noticed Mike shifting in his chair, tossing a pen from hand to hand. Suddenly he stood up. "Permission to retire, sir!" he said in a soft drawl. "I'd like to look over tomorrow's surveillance charts."

Mike left the room abruptly as Major Turner nodded agreement. The major sighed. "That boy never slows down." He too stood up. "He keeps us all hopping!"

As his visitors followed his lead, Major Turner walked the group to the edge of camp. "I'll be having the DEA office in Santa Cruz check you out in the morning," he said as he shook Uncle Pete's hand. "Please understand this is a routine procedure." He nodded farewell and strode back toward the base.

Light clouds skittered across the face of the rising moon as they followed the path single-file back to the oil camp. At the edge of the uncut field, Justin noticed a tall, motionless figure outlined in the light of an unshuttered lab window. Dr. Latour was staring in disbelief at the DEA encampment.

As Alan stepped onto the cut grass, the geologist demanded with cold anger, "I demand to know the meaning of this, Green!"

He checked himself as Uncle Pete followed Alan into the rectangle of light, then added more calmly, "What is the Bolivian army doing squatting on our land?"

"It's a DEA camp," Alan explained again.

"A what?" Dr. Latour shouted.

"You know, the DEA men I met in Santa Cruz," Alan said patiently. "I've mentioned them before."

"What are they doing *here*?"

"Major Turner asked to use our camp as base, and I gave him permission. The camp is practically empty anyway, with the pumps shut down. They called me up while you were gone this last week and set up the day before yesterday."

"You had no right to invite them here!" Justin was surprised at the fury in the geologist's voice. "Why wasn't I consulted about this?"

Alan's pleasant tones turned cool as he answered, "Gerard, you may be in charge of exploration and development, but I'm still administrator of this camp. As for consulting you, I tried to get you on the radio. You know you're supposed to keep in contact during survey trips, but you haven't checked in once all week. Besides..."

He glanced over at Uncle Pete. "The DEA presence here has already been approved."

Dr. Latour didn't protest further, and Alan turned away. Uncle Pete and Jenny followed, but Justin looked back to where the head geologist still stared across at the twinkling lights of the DEA encampment. At that moment, the full moon broke through its cover; Justin caught his breath sharply as its silver rays touched Dr. Latour. *What is there at the DEA base that Dr. Latour hates so much?* he wondered.

CHAPTER THREE

An Angry Pilot

W iping the juice from his chin with a cloth napkin, Justin reached for another slice of sun-ripened pineapple. "Boy, this is the best stuff I've ever eaten!"

It was early morning, and he was enjoying the typical Beni breakfast of rolls and tropical fruit. Though it was barely past dawn, a warm, moist breeze blowing across the verandah where they ate promised another scorching day.

"Where are Dr. Latour and Rodrigo?" Jenny asked, waving a sugar bun in the direction of the lab. "Don't they eat breakfast?"

Alan poured himself a cup of steaming black coffee. "Yes, I heard them out here earlier. They like to get an early start at—"

He was interrupted as Dr. Latour strode up the verandah steps. Justin studied the tall, handsome geologist curiously. Dressed in a lightweight suit and tie, he looked businesslike and confident. Justin wondered if he could have imagined the doctor's fury the night before.

"I'm on my way out," he said abruptly. "I'll be needing the helicopter again."

Alan looked surprised. "You're leaving again already? What about Mr. Parker's investigation?"

"There are important tests I need to finish," Dr. Latour explained curtly. He nodded to Uncle Pete. "I'd have made other arrangements if I'd known you were coming, but these can't wait. We'll be back tomorrow."

"I planned to take Mr. Parker up, but I guess we can wait," Alan answered pleasantly. "Just keep in touch this time."

Dr. Latour looked annoyed. "We can handle our own affairs, Green."

"I'm sure you can, but that helicopter is Triton property and my responsibility."

Without answering, Dr. Latour turned and marched away. Alan grinned at the children. Now that he was no longer worried about his unexpected visitors, his friendly personality had returned.

"Orders are that we check in at least every six hours when we're out in the bush—in case of breakdowns or some other emergency," he explained. "However, Dr. Latour is used to working on his own."

Uncle Pete set down his empty coffee cup. "Not to change the subject, but it's time we got down to business."

He motioned toward the oil pumps in the distance, black shapes against the pink remnants of the sunrise. "I'm curious to know why you shut down production. The reports we received indicated large quantities of high-grade oil."

"Yeah, we thought we had a real find here," Alan answered gloomily. "We were getting ready to bring in a whole crew of American and Bolivian personnel when Dr. Latour's tests showed that the first wells we dug were running out. What's left is too low-grade to process."

"You realize that Triton can't maintain an unprofitable camp," Uncle Pete answered with regret. "If there's no oil, we'll have to pull out of this area."

"I don't think it will come to that," Alan responded quickly. "I told you Dr. Latour is a genius at exploration. He's been working night and day to find another site. He's brought in several promising surveys. I'm sure he'll have some good results soon."

Uncle Pete stood up. "That will be taken into account. I'd like to go over those surveys and test results myself this morning."

"Sure! They're on file in the office. Dr. Latour could explain them better, but I'll do my best."

Alan quickly swallowed the rest of his coffee and followed Uncle Pete to the edge of the verandah. He turned toward the twins. "You're welcome to look around, but stay on the camp grounds and keep your eyes open. You'll find snakes and an occasional wild animal even around here."

▼▼▼

The children spent the morning exploring the grounds, Justin snapping pictures everywhere they went. They thoroughly inspected all the buildings except the tightly shut lab. They even poked their heads into the kitchen, but the busy cook chased them out with a raised frying pan!

For an hour they watched Alan and Uncle Pete shuffle through stacks of paper spread out on the old, termite-chewed desk in the camp office. They lazily searched through a pile of outdated magazines, then wandered around the room, reading the captions below dusty pictures of early oil explorers. Finally, Uncle Pete ordered the restless pair out of the office.

At lunch time the twins found the verandah table set for only two. They were just finishing their meal when they saw the cook emerge from the office with a tray of dirty dishes.

"This is *boring!*" Jenny complained as the cook cleared the table. "I thought the jungle would be exciting."

Justin pushed back his chair. "Well, I'm not staying around here any more! Come on, let's go for a walk."

Jenny agreed, and the two children paused only to grab their hats before heading toward the overgrown field beyond the camp. Watchful for snakes, they tramped their way through to a small clearing, where one of the oil pumps sat motionless. The noonday sun blazed overhead, and they were glad to rest in the shade of the pump.

"It looks like a prehistoric *grasshopper*," Jenny giggled. It *did* look like some overgrown insect, the long, black body of the pump suspended by a metal frame that could be spindly legs. The insect's "head," which should have been nodding up and down to pump the oil, reared sightlessly against a deep blue sky.

Settling back against the cool metal, Justin idly watched the aluminum dome of the DEA office. The sudden roar of an engine broke the silence. Barely visible above the brush, the rotor blades of the DEA helicopter began slowly rotating.

Justin sat up suddenly. "I've got an idea! Let's go visit Major Turner."

Jenny shook her head doubtfully. "I thought Alan told us to stay on camp property."

"That *is* camp property," Justin insisted. He desperately wanted a closer look at that helicopter. "It's inside the fence, and that makes it Triton property."

Jenny hesitated briefly, but she was bored too. "I guess you're right. Anyway, it's better than sitting here all day!"

Uniformed guards again met them at the edge of the camp, but this time they let the twins pass by as soon as they recognized them. Now that it was daylight, Justin saw that the military helicopter was painted camouflage green. Jenny clapped her hands over her ears as the roar of the powerful engine greeted them, but Justin's eyes shone as he studied the long, gleaming lines of the body.

Only a few soldiers were in sight as Justin and Jenny walked past the temporary barracks, but as they reached the helicopter pad, Major Turner climbed out of the helicopter and joined them.

"Hi, kids!" he shouted over the noise, shaking their hands. "What are you up to?"

Justin had eyes only for the long, sleek machine. "That's a Huey, isn't it?"

The major smiled at his eagerness. "That's right. A little outdated, but we get the army leftovers down here. I suppose you want to take a look."

"Oh, could we? I've never seen one up close." In answer, the major motioned toward the open door of the helicopter, and Justin and Jenny scrambled aboard.

"Wow!" Justin exclaimed as he examined the stunning layout of instruments, careful not to touch anything. "This is great! I'd *love* to fly in one of these some day."

"Perhaps we could arrange that." Major Turner, keeping a watchful eye on their explorations from the helicopter's doorway, smiled broadly as Justin's eyes widened. "Mike! Mike, get out here!" he bellowed.

Mike emerged at a run from the aluminum office building. He was dressed in a white coverall of the type pilots wear. He slid to a halt when he saw the two children.

"What are they doing here?" he demanded roughly.

Ignoring his bad humor, Major Turner clapped him on the shoulder and announced jovially, "Mike, these kids have never flown in a Huey. You wouldn't mind giving them a ride, would you?"

He explained, "Mike is doing some photographic surveillance this morning. That means he will be taking pictures of the jungle. He won't mind a couple of passengers."

The look on Mike's face showed that he *did* mind, but he obviously knew his boss too well to protest. "Okay, let's go!" he ordered crossly.

Justin hesitated in the doorway. "Uh ... sir? I think we'd better let Uncle Pete know before we go anywhere."

"No problem! I'll send one of my men over to the oil camp to explain."

Justin was too excited to say more. Mike buckled himself into the pilot's seat. He curtly ordered the two children to find a seat and fasten their seat belts. The whole body of the helicopter vibrated as the slow turning of the rotors quickened to a blur.

The noise made speech nearly impossible, but the young pilot showed the twins how to adjust a set of earphones over their ears. A tiny microphone at mouth level allowed them to talk to each other.

"Testing, testing—one, two, three!" Jenny was trying out her microphone in the copilot's seat in front of Justin. Through a small side window, Justin watched the DEA base shrink away from the helicopter. Within minutes they were skimming over unbroken jungle, the trees so thick that the ground was invisible.

Mike frowned at his instruments as the helicopter swept back and forth across the unbroken growth. "I'm taking pictures now," he explained grudgingly.

Below, a strong breeze tossed the treetops into billowing waves across an endless green sea. Justin snapped a few pictures of his own through the thick glass of the window.

After half an hour of flying, Mike announced gruffly, "I think something's down there. Hold on! I'm going down."

The helicopter dropped so suddenly that Justin felt like his stomach would wind up in his mouth! Through the window he could see a wide clearing in the jungle. Part of it seemed to be devoted to corn and other food crops, but the biggest share of the cleared land was filled with rows of a leafy green plant.

"A coca field! I'm going in for some close-up shots." The twins were startled at the anger in Mike's voice.

Slipping sideways, the helicopter turned to make several passes across the clearing. At the end of the field was a large bamboo hut with a tin roof instead of the usual thatch. As they flew over the hut, Justin caught a glimpse of some sort of vehicle parked under the tangle of trees and vines at the edge of the clearing.

A pile of leaves as high as a man was heaped beside the hut. Justin could barely make out the tiny figure of a man spreading the green mass with a rake. He pressed his camera against the window and shot another picture.

The sudden dive of the helicopter caught Justin unaware. He grabbed his camera just before it hit the floor. Glancing toward the copilot's seat, he saw Jenny clutching tightly to the armrests.

"What's going on?" Justin shouted over the roar that penetrated his earphones. Mike's vicious swearing was the only answer as he buzzed the bamboo hut so low that several figures scattered and ran for the protection of the jungle that surrounded the field.

"Mike, please! What's the matter?" Jenny asked in a voice that trembled as the helicopter pulled out of its dive and turned back over the jungle.

The bitter lines on the dark young face deepened as Mike waved angrily toward the cultivated fields. "THAT is what's the matter!" he burst out. "We come out here to fight drug traffickers, and all we do is take a few pictures ... maybe take the local boys on a few mock raids. In the meantime, these people keep on growing coca as though we were never here.

"And where's it all going? There's a cocaine ring buying it up and turning it into poison—*while we take pictures!*"

"But isn't that why you're here?" Jenny asked in confusion. "To find that cocaine ring and arrest them?"

"*Find* them? There are thousands of square miles of jungle down there—and a dozen hiding places in each mile! It would take a miracle to find them. And if we *do*, they'll just bribe a few local officials and be back at it in no time."

Mike gave a short laugh, but his angry eyes showed no humor. "You don't know how powerful these guys are. In fairy tales the good guys triumph, but in real life, the bad guys are definitely winning."

The twins were stunned at his outburst, but Jenny leaned over and touched Mike on the arm. "Please don't feel so bad, Mike. God will punish them in the end."

The black eyes blazed with anger. "God? You wouldn't believe that Sunday school garbage if you'd grown up in a black slum like I did—ten people in a three-room apartment, toilets that didn't work, cockroaches..."

He glanced down at the wide-eyed children, then added, "...and a lot of other things you don't need to know. The army got me out of there, but my sister wasn't so lucky. You tell me what kind of God lets a fifteen-year-old girl die of a cocaine overdose ... while the man who sold her the stuff walks off scot-free. I'd rather not believe in God than think He's letting creeps like that live!"

Justin shook his head in frustration. "Maybe Uncle Pete could explain it to you," he said.

Mike's soft drawl was loaded with scorn: "Sure, pass the buck! I figured you didn't have any real answers!"

Troubled, Justin said slowly, "Well, I don't know why those things happen, but I do know God didn't make us robots. He lets us choose what we do. It isn't His fault so many people decide to do bad things."

He thought back on the last few days and added, "But

I've learned one thing lately; God is more powerful than any cocaine smugglers, and He *will* punish them in the end."

"We're really sorry about your sister," Jenny added gently. "I wish there was something we could do to help..."

"There is!" Justin answered, remembering those long hours in the Cave of the Inca Re. "We can pray. We'll pray that you find that cocaine ring. Right, Jenny?"

"Sure, you do that!" Mike answered sarcastically. No one said another word during the remaining minutes of their flight back to base.

▼▼▼

An hour later, Major Turner and Mike were bent over the developed photos from the flight. Justin and Jenny stretched their necks to see over the men's shoulders. Straightening up, the major clapped Mike on the shoulder. "Great job, Mike! Those close-ups are excellent. Some of them look like they were shot almost at ground level."

Justin glanced up to see a momentary look of embarrassment on Mike's face. Mike shrugged, and Justin looked down. Major Turner moved away from the broad worktable where the prints were spread out. His hands in the pockets of his khaki-colored canvas trousers, he grinned at the impatiently waiting children.

"So, you kids want to check out what you've been doing this afternoon. Go ahead, take a look!"

Justin eagerly bent over the table. Most of the shots showed nothing but an unchanging view of the unbroken mass of jungle. Then he came to the pictures of the coca field. He could see the long green rows of coca plants, divided by protective ridges of earth. At one end a huge tangle of vegetation concealed a vehicle that might be a jeep or perhaps a small pickup. In another picture, a tiny figure stared upward, one hand shielding his eyes from the sun. A large hay rake lay abandoned on the green pile beside him.

"Hey, look at this one!" Jenny exclaimed, thrusting an enlarged photo under his nose. "You can practically see their faces."

The aerial camera must have still been running when Mike buzzed the hut, because the picture showed a close-up view of three dark-haired men standing in the doorway of the hut. Two stared up at the helicopter, mouths open with surprise. The third man had thrown an arm across his face and was frozen in the act of ducking into the hut.

Justin studied the third man closely. His close-cropped hair was dark but grizzled with gray, and he looked as though he would be tall if standing straight. It was impossible to distinguish facial features, but something seemed familiar about the pointed chin and the set of the broad shoulders.

Jenny put another print into his hands. This one showed three men diving away from the helicopter into the jungle. He took a closer look. From the helicopter window he had counted three men scurrying toward the cover of the trees. Now he noticed that one of the running men wore the same ragged clothing as the worker who had been raking coca leaves in the first picture.

Jenny pointed to a dark figure hidden within the shadow of the doorway. "That's the only one who didn't come out in the open," she commented. "It's like he knew we were taking pictures."

Justin glanced back and forth between the two prints. Suddenly he remembered a similar dark figure standing at the edge of the oil camp the night before, his sharp features shaded in just the same manner.

He shook his head, then looked again. It was a crazy idea, but he could have sworn that the third man in those pictures was the chief geologist of the oil camp, Dr. Latour!

CHAPTER FOUR

A Suspicious Conversation

J ustin awoke with a start the next morning. The first rays of the sun, filtered through the mosquito net, made a pattern of diamonds across the camp bed. He sat up suddenly. Something was wrong.

A high-pitched scream rang out again. "Uncle Pete! Justin! Oh, help! There's something horrible in here!"

Justin threw off the thin sheet that covered him. Without waiting to put on shoes, he rushed across the room. Uncle Pete was close behind him as he crashed open the door to the other room.

Jenny stood on top of a small metal dresser that looked as though it had been converted from an old filing cabinet. Dancing from one bare foot to the other, she pointed to the floor. She tried to speak, but only a squeak came out. She swallowed and tried again. "Th-*There! It's just horrible!*"

Justin followed the direction of her shaking finger. On the floor, just crawling out of one of Jenny's sneakers, was an insect about three inches long. It crouched on eight legs; a pair of claws extended out in front like those of a miniature crab. A wicked-looking, bony tail as long as its body lashed back and forth.

As Justin bent to look closer, Uncle Pete blocked his way with one arm. "Don't get too close, Justin. That thing packs quite a sting in its tail."

Grabbing a hairbrush from where it had been dropped on the floor, he whacked repeatedly at the strange insect. When it lay motionless on the cement floor, Uncle Pete lifted Jenny down. "Okay, what happened?"

Jenny gulped. "I was getting dressed and I picked up my shoes to put them on, and ... and I saw *that!*"

Picking up the hairbrush, Justin flicked the insect over. "I've never seen anything like this before," he said with interest. "I wonder if it's poisonous?"

Uncle Pete looked grim. "That's a scorpion. And, yes, they can be very poisonous. Now you know why Alan told you to shake out your shoes and clothes before putting them on."

"Well, I'll sure never forget again!" Jenny assured him.

Justin was careful to shake out his own clothes, and ten minutes later, the three Parkers joined Alan on his verandah for breakfast. After breakfast, Uncle Pete told the twins they would have to keep themselves occupied again, as he and Alan would be busy most of the day.

"Alan, I'd like to run a few tests of my own. Could you turn on one of the pumps this morning?"

Alan looked surprised. "Sure. But why? Is there a problem with Dr. Latour's test results?"

"It doesn't hurt to double-check," Uncle Pete answered vaguely.

Justin groaned inwardly at the thought of another long day sitting around camp. Catching his disappointed look, Uncle Pete added, "I know this trip hasn't been too exciting for you kids so far, but I haven't forgotten my promise to take you into the jungle. Before we left La Paz, Mr. Evans arranged for us to visit some friends of his. Our guide should be arriving tomorrow."

▼▼▼

The prospect of a trip into the jungle kept Jenny and Justin chattering like monkeys for much of the morning. Stretched out on a pair of worn-out lawn chairs, they talked about what they might see—neither having much idea of what the jungle was like.

But by about ten, they were bored again. Following Uncle Pete and Alan out to the oil field, they watched them gather samples of the black crude oil.

After lunch, the two men disappeared into the camp office. Jenny buried her nose in the pile of dusty magazines that Alan had found somewhere, while Justin whittled on a dry branch with a sharp pocketknife.

A sudden dig of the knife snapped the limb in two. Justin jumped to his feet and announced, "I think I'll head over to the DEA camp. I want to take another look at those pictures."

Jenny dropped her magazine. "Me, too! I'll go crazy if I sit around here much longer."

When the twins wandered into the DEA encampment, this time the guards merely glanced at them and went about their duties. Justin and Jenny paused in the open doorway of the office. Half-hidden behind a screen, Major Turner bent over a computer console. Mike stood over a table, shuffling through a pile of reports.

The sudden shadow across the doorway caught the major's attention, and he swung his office chair around to face the door. Regarding his visitors through alert gray eyes, he boomed, "Well, what are you waiting for? Come on in!"

As Justin and Jenny stepped into the main work area, the major demanded warmly, "Okay, you didn't come just to visit an old soldier. What is it you want?"

Justin asked hesitantly, "Uh, we were wondering if we

could see those pictures again. You know, the ones Mike took yesterday?"

Major Turner waved them across the room. "Go ahead and look. They're still on the table there. Just don't touch anything else. Turn on that overhead lamp if you need more light."

Justin quickly found the pictures he had studied the day before. Holding them up to the light, he examined them closely. He searched through the rest of the prints, looking for other close-ups of the clearing. Yes, there was another shot of the third man hiding in the doorway of the hut. Once again, his features were indistinct, but the profile looked familiar.

He held out the prints to his sister. "Does this guy remind you of anyone?"

Jenny glanced at the pictures and shook her head. "Not really."

"Come on! You didn't even look!"

Jenny shrugged. "What difference does it make! Who would we know out here, anyway?"

Justin ignored the question as he bent over the pictures again. No, he must be mistaken. After all, there were a lot of tall, dark-haired men in the world. Still! He held the last picture up to the light.

Jenny picked up another print that showed the carefully spaced rows of coca plants. "Major Turner, why do the farmers grow this stuff? I mean, can't the government tell them to plant something else? Then you wouldn't have to worry about cocaine anymore."

Mike looked up from the stack of reports he was reading. "It isn't that easy!" he answered bitterly. "There's no law against growing coca, and who's going to stop growing it when you can make ten times as much money as with any other crop?"

Major Turner swung his chair around to face the two children. "That's right. The cocaine dealers have made coca a high-paying crop. And with so much money to be made these days, more and more land is being cleared for coca growing. Fifteen years ago, Bolivia grew only 30,000 acres of coca—mainly in the Chapare, the southeastern corner of Bolivia—just enough for their traditional chewing. Now, 150,000 more acres have been slashed out of jungle areas to produce cocaine—thousands of acres out of this part of the Beni. It's illegal to open up new coca cultivations, but that law is rarely enforced."

"But don't they care about all the crimes and people who get killed from cocaine use?" Jenny asked in disbelief.

"Jenny, most of these growers are just dirt-poor peasants who see coca as the best way of providing for their family. All they know is that their children can grow strong and healthy on good food if they grow coca. And there is money for school, where once their kids could never have had an education. Few have ever seen what cocaine does."

Major Turner leaned back in his chair and waved a pencil. "You've got to remember that Bolivia is very poor. The only thing keeping the country going is money from coca. The U.S. and other wealthy countries are sponsoring programs to grow soybeans and other crops instead of coca, but they aren't working very well."

Justin was thinking hard. "What about the ones who buy the leaves? Couldn't you find out who's buying up the leaves and arrest them?"

Mike laughed harshly. "Anyone who wants to can buy coca leaves. You'd have to prove it was being turned into cocaine. Besides, we can't arrest anyone!"

"Mike is right, Justin," the gray-haired major stated. "The U.S. and Bolivian governments made a deal to bring us here, but we really don't have any authority. We teach their soldiers how to track down cocaine labs. And we gather evidence against drug traffickers. But only the Bolivian Narcotics Force, the UMOPAR, can arrest them—and even *they* are under orders from government officials."

"And there are plenty of them who wouldn't arrest a drug trafficker if we dropped one in their living room!" Mike added angrily. "Why, we know one man who has made millions from drugs. He's got a fabulous estate and a private airfield. The locals call him the 'Cocaine King.' "

"But why doesn't someone just arrest him?" Justin demanded.

"Because the police know that anyone who arrests him would be out of a job tomorrow!" Mike answered angrily. "He has a lot of friends in high places and plenty of money to pay out in bribes."

"The president and many government officials are beginning to see the problems that cocaine brings," Major Turner added. "They back us and the UMOPAR force all the way. But there are others who are only interested in getting their share of the cocaine money—and they have a lot of influence. They would use any excuse to kick us out of the country. So we can't do much unless we actually catch traffickers in the act."

Justin waved an arm around the room. "Why do you even bother trying to help, then? Why don't you just stay home?"

"Because cocaine and drug smuggling isn't just our country's problem," the major answered seriously. "It hurts people all over the world. And it won't be stamped out until countries and people start working together."

Looking at Justin and Jenny's unhappy faces, he suddenly smiled. "It isn't all bad. If we track down a cache of cocaine, we have authority to destroy it."

Jenny latched on to an unfamiliar word. " 'Catch'? You mean, like 'catch the ball'?"

Major Turner smiled. "No, a *cache* ... a deposit.

Somewhere out there is a cocaine lab producing hundreds of pounds of the drug. If we can find out how the cocaine is leaving the country, we can arrest the smugglers on the other end."

Justin was still shuffling through the aerial photographs. Suddenly he exclaimed, "Hey, look at this clearing! Maybe it's that lab you've been looking for."

Carrying a photo of thick jungle over to Major Turner, he excitedly pointed out a bare spot among the trees. Glancing at the picture, the major laughed. "Sorry, Justin. If we checked out every open space in the jungle, we'd never get this job done. That's probably some poor farmer's field, or even a natural clearing."

He patted him on the shoulder. "You've got a good eye, though, so I'll tell you what we're looking for. When you find an open strip in those aerials long enough to land a small plane, there's a good chance you'll find a lab nearby."

"There wasn't anything like that in the pictures," Justin said with disappointment. "Maybe the cocaine lab is somewhere else."

Mike whirled around. "Who do you think is buying up all that coca we saw? No, they're out there. We've just got to find them!"

Moving over to the open door, he stared out toward the line of jungle that bordered the camp, his broad face full of anger. "If I had my way, we wouldn't just be sitting here taking pictures. I'd blast every coca field out of existence—along with the creeps who peddle that poison!"

His hands at his sides in hard fists, Mike hurried out the door.

Major Turner sighed as he looked after him. "Don't mind Mike. He takes this job very seriously."

Jenny nodded. "Yeah, he told us about his sister."

Major Turner went on. "Mike was just out of high school

when that happened. He joined up with the Narcotics Division shortly afterward. He's turned his job into a personal war against drug traffickers."

Justin returned the photo to the table. "Well, I guess we'd better be going. Thanks for your time, sir. It's been very interesting." Jenny followed him toward the door.

"Any time!" Major Turner walked them across the cut lawn that surrounded the base. "I wish every kid knew a few facts about cocaine. We'd have a lot less work to do."

At the edge of the encampment, Justin suddenly stopped. "Sir, do you know Dr. Latour very well? You know ... the chief geologist at the oil camp?"

"We checked out all the camp personnel before we came down," Major Turner answered. "He has an excellent record and, I understand, a lot of friends in high places in the government. But I've never met him. He hasn't been around here since we arrived."

His keen eyes suddenly sharpened with interest. "Why do you ask?"

"Oh, I was just wondering," Justin answered hastily. "Thanks!"

The sun was setting in the short twilight of the tropics by the time The twins set off for the oil camp. Jenny broke into Justin's thoughts.

"I sure learned a lot today. Poor Mike! I wish he wasn't so angry all the time, but I can't blame him for hating drug dealers."

"Well, there isn't much we can do about him or the drug dealers ... except pray, like we promised," Justin answered.

"Why don't we pray right now?" Jenny suggested. The twins stopped where they were and bowed their heads.

The instant night of the tropics had fallen by the time Justin and Jenny drew near to the lights of the oil camp buildings. The narrow path, lit only by the hard glitter of countless stars, led along the back side of the lab. Justin had just passed under the window that had stood open their first night—it was now shuttered tight—when he suddenly put out an arm.

"Shh! Listen!" he hissed.

A faint gleam shone from a triangular-shaped break in the shutter just above them. Jenny stopped, staring at Justin in surprise. Over the stillness, angry voices rose from inside the lab. Jenny pushed past her brother. Standing on tiptoe, she peered through the small hole.

"It's just Dr. Latour and Rodrigo, back from their trip," she whispered loudly.

Justin quickly pressed a hand against her mouth as he placed his own eye to the opening. He could see only a small section of the long, narrow lab, but he saw Dr. Latour's assistant leaning against the counter across the room.

"This has really loused things up badly!" Dr. Latour paced into Justin's sight, blocking off his view of the room. His back was to the window, but Justin could tell he was very angry.

"Why didn't I know about this DEA operation—or Parker's coming? It was your job to keep an eye on Green's communications."

"Don't go putting the blame on me! I wasn't even here at the time." Though Justin couldn't see him, a slight accent identified Rodrigo as the speaker. "If you had reported in last week, we wouldn't have this problem."

"You know that was impossible," Dr. Latour answered coldly.

"And it was those tests you sent in that brought Parker down. Now he's even talking about closing down the camp. Our whole operation is in jeopardy!"

Dr. Latour suddenly moved toward the counter that ran along the back wall of the lab. Justin ducked as the geologist paused just inside the window. "It doesn't matter now," he said clearly, in calmer tones. "This is our last haul anyway. We'll be done in a week."

"But the DEA is swarming all over the place!" Rodrigo grumbled.

"Don't worry about the DEA." Dr. Latour moved away from the window, and Justin inched up to peer in again. "They aren't interested in us. It's Parker and those kids I'm concerned about. I don't like them prowling around the place. See to it they stay off my back until it's all over."

The two men moved out of sight, and Justin heard the heavy metal door of the lab swing open. "Don't you worry!" Rodrigo's slight accent floated back. "It's all taken care of."

His gloomy words changed to triumph. "I've got just the person to deal with them! And if that doesn't work, there are other ways to get them out of camp!"

CHAPTER FIVE

Stranger in Black

"**R**ise and shine!" Justin opened his bleary eyes. In the faint pre-dawn light, he could barely make out Uncle Pete standing beside his bed. When he didn't move, Uncle Pete grabbed the edge of the camp bed and tipped Justin onto the hard concrete floor.

"Let's go, Justin! We're leaving in less than an hour—with or without you."

Uncle Pete tossed a small canvas backpack onto the floor beside him. "You and Jenny can take anything that will fit in there. Just remember, you'll have to carry it!"

Justin was instantly wide awake as he realized this was the day of the promised jungle trip. He hurriedly pulled on his clothes and shoved spare underwear, T-shirts, and an extra pair of jeans into the backpack. Then he added a small, leather-bound Bible.

"Here's my stuff," Jenny said, dumping a pile of clothing on the bed.

"Hey, you can't take all that!" Justin protested. "We're going to the jungle, not a party!"

Ruthlessly sorting through the pile, he shoved back half the clothes. Jenny reluctantly began folding the remainder.

Justin checked through his camera case and added several more rolls of film. This reminded him of their visit to the DEA base the day before.

"Hey, Jenny," he asked, "are you sure you didn't recognize anyone in those pictures yesterday?"

Jenny shoved her clothes into the backpack. "Yes, of course I'm sure. Why? Did you?"

Justin ran a hand through his hair, making it stand straight up. "I could have sworn one of those guys in the hut was Dr. Latour."

"Don't be silly!" Jenny answered scornfully. "What would *he* be doing there?"

"Well, you heard what he said last night. Maybe he's mixed up in that business Major Turner is looking into."

"Yes, I heard what he said. He's worried about Uncle Pete shutting down the camp, and he wants us out of here. So what? He's probably afraid he might lose his job."

She headed toward the door. "You heard what Major Turner said. They've checked out everyone in the oil camp. Besides, why shouldn't he be out there? Alan said he was doing surveys in the jungle. Maybe he's found oil near there."

Justin was half-convinced. Maybe his suspicions *were* silly. After all, wanting visitors to clear out didn't make a man a criminal. His dad was the same way when *he* was working on some big project. Besides, it was none of their business.

▼▼▼

Pink barely stained the eastern sky as Justin and Jenny joined Uncle Pete for a quick breakfast. Alan was nowhere in sight, but seated beside Uncle Pete was a slim man of medium height who had the thin, dark features and curly hair common to people of the Beni-Brazil border area.

"This is Eduardo," Uncle Pete introduced. "At least I think it is. I couldn't understand much of what he said, but he mentioned Mr. Evans' name, so I assume he is our guide."

Justin glanced around. "Where is everyone else?"

"Dr. Latour and Rodrigo aren't up yet," Uncle Pete answered. "Alan is refueling the camp helicopter. He will drop us off at the river Mamorè, where we'll catch a boat."

He was interrupted by the loud drone of an approaching aircraft. Moments later, the small helicopter the twins had seen the day they arrived settled onto the gravel driveway. Alan jumped down as the rotor blades slowed to a stop.

"There's no rush," he grinned as Justin and Jenny looked with dismay at their untouched breakfast. "I could use another cup of coffee myself."

"Maybe you could help us out while you're here," Uncle Pete interjected. "I've picked up a bit of Spanish in my travels, but not enough to understand Eduardo here."

He gestured toward their silent visitor. "I'd like to know a bit about him and our destination before we end up in the middle of the jungle without a translator."

Alan turned to the man. At the sound of his strongly accented Spanish, the solemn, dark face brightened into a wide smile. Justin strained to listen, but he couldn't pick out a single word he understood.

"His name is Eduardo Villaroel," Alan translated, turning back to the three Americans, "and he is taking you to his village far up the Mamorè river. He is very glad to meet friends of Mr. Evans."

"How did he meet Mr. Evans clear out here?" Jenny asked. Alan repeated the question.

"I, like all my family, was a grower of the coca," Alan translated. The twins looked at each other in startled surprise.

"Mr. Evans came to our village many months ago," Alan continued. "He told us things we had never heard before about the Son of God, Jesus Christ—about how He loved all men and had given up His own life to pay for the sins of men. He told us how Jesus Christ had come to life again and has the power to change our lives, if we will follow Him. I knew in my heart that this gringo spoke the truth. My wife and I made up our minds to follow this Jesus."

Alan knit his eyebrows together as he tried to put Eduardo's exact words into English. "After Mr. Evans left, we began to walk long distances to hear more of Jesus. One day, Mr. Evans came and took me to Santa Cruz to learn from God's Word with many other followers of Jesus.

"It was there that I learned of the evil of the cocaina—the white powder made from our coca leaves. I saw even young children dying from taking this powder. I thought of my *gua-gua*, my little girl."

He made a motion of cradling a baby. "What if someday *she* learned to do this evil? I decided to stop growing coca."

Eduardo broke into another flood of Spanish. "Mr. Evans came and helped us to plant soya and food for my family instead. Now others of my family have also decided to follow Jesus and have left the coca. We have even built a church."

Eduardo stood up, motioning excitedly with his hands. "Come with me! I will show you my village and my family and the church we have built."

As Alan finished translating, Eduardo marched down the verandah steps, ready to leave immediately. Uncle Pete chuckled. "I guess we'd better go before we get left behind."

The twins had been listening intently, but now hurriedly swallowed the last of their breakfast and followed the three men to the helicopter. They had just buckled their seat belts when Dr. Latour and Rodrigo came down the steps of the bungalow next to Alan's.

"Just a minute!" Uncle Pete said, tapping Alan on the shoulder. Leaning out, he called, "Dr. Latour! Could I have a word with you?"

Dr. Latour strolled over to the helicopter. "Leaving, eh?" he said pleasantly.

"Just overnight," Uncle Pete replied. "I've finished going through your reports. I found some of your surveys very interesting. When we get home tomorrow, I'd like to fly out and investigate the sites for myself."

Dr. Latour looked displeased. "Don't you trust my work?"

"I'm sure your work is of the highest quality," Uncle Pete answered flatly. "But my job requires that I check things out for myself."

Dr. Latour nodded abruptly. "Of course! I'll be available when you're ready."

He was turning away when Jenny leaned forward. "By the way, Dr. Latour, we saw a picture of you yesterday. I mean Justin did... I mean, he *thinks* he did."

Startled, Dr. Latour turned around. "What do you mean, girl?"

"When we were flying with Mike, the DEA pilot, yesterday," Jenny explained chattily. "He took pictures from the helicopter. It *was* you, wasn't it?"

Dr. Latour looked displeased. "It's possible, I suppose. We did hear a helicopter fly over at one of the survey sites. Now, if you'll excuse me..."

"A helicopter just *flew over*?" Justin whispered fiercely to Jenny as the camp copter lifted off. "Why did you bring that up, anyway?"

"You said you wanted to know!" Jenny answered reasonably. "Now that the mystery's solved, let's enjoy the trip."

Jenny was right, Justin had to admit. He had looked forward to this trip too long to let anything spoil it. He turned his attention to the window. In less than an hour, a broad river spread out beneath them. Sitting behind the pilot's seat, Justin exclaimed, "Wow, look at all those boats! I thought hardly anyone lived here."

Below the rapidly descending helicopter, hundreds of

strangely assorted boats plowed a passage up and down the waterway. Their wake stained the rocky shoreline a muddy brown. A few dilapidated piers, extending far out over the beach, indicated how high the river would rise in rainy season.

"You'll find a lot more boats in the Beni than cars," Alan answered as he landed gently on the beach. "There aren't many roads out here, and the rivers are the lifelines between villages and towns."

The helicopter had landed only yards away from the river's edge. The party of four climbed out. As Uncle Pete gave Alan final instructions, Justin reached for the backpacks. He lifted Uncle Pete's, grunting in surprise. Justin was a husky boy, but he was puffing as he lowered the pack to the ground.

As Alan took off, spraying his passengers with sand, Justin demanded, "What in the world do you have in there, Uncle Pete?"

"Oh, just the radio and a few odds and ends." Uncle Pete shouldered the pack with ease. "Oh, and a car battery, of course, to power the radio."

Justin eyed Uncle Pete with new respect as he shouldered his own lighter pack. Eduardo hadn't said anything since they left camp, but now he mumbled something to Uncle Pete. Justin caught the word "barco." Uncle Pete pulled out a pocket Spanish-English dictionary and leafed through it.

" 'Barco' means boat," Uncle Pete said at last. As Eduardo nodded and pointed down the beach, he added, "I think we're supposed to follow him."

The three Parkers followed Eduardo along the waterfront to where a funny-looking boat bobbed beside the pier. Its deck was wide and flat like a cargo barge, its low railing only a few feet above water level.

In the center, a ramshackle structure of scrap lumber and

tin rose two stories above the deck. Rusty barrels, boxes and bags, and even livestock, crowded the deck. A steady stream of passengers was making its way up the wide wooden plank that connected the boat to shore.

"Look!" Jenny pointed. "That must be how they drive the boat!"

"*Steer* the boat!" Justin corrected, his gaze following her finger. On the second story, a small, rail-lined deck protruded in front of a tiny cabin. Above the rail was a large, spoked wheel. A man in a faded blue uniform leaned calmly against the wheel, a battered seaman's cap slanted over one eye. Catching sight of the two young Americans, he straightened up and waved in their direction. Jenny waved back.

Uncle Pete was already following their guide up the gangplank. Justin pushed his sister along in the direction of the boat. At that moment, the passenger in front of them stumbled, dropping a heavy burlap bag. Justin stopped so suddenly that he lost his balance, bumping into the person behind him.

Catching himself, Justin turned to apologize, then opened his eyes wide in surprise. Dressed in new jeans and cowboy-style shirt, the man behind him was so thin that his skin seemed to be stretched tight over bare bones. In spite of the heat, a black leather jacket hung loosely from skeletal shoulders. What could be seen of his face behind a pair of oversize sunglasses had an unusual yellow tint.

"I'm sorry!" Justin stammered, stepping backward. The man slowly lifted his sunglasses, and strangely unfocused eyes, rimmed with red, stared back at the twins. Without a word, the man turned and disappeared into the crowd.

Justin stared after him until he heard a familiar voice calling, "Justin! Jenny!" It was Uncle Pete, leaning over the rail of the boat. A foghorn bellowed, and he realized that the gangplank was being pulled away from the shore.

"Wait for us!" Justin grabbed his sister's hand and ran for the boat.

Joining the others at the rail, Justin and Jenny watched the boat putt putt slowly away from the bank. Just yards away, an oversize canoe slid by, propelled by an outboard motor. It was so heavily loaded with people and goods that the wooden sides rose only inches above the water level.

"Hey, there's people *living* on that one!" Justin pointed out a smaller, one-story version of their own boat. A woman stood on the deck, hanging wet clothing on a rope stretched from the cabin to the rail. A toddler played in the middle of barrels and boxes, a rope around his waist keeping him from falling into the water.

A shrill whistle turned their attention upward. The boat pilot leaned down from above, grinning broadly. Casually turning the big wheel with one hand, he motioned for them to come up with the other.

Justin glanced toward Uncle Pete. Deep in conversation with Eduardo, he was shuffling through the Spanish-English dictionary to find words to supplement his meager Spanish vocabulary.

"Come on!" he urged his sister. "I've always wanted to meet a real riverboat pilot."

The two quickly climbed up the steep ladder that led to the second-story deck. The pilot, his seaman's cap smartly pushed to one side, greeted them with a grin and a flow of Spanish.

When Justin and Jenny shook their heads regretfully, he resorted to sign language. Waving around at the boat, he pointed to himself. *"Capitàn!"* he repeated.

"I think that means he is the captain of the boat," Justin said. He pointed to the pilot and asked loudly, "Captain?"

The man nodded. "Sì! Sì! Capitàn!" Waving his graceful dark hands, he indicated that Justin should take the wheel.

"Me? Steer the boat?" Justin carefully took the wheel with both hands. A stiff breeze cooled his freckled face as he watched the river flow slowly past the sides of the boat.

"Wow! This is great!" he exclaimed, turning the wheel as he had seen the captain do.

"No! No!" The riverboat captain snatched the wheel from Justin's hands. Looking down, Justin saw that the boat was drifting close to the shore. The captain yanked the wheel, and the prow of the boat slowly moved away from shore.

This done, the captain grinned, his good humor restored. But he didn't offer them the wheel again. Justin watched the captain effortlessly rotate the wheel back and forth, keeping the boat on a straight course upriver.

"There's more to steering this thing than I thought," he said gloomily.

The twins moved over to the railing. They were out of sight of the small river town now, and thick jungle pressed down to the river's edge. Jenny scanned the deck below, searching for Uncle Pete and Eduardo. Suddenly she stiffened, and poked her brother in the ribs. "Hey, isn't that the guy we bumped into on the beach?"

Justin looked down. Leaning against the rail was a skeletally thin man in a black leather jacket. As though he felt their gaze, the man looked up. He stared at the two for a moment, then turned and disappeared around the side of the cabin.

Jenny shuddered. "That guy gives me the creeps!"

"I wonder how he got on the boat," Justin answered thoughtfully. "He was heading in the opposite direction when we saw him, and we were at the end of the line. He must have circled around and cut in front of us."

Jenny suddenly lost interest in the man. "Hey, take a look at that!" She scrambled down the ladder. Hurriedly thanking the captain, Justin followed her to the bow of the boat.

The river was narrower here, and the boat passed close to

the shore. A rotting log as thick as a man was tall extended down to the river.

"What's the big deal?" Justin grumbled. "It's just an old log!"

"Not the *log!*" Jenny answered impatiently. "Look what's *on* the log!"

Justin looked more closely. What looked like one of the heavy vines that covered the jungle trees was draped across the log; it was about eight inches thick. Then he saw the vine move.

"It's a boa constrictor!" he exclaimed. "And what a big one!"

The giant snake slowly slithered its way down into the underbrush. Justin and Jenny watched as more and more of its length moved up over the log and down the other side. The tail came into view just as the log fell behind the boat.

Justin lowered his camera in awe. "It must have been thirty feet long!"

Uncle Pete moved up beside them. "They get bigger than that north of here. A friend of mine once told me an amazing story. He was working with the Indians on a jungle river up north. A gigantic tree had fallen into the water there. He says he watched a snake a full yard thick come up out of the water and over that log. He got out of there pretty quick, so he never did get to measure the thing, but he figures it must have been at least a hundred feet long."

"Do you think it was a true story?" Justin asked doubtfully.

Uncle Pete's green eyes crinkled with a smile. "Yes, I believe it. You see, he had a photo with him. It showed an Indian guide standing on the bank with that snake sliding over the log behind them. There must have been a good forty feet of the snake showing above water."

His explanation was interrupted by a squeal from Jenny.

Justin drew in his breath sharply as he followed the direction of her gaze. A patch of white, sandy beach lay between the river and the jungle. Stretched out lazily on the warm sand was a cat-like animal the size of a large dog. Odd-shaped black circles dotted its short, golden fur, and its short tail twitched, apparently from a bad dream.

"Is that a real tiger?"

"Of course not, it's a jaguar!" Justin told his sister. "Isn't it, Uncle Pete?"

"Well, it looks just like a big kitten!" Jenny answered. "I'd love to pet it."

"Don't kid yourself," Uncle Pete answered. "The jaguar is one of the most vicious fighters of the jungle. It'll even hunt down a man if it finds one alone and defenseless."

Justin watched the sleeping animal with more respect. "I think I'd just as soon keep the river in between us!"

As though aware of their conversation, the jaguar lazily turned gold-green eyes toward the intruders who had interrupted his nap. It gave a wide, bored yawn, the boat passing so close that Justin could see the pink of its long tongue.

The twins watched breathlessly as the graceful animal stretched, its muscles rippling under the sleek pelt. Without looking back at its spellbound audience, it stalked leisurely into the tangle of trees. Justin sighed with pleasure. This was his idea of jungle!

Shortly after noon, the riverboat docked at a small landing on the edge of the jungle; it actually was nothing more than a cluster of thatched huts along a strip of muddy shore. Justin half-slid down the steep wooden plank onto the shore. Jenny and the others followed.

"Is this where we're staying?" Jenny waved around at the handful of huts. But Eduardo said something and was motioning toward the thick, unbroken trees behind the tiny village. He held up two fingers.

"We have to walk in two hours," Uncle Pete told the twins after consulting his dictionary again.

Jenny looked at the mass of green. "Through that?"

"Of course!" Uncle Pete answered sternly, but his green eyes crinkled with amusement at her worried expression. "You said you wanted to see the jungle!"

Justin and Uncle Pete adjusted their backpacks, and the Parkers followed Eduardo up a narrow path that pierced the jungle. Fresh hoof marks showed that it was well-traveled. Tall hardwoods, covered with vines and orchids, shut out the sun but locked in the steamy heat. Eduardo swung a machete at undergrowth that threatened to overrun the path.

Shifting his backpack to a more comfortable position, Justin wiped beads of sweat from his face and wished that he had brought mosquito repellent. The air was noisy with the chatter of birds and the "ooh, ooh" of the small brown monkeys that lived in the tall trees. One tiny, wrinkled face peered out curiously from under fan-shaped, green leaves before a hairy arm reached out to snatch the infant away.

Several times as they hiked along, Justin heard crackling in the underbrush along the path. *More wild animals*, he thought with satisfaction. An hour into their hike, Uncle Pete called for a rest break and uncapped a canteen of boiled water. As Justin tipped up the canteen, he again heard the snap of a branch close behind. Jenny grabbed his arm.

"Look! Someone's following us!"

Justin whirled around. A dozen yards behind them, a man had stumbled into the path. The man ducked behind a tree. Justin dropped his backpack and ran back down the path. The man had disappeared by the time Justin reached the spot where he had stood, but not before Justin recognized a now-familiar black leather jacket!

CHAPTER SIX

Fire!

enny hurried to catch up as Justin stared into the gloomy tangle of trees. "That was the man we saw earlier, wasn't it?" she panted. "I *know* he's following us."

"What are you talking about, Jenny?" Uncle Pete asked as they rejoined the others. "What man?"

Justin explained about the man they had seen on the dock and later in the boat. "He really *was* watching us," he concluded.

Uncle Pete turned to Eduardo and again pulled out his Spanish-English dictionary. But Eduardo only shook his head at Uncle Pete's halting questions.

"We sure could use a translator *now!*" Uncle Pete said with exasperation. "At any rate, Eduardo didn't see the man and doesn't know who it could be."

"Well, he sure looked creepy!" Jenny said with a shiver.

"I think you kids are making too much out of this," Uncle Pete answered firmly. "He was probably a local on his way home to his village."

"Then why was he staring at us—and sneaking around in the bush like that?" Jenny demanded.

"Maybe he's never seen foreigners before." Uncle Pete dismissed the subject. "Anyway, if we're going to get anywhere today, we'd better get moving."

Justin and Jenny exchanged an unconvinced glance, but began walking. An hour later, a good-sized town spread out in front of them. Thatched houses, with a few brick buildings mixed in, lined broad, muddy streets. There were even a few storefronts and a tiny central plaza.

A road divided the village in half. Though it was unpaved and rutted, it was at least as good as the road that led to the oil camp. Beyond the wide-spaced buildings, the twins glimpsed what looked suspiciously like a grass-strip runway.

"Welcome to Magdalena," Uncle Pete boomed with a broad smile.

Hands on her hips, Jenny looked up irritably at her uncle. "And you made us walk all this way? We could have flown into here!"

Uncle Pete's eyes were playful. "You *did* say you wanted to see the jungle!"

Jenny's indignant glare relaxed into a grin. "Yeah, I guess I did."

"At any rate, you'll get your chance to fly tomorrow." Uncle Pete tapped the backpack he carried. "That's why I brought this two-way radio. When we're ready to go, I'll give Alan a call and he'll fly in to pick us up."

"Tomorrow?" she asked in dismay. "So soon?"

"That's right! I have a job to do back at the oil camp, remember?" A frown wrinkled Uncle Pete's forehead. "There's a few things I just don't understand…"

Jenny looked puzzled, but Justin suddenly realized it was long past lunch time. Clutching his stomach dramatically, he moaned, "Do you realize we haven't eaten since breakfast? I'm starved!"

"What do you mean you haven't eaten?" Jenny answered. "What about all that junk you bought on the boat?"

She counted on her fingers. "Let's see, cheese rolls, and tamales, and those meat shish kebobs..."

"Those didn't count!" Justin interrupted hastily. "That wasn't a real meal. Besides, I'm a growing boy!"

Uncle Pete laughed. "Come on! Let's find something to eat before you collapse in the street."

A short time later, Justin dipped into a bowl of hot, thick soup. "This is great!"

"What's in it?" Jenny asked doubtfully, dipping into her own bowl. She picked something out of the stew—and dropped it. "Justin! What's this?"

Justin leaned over and lifted out a long, narrow piece of bone. Running along the top of the bone was a perfect set of oversized molars!

"Uncle Pete," he asked faintly, "what kind of soup did Eduardo say this is?"

Eduardo had obviously caught the drift of the twins' remarks. Justin was sure he detected a twinkle in the dark eyes as he motioned toward the soup and repeated, "Es sopa de cabeza de vaca."

Justin reached for Uncle Pete's dictionary. "Cow head soup!" he exclaimed, giving his own bowl another stir. He swallowed hard as a round, rubbery object floated to the top. "An eyeball!"

Jenny shuddered. "Well, you can have my piece of cow head!"

Justin and Jenny felt much better when the smoky odors in the small kitchen behind the open air restaurant resulted in plates heaped high with rice, potatoes, and what looked like fried bananas but was actually plantain, a starchy cooking banana. A smiling waitress topped each plate with one of the thick steaks that sizzled on a homemade grill made of heavy wire stretched six inches above a vast bed of coals.

"This is more like it!" Justin exclaimed, digging into the mound of food.

Full at last, the twins followed the two men across the small plaza. Justin kept an eye out for the man who had been following them, but saw no sign of a black leather jacket. Eduardo turned down a muddy alley which ended in a grove of palm trees. Sheltered under their long leaves was another of the now-familiar thatched huts.

This was the first time Justin had seen one up close. He studied the construction with interest. Saplings had been stripped of leaves and cut into poles the height of a man. Thrust into the ground close together to form walls, they were bound together with jungle vines to help keep them upright. Gaps between the poles allowed every breeze to cool the hut.

Laid over a wooden frame, a thick layer of palm and banana leaves formed the roof and hung down over the edges of the walls to keep the frequent rains out. A mat of lightweight reeds hung over the narrow doorway.

Eduardo knocked sharply against the wooden door frame. An elderly woman, a still-black braid hanging to her waist, lifted the mat and peered out cautiously. After a few exchanged remarks, Eduardo disappeared into a field behind the hut.

He returned a few minutes later, leading a pair of hump-backed Brahman cattle. Harnessing them to a two-wheeled cart parked under the palms, he waved the Parkers into the cart with the same air of pride with which Justin's father showed off his new Aerostar minivan.

"So this is the family car!" Jenny giggled as she tumbled into the cart. "But where are we going? Isn't this Eduardo's village?"

Uncle Pete shook his head. "Alan mentioned that Eduardo owned fields out of town a ways."

Eduardo cracked a rawhide whip over the bullocks' longhorned heads, and the wooden cart jolted into slow motion. He turned into the rutted road they had seen coming into town, and soon Magdalena faded from sight.

Small fields, chopped out of the jungle, led off from both sides of the road. Huge, vine-covered trees pressed against the edges of the small clearings—determined to take over the moment the farmers turned their backs. Justin noticed row after row of the same coca plants they had seen from the air two days before.

Braced against the side of the cart, Justin lifted his hot face to catch a late afternoon breeze, and breathed in deeply the sweet, damp smell of tropical flowers. Suddenly he sat up straight.

"Something's burning!" he exclaimed. Peering over one high wooden wheel, he saw a haze rising above the trees some distance ahead. "It looks like a forest fire!"

"Maybe some farmer is burning off a field," Uncle Pete remarked, but Eduardo too had suddenly straightened up. He leaned forward, staring in the direction of the smoke haze. Then with a loud crack, he struck the bullocks with his rawhide whip.

The twins tightly gripped the sides of the cart as the bullocks broke into a shambling run. Uncle Pete grabbed for his backpack just before the radio smashed against the cart wall. Hunched tensely over the reins, Eduardo urged the animals to move faster.

Minutes later, Eduardo jerked the bullocks to a halt. He was out of the cart and running before anyone else could move. Justin stared with horror at the scene before him.

It could hardly be called a village—just a dozen thatched huts built close together, with cleared fields fanning away on all sides. It had been a pleasant area, with orange and lemon trees shading the simple homes, and groves of young banana plants bordering the fields. Judging by one field to the left with waist-high rows of healthy green plants, the ground was fertile.

But now there was nothing pleasant left. Blackened heaps now smoldered where there had once been thatched huts. Bursts of flame shot through the heavy, black smoke that cloaked the once green rows of soybeans, while banana plants lay smashed into the ground.

A group of dark-haired people milled about among the ruins, the wailing of children rising above the anguished cries of adults. Catching sight of the new arrivals, a young woman with a toddler on one hip broke away from the group and ran to meet Eduardo. Her waist-length, blue-black braids were scorched, and tears streamed down her pretty, dark face.

"This doesn't look like an accident," Uncle Pete said grimly, stepping down from the cart and swinging his backpack to the ground. "Look at that house over there!"

Justin suddenly noticed that one of the houses of the group remained untouched. It bordered the one green field that remained. Eduardo loosened his wife's clinging arms and walked over to the remaining hut. A moment later, a man who could have been Eduardo's brother stepped out.

The man leaned against the door frame, his arms crossed over his chest. Eduardo spoke angrily, waving his arms toward the ruin around him. The other man answered sharply, then stepped back into the hut and dropped the mat shut behind him.

"What's going on, Uncle Pete?" Jenny inquired anxiously. "Why isn't that man helping the others?"

"Yeah, and how did this fire start, anyway?" Justin answered, staring around in dismay.

"I don't know," Uncle Pete answered, still grim. "But we'd better do something to help. I'm calling Alan in."

He pulled a rectangular black box from his backpack and set it on the back of the cart, then added a car battery. Hooking cables to the battery terminals, Uncle Pete quickly stretched out a length of wire and looped the antenna over a nearby branch. Moments later, he was speaking into a small, hand-held microphone.

Switching off the radio, he turned to the waiting children. "Alan should be here within the hour. Then we'll find out what's happened here. In the meantime, let's see what we can do to help."

He paused for a moment. "I'm really sorry about this, kids," he added. "This has put an end to your jungle trip."

"That doesn't matter!" Justin answered quickly. "I just feel sorry for all these people."

"Poor Eduardo!" Jenny exclaimed. "How awful to come back to this. And he was so proud of his farm and his church."

"What can we do, Uncle Pete?" Justin added. "We'd like to help, too."

Uncle Pete gave them an approving look, then pulled a first aid kit out of his spacious backpack. "Okay, then! Let's see if there are any injuries. Justin, you get Eduardo. Jenny, help me unpack this stuff."

Justin found Eduardo standing among the half-burnt timbers of a larger thatched building, his dark eyes sad. Red-orange tongues of fire still licked the blackened remains of what had once been simple wooden benches. Justin guessed that this was the church Eduardo had told them about. Catching sight of him, Eduardo greeted Justin with a determined smile and followed him over to the cart.

For the next hour, Uncle Pete dressed burns and treated scratches and grazes. Eduardo worked with Uncle Pete, urging those in need of treatment over to the makeshift first aid post Uncle Pete had set up at the back of the cart. Only one person had been seriously hurt—a young woman who had tried to re-enter her burning hut. She had only slight burns, but a falling branch had cut a deep gash across her forehead.

Jenny cuddled the woman's newborn son while Justin helped cut bandages and spread burn ointment. Those who didn't need treatment poked through the embers, searching for the few items that had escaped the flames—a few battered tin pots and pans, a twisted spoon, a blackened spade.

Uncle Pete was bandaging the last patient when they heard the drone of an approaching aircraft. Justin looked up from the roll of gauze he was packing away to see the camp helicopter lower onto a flat spot in the road. The rotors blew dust across the cart, then Alan was running toward them.

"What in the world is going on here?" he exclaimed, staring around in amazement.

"We hope you'll tell us!" Uncle Pete answered. Alan turned to Eduardo, who had just dumped a pair of blackened ax heads he had salvaged beside the cart. In answer to his question, Eduardo poured out a flood of words, motioning angrily toward the ruins of his home.

Alan flushed red with anger as he listened. He turned to Uncle Pete. "He says an armed band of men came earlier today. They herded all the people out, then poured gasoline over the buildings and across the fields. Then they set everything on fire. They told the villagers it was a warning from the *narcotraficantes*—the cocaine dealers."

"But what about *that* house?" Justin asked suddenly. "How come that house and field didn't get burned?"

Alan turned to question Eduardo again, then answered, "The man who owns those agreed to start growing coca again. That's why he wasn't burned out."

A slow anger had been building up inside Justin ever since they had arrived. Now, gazing at the small group of children huddled fearfully on an unburned patch of grass, and the adults poking through the blackened embers of their homes, he suddenly understood Mike's bitterness toward the traffickers who had destroyed so many lives.

"Maybe it *is* none of my business, but I'm going to do anything I can to help stop them!" he vowed silently.

"We can't leave these people here like this," Uncle Pete said, interrupting Justin's thoughts. "Alan, ask Eduardo if he'd like us to ferry them into town. Maybe they can find land elsewhere."

Eduardo listened carefully as Alan explained Uncle Pete's idea, then moved away to talk with the rest of the fire victims. Moments later he was back, a group of the others with him.

Alan translated his exact words as he shook his head emphatically. "Thank you for your kindness, but we will not go. If we go, who would tell the people here of Jesus? No, we will not be driven out by these evil men."

He waved an arm toward the blackened fields. "We will stay here and replant our crops. God is with us, and He will help us to rebuild our homes and our church again." Behind Eduardo, dark heads nodded solemn agreement.

It was getting late by the time the four Americans were ready to leave. Eduardo had agreed to let Alan fly the one badly injured woman to the health clinic in Magdalena. As they helped the injured woman and her mother and the baby into the helicopter, Justin saw Uncle Pete shove a roll of bills into Alan's hand.

Eduardo stared in disbelief when Alan returned an hour later with a load of blankets, sacks of flour, sugar, powdered milk—even a crate of live chickens.

As villagers crowded close to finger the bundles in

amazed silence, Eduardo gave each of the Americans a hard "*abrazo*," the traditional Bolivian hug. "I thank you on behalf of our people. We will never forget you."

As Alan translated, Eduardo added, "Please do not forget us, either. These men are evil and strong. It would be easy to give in and grow the coca. As you have seen, some Christians have already gone back to the coca fields. Pray that we may stay strong to follow Jesus."

Uncle Pete lifted their backpacks into the helicopter. "Hop in, kids! We'd better leave if we plan to make it home before dark."

"*Hasta luego!*" the twins called good-bye in halting Spanish. Turning to go, a flicker of movement at the side of the road caught Justin's attention.

It was the man with the black leather jacket. He stood hidden in the long shadow the setting sun cast across the helicopter, his unfocused eyes closely watching the little group.

Justin grabbed Alan's arm and pointed. "There he is!" he said urgently. "That man's been following us. Ask Eduardo if he knows who he is."

Realizing he had been seen, the man dove into the tall brush that lined the other side of the road, but Alan had already pointed him out to Eduardo. The young man shook his head violently. Alan translated his agitated words.

"No, we do not know him. But can you not tell from his eyes what he is? That man is a '*drogadicto*'—one of the takers of the cocaine!"

CHAPTER SEVEN

A Lab Discovered

A s the camp helicopter lifted off, Jenny looked questioningly at Alan. "Why would those men burn everything down like that? It's just awful!"

Alan's mouth tightened. "It's not a new story. This is one reason it's so hard to stop cocaine production. If a farmer turns from coca to other crops, the cocaine dealers figure he has turned police informer. Besides, they don't like any interference in their supply of coca leaf."

He waved toward the black and smoldering ruins below. "So they decided to teach your friends a lesson—*and* discourage anyone else from following their example."

"Well, I'm glad they decided to stay and stand up to those bullies!" Jenny answered forcefully.

"What I'd like to know is why that cocaine addict was following us," Justin said from his seat behind the pilot. "I wonder what he wanted?"

"He was probably a thief," Alan answered after Justin quickly filled him in on their past run-ins with the stranger in the black leather jacket. "Addicts often turn to stealing in order to buy drugs. Tourists are usually the easiest targets. At any rate, he can't possibly know where you've come from. I'm sure you've seen the last of him."

"I wonder," Justin muttered. Jenny looked back at him curiously, but he said nothing more.

It was dark by the time they reached the oil camp, but the helicopter lights and a faint glow from the lab building enabled Alan to set down on the field behind the camp buildings. The four quickly scrubbed off soot from the fire in the camp's makeshift shower and tumbled into bed. Justin remembered to pray for Mike and his search as he drifted off to sleep.

▼▼▼

Justin was biting into a fresh, hot cinnamon roll the next morning when Dr. Latour and Rodrigo joined the group on the verandah. Justin secretly studied them as they pulled out a chair and sat down. The two men ate quickly without joining in the conversation, and were finished eating while the others were still leisurely drinking a second pot of coffee. Dr. Latour rose abruptly, but before Rodrigo could follow, Jenny leaned over and asked, "Are you going to be working around here today?"

White teeth flashed as the young, dark assistant answered, "Sì, we will be in the lab all day. We have a lot of samples to process."

"Can we watch?" Jenny begged. "There's nothing else to do!"

"No, you may not!" Dr. Latour snapped before his assistant could answer. "Now, if you will excuse us..." He marched down the verandah steps. Rodrigo reluctantly put down his coffee cup and followed.

Uncle Pete drained his cup and stood up. "If you two are looking for something to do, you can help Alan sort through the office files."

"That's not exactly what I had in mind!" Jenny whispered to Justin, but the two children obediently followed Alan and Uncle Pete to the cinder-block office building across the gravel driveway.

Alan pulled out a key ring, but as he reached for the doorknob, he exclaimed, "That's strange! I know I left this door locked!"

He bent to examine the lock. Peering over his shoulder, Justin noticed that the wooden door stood slightly ajar. "It looks like it's been forced!"

Alan pushed the door open, then stood in dismay. Crowding up from behind, the twins saw that it looked like a small cyclone had gone through the office! The desk and file cabinet were tipped over, and the drawers were scattered across the floor. Pens, pencils, bottles, and other office items were scattered everywhere. A dried-up puddle of ink stained the tiles.

Alan stepped carefully over the shards of a glass container and looked around. Uncle Pete stepped up behind him. "Can you tell what's missing?"

"The files!" Alan answered immediately. "The ones with the test results and Dr. Latour's surveys. They're all gone!"

Justin suddenly realized what had been missing in the mess on the floor—there was no paper.

Dr. Latour was suddenly in the office door, Rodrigo behind him. "What is all the commotion?"

Taking in the situation with one glance, he said coolly, "It would appear that someone broke in here while you were gone yesterday."

"Everything was fine when I went to pick up the Parkers," Alan insisted. "Gerard, did you see any strangers around after I left?"

"No, I didn't!" Dr. Latour answered firmly. "But Rodrigo and I didn't leave the lab until well after dark. Have you checked the other buildings for signs of a break-in?"

The twins trailed behind the adults as they checked through the camp. Their own bungalow was untouched, but Alan discovered scratch marks on his own lock that he hadn't noticed in the dark. Checking through his belongings, he found that a small radio and a pair of cufflinks were missing.

"It must have been a petty thief looking for cash," he decided at last. "But why would he take the files?"

"He obviously thought they might contain something worth selling," Dr. Latour answered curtly. "Now if you will excuse us, Rodrigo and I had better get started redoing those reports. This means a lot of extra work for us."

Uncle Pete raised his reddish-brown eyebrows. "But surely you keep copies of your reports. I had planned on checking out those survey sites today."

"I only keep rough notes in the lab. They wouldn't make any sense to you," Dr. Latour answered. "It would do no good to fly out there without the information in those reports. And it will take days to redo all the field work."

Surprisingly cheerful, considering he had lost several weeks of hard work, he added, "There is really no need for you to fly out to the survey sites personally. I know you had only planned on spending a few days here. Why don't you return home? I'll forward the surveys and test results as soon as I redo them. Then you can make your decision as to the future of this camp."

Uncle Pete nodded. "I'll think about it. In the meantime, Alan and I will get the office cleaned up."

"Fine," Dr. Latour answered crisply. "In that case, Rodrigo and I will return to work."

As Rodrigo and Dr. Latour turned to leave, Justin called out, "By the way, Dr. Latour, did you hear about the strange man that followed us on our trip? He turned out to be a cocaine addict."

Dr. Latour's broad back stiffened instantly. Justin saw

him threw a startled glance at Rodrigo. He turned around slowly.

"No, I hadn't heard. You were fortunate that you suffered no harm." The two men stalked off in the direction of the lab.

"What was that all about?" Jenny demanded.

"Just an idea I had," Justin whispered back.

The twins spent the next hour helping clean up the mess in the office. When they were done, Justin turned to Jenny. "Come on! I want to talk to Major Turner."

They found the major outside the aluminum office building, loudly lecturing a guard who stood stiffly at attention, a gloomy look on his face. When he saw the twins, he dismissed the guard.

"Taking a siesta on duty! What kind of soldiers are they making these days?" Turning to Justin and Jenny, he demanded gruffly, "Okay, what is it this time?"

Justin told him about the break-in, and about the man who had followed them the day before. "Maybe you could arrest the guy and find out something that would help," he finished hopefully.

The major's stern expression lightened. "Thanks for thinking of us, Justin. Any information is helpful at the moment. But I'm afraid we have no authority to arrest a man just because he is an addict. What we need is the man who is supplying the drug."

Justin's face fell, but Jenny suddenly added, "Maybe we *do* know something that will help!"

Justin brightened. "Yeah, Eduardo's village!" Major Turner's gray eyes sharpened with interest as the twins filled him in on what had happened.

"It's unlikely we'd catch the guys now, but we'll pass the information on to the DEA office in Santa Cruz," he told them. "In the meantime, keep your eyes open. If you see that man again, or anything else of interest, let me know."

"We will!" Justin promised eagerly. At that moment, Mike emerged from one of the sleeping tents wearing his flying outfit. His black eyes lit up momentarily, but he scowled fiercely. "So you're back again!"

He strode toward the helicopter. "I suppose you want another ride," he growled as he swung open the door. At Jenny's excited squeal, he continued sourly, "I thought so! Okay, get in. I don't have all day!"

Reaching down, he pulled Jenny up the steps. Justin hung back. "If you don't want us…" he said in what he hoped was a dignified tone.

"Who said I didn't want you?" Mike snapped. "I can use some extra pairs of eyes today. Get in!" In spite of his scowl, Justin decided that Mike really was glad to see them.

"Well, kids, we are as close to nailing that cocaine ring as the last time you were here," he said sarcastically as the rotor blades disturbed the still heat. "Do you still think God is going to help us catch them?"

"Yes, we do," Jenny answered firmly. "We've been praying for you, haven't we, Justin!"

"Well, you just keep on," Mike answered more softly. "I don't suppose it hurts anything. Anyway, I thought we'd track down that clearing we photographed on the last flight. That's why I need you. You kids keep your eyes peeled and let me know if you see a break in the trees. We're especially looking for anything long enough to be an airstrip."

An hour later, they had examined three natural clearings and a sugar cane farm. "Everything looks the same from up here!" Justin complained.

Slumped back in his seat, Mike was scowling again. "I told you praying wouldn't help. We're heading back to base!"

"Oh, couldn't we try just a little longer?" Jenny pleaded. "Look! There's another little clearing over there. It might be something important!"

"Someone else's farm," Mike muttered. "Okay, we'll give it fifteen minutes more."

A strong wind buffeted the helicopter and bent the tops of the trees as they swung over to the opening Jenny had spotted. As they hovered above the break in the trees, Justin saw that it was not really a clearing, but only an opening where the trees grew less densely. Raw stumps showed that some of the trees had recently been removed.

He swallowed hard with disappointment. As though reading his mind, Jenny said mournfully, "It's not a coca field *or* an airstrip. I guess we'd better give up."

"Just a minute!" Mike bent forward, staring intently into the thick foliage beyond the small clearing. His scowl suddenly disappeared, and there was a note of excitement in his voice. "I don't believe it! Kids, I think we may have hit the jackpot!"

They swung leisurely away from the opening in the trees. A strong gust of wind again tossed the trees below, and Justin saw what Mike had seen—a glimpse of what could be olive-green canvas. It would normally be invisible under the thick leaf cover.

He gulped. "You mean there might be a cocaine lab down there?"

Mike nodded. He turned the helicopter away from the site. "Those were camouflage tents down there. Not the sort of thing the average family around here owns."

Jenny spoke up. "But we didn't find an airstrip. How can there be a lab?"

Mike pointed out the window. "That must be the answer. There's a four-wheel-drive track hidden under those trees."

Below, Justin could trace a faint line through the jungle that might possibly be a road. As Mike flew on, the territory they covered began to look vaguely familiar. "That track goes to the coca farm!" he exclaimed.

Mike nodded approvingly. "That's right. And there's a passable dirt road from there out to the main road. But they still have to fly their goods out of the area. I wonder how? We've got every known airstrip covered."

"Are we going to land?" Jenny asked eagerly.

"No!" Mike was now the professional DEA agent. "If that *is* a cocaine lab down there, the workers will be armed and dangerous. I want you kids to stay out of this."

Seeing their downcast expressions, he added, "You don't think *I'm* stupid enough to go down alone either, do you? I'm radioing for help."

He was already on the radio. When he set the microphone down, he turned to his passengers. "Major Turner will be sending UMOPAR troops right away. I've given them coordinates for finding that road. I'm heading back to base now to pick up the major and some men."

"Won't they get away by the time you get there?" Justin asked anxiously.

"Why do you think I flew on by?" Mike explained reasonably. "That place is practically invisible from the air. We've flown over the area half-a-dozen times and never seen a thing. They have no reason to think we've seen anything this time.

"And we wouldn't have, if the wind hadn't been blowing right when we were over the spot." The young agent was actually smiling. "Maybe there *is* something to that praying business."

A half hour later, they approached the oil company property. Below them, billows of dust masked the rutted dirt road that led past the two camps. Mike dropped low, and the dust cloud separated into a pair of army jeeps and the transport truck Justin had seen parked beside the DEA office. Soldiers in khaki uniforms, machine guns and rifles slung over their backs, waved as they swooped down over their heads.

"They're on the way!" Mike announced jubilantly. "Those filthy drug dealers won't get away this time. Come on, let's pick up the boss!"

The major, four armed UMOPAR agents at his back, was waiting impatiently beside the helicopter landing. As Mike set the helicopter down, he ran toward them, one arm sheltering his face from the strong wind of the rotors. He was aboard almost before the helicopter touched the ground. The other men scrambled through the open door at his heels.

Afraid he would be ordered out, Justin made himself as small as possible. He noticed that Jenny was also holding her breath, but the major didn't even glance at the twins as Mike lifted off within seconds of landing. The soldiers squatted on the floor while the major gave orders in Spanish. One man was hooking a coil of nylon rope to a thick metal rod above the door.

"What's that for?" Jenny whispered in her brother's ear. But she soon found out as Mike headed back to the tiny clearing. The wind had died down, and there was no sign of human habitation below. But Mike easily maneuvered the helicopter to a position near the glimpse of camouflage they had seen earlier.

Lowering the helicopter, he hovered barely above tree level while one of the soldiers slid open the door and tossed out the coils of rope. Seated closest to the door, Justin was glad he wore a seat belt as he glimpsed the ground far below the widespread branches.

The soldier who had tossed out the rope snapped a hook on his belt to the rope and slid over the edge. One by one, the others followed, skillfully dodging branches, their weapons carefully balanced across their backs. When the last one hit the ground, Major Turner slammed the door.

"They'll guard the place until the main troops arrive," he

informed Mike. Then he seemed to notice the children for the first time.

"What are you doing here?" he growled. "You should have been dropped off at the base. This isn't a school picnic we're on!"

He looked so stern that Justin was sure he would order Mike to take them home. But after a long moment, he shrugged. "Well, we don't have time to take you back now. You'll have to come along."

Justin and Jenny couldn't suppress excited grins. As he buckled himself into the copilot's seat, Major Turner warned gruffly, "Don't get any funny ideas about seeing action. You'll stay in the chopper with Mike, well out of the way of any trouble."

But as they circled back across the small opening in the trees, Mike exclaimed angrily, "Sir, didn't you tell those clowns to stay out of sight and keep quiet?"

"I sure did," the major answered grimly.

He leaned forward as Mike moved in for a closer look. An area just large enough to land a helicopter had been completely logged off. Two men stood in the center, their uniforms clearly marking them as members of the UMOPAR team they had dropped off fifteen minutes earlier. They waved violently as the helicopter hovered overhead, and a flow of Spanish blasted from the radio.

Major Turner nodded grimly to Mike. "There's a cocaine lab down there all right, but the place was abandoned by the time our men got here."

"What? That's impossible!" Mike burst out.

Striking the armrest of his seat with a blow of his clenched fist, he swore so loudly and viciously that Justin had to strain to hear as the major added, "Both the men and the cocaine are gone. I'm sorry, Mike!"

CHAPTER EIGHT

Nightmare Creature

"**S**et her down, Mike!" Major Turner commanded. "We're going in!"

Mike carefully maneuvered into the tiny opening below. Major Turner had the door open and was following the two UMOPAR men into the underbrush before Justin managed to unbuckle his seat belt. Jerking off his earphones, Mike barked, "You kids stay with me and keep out of trouble!"

Justin looked around. A dozen yards beyond the clearing, a bunk tent of dappled olive-green and brown canvas hid under a thick grove of trees. Green walls of heavy screen stood about four feet high, while the peaked roof allowed room for a man to stand upright. Through the open tent flap, Justin could see a line of camp cots inside.

Mike was examining the small patch of cleared ground around the helicopter. "We aren't the first helicopter to land here!" he said with satisfaction. "No wonder we haven't found signs of an airstrip. They've been taking the cocaine out by helicopter!"

He added, "This could be a real clue. There aren't many

helicopters in Bolivia. If we could trace their recent where-abouts..."

A clear picture of the oil camp helicopter suddenly popped into Justin's mind. It would fit easily into this space. Mike straightened up. "Okay, let's go! You two stay right behind me and keep your hands in your pockets."

Carefully picking his way across fallen branches, Justin followed Jenny and Mike around the bunk tent and soon noticed two buildings made of wood planks—one the size of their tool shed back home, the other several times bigger. Camouflage nets kept them from being seen from more than a few yards away.

Mike strode over to a picnic table which sat under over-hanging branches in between the buildings. He seemed to have forgotten the twins, but they trailed obediently behind.

The table had been set for a dozen men, and a half-eaten meal sat on the plates. A coffee mug lay on its side, its contents forming a dark-brown pool on the weathered wood. Mike picked up a tall metal glass and looked inside.

"There's still ice in here!" he shouted in disgust. "They must have left in the last half hour."

"Mike! We found the lab!" Major Turner exclaimed, thrusting his head out the doorway of the larger building. Dropping the glass, Mike joined him, the twins close behind. Peering into the gloomy building, they saw a long, dark room full of unfamiliar objects.

The jeeps and transport truck bounced into the clearing minutes later, and soon the area was swarming with armed men. The major had discovered a portable electric generator, and lights now brightened the largest building.

Jenny had slipped out to explore the rest of the camp, but Justin was more interested in the strange equipment that sev-eral UMOPAR agents were now taking apart. The major stood over a metal frame the shape and size of a dining table.

Suspended from the frame was a thick white cloth, like a bed sheet, giving it the look of a sunken trampoline.

"What's this for?" Justin asked. In answer, Major Turner rubbed his fingers against the cloth, then held out his hand. Justin looked closely at the white powder that clung to it.

"This is the filter for the cocaine," the major explained. "Those leaves you saw the other day are turned into a paste we call cocaine base. The base is brought here and filtered with chemicals through this cloth until it turns into white crystals."

He motioned across the room to where a dozen heat lamps hung over a long wooden table. "The crystals are spread out under those to dry, then packaged."

His expression grew hard. "The final step in the process is smuggling it out to the U.S. and other countries to ruin the lives of millions of people!"

He was interrupted as Jenny bounced in the door. "There isn't anything very interesting out there," she announced. "That other building is just the kitchen. But you wouldn't believe what they found hidden in the bushes—a great big freezer and even a clothes dryer!"

She looked around the big room with interest. "What's all this?"

She bent over the filter, then glanced at the major. "Oh, I forgot! They found a whole bunch of garbage cans hidden behind the kitchen, too—way back in the brush. You know, those big plastic ones of all different colors."

She wrinkled her nose in disgust. "They smelled awful! The soldiers were acting all excited, but they wouldn't let me take even one little peek inside!"

Justin grinned. If he knew his sister, she was probably going crazy with curiosity. Mike straightened up from a jumble of bottles and boxes he was sorting. "Did you say garbage cans?" he asked. "I wonder..."

But two soldiers were already carrying in a pair of large orange pails. They set the pails on the floor, and Mike tore off the plastic lids.

"Chemicals for producing cocaine!" he announced. "And illegal to own in Bolivia. There must be thousands of dollars worth here!"

A bleak expression wiped the triumph from his face. "But there's no sign of the cocaine nor any evidence that points to those in charge. If we had caught just one of the workers!"

He slammed a fist into the palm of his other hand. "How could they have cleared out of here so fast? We *had* them! I know I didn't give anything away when I flew over."

Jenny piped up, "Maybe they overheard the radio."

Such scorn blazed from Mike's black eyes that Jenny stepped back. "Not unless they had the equipment to bypass half-a-dozen scrambling devices. No, they were warned! But how?"

He was interrupted by a soldier in lieutenant's uniform who mumbled something in his ear. Mike turned to the major, "Sir, we've detained the coca grower. He insists he doesn't know anything about the lab—or the track that leads here. He says he just sold his crop to strangers who offered him a good price. Do you want us to hold him?"

Major Turner nodded his head. "I have a feeling he knows more than he's telling. I'll interview him myself."

He marched toward the door. "We've gone over everything there is to see here. We'll leave the UMOPAR agents—they will go through the area with a fine-toothed comb. Pick out a dozen good men to stand guard just in case someone comes back. And get those kids back to the oil camp before someone starts worrying."

Deep, bitter lines again grooved Mike's face as he hurried the twins into the helicopter. He was so obviously lost in his own angry thoughts that neither twin dared say a word on the flight back to camp. Dropping them off in the field behind the camp buildings, he took off again without a glance in their direction.

There was no one in sight as they came around the back of the administration building, but the camp jeep stood at the door of the lab. As they sauntered down the gravel driveway that divided the property, Rodrigo walked down the lab steps.

"Hi, there!" Jenny called gaily.

Visibly startled, Rodrigo stumbled on the bottom step, dropping a bundle of what looked like burlap bags. "Wh ... what are you doing here?" he gasped.

Recovering himself, he picked up his bundle and tossed it into the back of the jeep. "I thought you kids were gone for the day," he added more calmly.

Jenny looked around. "Where's Uncle Pete and Alan?"

Rodrigo glanced nervously behind him. "They left right after you did—took the camp helicopter."

He reached into his pocket and pulled out a folded piece of notebook paper. "Here, they left you a message."

Justin leaned over the back of the jeep. Besides Rodrigo's bundle of sacks, there was only a folded canvas tarp, of the type used to protect cargo from the weather, and a large metal tool chest.

"Did you hear about the raid on the cocaine lab?" Justin asked, watching the lab assistant closely. "Things got so hot we had to come home."

"Yes... Yes, we did." Rodrigo didn't look at all well. He glanced toward the lab again.

Dr. Latour loomed up behind Rodrigo. "What nonsense are you kids talking about?"

"The DEA just raided a cocaine lab," Justin answered.

"We were there and saw it all. They didn't catch anyone, though. Someone warned them before the DEA got there."

"Rodrigo said you already knew," Jenny added brightly. "How did you find out? I didn't think anyone else was back."

Casting an annoyed glance at Rodrigo, Dr. Latour said sharply, "We haven't heard anything. But when the entire complement of UMOPAR goes out the front gate armed to the teeth, there's obviously more than a drill going on!"

Without another word, the chief geologist pushed past the children and climbed into the driver's seat of the camp jeep. Avoiding eye contact with the children, Rodrigo climbed over the tailgate and began shuffling through the tool chest. Peering over the side, Justin opened his eyes wide as he glimpsed what looked like a semiautomatic rifle. Dr. Latour snapped a curt order, and Rodrigo slammed the lid shut.

"Where are you going?" Jenny asked as Rodrigo sat down. "It might be dangerous out there with all those cocaine dealers on the loose."

Dr. Latour was so angry that his hands shook as he turned the ignition key. "You are far too nosy, kid!" he hissed. "Mind your own business or you'll find yourself in a lot of trouble!"

"What got into him?" Jenny asked, staring after the speeding jeep. "He didn't even ask about the drug raid. You'd think he'd want to know!"

Justin watched as Rodrigo climbed out to unlock the gate, then he grinned at his sister. "Not everyone is as nosy as you!"

"You're the one who's always poking your nose into things!" Jenny gave her brother a playful push that sent him sprawling into the gravel driveway.

"Okay, you asked for it!" Picking up a handful of pebbles, Justin jumped to his feet and chased after his sister. Jenny was a fast runner, but she was laughing so hard that he soon caught up. As he dumped the handful of gravel down the neck of her T-shirt, he pushed Dr. Latour and Rodrigo's strange behavior to the back of his mind.

The note Rodrigo had given them told Justin and Jenny to stay put if they got back before Uncle Pete and Alan, and that the two men planned to be back for supper. The twins ate lunch alone, then leafed through magazines on their bungalow verandah, keeping an eye out for either the helicopter or the jeep.

The sun was setting as Uncle Pete and Alan finally flew in. The twins were now accustomed to eating supper at eight o'clock or later. Jenny was still recounting her version of the morning's adventures between mouthfuls of a sticky custard dessert, when Justin heard the familiar roar of the jeep engine. He kept one eye on the front of the lab as he ate, but the headlights of the camp jeep never appeared in the driveway. *They must have circled around back,* he decided.

"You kids stay away from the DEA camp until we leave," Uncle Pete ordered when Jenny had finished. "They'll be up to their ears in work over there."

Jenny nodded, then asked, "When *are* we leaving?"

Justin looked up from his dessert in dismay. "We aren't leaving yet, are we, Uncle Pete?"

Uncle Pete raised his eyebrows. "I hadn't planned on it. I haven't finished my investigation."

"But I thought you couldn't!" Jenny said. "I mean, with all those reports and things stolen..."

Uncle Pete's green eyes twinkled. "Don't you worry about that! I have all the information I need."

He didn't add anything more, and Justin and Jenny soon excused themselves and returned to the bungalow. They had exhausted Alan's pile of old magazines, so Justin pulled out a set of checkers. But after two games, both of them decided to call it a night. Uncle Pete and Alan were still bent over a sheet of scribbled numbers when the twins called a goodnight from the office door.

Back in the bungalow, Justin spread toothpaste on his toothbrush and poured a glass from the pitcher of boiled water the cook had provided. With the tropical heat, he and Jenny had traded the sweat suits they used as pajamas for shorts and T-shirts.

"You can have first dibs on the outhouse, Jenny," he called as he brushed his teeth. "The flashlight's right here."

Jenny emerged from her bedroom. Accepting the flashlight he offered, she opened the front door and hesitated. "It's awfully dark out there. Why don't you come with me, Justin?"

Surprised, Justin demanded, "Why? You've always gone by yourself before!"

Jenny lifted her shoulders. "I know, but ... today's been kind of spooky and all ... and anyone could be out there. Maybe that man's still following ... or one of those cocaine dealers. Please come!"

"Don't be such a sissy!" Justin growled. But he reluctantly followed her out to the verandah.

"Girls!" he muttered under his breath as he took the flashlight Jenny shoved at him. Walking single file behind his sister, he made a narrow path of light for their feet.

The outhouse sat in a patch of beaten-down brush about a hundred yards behind their bungalow. Justin had gotten used to the long trip, but even he had to admit he preferred the walk by day. A three-quarter moon stained the open spaces with silver, but the bushes and trees loomed black and menacing. It reminded him of younger years when he and Jenny had played in their own back yard after dark, imagining monsters or enemies behind every bush. But then, safety had been only as far away as the warm, shining light of their kitchen door.

The night seemed unusually loud, with strange rustles and noises. Justin couldn't suppress a shiver as something dropped at his feet. Jenny slipped a hand into his as he turned the flashlight downward. An oversized toad blinked up at him. With a deep croak, it was gone.

He was relieved when the familiar form of the outhouse was before them. Twice the size of a telephone booth, it was built of locally cut planks of wood, somewhat carelessly nailed together. Although fairly new, tropical storms and sun had already weathered the boards to a silvery-gray. A rusty latch held shut a rickety handmade door.

"See, I told you there was nothing to be scared of!" Justin told his sister. "Go on in. I'll wait right here."

Jenny opened the outhouse door. The interior was inky-black. Justin handed her the flashlight. She stepped inside and closed the door, and Justin leaned against the weathered doorjamb to wait. Then a terrified scream shattered the night!

Justin yanked open the door as Jenny stumbled backward. "Don't tell me you've seen another scorpion," he sighed loudly, catching her as she half-fell down the one high step. His eyes followed the narrow beam of the flashlight, and suddenly his own heart skipped a beat.

Against the back wall of the outhouse was a square wooden box the size of a toilet. A hole in the top led to the pit below, and on top of this had been fastened a regular plastic seat taken off of a discarded toilet.

The toilet lid leaned up against the wall. Over the top, curling and uncurling like grasping claws, reached two pair of black, hairy legs. As the twins watched in frozen fascination, the toilet lid crashed down with a force that wrung another scream from Jenny and a startled yelp from Justin.

For there—with eyes glittering gold in the flashlight

beam, its circular, mouse-sized body humped high, and its eight hairy legs extending the width of the toilet lid—squatted a creature straight out of a nightmare!

CHAPTER NINE

Evidence Discovered!

Justin and Jenny stood frozen for a long moment as the creature reared, its velvety front legs clawing the air. A beak-like mouth snapped, and they caught sight of fangs like those of a rattlesnake. Justin pulled Jenny away from the door. "Stay out of there," he ordered hoarsely. "I'll get a stick."

But someone else had heard Jenny's scream. Uncle Pete was already pushing past them, and they heard the sound of heavy blows. Then Uncle Pete appeared in the doorway of the outhouse, and Jenny threw herself into his arms. Alan appeared moments later, demanding breathlessly, "What happened? Has anyone been hurt?"

Alan shone his flashlight around the interior of the outhouse. "It's okay, kids!" he assured them. "It's only a tarantula spider. They look awful, but they aren't really that poisonous. One that size would certainly give you a bite you'd remember, but they aren't deadly."

Peering around Uncle Pete's arm, Jenny looked unconvinced. With the branch Uncle Pete had used to kill it, Alan swept the tarantula out onto the path. The giant spider now lay on its back, its furry legs curled unmoving over its body.

Justin bent down to study the ugly creature. It looked much smaller now than he had remembered.

Alan, too, bent over the spider. He looked puzzled. "I don't understand how this happened, kids. We always keep that door latched, and I was just out here myself an hour ago."

Nudging the creature with the toe of his shoe, he shook his head in amazement. "I've heard of tarantulas this big in the deep jungle, but I've never seen one around here!"

"Well, I hate spiders, and I'm not staying here if there are any more of those around!" Jenny cried. She was still clinging to Uncle Pete.

"What exactly is going on here?" a smooth voice demanded. Startled, Justin jumped to his feet as the tall form of Dr. Latour loomed out of the dark. Justin stifled a momentary suspicion as he caught the look of genuine surprise on the geologist's face. The look turned to cool amusement as he took in the spider and Jenny's face, still wet with tears.

"Mr. Parker, it's evident that your family isn't cut out for the jungle," he said. "I suggest you all go home before you run into something much worse than a spider. I'd be glad to run you in to Trinidad."

Uncle Pete's voice was suddenly cold as ice. "Are you suggesting that I drop my investigation, Dr. Latour?"

The cool gray eyes narrowed as Dr. Latour answered. "As I've said before, there is nothing more you can do at the moment. I've already told you what the situation is here. You've found nothing in the records that shows my analysis to be at fault."

"I would have to agree," Uncle Pete answered dryly, "since most of the records are unfortunately unavailable!"

Looking deeply offended, Dr. Latour demanded, "Are you suggesting I had something to do with that?" He drew himself up arrogantly. "You know my reputation! Have you any possible reason to doubt my commitment to finding oil for Triton and for this needy country?"

"No, I don't," Uncle Pete admitted. He dropped his gaze to his nephew and niece.

"Well, Justin, Jenny. What do you think? Are you ready to pack it in and go home?"

"No!" Justin's answer exploded in the silence. He continued more quietly, "Please, Uncle Pete! I want to stay."

"Well, I'd just as soon go..." Jenny said with quivering voice. She stopped as Justin caught her eye; he was shaking his head violently. "I ... I mean I guess I'd like to stay, too."

Uncle Pete nodded. "That settles it. We'll finish this investigation from here."

Dr. Latour seemed annoyed, but he shrugged his broad shoulders. "It's your decision."

▼▼▼

The lights were out across camp when Justin slipped into Jenny's small bedroom. The faint moonlight entering through the open shutter showed Jenny still sitting cross-legged on her camp cot.

When she saw her brother, she demanded, "What's the big idea? Why did you make me say we'd stay? It's not like there's anything to do here!"

Justin sat down on the edge of the cot. "Because," he said calmly, "I think something funny is going on here—and I know Uncle Pete thinks so too. I don't want to go until we find out what it is."

With the practice of years, Jenny instantly read his mind. "You mean Dr. Latour, don't you?"

Justin nodded. "Dr. Latour seems awfully anxious to get us out of here. And I think I know why. I'm pretty sure he and Rodrigo are mixed up in the drug traffic."

Jenny dropped her brush in astonishment. "What makes you think *that?*" She added suspiciously, "I hope you aren't going to start in again about seeing Dr. Latour in those pictures!"

Justin looked stubborn. "Well, what if it *was* him? Don't you think it's strange that there's a track leading from the cocaine lab right to that field? Besides, he was so angry about the DEA being here."

Thinking of the look he had seen on the geologist's face, he added, "I got the impression that ... well, that he almost hated them! Then other things started adding up."

Justin ticked the points off on his fingers. "First, do you remember what we overheard that night? He didn't want us snooping around because he had 'one last haul' to make.

"Then there's that man who's been following us. All right, maybe he was just a thief, but he never did try to steal anything from us! And we heard Rodrigo say he was going to have someone keep an eye on us. Who better than a drug addict, if they really are mixed up in cocaine dealing?"

Jenny still wasn't convinced. "If this is all true, why hasn't the DEA found out about it? They saw those pictures too!"

"Major Turner said they'd never actually met Dr. Latour or Rodrigo. Those two have been very careful to stay away from the DEA camp," Justin answered. "And don't forget Dr. Latour's perfect record. There's no reason to suspect him."

Leaning back against the wall, Justin continued, "This morning, Mike said the cocaine was going out by helicopter. Alan told me the other day that the oil camp had the only helicopter in this area. I got to thinking about how easy it would be for Dr. Latour to fly in there and get cocaine out."

"So that's why you asked Rodrigo about the raid!" Jenny exclaimed. "If they saw all the soldiers going by, I suppose Dr. Latour could have called the lab and warned them there might be a raid."

"That's right!" Justin said. "Remember my friend Nick back home? His dad has a ham radio like that one in the lab.

It can reach anywhere! And then, the way they took off this afternoon... Where did they go? And what were all those burlap bags for? Maybe they were meeting someone."

He made his last point. "And finally, how *did* that tarantula get in the outhouse? I was in there myself after supper and I shut the door. Dr. Latour and Rodrigo are always exploring out in the jungle..."

"Then you think Dr. Latour put that spider in the outhouse?" Jenny asked doubtfully.

Justin shook his head. "That isn't his style. Besides, he looked awfully surprised. No, I think that was Rodrigo's idea. Remember when he told Dr. Latour he could get rid of us? He must think we're real sissies!"

"Well, a spider that big would scare anyone!" Jenny declared, shame-faced. She added, "But I can't imagine Rodrigo being mixed up in something like that. He seems so nice!"

"You just think that because he kisses your hand and all that stuff!" Justin answered scornfully.

"Well, it still seems to me you're doing a lot of guessing," Jenny replied. "And if you're right, what can you do about it? We got into enough trouble poking into things *last* time."

"Yeah, I know!" Justin admitted. "I'm going to tell Uncle Pete about this. If he thinks there's something to it, he'll check it out and tell Major Turner."

He opened the door. Hearing a steady snore, he added with a grin, "I'll tell him in the morning, that is!"

▼▼▼

A tap on the shoulder awoke Justin the next morning. Opening bleary eyes, he saw that it was still dark. Uncle Pete bent over his cot and whispered, "Justin, Alan and I are leaving to check out the rest of those survey sites. This should finish the investigation. You and Jenny stay out of trouble while we're gone."

"Sure, Uncle Pete," Justin answered sleepily, burrowing back into his pillow. Then he was suddenly wide awake.

"Oh, Uncle Pete, I wanted to tell you…" It was too late. The screen door banged shut behind his uncle, and moments later he heard the camp helicopter lift overhead.

The first weak rays of dawn provided enough light for Justin to find his clothes. Shaking them out, he dressed quickly, then woke his sister.

"What do we do now?" she asked with dismay.

Justin shrugged. "We can at least look around a little—just to see if Dr. Latour and Rodrigo brought anything back last night."

"Not until after breakfast," Jenny said firmly. Justin nodded agreement, but as the twins stepped onto the verandah, Justin heard the sound of an engine.

"Get down!" he hissed, pulling Jenny down behind the verandah railing as Rodrigo backed the camp jeep around to the front steps of the lab.

"Why?" Jenny hissed back.

"I want to see what they're up to!" As Rodrigo disappeared inside, Justin swung a leg over the railing. "You wait here. I'll be right back!"

Out of sight of anyone who might be looking out the lab windows, he moved quietly to the back of the jeep. He was back within a minute. "Nothing in there," he announced triumphantly. "Not even those bags they loaded yesterday. If they did bring anything back last night, it's still inside."

The twins ducked down again as the lab door opened. Though unable to see, the two children could hear footsteps on the gravel and Dr. Latour's voice raised in anger.

"How dare they take off without notifying us! We've got to have that chopper!"

"Why not just wait until they return?" replied Rodrigo in accented English.

"With the DEA swarming all over? No, we've got to get that stuff out this morning."

Rodrigo muttered something, and Dr. Latour's voice rose again. "Yes, you were so sure you could get rid of them. When you said you had a plan, I thought you had something a little more subtle than that stupid spider. I had a collector willing to pay big money for that thing!"

Justin nudged his sister, then strained to hear as Rodrigo answered gloomily, "Well, at least they're gone for a few hours."

"No thanks to you! We'd better move things out before they get back."

"It would save a lot of time to radio from here."

"Are you kidding? This is one day when the DEA will be monitoring every broadcast in the Beni!" Dr. Latour answered. "No, we've got to be off Triton property to make this call."

The engine started again, and the men's voices could no longer be heard. The twins waited until the jeep had faded from hearing before they came out from hiding.

"Boy, it *does* sound like they're up to something!" Jenny admitted. "Maybe we'd better go tell Mike and Major Turner about this."

"No, not yet!" Justin shook his head. "We still need proof. We can't call Major Turner over here just because we heard those guys talking."

He disappeared inside the bungalow. A few moments later he emerged, camera in hand. He handed his sister a spare roll of film. "Here, can you hold on to this?"

"What's it for?" Jenny asked as she tucked the film into a jeans pocket.

"I want to see what those guys are in such a hurry to get rid of. And I want to take some pictures. Remember how

Major Turner said they can't touch the cocaine dealers unless they actually catch them in the act?"

"Sure. So what?"

Justin slung the camera around his neck. "So if they haul off whatever they've got hidden before we can get Major Turner, we've got to have some proof it was there!"

"And what if Dr. Latour and Rodrigo come back before you're done? They think we're gone for the day."

Justin shrugged. "So we're just a couple of kids out exploring!"

Jenny shook her head doubtfully. "I don't know. It sounds dangerous!"

Justin suddenly remembered Eduardo's burning village. "I don't care!" he declared. "Those cocaine dealers need to be stopped! If I can do something to help, I will!"

"Besides," he added more calmly, "I figure it'll take them at least an hour to go make that radio call..."

Jenny was suddenly excited. "Wouldn't it be wonderful if we *did* find some kind of proof? Mike would see that God really does answer our prayers!"

Forgetting about breakfast, she added impatiently, "Well, where do we start?"

"The lab!" Justin answered. "Dr. Latour and Rodrigo are the only ones who ever go in there. Come on!"

Jenny at his heels, he trotted across the gravel and up the lab steps. Then he stopped in sudden dismay. Thrust through the latch of the sturdy wood door was an oversized, shiny new padlock. He glanced at the large window to the right of the door. Its heavy wooden shutters were pulled tight, the black metal bars protecting them from prying fingers.

Turning to Jenny, he hunched his shoulders in disappointment. "We can't even get a look inside!"

"Well, you didn't really think they'd be stupid enough to

leave anything out where we could see it, did you?" Jenny answered.

Justin grinned suddenly. "No, but I was hoping."

"Besides," Jenny added triumphantly, "we didn't have any problem seeing in the other night."

"Of course!" Justin exclaimed. "That hole in the back window. Come on!"

He led the way around to the back. There was nothing beyond the lab except open field and the shimmering metal roof of the DEA office building in the distance. The brush grew tall and thick here against the back wall, except for the narrow path that feet had pounded out toward the DEA camp.

As they neared the back window, the twins saw that the tangled bushes they'd crouched under three nights before were trampled and broken, as though by heavy boots. A double line of crushed grass indicated a track where a vehicle might have pulled up to the window.

Justin examined the faint track. "This must be where they parked the jeep last night."

Jenny was already inspecting the back window. "Look at this!" she cried excitedly. "They've taken off the bars!"

Justin joined her at the window. From a distance, everything had looked normal. But now Justin could see that the black bars that had protected the window were only leaning up against the wooden shutters. Crumbling holes in the plaster around the window showed where they had been forcibly removed. As on the front window, the heavy shutters were closed tight, but at the bottom left-hand corner was the hole where something had eaten away at the wood.

"Why would they go to all this trouble when all they had to do was open the front door?" Jenny asked curiously.

"So we wouldn't see them unloading, of course!" Justin stated proudly, lifting the bars down and stacking them against the whitewashed wall. "This means they really *did* bring something in last night that they didn't want anyone to see. They brought it back here and passed it through the window."

The bottom of the window was level with Justin's chin. He put an eye to the hole, but blackness filled the interior of the lab. "You can't see a thing through here," he informed his sister.

Standing on tiptoes, he pushed hard at the shutters, but they didn't budge. "Must be barred from the inside," he commented. "I'm going to climb up and see if I can get them open."

The shutters fit into a wooden window frame. At the bottom of the frame was a windowsill about six inches wide. With both arms on the sill, Justin tried to haul himself up. But as he applied his whole weight to the wood, he heard a crack. A section of wood gave way under his hands, and he tumbled backward into the bushes.

"Great!" Jenny exclaimed as he scrambled to his feet. "Now you've broken the window."

Justin picked up the piece of wood and turned it over. "No, I didn't break it," he said in an odd tone. "Look! It's been cut!"

Jenny took the piece of wood from his hand and examined it closely. About a foot long, its sides were smooth and showed marks of a saw. Justin reached up and felt along the window. "There's room under here to hide something.

"See? This wood fits right over, so no one can see it." He reached inside a small hollow. "Here it is!" He pulled out a rectangular, plastic-covered object and handed it to Jenny. Jenny quickly unwrapped it. Inside the plastic was a small, leather-bound notebook.

"Rodrigo was writing in a notebook just like this the night we came," Jenny commented, flipping through its pages. "Remember how he hid it away when Dr. Latour took us into the lab?"

Justin studied the notebook over her shoulder. Small, precise writing covered the pages with numbers, slashes, letters, and an occasional name. There were no words. He handed it to Jenny. "It's just jumbled-up letters and numbers!"

"Maybe it's in code," Jenny suggested.

"Well, it must be important or it wouldn't be hidden like that. We'll take it for evidence," Justin decided. He tucked the notebook into his belt and pulled his shirt down to hide it.

"I still want to see inside the lab, though. If they bothered taking those bars down last night, then they certainly weren't hauling some experiment. It must be something illegal … maybe the stuff that disappeared from the cocaine lab."

Justin climbed back onto the window ledge, but he couldn't budge the heavy shutters. "We'll just have to make this hole bigger," he said at last. "I've got my penknife, and this wood's half-rotten anyway. Jenny, why don't you go get the flashlight."

By the time Jenny returned with the flashlight, Justin had whittled away enough of the termite-eaten wood for him to put his arm through. Finding a good-sized rock to stand on, he leaned carefully against the sill and thrust the flashlight through the hole. He gave a low whistle as he saw what lay in the beam of the flashlight.

"We were right!" he announced excitedly as he slid down. Handing Jenny the flashlight, he moved aside to let her step up on the stone. She too whistled when she saw what he had seen. A dozen burlap sacks filled to overflowing leaned up against the back wall. Right under the window, one stood open. Its contents had obviously been under inspection, because several plastic bags filled with a white, powdery substance lay scattered on the top.

"That looks just like that white stuff on the cocaine filter

Major Turner showed us," Jenny exclaimed as she handed the flashlight back to Justin.

"It must be the cocaine from the lab we saw yesterday," Justin agreed. "This'll cheer up Mike!"

He flashed his light around the lab. "They must have warned their men in time to get it away. And when they left in such a hurry yesterday afternoon, they were on their way to pick it up. They can't know anyone suspects them, but they must be going crazy having all this stuff here—especially with visitors in the camp. No wonder they wanted us to leave!"

Jenny moved away from the window. "We'd better get out of here before they come back. Let's find Major Turner and let him take care of it."

"Just a minute," Justin answered as he removed his camera from around his neck. "We've got to get pictures."

It was now fully daylight, but he set the flash for the dark lab interior, then maneuvered the camera through the hole. Though he couldn't see what he was shooting, he slowly moved the camera in a half-circle, taking one shot after another until he was sure he had photographed the whole room. He finished off with at least half-a-dozen shots of the open burlap bag.

He had just heard the click that meant the roll was finished when Jenny said urgently, "They're coming back, Justin! I can hear the jeep. Hurry!"

Justin looked up in dismay. "Already?"

The camera stuck as he pulled his arm out, and he lost precious seconds before he managed to tug it free. Hurriedly, he rewound the film, yanked open the back of the camera, and pulled it out. Taking the fresh roll from his sister's pocket, he quickly fitted it into the camera.

He thrust the camera into Jenny's hands and whispered, "Quick! Take some pictures! *Any* pictures!" Turning back to the window, he swiftly put the cut section of sill back into place. Leaning the bars up again, he brushed the wood splinters from the sill.

"Let's go before they see us!" he ordered urgently, reaching for the camera as Jenny snapped a final shot. But it was too late. Rodrigo was already striding around the side of the building.

He came to a surprised halt when he saw the children. He wore his usual bland smile, but his dark eyes darted suspiciously from one to the other. "What are you kids doing here? I thought you were gone for the day!"

"We were just out taking a few pictures," Justin answered calmly as the twins edged backward. But they hadn't taken two steps before Rodrigo caught sight of the freshly widened hole in the shutter. The smile disappeared as he lunged for the children.

"Boss!" he shouted. "These kids have been snooping in the lab!"

CHAPTER TEN

The Pursuit

"**C**ome on!" Justin whispered. "We've got to get this stuff to Major Turner."

Grabbing his sister's hand, he turned to run—and collided with a solid object. He looked up to see Dr. Latour, dark with anger, looming over him. Steel-strong hands bit into Justin's shoulders.

"What do you think you're doing here?" the geologist asked, giving Justin a hard shake.

"We ... we were just taking pictures," Justin said, trying to appear calm.

Steely-gray eyes seemed to bore right through his thin clothes to the notebook and film he had hidden. Then Dr. Latour released Justin so suddenly that he almost fell. Stepping over to the broken shutter, he examined it with a frown. Justin was too shaken to move, and before he had a chance to recover, Dr. Latour was back at his side.

"I don't think they could see anything," he informed Rodrigo. "It's pitch dark in there."

His anger seemed to have evaporated, and he was smiling as he turned back to the children. "Do forgive us," he said. "My assistant has overreacted. You see, we have some very delicate experiments set up in the lab. Rodrigo was afraid that you had disturbed them, and... What's this?"

He bent down to pick up an object lying in the grass. Justin's heart sank as he recognized his flashlight. Dr. Latour straightened up slowly. "And what, exactly, was this for?"

He spoke softly, but something in his voice made the twins press closer together. When neither answered, he took a step closer. "Answer me!" he commanded sharply.

Justin kept his mouth stubbornly shut, but Jenny answered truthfully enough, "We saw that the bars were loose and thought we'd take a look. We were just curious about what was in the lab. We didn't get inside."

The geologist pinched Jenny's chin with two strong fingers. Tilting her head back, he asked smoothly, "And what did you *see?*"

"Only ... only burlap sacks." Jenny's voice trailed off at the menacing look in the two men's eyes.

"And they were taking pictures!" Rodrigo growled. He yanked the camera from Justin's hand. Opening the back with a violent jerk, he tore out the film that Justin had just replaced and trampled it into the ground.

"That settles it!" Dr. Latour snapped. "They're coming with us. I'll clear the stuff out of the lab. You get the kids in the jeep. And make sure you search them well first."

Without so much as another glance at the twins, he marched away. At the corner of the building, he turned. Pulling a small pistol from his pocket, he checked the safety catch and tossed it to Rodrigo. "Here! You may need this to keep the brats in line."

But Justin had seen his chance the instant Rodrigo turned his back to catch the gun. Dropping his sister's hand, he whispered urgently, "Run!"

They had only a few steps head start before angry shouts broke out behind them, but it was enough to bring Justin to the edge of the tall grass that lay between him and the DEA camp. A shot rang out, and he glanced backward as he dived under cover. To his dismay, he saw Jenny trip over Rodrigo's outstretched foot and sprawl on the ground. She seemed unhurt, and a moment later he heard her shout, "Let me go! You can't do this! Let me go!"

He hesitated only momentarily, wondering if he should go back and help, but it was enough to show him the tall figure of Dr. Latour rapidly closing the gap between them. In a fraction of a second, he made a decision. The only help available was at the DEA camp. He turned and ran.

His feet found the beaten-down path that led across the field to the DEA camp. Glancing over his shoulder, he saw that he was getting away from Dr. Latour as the tall geologist struggled through the thorny mass of bushes surrounding the lab. Elated, he settled into a running stride and saw his pursuer fall even farther behind. His heartbeat pounded loudly in his ears, but over it his mind repeated triumphantly, "I'm going to make it, I'm going to make it!"

He didn't know how many seconds had passed before he realized he was no longer moving away from Dr. Latour. The geologist was now through the brush and into the high grasses that covered most of the field. His powerful arms pushing aside the thick grass, he trotted at a diagonal toward the running boy.

Justin produced a desperate burst of speed, then his heart sank as he suddenly noticed what Dr. Latour was obviously well aware of: The path he had been following with such ease curved gradually to the right to avoid a patch of deeply rooted thorn bushes. It would lead him straight into Dr. Latour's waiting arms.

Justin swerved left into the briar patch. Thorns grabbed at his clothes as he dodged through tiny openings among the brambles. One long, sharp branch reached over his shoulder to slap him across the cheek, leaving a streak of red. Then the waving grain closed over his head. Grateful for the temporary shelter, he pushed deeper into the tangled grasses, using both hands as though he were wading in a chest-deep pool.

Sweat ran down his face, but he didn't dare stop to wipe it away. The notebook he had tucked inside his shirt rubbed against him, making it harder to run. *God, please don't let them hurt Jenny!* he pleaded silently. He stumbled over a root as his eyes suddenly blurred.

Now in the middle of the field, he could no longer see Dr. Latour. He was conscious only of the already glaring heat of the sun, an increasing fire in his chest, and a dusty-sweet scent that came from the drying grasses. He'd had this nightmare before, he suddenly realized—the one where you ran forever from some unseen enemy—only this time he couldn't seem to wake up.

He almost fell when his groping hands pushed ahead and met only air. Catching himself, he realized where he was. Here, a circular clearing had been clipped out of the grass, and in the center stood the grasshopper-like oil pump where he and Jenny had rested several days earlier. In the same instant, Justin also realized he had come far out of his way. The path he had followed and the metal roof of the DEA office now lay far to his right, even farther away than before.

Standing on tiptoe, Justin raised his head cautiously above the concealing brush. He froze as he caught sight of Dr. Latour standing directly between him and the safety of the DEA encampment. Head and shoulders above the surrounding grass, the tall geologist shielded his eyes with one hand as he scanned the field. Justin ducked down as Dr. Latour moved in his direction.

"Well, they won't get *these*, anyway!" Justin mumbled fiercely. Yanking the notebook from his belt, he slipped the roll of film into its plastic covering. Kneeling beside the oil pump, he thrust the bundle into a slight hollow behind one of the great iron legs. Certain that the package was invisible, he was up and across the other side of the clearing a few seconds later.

But he had lost much of his head start. Other oil pumps dotted the field here, and the grass grew only knee-high and not so thick. He lengthened his stride, but a shout from behind told him he had been seen. Glancing back, he saw that Dr. Latour too had broken through to the shorter grass. Running easily, he was now a scant thirty yards away.

It was then that Justin saw the other man. He stood at the edge of the field some distance away, where the grassland gave way to uncut jungle. Justin could only make out a vague form as sweat and a few tears blurred his vision. He turned his leaden legs in that direction as he croaked out a call for help. Whoever the man was, he might be able to assist Justin. It might even be someone from the DEA camp.

An answering shout rang out ahead of him. Wiping a sunburned arm across his eyes, he pushed on as the distant man waved an arm in his direction. Then fresh horror gripped Justin as an all-too-familiar black leather jacket came into focus.

The man stood casually, watching the boy come closer. Freezing, Justin looked back frantically. Now even closer, Dr. Latour called out a command in Spanish, and Justin's new enemy pounded across the field.

For one long moment, Justin didn't move. A red haze danced before his eyes as he tried to draw air into his burning chest. His legs seemed incapable of carrying him any farther. His lips moved silently as he repeated desperately, "Please help me, God! Please help me!"

The haze cleared. He was looking straight at the tangled mass of the uncleared jungle only yards away. If he could only lose himself in there, he thought, he might still be able to circle around and reach the safety of the DEA camp. With new strength, he turned and ran for the shelter of the trees.

He could hear hoarse breathing close behind as he reached the edge of the field. Pushing Alan's many warnings out of his mind, he crashed through the underbrush, intent only on putting distance between himself and the two men who followed him. He was brought up short by a low, menacing growl.

Justin froze. Here, near the open fields, the trees were not the massive giants of the deep jungle, but they grew thick and close together. Their leafy canopies filtered the brilliant sun, letting through a dim green light that gave an illusion of coolness.

Just ahead, two small trees grew so close together that their branches interlocked to form a shady thicket. Emerging from the thicket, its heavy paws making no sound as it stepped gracefully around a massive fallen log, was an animal Justin recognized at once.

Muscles rippled under the short, yellow fur. The black circles that dotted the golden pelt blended with the earth and branches to make the long, sleek body seem a part of the dancing shadows and dim sunbeams. A heavy, cat-like head turned, fixing Justin with an unblinking, golden-green stare. Justin suddenly remembered what Uncle Pete had told him about jaguars attacking defenseless human beings. Could the big animal sense his fear?

The jaguar paused, half in, half out of the thicket. The rumble of its low growl seemed to hold curiosity rather than anger. Without taking his eyes off the animal, Justin edged quietly backward. This new danger had temporarily driven his pursuers out of his mind. He stumbled over a dry branch, and a loud crack broke the silence. Justin's mouth went dry as the sleek muscles tensed under the smooth skin, and the low rumble rose to a roar.

A crash in the underbrush to his left diverted the animal's attention. The jaguar jerked its cat-like head around and sank back on its haunches as, some ten feet away, Dr. Latour lunged toward Justin.

"We've got him!" he called triumphantly. The steel-gray eyes narrowed as he took in Justin's frozen expression and realized that the boy hadn't even turned to look at him. Then he too caught sight of the jungle cat and froze in mid-step. The jaguar rose to four paws again and crouched down to face the geologist.

Another crackling in the brush, and the jaguar swung to Justin's right. Its muzzle pulled back in a snarl as the man in the black leather jacket broke into the open. The man took two long steps toward Justin, then his face twisted with terror as the golden-green eyes turned in his direction. Shaking, he stumbled back against a tree trunk.

This was the first time Justin had seen this man up close since they had boarded the boat two days earlier. The dark sunglasses were gone, and the thin face seemed yellower than ever. Drops of perspiration beaded his upper lip, but the man shivered in spite of the heat and the black leather jacket. His eyes, red and dilated, roved ceaselessly from side to side.

The fire in Justin's chest was easing, and he felt less fearful now that he stood face to face with this thin, shivering man who had frightened him so much. He didn't look strong enough to be a threat to anyone—much less a husky, athletic thirteen-year-old. It should be an easy matter to push past him and escape into the field while his two pursuers dealt with the jaguar, Justin thought. Justin took one small step to the right.

"Don't let him get away!" Justin realized with dismay that Dr. Latour had easily read his thoughts. The other man took a step toward Justin, an unpleasant grin stretching his thin lips. A wicked-looking knife appeared suddenly in one hand.

"I understand you've already met my old friend Choco," Dr. Latour spoke across the small clearing.

"So you *were* the one who had him follow us!" Justin said with a glare toward the geologist. "I knew it!"

Dr. Latour shrugged his shoulders. "He had strict orders to stay out of sight. But he's not too bright. They never are when they're this far gone on cocaine."

As Justin glanced at the tensed and waiting addict, Dr. Latour added, "He may not be bright but he's loyal—at least to anyone who will give him his daily cocaine ration. He'll cut you to pieces rather than let you by. In any case, there's no reason for you to run away. You and your sister will be released just as soon as Rodrigo and I are well away from here."

The hand he held out was long and slim, but Justin had already experienced the strength of that grip. "Now step over here quietly, and we'll get out of here. Unless you'd rather we left you to the jaguar!"

Justin stubbornly remained where he was. "You and Rodrigo are the cocaine dealers Major Turner is looking for, aren't you? I'll bet it was you who stole those files—and scared Jenny—just to get us to leave here!"

Dr. Latour looked amused. "Your uncle was getting too nosy. You wouldn't be in all this trouble if you'd left camp like we planned. You really messed up this operation!"

"And you burnt Eduardo's farm and house down!" Justin accused. "How could you do that? He wasn't hurting you!"

The look of amusement turned to annoyance. "What are you talking about?"

"You know, our friend's village! You burned it down because they wouldn't grow coca."

"Oh, yes, the village Choco told me about." Dr. Latour forced a friendly smile. "Look, kid, I just buy coca leaf from the local dealers. It's none of my business what they do to get it. I didn't hurt your friends. I'm just trying to make some money like a lot of other people."

"You'll never get away with it!" Justin answered defiantly. "Uncle Pete and Alan will be back any time. They'll stop you!"

He glanced sideways at the crouching jaguar, shaking inwardly in spite of his brave words. The big cat seemed confused, its short tail lashing the ground as it swung its head from side to side as though trying to decide who to attack first. It didn't seem possible that scarcely two minutes had elapsed since Justin's wild dash into the jungle.

Dr. Latour laughed without humor. "Don't be a fool! We'll be out of here long before your busybody uncle gets back. This was our last haul anyway. And you and your sister are our insurance that no one tries to stop us."

He again reached out his hand. "Now step over here, and we'll leave while Choco distracts that animal."

Without moving, Justin looked at the geologist with disgust. "You'd just leave your friend to the jaguar while we get away?"

Dr. Latour was annoyed. "He'll get away just fine. Besides, he's just a drug addict. He's no good to anyone, and he won't last much longer anyway!"

Justin remembered the sadness in Mike's eyes when he talked of his sister. "Maybe he has a family somewhere that still cares about him," he said slowly.

"Well, I can promise he won't give you the same consideration," the geologist said dryly. Justin looked over at the addict. Catching his glance, the man stretched his thin lips in a crazed smile. Justin took an involuntary step backward. The geologist's voice sharpened suddenly. "Choco!"

Then everything happened at once. As Justin turned to make a final dash for escape, his leg became tangled in a vine. He sprawled backward just as the crazed addict lunged toward him, knife held high.

An ear-shattering roar drowned out the addict's sudden terrified scream. The jaguar had finally made up his mind. Staring up helplessly, Justin saw the powerful muscles bunch up under the smooth yellow and black skin. Then he shut his eyes as the jaguar launched itself straight at him.

CHAPTER ELEVEN

Jungle
Chase

A s Justin braced himself for the impact of the jaguar's heavy body and sharp claws, the crack of a gunshot stung his ears. He didn't move for a long moment, then he let out his breath slowly and cautiously opened his eyes, scarcely able to believe that he was unhurt.

He felt his arms and legs. They were unmarked. Reassured, he freed himself from the vine that had tripped him and stood up. Glancing around, he saw the man Dr. Latour had called Choco slumped back against the moss-grown log, a faint pulse at his throat the only indication he was still alive. The jaguar lay unmoving across his chest.

There was no sight of the camp geologist, but Justin was vaguely aware of a crackling of dry twigs receding to his left. The loud thud of heavy boots jerked him around. He tensed for flight, then went limp with relief as Mike plunged into view, a 30-30 caliber hunting rifle over one shoulder.

Lowering the rifle to the ground, the young DEA agent leaned on it as he looked from Justin to the dead animal and back again. His chest still heaving from running, he demanded, "Are you okay, kid?"

When Justin nodded weakly, Mike leaned the rifle against a tree. Rolling the heavy body of the jaguar away from the unconscious cocaine addict, he examined the gunshot wound.

"A perfect head shot!" he announced as Justin knelt beside him. "There's a souvenir for you to take home, kid!"

He glanced aside at Justin, his expression still grim. "When I saw that cat going right for you ... well, I didn't think I'd get a shot off in time!"

"Yeah, I guess you saved my life," Justin responded, eyeing the outstretched claws of the big cat with respect. "Thanks!"

Mike turned his attention to the unconscious man. Now that the jaguar had been rolled away, Justin could see that the black leather jacket was ripped to shreds where a vicious claw had raked down one arm. Long, shallow cuts stretched from the man's shoulder to his wrist.

"This guy really saved you!" he answered as he slipped a hand under the unconscious man's head. "I'd have been too late if he hadn't jumped in the way."

Lightly holding one skeletal wrist with a thumb and forefinger, he added, "He's really lucky! He must have knocked himself out against that log—he's got a lump the size of a baseball on the back of the head. But his pulse is strong, and that arm is only scratched."

He began to ease off the leather jacket. His eyes opened wide as he noticed the knife still clenched in Choco's fist. Twisting it loose, he motioned to the jaguar. "Was this for the cat ... or for you?"

His question suddenly reminded Justin of the reason he was there. He jumped to his feet. "Mike, we've got to go!" he said urgently. "They're going to get away if we don't hurry!"

Mike glanced up at him sharply. "What are you talking about? *Who's* going to get away?"

Justin was almost dancing with impatience. "Dr. Latour and Rodrigo ... they're the cocaine dealers! They made this guy follow us ... and they took the cocaine ... *and Jenny!* They're getting away with her!"

Leaving the now moaning Choco, Mike rose slowly to his feet. "Just a minute. Are you telling me you actually saw the cocaine?"

Putting a hand on Justin's shoulder, Mike looked into his eyes. "Look, kid, you aren't pulling my leg, are you?"

"No! I saw it! We both did! In the lab!" His words tumbled over each other as he poured out all that had happened since Mike had dropped them off the day before.

Mike stared at Justin uncertainly. "Are you trying to tell me that, after all our searching, you just happened to stumble over the leaders of the cocaine ring?"

Shaking his head in disbelief, he pulled a walkie-talkie off his belt and barked out a few short orders in Spanish. Slapping Justin on the back, he said with admiration, "We send you home to keep you out of trouble, and instead you turn up a million dollar cache of cocaine. Things sure do happen when you're around!"

He caught a motion at his feet. Choco, now fully conscious, was reaching feebly for the knife that still lay beside him on the ground. Kicking it out of his reach, Mike then tucked it into his own belt. "He'll keep until my men get here. Come on!"

Justin was still winded, but he followed Mike back across the oil field at a steady trot. Beyond the open field, he could already see several uniformed men running in their direction. As they slowed down to push through the thicker brush, he asked curiously, "Mike, how did you know I needed help?"

"I didn't!" Mike used his rifle to beat a path. "I was on my way over to see you—thought you might want an update on the raid yesterday. I took my rifle to do a little hunting—

I've been out several times but never did see any big animals until today—and was cutting across the field back there when I heard that first roar. It's quite a coincidence that I happened to be passing through just when you ran into that jaguar."

"That was no 'coincidence,' " Justin answered soberly. "I prayed for help, and God sent you."

Mike looked at the boy strangely, but said nothing. They were now passing the oil pump where Justin had hidden the notebook and film. Justin paused to grab the package and stuff it inside his shirt, then broke into a run to catch up with the DEA agent.

As the buildings of the oil camp came into sight, Mike pulled Justin to a stop. "Take it easy!" he told the impatient boy. "I know you want to help your sister, but you can't just run out there. First, we'll take a quiet look around."

Pushing Justin behind him, he added firmly, "A *very* quiet look!"

There was no one in sight as they reached the cut lawn around the camp. Avoiding the lab, Mike silently led the way behind the closest bungalow. Crouching down at the corner, he whispered to Justin, "Stay here and keep out of trouble. I'll see if anyone's out there."

Justin opened his mouth to protest, but the roar of an engine drowned out his words. Before Mike could stop him, Justin was running around the corner. He reached the front of the bungalow just in time to see the camp jeep, with Dr. Latour at the wheel, careening through the open gate. As he reached the gravel driveway, one small figure in the front seat twisted around and waved frantically.

"Come back here!" Justin was running down the dusty track when Mike yanked him to a stop.

"Justin, I know how you feel." From the grim look on Mike's face, Justin knew he *did* understand. "But you'll do no good on foot. We'll have to use the helicopter. Come on! If they reach the cover of the jungle before we track them down, we'll never find them."

Following the footpath, Justin and Mike reached the DEA encampment just as two soldiers herded Choco into camp. He stumbled along, cradling his injured arm, but prodding machine guns at his back kept him moving. He had salvaged the torn leather jacket, which he held around his thin shoulders with his good arm. His black eyes glistened with hate as he caught sight of Justin and Mike.

Major Turner met Mike and Justin outside the DEA office. Justin shifted impatiently from one foot to another while Mike rapidly updated the major. Before Mike had finished, the two DEA agents were already trotting briskly back toward the oil camp lab, Justin panting along behind. The rumbling of his stomach reminded him that he had missed breakfast.

Major Turner glanced only briefly at the back window, where the metal bars still leaned against the wooden shutters, before heading around to the main door of the lab. To Justin's surprise, the lab door was unlocked. Major Turner gave him a sharp look as he pushed it open.

Following the major and Mike inside, Justin blinked as his eyes adjusted to the sudden dimness. He looked around. The burlap bags he had glimpsed through the back window were gone. The big room looked much as it had on his first evening in camp. Then he noticed the empty space in the far corner where the two-way radio had been.

Major Turner and Mike quickly searched the room. Straightening up at last from the tall file cabinet beside the door, the major said firmly, "This is just standard geological and lab equipment. I don't see a thing out of place."

"But there was!" Justin answered urgently. "There was a big ham radio in that corner. And there were a whole bunch of big sacks right there against the window. Jenny and I saw some little bags of white powder sitting on top—just like the stuff you showed us. They said they were going to 'haul' it all somewhere."

Major Turner turned to Mike. "Did you see actually see Dr. Latour in pursuit of Justin?"

"Well, no," Mike admitted. "I just saw the man my men hauled in. The kid says he's been following them. But I did see the camp jeep take off out of the gate mighty fast."

Major Turner's usually smiling eyes were stern. "Justin, I know you've had a real scare with that jaguar, but this is quite an accusation you're bringing against Dr. Latour. He is a very well-known man with an excellent reputation."

"I'm telling the truth—I promise!" Justin insisted anxiously. "He said he was taking that radio out of camp to call his men. He said you would be monitoring calls. Didn't you hear anything?"

Justin held his breath as Major Turner admitted, "Well, we did overhear one radio call from this general area about an hour ago. Just a couple of hacienda owners talking prices on beef."

As Justin swallowed with disappointment, Mike spoke up. "That could have been a code, Major."

Justin looked up eagerly as Mike added, "I mean, I've been thinking ... Dr. Latour has had access to a helicopter! And he's got big-shot buddies all over the country. It's the perfect setup!"

"Mike, I do know my job!" Major Turner answered dryly. He looked down at Justin. "I'm not saying you're lying, Justin. I've given some thought to Dr. Latour myself. He does have both the know-how and connections to run an operation like this—as well as an available helicopter.

"But he also has a perfect record and a lot of very powerful friends in the Bolivian government. I told you before that there are government officials are looking for any excuse to get us out of the country. If we call out a full-scale pursuit of Dr. Latour and he turns out to be clean, he'll have us thrown out of the country tomorrow. All our work would be down the drain."

He looked sternly down at Justin. "Justin, are you sure that was cocaine you saw and not a trick of your imagination?"

"Yes, I'm sure!" Justin cried. "Besides, he's got Jenny! And he's getting away with her! You believe me, Mike, don't you?"

Mike nodded. His drawl even broader than usual, he urged, "Major, I'm sure the kid's telling the truth! We've finally got a chance to hit those drug traffickers hard. But we're going to lose them if we don't hurry!"

Justin and Mike both held their breath for a long moment, then Major Turner nodded abruptly. "Okay, we'll go after them. But you'd better be right, Justin!"

Feeling as though he'd been running for a lifetime, Justin struggled to keep up with the two men as they headed back to the DEA encampment. The major was shouting out commands even before they reached the edge of the base, but by the time the helicopter was airborne, Dr. Latour had a full hour head start.

"They were heading north from camp," Mike informed Major Turner as the major settled himself into the copilot's seat. Behind him, semiautomatic weapons cradled across their knees, four men in battle fatigues sat straight-backed, their dark eyes watchful.

Looking down at Justin, who sat squeezed in between the two DEA agents, Mike added, "They'll leave the main road as soon as possible and try to lose us in the jungle. We'll have to pick them up before they leave the road."

Perched on the edge of the major's armrest, Justin kept

his eyes on the narrow, dusty ribbon that whipped past below them. His reddish-brown eyebrows knit together in unconscious imitation of Uncle Pete as he wondered what was happening to Jenny.

"It's all my fault!" he said aloud. "If I'd stayed away from that lab, none of this would have happened."

"And they'd be getting clean away," Mike answered dryly. "Don't worry, kid. We'll get your sister back."

When Justin's gloomy expression didn't change, he added encouragingly, "Come on, Justin! You're the one who's been praying that we'd catch the drug dealers. Don't you believe what you preach?"

"Yeah, you're right!" Justin's face suddenly brightened as he caught sight of a moving, dust-colored cloud far ahead. "Hey, that must be them!"

As the helicopter gained on the moving cloud, they soon made out the tiny shape of an open jeep in the center of the billowing dust.

"We've got them now!" Mike announced triumphantly. But, as though in answer, the jeep suddenly swerved under the cover of trees. The young DEA agent struck the control board with his fist. "Blast it!"

Major Turner spoke a few Spanish phrases into the microphone of the helicopter radio. "I relayed their last coordinates to the ground vehicles," he said to Justin. "But I'm afraid they will be long gone by the time our men get here."

"What are we going to do now?" Justin asked anxiously as they hovered over the spot where the jeep had disappeared.

"I suggest you do some more of your praying, kid," Mike answered grimly. "Finding them now will be like looking for a needle in a haystack!"

"There's no need to give up yet," Major Turner said calmly. "They have to stick to some kind of track. We just need to find some indication of which direction they are heading. Mike, begin aerial search procedure."

Justin kept his eyes glued to the unbroken green canopy below as Mike swung the helicopter in ever-widening circles. There wasn't even the faint line against the trees that he had noticed when they had traced the road from the cocaine lab to the coca farm. If there was a road somewhere below them, it was no more than an undeveloped track.

They had been scanning the jungle for a full hour when Justin sat up with a jerk. "What's that?" he demanded excitedly, pointing out an open slash in the tangled mass of green, to the left of the wide circle that the helicopter was now tracing.

The clearing ahead was just like the many others he had seen during Mike's aerial surveillance flights. Thousands of similar clearings dotted the vast jungle area of the Beni where local inhabitants had hacked out small farms. They would cultivate their few crops until the poorly nourished soil gave out, then move on to begin the process all over somewhere else. This clearing had obviously been abandoned for some time, but what excited Justin was the faint line of a dirt track that angled across the overgrown fields.

"Couldn't that be the road they're on?" he asked eagerly.

"You could be right, kid!" Mike answered, a hint of excitement in his voice. "I'm going in for a closer look."

Just as Mike maneuvered over the abandoned fields, an open jeep bumped slowly onto the deeply rutted, overgrown track. "Look! There they are!" Justin called out.

As Mike dropped lower, Justin could make out three startled faces staring upward. Then a cloud of dust hid them from view as the jeep put on a burst of speed.

"We've got to stop them before they get to the other side!" Justin cried desperately.

But Mike was already acting. The tall weeds that had

overtaken the field bent under a sudden violent wind, as Mike gently lowered the helicopter right into the path of the speeding vehicle. Justin saw Rodrigo slam against the windshield as the jeep slid to a stop.

Justin was already out of the helicopter and running. The four armed soldiers were close behind, surrounding the jeep before its occupants could move. Justin caught a glimpse of Dr. Latour, his arms held high and his narrow face tight with anger. Beside him, Rodrigo held a handkerchief to a cut on his forehead.

Jenny had instinctively grabbed the back of the seat to keep from following Rodrigo into the windshield. Now she climbed shakily over the seat and jumped to the ground. Hugging Justin tightly, she cried, "I knew you'd bring help!"

"I demand to know the meaning of this!" Dr. Latour protested as Major Turner and Mike strode over to the jeep. His steel-gray eyes fastened on Justin. "What has this boy been telling you?"

"We have been informed that you are carrying cocaine," Major Turner answered bluntly. But Justin had already scrambled to the back of the jeep.

"It's gone!" he cried in dismay.

"I don't know what you're talking about." Dr. Latour had recovered his usual self-confidence. He stepped out of the jeep. "We've been on a normal oil exploration trip. These kids have been pestering us for a ride. The boy ran off before we left, but we let the little girl come along with us."

Jenny gasped. "That's not true! You kidnapped us with a gun!"

Major Turner reached under the front seat of the jeep and pulled out a semiautomatic rifle and the pistol Justin had seen earlier. "Do you always carry these weapons?"

"Of course!" Dr. Latour answered scornfully. "There are wild animals in these parts."

"If you're innocent, why did you run away?" Mike interrupted angrily. "You saw us chasing you all over the jungle!"

Dr. Latour looked down his long nose at the angry young agent. "Certainly I saw you. I assumed you were on one of your usual training maneuvers. Am I supposed to stop every time I see a helicopter overhead?"

Justin was still frantically searching the back of the jeep. "I know it was here! Wasn't it, Jenny?"

Jenny tugged on the major's arm. "There *was* cocaine back there—big bags of it. They were afraid you'd catch them so they dumped them—*and* a big radio!"

Her face fell. "They hid them awfully well, though, back in the trees. And they kept changing tracks. I don't think we could ever find it."

Dr. Latour's eyes swept over the twins. "These children are telling a pack of lies!" he said coldly. "You don't have one shred of evidence against me. Do you think anyone would believe their word against mine? I'll have your jobs for this!"

Major Turner looked like a thundercloud. At his quick motion, the soldiers lowered their weapons and stepped back. His arms now at his sides, Dr. Latour smiled with satisfaction.

Dropping his gaze to the two children, Major Turner said sharply, "Kids, if this is your idea of a practical joke…"

His hands clenched into fists, Mike muttered bitterly to Justin, "So this is the kind of help you get for praying! These guys are going to get away with this, and there's nothing we can do to stop them!"

But Justin had suddenly remembered something. He broke into a grin of relief. "Oh, no they won't!"

Reaching inside his shirt, he pulled out a small, rectangular package wrapped in plastic and handed it to Major Turner. Turning to Dr. Latour, he said triumphantly, "You thought you'd destroyed the pictures we took of the cocaine in the lab, Dr. Latour—but you got the wrong roll of film! And I think Major Turner might be interested in this notebook we found under the back windowsill of the lab."

"Give me that, you little...!" Dr. Latour lunged toward Justin, but Mike stepped between them and strong hands grabbed Dr. Latour from behind.

Major Turner seemed to get more meaning out of the small notebook than Justin had. As the major leafed through the pages, nodding with satisfaction, Mike burst out, "You're a well-known scientist, Dr. Latour. You've even won medals for helping other people. How could you do this?"

"Why not?" Dr. Latour sneered. "Where did my skills and good will get me? Another second-rate job in a third-rate country, making money for other people. I figured it was *my* turn to get rich!"

Mike scowled. "And I guess it didn't matter how many innocent people got hurt in the process!"

Turning away in disgust, Mike motioned to the soldiers. As two UMOPAR agents led him by the children, Dr. Latour glared down with hate, his usual self-confidence erased by defeat.

CHAPTER TWELVE

Successful Operation

Uncle Pete and Alan walked into the DEA base in search of the twins just as the handcuffed prisoners were being unloaded from the helicopter. Mike had stayed behind with several UMOPAR soldiers to drive the camp jeep back.

Much to Justin's disappointment, Uncle Pete only nodded with satisfaction when he learned that Dr. Latour and his assistant were the heads of an international cocaine ring.

"So that's it!" was his only comment. After a brief conversation with Major Turner, he ordered Justin and Jenny back to the oil camp.

"I'll be over as soon as possible to let you know how things turn out," Major Turner promised the children. He gave Uncle Pete a strange look. "I have a few questions for Mr. Parker and Alan as well."

A few minutes later, the twins joined Uncle Pete and Alan on the dining verandah. Over a long overdue meal, they recounted all that had happened since Uncle Pete and Alan had lifted off that morning.

"After Justin got away and Dr. Latour went after him,"

Jenny explained, "Rodrigo made me help load the stuff from the lab into the jeep. He kept waving that gun around till I was sure it would go off. And here I thought he was such a nice guy!

"We had just finished when Dr. Latour came running up like he was being chased by hornets. Boy, was he angry! He said we had to get out of there fast, so Rodrigo shoved me into the front of the jeep. I was afraid Dr. Latour had hurt Justin, until I saw him running after us.

"I was praying that Justin would bring help. Then, just before we turned into the jungle, I heard a helicopter. But when we got under all those trees, I couldn't hear anything. I was getting pretty discouraged. The road was really bad, and the jeep was going so slow that I thought of jumping out and running into the jungle. But they made me sit between them, and Rodrigo held onto my arm the whole time.

"Then they stopped to hide the sacks and radio. They wouldn't let me see where they took the stuff, but it couldn't have been very far from the track. I thought maybe I could get away then, but they took turns watching me. A little while later, we drove out into that clearing and saw the heli-copter... I was never so glad to see anyone in my life!"

When Jenny finished her story, Uncle Pete shook his head in disbelief. "It seems I can't leave you two alone without you tumbling into some kind of trouble!"

He eyed them sternly. "I thought you promised to let me know before you started chasing bad guys again."

"We *were* going to tell you, Uncle Pete!" Justin protested. "But you took off so fast this morning, we didn't get a chance! Anyway, we didn't really know anything for sure—just what we overheard. We thought we'd better check it out before accusing anyone of anything."

"Next time, try jumping out of bed a little faster," Uncle Pete responded dryly. But there was a twinkle in his eye as he added, "Given the circumstances, I must admit I would have done the same thing."

He was interrupted as the camp jeep, with Mike at the wheel, roared into the gravel driveway and braked to a stop at the edge of the verandah. Mike hopped out, waving his arms excitedly. The bitterness that had lined his face was gone. As Major Turner stepped out on the passenger side, Mike announced jubilantly, "We found the cocaine! Every last bit of it!"

Running up the steps, Mike clapped Justin on the shoulder. "That stuff was so well hidden, we'd never have found it on our own. It was Justin's evidence that did it. When Rodrigo saw that we had the notebook and film, he just collapsed and told us all he knew. His directions led us right to the cocaine."

As Justin turned red with pleasure and embarrassment, Major Turner, who had followed Mike onto the verandah, pulled out a chair and sat down. Leaning forward, he fastened keen gray eyes on Uncle Pete. "Mr. Parker, you don't seem too surprised by the arrest of two of your key personnel. Why? Did you have some idea of what was going on?"

Uncle Pete shook his head. "No, I had no idea that Dr. Latour and Rodrigo were involved in drug trafficking. But I wasn't too surprised to find out. I knew that *something* strange was going on here."

"What do you mean by that?" Major Turner asked, raising an eyebrow.

Uncle Pete tilted his chair back against the wall as he responded, "I was sent here because we had received reports that the oil discovered here had turned out to be too low-grade and in too small quantities to be worth developing. The samples Dr. Latour sent in confirmed his reports. This was surprising, as earlier reports had indicated a large reserve of high-grade oil. But it wasn't the first time preliminary reports had proven overly optimistic."

As he paused, Alan explained, "Because of Dr. Latour's reports, we shut down the oil pumps and dismissed the workers. He's been out ever since prospecting for other possible oil sites—or so we thought!"

"You mean he wasn't looking for oil all those times that he took out the helicopter?" Jenny interrupted eagerly.

Uncle Pete held up a hand for silence. "I came down here with the intention of shutting down the whole camp. When I arrived, I reviewed Dr. Latour's reports as a matter of course. They were very well done, but I never take reports at face value. So I took a few samples of my own.

"I've been around oil long enough to know high-grade oil when I see it. I sent the samples to Santa Cruz for processing, then decided to check out the fieldwork Dr. Latour claimed to have done in the last few months. I informed Dr. Latour that I would be flying out to inspect his survey sites, and of course you know that the office was robbed the next day."

Uncle Pete smiled with satisfaction as he pulled a small notebook out of his breast pocket. "What Dr. Latour didn't know is that I have a habit of jotting down any information pertinent to my investigation. By that time, I was quite sure Dr. Latour had been falsifying his reports. The robbery of the office files was just too convenient, and he was too determined to get me out of camp. What I couldn't figure out was why!

"Anyway, Alan and I decided to check out his surveys of promising oil fields on our own, using the coordinates I had jotted down. We discovered that there *were* no so-called 'survey sites.' In fact, one set of coordinates put us smack in the middle of a river. We planned to confront him today, but of course, you got to him first."

"It never occurred to me to check up on Dr. Latour's lab reports and field explorations," Alan added gloomily. "After all, I'm no geologist, and Dr. Latour is one of the best in his field. He must have taken those faked samples from other oil sites around the area. What I can't figure out is what he was doing all those weeks that he had the helicopter out. He couldn't have just been flying out to the cocaine lab and back."

"I can answer that!" Mike announced from his perch on the verandah railing. "Rodrigo has agreed to testify against Dr. Latour, who was head of the drug ring, in return for a lighter sentence. He has admitted that they were using the helicopter to ferry the cocaine to a friend with a large estate near Santa Cruz. Those times that they didn't check in on the radio, they were in Santa Cruz, out of radio range—*not* checking out oil sites around here."

"It wasn't that drug lord you told us about, was it?" Justin asked eagerly. "The one with his own airplane and everything?"

Mike grinned broadly. "That's right. Between Rodrigo's confession and the information in that notebook you found, the UMOPAR has managed to put *him* under arrest as well."

"So their so-called 'exploration trips' were a cover-up for their drug dealings," Major Turner commented thoughtfully. "It gave them a reason for traveling in the jungle without arousing any suspicions. I imagine Dr. Latour faked those samples because he didn't want the area swarming with oil crews."

Mike spoke up again. "Rodrigo has admitted that they had Choco, one of their drug contacts, follow you. Choco put the tarantula in the outhouse, too. And they faked the robbery the other day. We found Alan's missing cuff links and radio tossed into the bushes behind the lab. They wanted to get the Parkers out of camp so they could get this last pay-load of cocaine out."

Justin couldn't contain his curiosity any longer. "What about the notebook I found? Did you discover what was in it?"

"We sure did!" Major Turner answered with satisfaction. "That notebook is the most important haul we've made yet. It was written in code, but we had no trouble breaking it, once we fed the contents into the computer. It contains names and information about people involved in the drug traffic, as well as dates and details of cocaine shipments. We'll turn that information over to the UMOPAR—at least that relating to Bolivian nationals."

"What's going to happen to Dr. Latour and Rodrigo now?" Jenny asked.

"They'll be sent to the U.S. for trial," Major Turner answered. "It seems that Rodrigo took out U.S. citizenship during his years in Miami. So he too will have to stand trial in U.S. courts. No clever lawyers are going to get them off this time."

Mike turned to Justin. "Your pictures turned out beautifully. With those and the other evidence we've collected, we have a clear case against the two of them."

"I've got just one more question," Justin said. "Whatever happened to that lab we found in the jungle?"

Mike laughed. "That's right! I was on my way to tell you about that when things got crazy this morning. UMOPAR men are removing all the equipment and chemicals for evidence. Then the place will be burned to the ground. That's one cocaine lab that will never be used again!"

Major Turner stood up. "Mike and I had better be on our way. We have a lot to do. We've finished our training operation here, and it has been a bigger success than we ever dreamed it would be. But there are still cocaine rings in other places to go after. We're moving out in two days."

Standing up, Mike looked down at Justin and Jenny. "Maybe you were right about good winning out in the end. At any rate, we owe you kids a lot!"

Jenny shook her head. "We didn't really do anything!"

"I suppose you're going to tell me it was God," Mike answered with a skeptical twist of the lips. But his tone was thoughtful this time, not mocking.

Major Turner shook hands all around. Stopping at Justin, he said briskly, "You have quite an eye for digging out information, Justin. Why don't you look me up in a few years? There will always be a place for you on my team!"

As he shook Uncle Pete's hand, Uncle Pete said, "We will be pulling out of here as well—tomorrow morning, in fact. My job is done, and it's time to be heading home. Right, kids?"

Jenny frowned. "I admit I'll be glad to say good-bye to the wildlife!"

Everyone chuckled, but Justin wondered how he would ever settle down to suburban Seattle after all the excitement of the last couple of weeks.

Major Turner turned to Alan. "I suppose you will be moving out as well, if the oil camp is shutting down."

Alan grinned. "Maybe not. We should be hearing back from Santa Cruz any time on those samples we sent in. If they prove as profitable as Mr. Parker thinks, this camp may be booming again."

▼▼▼

The next morning, Justin sorted through his belongings. Picking up his Bible, he leafed through the pages. It was a very nice Bible, with colorful maps and interesting charts and facts about Bible times in the back. Laying it aside, he shoved the rest of his clothes into the suitcase.

By breakfast time, all three Parkers were packed and ready for the two-hour drive into Trinidad. They would fly out to Santa Cruz later that morning, where Uncle Pete planned to buy tickets to Miami. Justin was loading suitcases into the back of the jeep when he saw Mike hurrying across the driveway. The tall DEA agent was carrying a heavy-duty plastic garbage sack, the opening knotted tightly.

"Just thought I'd see you off," he commented briefly, casually dropping the garbage sack on top of the other luggage.

Alan dropped the group off at the airport on the outskirts of Trinidad. It consisted of a galvanized-metal warehouse that had been converted into a terminal, with a single strip of asphalt runway. As they unloaded the luggage, Mike swung the black plastic sack over his shoulder.

"Your plane won't be in for another hour," Alan informed Uncle Pete. "I'm going to make a quick run to the post office. I'm hoping the results of those oil samples are in by now. I'll be back in time to see you off."

With Mike's help, Uncle Pete checked their luggage in at the long table that served as a checking counter. Alan still hadn't returned by the time the boarding of Flight 903 to Santa Cruz was announced. Most of the passengers had filed out the double doors that led to the waiting forty-passenger DC-3 prop plane, when Uncle Pete finally declared that they would have to leave.

The last call for boarding echoed from massive loudspeakers near the vaulted metal ceiling. Reluctantly, the twins turned to say good-bye to Mike, who still carried the plastic garbage sack over his shoulder.

"I wanted you to have this to remember us by," Justin told him somewhat hesitantly.

He handed Mike a newspaper-wrapped package. Mike unwrapped it and held up Justin's Bible. Quickly leafing through it, he looked curiously at Justin. "Well, kid, knowing you has certainly made me wonder if maybe there isn't a God out there controlling things. I promise I'll read it."

He lowered the garbage sack to the floor. "I've got something for you too, kids. Not that I think you'll ever forget the last few days." Untying the sack, he dumped out a rolled-up bundle of fur that glinted gold and black in the fluorescent lights that illuminated the dim warehouse.

"It's the jaguar skin!" Justin exclaimed.

Mike grinned. "I promised you could have it as a souvenir. It's been salted down, but you'll have to cure it when you get home."

Handing Justin an official-looking envelope, he explained briefly, "Under normal circumstances, you aren't allowed to hunt jaguar. This gives you permission to take the pelt through customs."

Jenny gently stroked the kitten-soft fur. "It's beautiful!"

A flight attendant in a spotless blue and gold uniform was now frantically waving at the group from the wide double doors that led to the runway. Calling a final good-bye, the twins followed Uncle Pete across the asphalt to where the plane waited, its jet engines roaring impatiently. Justin looked back to see Mike still watching them. He smiled and waved again, and held up the Bible Justin had given him.

They were climbing the steep staircase that led into the airplane when they heard running footsteps behind them. Alan hurried up the staircase, waving an envelope. "It came!" he panted. "The sample results. That field behind the oil camp is rich with high-grade oil! I'll have the work crews move in next week."

He handed Uncle Pete a long slip of yellow paper. "There was a telegram for you, too."

Uncle Pete opened the telegram. He read aloud: CONGRATULATIONS BENI JOB. STOP. PROBLEM IN HEAD

OFFICE, BOGOTA, COLOMBIA. STOP. REQUEST BRIEF EXTENSION OF TRIP TO INVESTIGATE. STOP.

He glanced up. "It's signed by my boss in Washington. We called him by radio-telephone last night. How about it, kids? Would you mind just one more stop before we head home?"

The twins' ear-to-ear grins were all the answer he needed.

The flight attendant, standing in the doorway of the plane, waved again. She now looked distinctly annoyed. The twins hurried up the stairs behind Uncle Pete and followed him to the back of the plane. The plane was already taxiing down the runway.

Justin checked his seat number and slid into a window seat. Belting herself in beside him, Jenny chattered, "I wonder what Bogota will be like. It's supposed to be as big as New York City. The jungle was interesting, but it'll be nice to see a real city again."

Justin was listening with only half an ear. As the plane soared into the air, he exclaimed, "Take a look over there!"

Jenny leaned over to peer out the small, round window. Like an endless, wave-tossed green sea, the vast tangle of the Beni jungle stretched below them as far as they could see. Far off to their left, a column of smoke billowed high above the trees—all that was left of the cocaine lab that had produced so much wealth and misery.

The two children watched as the column of smoke grew fainter and fainter. The plane banked right, and the last reminder of their jungle adventure faded out of sight.

BOOK THREE

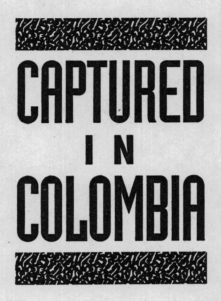

CAPTURED
IN
COLOMBIA

A Deadly Flood

t was the stillness and grayness that caught Justin's attention. He stopped struggling against the tightly knotted ropes cutting into his wrists long enough to draw a hot breath into burning lungs. The cliff-top above them was empty. The hoarse voices and the jingle of mules' harnesses had long since died away. The hail of pebbles and grit that had stung his face was over now, too.

No birds twittered in the wind-stunted tamaracks. And not a single cricket scraped the incessant song Justin had heard since his captors dragged him into the guerrilla camp. His sister and uncle, working at their own bonds, were silent. They had said all there was to say. Even the tangled branches of the bent cypress and junipers that lined the narrow creek and grew up the steep sides of the canyon hung silent and still. The only sound was a faint rushing in the distance that carried the promise of a faraway waterfall.

An onlooker might have thought it was snow that cast a cloak of ghostly white across the ground, the camp, and the three people tied fast to a branch that overhung the creek ... if it weren't for the strange breathlessness and the taste of sulfur in the air. Even the prints of men and animals, and the dead grass where tents had stood just a short time ago, were slowly being covered.

Justin blew uselessly at the cloud of grayish-white that drifted down from the evergreen needles to blind his eyes and choke his nostrils. Sweat trickled into his eyes and traced dark streaks down his face. He no longer felt the early morning chill of this high Andes gully.

Most of Justin's attention was focused on a broken piece of glass on the ground that offered hope of escape. But a corner of his mind eventually became aware that the quiet of the imagined distant waterfall had been transformed until it now resembled the grinding of an enormous cement mixer, churning rock and concrete in its massive metal belly. He looked up in surprise—then froze in fear.

Far up the mountain canyon, the eruption had fulfilled its promise. Released by the volcanic heat of the simmering Andes peak, thousands of tons of melted snow had plummeted downward, gobbling up dirt, boulders, trees, and any animals unfortunate enough to step in its path. Squeezed to unbelievable heights by the narrow canyon walls, the churning gray-brown mud flow—or *"lahar"*—now swept down the gully with enough force to bury a town.

The distant wall of mud and ice that met Justin's stunned gaze seemed to crawl at a turtle's pace, but Justin saw it scrape tangle-limbed trees and bushes from the canyon walls with the ease of a toddler snapping a toothpick in two. He saw a leaping wave sweep a boulder the size of a small house from the cliff-top. It bobbed a moment, then disappeared below the surface.

Justin now pulled frantically at the ropes that held his hands outstretched overhead. Warmth trickled down his arms as the harsh strands cut into his wrists. He glanced upstream once more. Already the solid, gray-brown mass had doubled in size as it moved closer. He could see uprooted trees tossing about on the crest of the wave.

He tugged again, desperately, at his bonds, but there was no more time. Towering above the three small figures on the canyon floor, the "lahar" was now swallowing, one by one, the long line of evergreens that shaded the creek only half-a-mile upstream.

Justin stopped struggling. No longer afraid, he stared in helpless horror as the wave of mud and ice swept down upon the camp.

CHAPTER ONE

A Steaming Peak

"**J**ustin, are we riding clear to Colombia like this?"

Nose pressed to the small round window of the DC-3, Justin Parker watched the distant carpet of the jungle canopy sweep under the wing just below him. A heavy wind tossed the treetops into a choppy, dusty-green sea.

"Justin!" his twin sister, Jenny, repeated above the roar of the propellers. Running his fingers impatiently through short, red curls, the husky thirteen-year-old reluctantly looked away from a mass of darkening clouds that drifted across the horizon.

Justin grinned as he noticed his sister's pale face and the folded paper bag in her hands, but he quickly changed his freckled face to a look of concern as he exclaimed, "Jenny, you look awful!"

"Thanks a lot!" Jenny answered, gold-brown eyes flashing indignantly. She sat up straight. One slim, tanned hand used the paper bag as a fan while the other pushed back damp, dark curls. But as another wind gust shook the plane, Jenny slumped back in the hard seat and moaned, "I'm going to be sick!"

"It's the altitude," Justin explained patiently. "These old planes don't have pressurized cabins."

Justin and Jenny Parker were opposites in more than just appearance. Tall for his age, Justin was usually calm and even-tempered, but those who knew him well understood a certain stubborn set of his jaw. Steady, blue-green eyes noticed everything that went on around him.

As tall as her brother, Jenny moved through life at a run. But a strong streak of common sense rounded out her outgoing personality.

A flight attendant, her dark hair tucked up inside a blue cap, smiled at the twins and held out a tray. Jenny shook her head violently, but Justin reached for a plastic cup half-filled with Coca-Cola®.

He had barely lifted the cup to his mouth when his seat seemed to drop away beneath him. Justin grabbed for his armrest as his stomach leapt into his throat. When the plane leveled off, he looked at the almost-empty cup in his hand, then at the ceiling as something wet dripped down his neck. Another drop of Coca-Cola® landed on his freckled nose.

"*Disculpa!* I am so sorry!" said the flight attendant, wiping a handful of paper towels across the light panel above Justin. Glancing around, Justin saw that he wasn't the only one to lose his drink.

"The plane fell!" Jenny gasped. "Uncle Pete, what happened!"

Across the aisle, a tall man with the build of a youthful Santa Claus wiped a paper towel across a full beard as red as Justin's hair. "We hit a down draft. The plane just dropped a few meters—nothing to worry about."

"Nothing to worry about!" Jenny wailed, clutching her paper bag again.

Shaking his head at the remainder of his drink, Justin

handed the cup to the flight attendant. "I guess I didn't want it, anyway!"

"Oh, no!" Jenny wailed. Justin swung around as she motioned toward the window. The bank of storm clouds he had seen earlier was now just ahead—a menacing, dark mountain looming over the small plane. Moments later the interior of the plane turned to night as the storm closed around them.

The twins clutched their armrests as the small plane shook violently. Rain streamed down the windows. Looking over Justin's shoulder, Jenny gasped, "Justin, look! The wings!"

Justin again pressed his nose to the window. Just outside the window, the propeller fought against the driving rain. Lightning lit up the misty interior of the cloud, and Justin swallowed hard as he watched the wings shiver under another blast of wind.

As another flash of lightning crashed just beyond the wing tip, a light went on across the aisle. Swaying gently with the movements of the plane, Uncle Pete calmly held a sheaf of papers up to the dim glow of the cabin light. The man seated next to him, his eyes squeezed shut, was muttering what Justin guessed to be Spanish prayers.

Jenny eyed her uncle indignantly. "Uncle Pete, how can you work in this? We could be killed!"

Uncle Pete raised reddish-brown eyebrows at the anxious expressions of his niece and nephew. "You aren't worried, are you, kids? These planes are used to this kind of weather. They don't have the power to get up above the clouds."

Laying the sheaf of papers carefully on his lap, he added thoughtfully, "Of course, this particular plane is a World War II leftover. I don't suppose it's been maintained too well…"

As the sound of an infuriated kitten exploded from Jenny, he added hastily, "There's nothing to worry about, kids!

Look! We're already breaking through the storm. We'll be in Santa Cruz in twenty minutes.

"And, no," he answered Jenny's original question as he turned back to his paperwork, "we won't be flying this crate clear to Colombia. We'll be flying to Bogota tomorrow in a Boeing 727." Glancing at Jenny's still-pale face, he added, "With a pressurized, air-conditioned cabin, and well above any kind of weather!"

A top consultant for a major oil company, Triton Oil, Pete Parker spent much of his time jetting around the world, taking care of any problems that arose at the company's scattered work bases. His special hobby was befriending missionaries in the many countries he visited on business, and he liked to blame his size on their hospitality and the many new dishes he had to sample.

Justin and Jenny Parker had always looked forward to the interesting gifts and stories Uncle Pete brought on visits to their Seattle, Washington, home. When Uncle Pete decided to combine some vacation time with business in the small South American country of Bolivia, he had invited his nephew and niece to come along.

Exploring Inca ruins less than two weeks ago, on a visit to the highland capital of La Paz, the twins had encountered a pair of artifact smugglers. Their escape from the cursed Cave of the Inca Re had shown their young guide, Pedro, a descendant of the ancient Incas, both the love and power of God.

Just this past week, at one of Triton Oil's jungle bases, they had helped bring about the destruction of a cocaine lab and the arrest of a ring of drug dealers. Then, just this morning, as they boarded the DC-3 to leave the Bolivian jungle behind, Uncle Pete had received a request to check out the company's main Latin American office in Bogota, the capital city of Colombia.

▼▼▼

It was noon the next day when the loudspeaker at the front of the Boeing 727 first-class cabin announced that they were now over Colombian airspace and would be landing in Bogota within the hour. Their appetites by now restored, Justin and Jenny bent over the lunch the airline had provided.

Justin lifted the tinfoil that covered his plate and sniffed gratefully at the perfect sirloin steak that nestled beside a baked potato. Adjusting the flow of cool air above her, Jenny sighed with contentment as she peeled the gold foil from a wedge of French cheese.

The flight attendant had just cleared away the trays when the warning light above their seats blinked on. The twins quickly fastened their seat belts for the landing. Jenny now sat beside the window, but Justin bent his neck to look over her shoulder. Still far below, a circle of snow-capped peaks enclosed a vast valley. As the plane curved downward, Justin could make out a patchwork of dark-green evergreens and yellow-green mountain meadows.

"Uncle Pete, isn't Colombia on the equator?" he asked with surprise. "I thought it would be all jungle."

"Yes, it is on the equator," Uncle Pete answered without lifting his eyes from his spread-out briefcase contents. "And there is plenty of jungle. But the Andes Mountains here form a valley at about eight thousand five hundred feet in elevation. It's cool enough to have vegetation much like the mountains back home."

"It's beautiful!" Jenny said with awe, as pine forests and meadows bright with wildflowers rolled away below.

"Why are the capital cities all so high?" Justin asked, remembering the vast mountain crater in which the Bolivian capital of La Paz sat.

"Most of the main cities in the Andes were built in high mountain valleys," Uncle Pete answered, absently shuffling through a stack of computer readouts, "to get away from the heat and danger of the jungles. The Andes here in Colombia get a lot more rain, so they have more vegetation—"

His explanation was interrupted by an excited squeal from Jenny. "Hey, look at that! That mountain is smoking!"

Justin leaned over to study the mountain peak his sister was pointing at. The slightly lop-sided peak was as snow-covered as its neighbors. But sure enough, from the snow fields rose clouds of steam—as though the mountain were indeed smoking.

"Is that a volcano?" he asked curiously.

"Most of the Andean mountains were once active volca-noes," Uncle Pete said, looking up again. "Hmm, that one does look like it's still alive! It must be the Nevada del Ruiz."

Laying down his papers, he added thoughtfully, "That peak made world news not too long ago."

Jenny could always sense a story. "Please tell us about it, Uncle Pete!"

Uncle Pete closed his briefcase and sat back. "Well, like most of its neighbors, the Nevada del Ruiz had been asleep—dormant—for many years. Then one day it woke up and blew its top. It wasn't much of a blow as volcanoes go—not much lava flow at all. But the heat of the volcano melted much of its snow and ice cap. Half the mountainside washed down, creating a mud flow more than forty feet deep that wiped out thousands of farms. One entire town of twenty-thousand people remains buried under the mud."

Justin eyed the steaming peak respectfully as the plane banked and left the mountain range behind. Still far below sprawled the city of Bogota. Box-like skyscrapers reached for a cloudless sky, and a maze of roads climbed over and under each other like some toy construction set.

"It's so big!" Jenny gasped.

"More than eight million people," Uncle Pete commented. "Bigger than New York City."

"Well, there should be some good shopping in a place that size!" Jenny concluded with satisfaction.

The landing wheels touched down just minutes later. Slinging his handbag over his shoulder, Justin pulled his jacket tight against a brisk wind that whistled through the cracks of the inflated plastic tube that connected the Boeing 727 to the airport terminal.

As they trudged up the long corridor from the unloading gate, the twins eyed with interest the shops that lined both sides. They had stopped to admire some hand-blown glass swans when a voice questioned softly, "*Cafe*, señores?"

The two children whirled around. A square booth stood in the center of the wide hallway. On its side the words "Asociacion de Cafeteros Colombianos" were written under a picture of a man dressed in a poncho and sombrero. On the counter, a tall percolator steamed next to a collection of fine china cups. A smiling, dark-haired girl leaned over the counter. Catching their puzzled expressions, she repeated in careful English, "Would you like to try a cup of Colombian coffee?"

Jenny grimaced. "No, thanks! I don't like coffee."

Uncle Pete reached over their heads to accept a cup of coffee. "Try it, kids! You've never tasted coffee like this."

Justin breathed in the rich smell of the percolator. "I guess I'll try a cup!"

"I will make you my specialty," the girl offered. " '*Cafe con leche*'—coffee with milk."

Justin raised reddish-brown eyebrows in surprise as he took a cautious sip of the milky-brown liquid. It was sweet and strong but had none of the bitter taste he usually associated with coffee.

Jenny doubtfully sipped her own cup, then her eyes lit up. "Mmmm! It tastes almost like hot chocolate!"

The hostess smiled with pleasure. "It is pure, mountain-grown Colombian coffee—the best in the world!"

Jenny giggled. "Just like the commercials back home!"

Uncle Pete set down his cup. "OK, kids, we need to check through customs and pick up our baggage."

In the center of the long corridor ahead stood what looked like a metal doorway just wide enough for one person. At table height beside it, a conveyor belt carried hand luggage through a similar—though much smaller—door. Soldiers in camouflage, machine guns cradled across muscled bare arms, made sure that every passenger passed through the doorway.

The passenger in front of the Parkers had just set his handbag on the conveyor belt when someone with an American accent called, "Mr. Parker?"

A young man of medium height with clipped, dark hair pushed unhindered past the armed guards and stepped around the metal door. His gray business suit didn't hide the tough, wide-shouldered build of an athlete. Or a soldier, as Justin thought.

His dark-brown eyes were unsmiling as he handed a card to Uncle Pete. "Pete Parker, Triton Oil, right? I'm Steve Cardoza, American embassy. I'm here to pick you up."

"Well, I appreciate this," Uncle Pete answered, studying the card with a puzzled expression. "But it isn't necessary. I'm expecting one of my own men to pick me up."

"I'm afraid that won't be possible," Steve Cardoza answered shortly. He glanced around at the still-waiting passengers. "I'll explain later. This place is too public. Right now, let's get your things cleared through customs."

An impatient official was now waiting for the Parkers to move ahead. As Uncle Pete stepped through the metal doorway, Mr. Cardoza swung Jenny's handbag to the conveyor belt. Jenny hung back. "Why do we have to go through that? What is it?"

"It's an X-ray machine," Mr. Cardoza explained shortly. "It makes sure you're not bringing in anything you aren't supposed to."

"Drugs, you mean," Justin commented, remembering the customs search in Bolivia.

The dark-haired embassy aide looked grim. "Not drugs. Bombs!"

The surprised children meekly stepped single-file through the doorway. As Justin walked through, an alarm sounded and a red light above the doorway began blinking. An unsmiling soldier moved to cut him off, then stepped back as Justin sheepishly pulled out the pocket flashlight that had triggered the alarm.

Justin noticed many other heavily armed soldiers as they pulled their suitcases from the baggage conveyor and went through another customs check. When they had repacked their suitcases, Steve Cardoza flagged a porter who wheeled the luggage to the parking zone. Here too, alert and unsmiling soldiers patrolled back and forth, machine guns held ready across their chests.

"Wow! Is there a war going on?" Justin whispered to Jenny as Mr. Cardoza unlocked the back of a dark-blue Toyota Vanette and tossed in the suitcases.

Giving the minivan a disappointed look, Jenny whispered back, "That's an embassy car? I figured it would be red, white, and blue with an American flag flying from the top!"

The embassy aide obviously had sharp ears. As he motioned them into the minivan, he remarked grimly, "In Colombia we'd rather not stand out! And yes, you could say there's a war going on!"

Mr. Cardoza expertly maneuvered the minivan through a

long line of buses and taxis. Justin was surprised to pass several more terminal buildings, the signs in front announcing the services of dozens of airlines. AVIANCA, the national Colombian airline, predominated. One of the terminals was air force, Justin guessed, eyeing the fighters and combat helicopters outside.

Mr. Cardoza turned onto a broad boulevard. Squat, gray factories stretched out alongside towering office buildings.

"Just like Seattle," Justin commented, feeling suddenly homesick for the busy streets of his home city. Then, as the embassy aide suddenly slammed on the brakes and cut across a lane of traffic, he added dryly, "Well, maybe not quite!"

Justin counted five lanes clearly marked on the road flowing toward the city, but he was startled to notice that seven or eight vehicles rushed abreast ahead of the van. With total disregard for traffic rules, the smaller cars zipped back and forth across the path of buses and trucks while the larger vehicles seemed ready to ram anything that got in their way.

Jenny squealed as Mr. Cardoza changed lanes again, almost under the wheels of a massive refrigerated truck. Glancing back, the embassy aide's bronzed face broke into a grin. "It's not much like driving back home, but it's really a lot of fun when you get used to it. Kind of like the Indy 500."

Justin suddenly sat up straight. Just ahead, a mass of blackened rubble and the shattered remnants of a tall building broke the solid line of factories. "Wow! What happened there?" he asked. "It looks like the place exploded!"

Over the back of the seat, Justin could see their driver's strong hands tighten on the steering wheel. "Yesterday's bomb," he answered grimly. "The reason for all the stepped-up security at the airport."

"You mentioned a war, Mr. Cardoza," Uncle Pete spoke up quietly. "I haven't had much access to the news in the last couple of weeks, but I understood that the guerrillas here in Colombia were in the middle of peace talks with the government. I wouldn't have brought the kids otherwise."

"Gorillas!" Jenny exclaimed, looking puzzled. "How can monkeys talk to a government?"

Uncle Pete's sudden cough sounded suspiciously like a laugh, but he explained patiently, "Not the kind of gorillas you find in a zoo. *Guerrillas* are bands of terrorists who want to overthrow the government so they can take over the country for themselves. Is that essentially right, Mr. Cardoza?"

"Just call me Steve," the dark-haired embassy aide said absently. Then he added, "You're exactly right, Mr. Parker. And yes, the guerrillas have consented to peace talks with the government. But as you can see, there are plenty of stray bands still tossing bombs."

"Well, I appreciate your concern for the safety of American citizens," Uncle Pete commented. "But I still don't understand. There must be dozens of Americans flying in and out of Bogota every day. Surely the embassy doesn't go to the trouble of picking them all up every time there has been a bombing!"

He added quietly, "There's obviously something else going on here. Maybe it's time you told me where you are taking us—and why my own men didn't come to pick me up."

"You'll see where we're going in just a minute," Steve answered politely. "My boss will be there to meet you. I'd rather let him explain."

They were now driving through a quiet residential neighborhood. Just then they turned into a narrow side street lined with four-story brick buildings. High-pitched, excited voices broke the quiet. Steve slammed on the brakes as a group of dark-haired children kicked a tattered soccer ball right under the wheels of the minivan.

A shrill bark caught Justin's attention. Pressing his nose

to the window, he realized that what looked like a dirty-white dust mop on the sidewalk was actually a small dog. The dog rolled over and whined with contentment as a girl—long, dark hair covering her face—leaned down to scratch its belly.

The children scattered as Steve leaned on the horn. Muttering under his breath, he pulled up in front of one of the townhouses. Only a pair of soldiers with tiny American flags on the shoulders of their uniforms gave any indication that the building was anything other than an ordinary house.

"This is the American embassy guest house," Steve informed them as they piled out of the minivan. Nodding at the soldiers' salute, he took out a bunch of keys. The twins watched in awe as he unlocked first one, then another of a series of five locks. "We had a hand grenade tossed in here a couple of months ago. So we're careful about who enters embassy property."

Picking up his suitcase as Steve swung open the heavy metal door, Justin glanced down the long street. The children were still playing, the small, dusty-white dog frisking around their feet. Suddenly, Justin heard a shrill whistle, and the dog broke free from the group of children. Just as Justin stepped into a wide, tiled hall, the dog dashed between his legs and into the hall.

"Get that dog!" Steve slammed the door shut and leapt for the dog. As he skidded across the polished tiles, the dog dashed back toward the door. Dropping his suitcase, Justin lunged for the dog.

Rolling over, Justin sat up, clutching the bundle of fur tight. Noticing a grimy handkerchief tied around a front fore-leg, he stroked the trembling animal gently. "Did you hurt yourself?"

He untied the dirty cloth, and a rolled-up piece of paper fell to the ground. Unrolling the paper, Justin stared with astonishment as he recognized the insignia that had been cut from some brochure and pasted to one end of the sheet of cheap notebook paper. It was the insignia of Triton Oil.

"Well, what is it?" Jenny asked impatiently, peering over his shoulder. Then Uncle Pete reached down and lifted the piece of paper from Justin's hands. The hall fell silent as he read aloud, "Release our men at once, or suffer grave consequences."

CHAPTER TWO

Trouble
for Triton Oil

"Give me the dog!" Justin blinked in astonishment as Steve snatched the dog away. Carrying him across the hall, he ran his hands over the animal, even checking its mouth. "No explosives!" he pronounced at last with relief.

Seeing the twins' look of surprise, he explained, "I've seen bombs delivered in some pretty strange ways."

As Steve put down the dog, Justin suddenly thought of something. Swinging open the heavy door, he peered down the street. It was now empty.

"Hey! Shut that door!" Something furry brushed against Justin's legs. Before he could move, the dusty-white dog had dashed around the corner of the building. Steve clapped Justin on the shoulder as he started to apologize. "Don't worry about it, kid. The dog probably wouldn't have helped us anyway."

He too studied the empty street. "That was good thinking, though. I'd say someone paid those kids to deliver this message."

As they stepped back inside, a tall, thin man with honey-colored skin and tight black curls came down a wide staircase at the end of the hall. "What's all the commotion, Steve?"

He held out his hand to Uncle Pete as Steve introduced him. "This is Martin Bascom, Secretary to the American ambassador here in Bogota—and my boss! Mr. Bascom, Pete Parker, consultant for Triton Oil."

Mr. Bascom led the group into a large living room off the hall while Steve explained what had happened. As they all sat down, Uncle Pete handed the diplomat the slip of paper they had found on the dog. "This seems to be directed at my company. What, exactly, is going on here?"

Instead of answering Uncle Pete's question, Mr. Bascom asked, "Mr. Parker, how much do you know about the situation here in Colombia?"

Uncle Pete rubbed his beard thoughtfully. "Well, I know that Colombia has one of the best records of democratic government in South America. They are not a wealthy country, but they've made a lot of social and economic advances over the last thirty years—including the development of their oil industry."

He added, "I also know that in the last few years guerrillas have brought the country to the brink of civil war and threatened to destroy every advance the government has made."

Mr. Bascom looked satisfied. "That's right! Guerrilla bands are the plague of Colombia. Each group is determined to overthrow the elected government and put themselves into power. The biggest is FARC—which is the Spanish abbreviation for the 'Armed Revolutionary Forces of Colombia.' Then there is the ELN—or the National Liberation Army. And of course, there are dozens of smaller groups. Many are being funded by the drug trade."

As the twins sat up with sudden interest, he added, "Drug traffickers use guerrillas as their private armies—paying them in weapons. Many of these guerrilla bands are better armed than the Colombian army. And they will do just about anything to achieve their goals—from tossing a bomb that kills dozens of innocent bystanders to blowing up the pipelines that carry oil across the country."

Uncle Pete's hazel eyes sharpened with interest. "Is that where Triton Oil comes in?"

Mr. Bascom nodded. "At the moment the major guerrilla groups have signed a cease-fire with the government. But there are still plenty of smaller groups running around loose. Two days ago, one of your American engineers was checking out your base in the eastern plains when he discovered two men setting an explosive to the pipeline near the oil camp. With the help of some local oil workers, he managed to capture them and turn them over to the Colombian police.

"It turns out that the two men were both members of some small guerrilla band. The Triton Oil office here has already received a phone call this morning, threatening to take action against the company if their men are not released."

An expression of worry clouded the man's face, but Mr. Bascom said firmly, "We really don't think there is much danger, but as a precaution, we have temporarily shut down your office and placed security guards at the homes of the two Americans who work there. Your head of operations here in Bogota asked if we would have you picked up at the airport."

"I certainly appreciate your cooperation," Uncle Pete said, glancing at his watch, "but I would like to meet with the head of operations as soon as possible. Can that be arranged?"

"Of course!" Mr. Bascom stood up. "I'll give him a call and take you over myself."

The twins jumped up eagerly, and Uncle Pete frowned.

"A business meeting is no place for you kids. You'd better stay here, where it's safe."

Catching their look of disappointment, Mr. Bascom raised a hand. "There's no need of that. Lieutenant Steve Cardoza is on loan from the U.S. Marine Corps to help with our security. He will be responsible for your safety while you are here. The children will be perfectly safe doing some sight-seeing with him."

Justin eyed with satisfaction the muscles that pressed against the seams of Steve's civilian clothes. "I *knew* you were a soldier!"

With a grin, the broad-shouldered Marine saluted smartly, then motioned toward the door. "Let's go, kids!"

▼▼▼

The quiet streets surrounding the embassy guest house could have been any middle-class neighborhood in North America. As Steve drove back onto a major thoroughfare, he asked, "Well, kids, what would you like to see first?"

"A pamphlet we got on the plane said something about the Gold Museum," Justin said.

"*I* want to go shopping," argued Jenny. "We saw the open-air market in Bolivia. It was pretty exciting, with all the Indian ladies sitting on the ground, selling their fruits and vegetables."

Steve looked from one to the other. "Tell you what! I'll show you how we do our shopping here in Bogota. Then we'll hit that museum you mentioned."

Moments later, the minivan turned into a large parking lot. Across the front of a two-story glass and brick building several blocks long, a massive sign announced, "UNICENTRO."

"Hey, this is a just a mall!" Jenny exclaimed with disappointment as Steve herded them toward the main entrance.

Inside, Justin read the signs that lined the vast, tiled corridor. "Wendy's, Burger King, Sears—just like back home!"

Steve grinned. "I'm afraid shopping in Bogota isn't much different than in the U.S."

Jenny was inspecting a dress displayed in the window of an exclusive boutique. "Except for the prices! Look at this ... $2,249! Who can afford to shop here?"

Leaving the mall with their savings intact, they drove toward the center of the city. Modern skyscrapers elbowed white colonial buildings with fancy iron balconies and red-tile roofs. Studying a space-age office building whose tilted roof jutted toward the sky like a fighter jet taking off, Justin commented, "I sure didn't expect everything to be so modern and beautiful."

"Yeah, I don't understand why anyone would want to overthrow the government when they have such a nice country," Jenny agreed. "Those guerrillas must be awful people!"

"You kids have only seen the best part of the city!" Steve commented, turning the minivan onto a narrow avenue lined with old, gray factory buildings. Soon the factories gave way to grime-stained apartment buildings. Doors swung on broken hinges, and scraps of lumber and cardboard darkened smashed windows. Startled, the two children sat up straight as even these buildings were left behind.

The houses just ahead—if such they could be called— clung to the edges of a vast garbage dump. Scavenged boards, tin, and even old tires were nailed together to form crude shelters. Lines of threadbare laundry dangled between low roofs pieced together from scraps of metal.

"Hey, look at that!" exclaimed Jenny.

Under the flat bed of an abandoned trailer was a cardboard box that had once protected a freezer. An entrance had been cut in the front, and a sheet of torn plastic stretched over the top to keep out the rain. But what caught the twins' attention was the small boy whose tangle-haired, dark head was pillowed on a gunny sack in the makeshift doorway. A ragged man's sweater was his only protection against the chill mountain winds.

"Does he *live* there?" Jenny asked in horror. "Where are his parents?"

The grim look was back on Steve's face. "He probably has no parents. There are hundreds of thousands of kids like him on the streets of Colombia. They are called the 'gamines'—street urchins. They stay alive by running errands, stealing, even eating garbage.

"You asked about the guerrillas," he added as they left the dump behind. "Many of the guerrillas come from poor families such as these. They've seen their families suffer while most of the country's wealth is concentrated in the hands of just a few."

"No wonder they get mad!" Justin said soberly, looking back at the flimsy cardboard home. "But if the government doesn't want the guerrillas to fight, why don't they do something to help?"

"The government *is* trying to do something," Steve answered seriously as he turned back onto a major boulevard. "But Colombia isn't a rich country, and improvement is slow. The guerrillas aren't willing to wait. They don't consider themselves criminals. They think of themselves as freedom fighters—fighting to free the poor from what they consider the 'oppression of the rich ruling class.'

"Unfortunately, while some guerrillas are real idealists who want to make the country better for the ordinary people, many just want to grab power and money for themselves. Instead of trying to change their country peacefully, they throw bombs and murder a lot of innocent people."

Glancing at their gloomy faces, he suddenly smiled. "Hey, kids, cheer up! On the whole, Colombia is a beautiful country, and we want you to enjoy your stay here."

Moments later Steve pulled up beside a wide plaza

where thick-trunked trees spread leafy branches over stone benches, and marble fountains splashed rainbows in the late afternoon sun. "Come on, kids! You're about to see the most fabulous gold collection in the world."

Steve led the twins through the center of the plaza to a new-looking brick and glass skyscraper. Justin stopped counting stories after the first two dozen and studied the sign above wide glass doors. "Hey, this is a bank! I thought we were going to the Gold Museum!"

Steve grinned. "Yes, it *is*—and we *are!* The Gold Museum is housed in the bank because it contains most of Colombia's national gold reserve."

"You mean it's just a bunch of gold bars?" Jenny asked in disappointment. "Like the American national gold reserve at Fort Knox?"

"You'll have to wait and see," Steve answered. He motioned them into the bank lobby and bought their tickets. When a small group of other tourists had gathered, a guide motioned them toward a broad staircase. An armed Colombian soldier stepped in front of the group, while another brought up the rear.

The guide paused outside a heavy metal door like that of a bank vault. An armed guard stood in front of the door. As the door swung open, the guide motioned for the group to step forward, one at a time.

"What is he doing?" Jenny asked Steve.

"That door works like the X-ray machine you stepped through at the airport," Steve explained. "They're checking for burglary tools, as well as weapons."

The twins were surprised when Steve reached inside his jacket and pulled out a small pistol. With a rapid stream of Spanish, he handed the pistol and some identification papers to the guard.

"Hey, you sure speak good Spanish!" Justin compliment-

ed as the guard handed back Steve's identification and pock-
eted the pistol.

Steve grinned. "You pick up plenty of Spanish growing
up in Southern California. That's what got me transferred to
Colombia."

Justin and Jenny followed him into a large, empty room
with no windows. Justin noticed a tiny video camera watching them from one corner. Across the room was another vault
door. When the entire group was inside, the first door closed
behind them.

"They sure aren't taking any chances with their gold, are
they?" Jenny giggled a bit nervously as the light dimmed
around them.

But her giggles ended in amazed silence as the second
door slid open and the crowd of people moved into the light-
ed vault beyond. A soft yellow glittered on all sides, but not
from stacks of heavy gold bars. Behind thick glass display
windows, gold bracelets, rings, and necklaces were piled in
careless abandon. Odd geometric designs etched cups and
plates of solid gold, hammered out centuries before for an
Indian noble's table.

"All that remains of Colombia's pre-Spanish riches,"
Steve said, looking amused at their open-mouthed awe. "It's
the largest collection of gold artifacts in the world."

Jenny paused to examine a headdress that gleamed green
against the delicate gold-work. Steve looked over her shoulder. "Those stones are emeralds," he told her. "The best coffee
in the world isn't all Colombia produces. They also export
most of the world's emeralds."

He leaned against a pillar. "You kids go on and look
around. I've seen this often enough."

The twins moved slowly along the rows of display windows. They stopped suddenly as a dark-skinned warrior

glared fiercely at them from behind a mask of solid gold. His out-thrust spear guarded a staircase that led to a lower level.

"He isn't real!" Justin said a little shakily as he realized the warrior was carved of some dark wood. From a lifeless chin jutted a pointed, golden beard. The gold helmet on the wooden head was topped with an ornate headdress of red, black, and gold feathers, and emeralds crossed a hammered breastplate. Golden earrings, curled like wood shavings, dangled from deaf ears.

"I *knew* he wasn't real!" Jenny answered scornfully as she started down the staircase. Justin looked unconvinced, but followed her to the lower level. Here tourists crowded around more showcases, exclaiming expressions of awe and greed in many languages.

Glancing up from an elegantly jeweled crown, Justin suddenly noticed that one face nearby didn't reflect awe or delight at the beauty that filled the vault. Her slim shoulders tight with concentration, a girl about the age of Justin and Jenny pressed against a glass window. The arrow-straight hair that cascaded below her waist was so black that it gleamed blue in the soft light of the display.

The girl moved slightly, and Justin caught a glimpse of delicate, pale features tight with anger. A thin hand hanging at her side clenched and unclenched as she stared at the heaped-up gold. *She must have come in at the last minute or I would have noticed her,* Justin thought. *She isn't like anyone I've ever seen!*

Reading his thoughts with the closeness of long practice, Jenny whispered, "She looks like a princess!"

Eyeing the neat but threadbare clothes, she added, "A princess in disguise, that is!"

"I wonder who she is?" Justin whispered back.

As though she had heard, the girl turned. Ice-blue eyes,

fringed with impossibly long, black eyelashes, gave them a disdainful look. Then she turned her back to them.

"Come on, Jenny!" Justin said, flushing with embarrassment as he motioned Jenny toward a large, square glass case that stood alone in the center of the room.

"Wow! Look at that!" They forgot the strange girl as they bent over the lone object displayed in the glass case. Somehow afloat on a tiny artificial lake was a raft of gold logs only six inches long. At one end knelt a paddler, steering the raft with a long golden pole. In the center, his jeweled eyes blindly watching the horizon, stood an Indian prince, his tiny gold adornments hinting his relationship to the warrior upstairs. The haughty lift of the royal chin brought back to Justin's mind the proud face of the girl they had just seen.

"That piece alone could keep every homeless child in Bogota off the streets for a month!" a voice said coldly in the precise, accentless English of a well-educated foreigner. The twins whirled around. Her silky-fine hair falling in a shimmering curtain across her face, the girl they had noticed earlier leaned over the glass case.

"This gold should belong to the people of this country— all of it!" Her eyes were now hot blue sparks as she threw out a slim arm to include the rest of the room. "It should be sold—used to help the poor of this country. Instead, it's kept locked up for a bunch of fat, wealthy tourists to stare at!"

Startled at the bitterness in the girl's voice, Justin answered reasonably, "I thought it *did* belong to the people of Colombia. I mean, they said it was the *national* gold reserve. Doesn't that mean these things belong to everyone?"

"And they are so beautiful!" Jenny broke in, brushing her fingertips over the glass case as though to touch what lay within. She added, "And here, everyone can enjoy them— including the people of Colombia."

"Beauty can't fill a starving stomach!" the other girl answered coldly.

The murmur of tourists filing by filled an awkward silence. Then Jenny turned away. "Come on, Justin! I'm ready to go!"

"Wait! Please! Don't go!" Her voice half-angry, half-pleading, the girl took a step toward them. "I'm..." The apology seemed to catch in her throat, then she said, "My name is Estrella."

She pronounced the name Es-stray-yu. As Justin mentally sounded out the strange syllables, she added, "It means 'Star' in your language."

Seeing Jenny's unfriendly expression, Justin held out his hand. "Why don't we start over. My name is Justin Parker, and this is my sister, Jenny. We're visiting your country with my Uncle Pete. He's an oil consultant. You may have seen the signs for Triton Oil. That's his company."

The girl's long lashes dropped to conceal a sudden gleam of satisfaction as Justin hurried on, "You sure speak good English! Where did you learn it?"

For a moment Justin thought the girl would refuse to answer, then she admitted, "My father was American."

Jenny's expression thawed noticeably. "Really! Then you're American like us! That's great!"

The blue eyes suddenly iced over again. "Do not call me American! *This* is my country!"

Justin and Jenny were both bewildered by Estrella's sudden changes of mood. Jenny answered rather coolly, "I just thought ... I mean, your father ... does he live here in Bogota?"

Estrella was silent a moment, then she said reluctantly, "I have no father anymore."

"Oh, I'm sorry!" Jenny answered sympathetically. "Does your mother live here, then? Is *she* American?"

Justin saw the cold curtain drop again over Estrella's face. Elbowing Jenny, he whispered, "Don't ask so many questions! You're going to make her mad again!"

Jenny's eyes sparked hot gold, and she elbowed him back. "Look who's talking! You're the one who wanted to know who she is!"

Catching Estrella's wide-eyed expression, they both smiled sheepishly, and Jenny asked, "Don't you ever argue with your brothers?"

Estrella looked sadly thoughtful. "I don't have any brothers—or sisters. And my mother died three years ago."

"Oh, that's awful! You aren't…" Jenny faltered. "You aren't one of those poor kids living on the street, are you?"

"You don't need to feel sorry for me!" Estrella answered proudly, "I have a new family now—a family of others like myself who have no home of their own."

Again she waved a slender arm around the room. "One day they will take all this gold and give it to those who really need it."

Justin raised unbelieving eyebrows. "Estrella, it would take an army to break in here and take out this gold—if anyone would be dumb enough to try!" He smiled encouragingly. "You're joking, aren't you?"

Her slim back straight as an arrow, Estrella answered firmly, "I am *not* joking! My family are special people. They are freedom fighters, and one day they will free our people from those who take all the wealth and keep it for themselves!"

"Freedom fighters!" Justin repeated in a whisper. He and Jenny stared at each other in horrified understanding. Then Justin demanded doubtfully, "You mean your 'family' are guerrillas? Like the terrorists who threw that bomb and killed all those people yesterday? You can't mean that you're really a member of a guerrilla band!"

CHAPTER THREE

Haunted!

The three children stared at each other for a long moment, then Jenny broke the silence. "You really live with terrorists?" she asked doubtfully. "How can *they* be your family?"

"Don't you dare call my family 'terrorists'!" Estrella's eyes were now the frozen blue of a winter sea. "Yes, they are guerrillas. They work for the freedom of my people. But they are not like those mad men who throw bombs. They would not hurt anyone!"

Jenny looked scornful. "If they are so kind and peaceful, how do they plan on getting all the gold out of here and giving it to the people?"

"I ... I don't know!" Estrella looked suddenly troubled, but she answered defiantly, "I just know they are good people. They found me on the street with no place to go, and they gave me a home—and food to eat. They even paid for lessons so that I would not forget the language of my father. I am very special for them because no other children are allowed."

She lowered her voice almost to a whisper. "Sometimes,

though, I think it would be nice to have a friend my age, or ...
or perhaps a brother!"

Justin saw sorrow and longing behind the defiance in
Estrella's eyes. He put out his hand. "Well, we'll be going
back to the United States soon, but we'd sure like to be your
friends while we're here!"

Estrella froze, scorn erasing the momentary softness in
the blue eyes. She quickly put her hands behind her back.
"The United States!" she repeated, her voice dripping with
disdain. "What do Americans know about friendship? You
are all alike. You pretend to care for people. Then you go
away and leave them! Your friendship means nothing!"

Justin was too hurt and puzzled at her reaction to answer,
but Jenny demanded angrily, "What do you mean by that?
What do you know about Americans?"

"I knew my father!" Catching an astonished stare from a
passing tourist, Estrella lowered her voice. "He was an
American—like you! He said he loved me, that he would
always love me. Then one day he just left. I was only seven
years old."

Her voice shook with anger and bitterness. "He never
even bothered to write or send money. When my mother
died, I would have starved if my 'family' had not found me."

She drew herself up proudly. "No, I don't need any
American friends. My 'family' are all the friends I need!"

Jenny bristled with anger. "If you hate Americans so
much, why did you stop to talk to us?"

Without waiting for an answer, she turned away. "Come
on, Justin! Let's go!"

Justin started to follow, then stopped and said awkwardly, "Well, it was good to meet—" He was interrupted by a
shrill whistle, and Steve called from the foot of the stairs,
"Hey, Justin, are you planning on spending the night?"

Justin suddenly realized the lights had dimmed and that

they were the only ones left in the vault. Even Estrella had disappeared. He hurried up the stairs. Ahead of him, Steve's clear baritone echoed down the stairwell as he answered Jenny, "So you really liked it, huh? Wait till you see Zipaquirà tomorrow. That's even better!"

At the top of the stairs, Justin glanced back. Estrella had stepped out from behind the display case where she had ducked. Perhaps it was only a trick of the light that made the young guerrilla girl look suddenly uncertain and lost as she stared up at them. Catching his glance, she ducked back into the darkness.

"Who's your little friend?" Steve asked as the guard returned his gun and he slid it into a shoulder holster. The rest of their group and even the guide had already left.

Jenny sniffed. "She isn't our friend! She made that pretty clear!"

The short dusk of the tropics had already fallen by the time they left the museum. Like so many fireflies, thousands of office windows twinkled against the black-velvet backdrop of a starless night. In the plaza, underwater floodlights turned the fountains into rainbow-colored cascades of light.

Justin checked his watch. "Only six o'clock and dark already!"

"We're on the equator here," Steve explained. "Days and nights in Colombia are just about exactly twelve hours long. It's light from six A.M. to six P.M. year around."

As they followed Steve across the plaza, the twins told Steve all about the strange girl they had met. As they climbed into the minivan, Jenny concluded, "She sure wasn't very nice, was she, Justin!"

Justin nodded agreement, but that last glimpse of the young guerrilla girl's troubled face popped into his mind. "Maybe not, but I still feel sorry for her. She ... I don't think she's very happy."

Jenny sniffed. "Well, we'll never see her again, so I guess it doesn't matter!"

Turning the minivan back onto a major thoroughfare, Steve suddenly asked, "You say she was the one who came over ... wanted to talk? Are you sure you didn't speak to her first?"

When Justin and Jenny emphatically shook their heads, the young Marine fell silent and seemed lost in thought as they drove back through the rush-hour traffic. As Steve swung the minivan off a traffic-congested overpass, Justin remembered his manners. "Thanks a lot for taking us, Mr. Cardoza."

"Yeah, that was great!" Jenny exclaimed.

"That's my job!" Steve answered. He looked at Justin. "I was telling your sister that I thought we'd head out to the salt mines at Zipaquirà tomorrow. There is less chance of anyone following us if we keep on the move."

There was a twinkle in the dark-brown eyes as he added, "That's a good excuse for sightseeing."

The narrow street was dark and quiet when they arrived back at the embassy guest house, but two American soldiers still stood at attention in the doorway. The four-story building echoed with emptiness as Steve swung open the heavy metal door and ushered the twins into the wide hall. There was no sign of Uncle Pete or Mr. Bascom.

Leading the two children into a gleaming-white kitchen at the rear of the building, Steve lifted the lid of a large pot that simmered on the back of the huge stove. Handing Justin a sack of crusty rolls and a pat of butter, he carried the pot across to a dining room that could seat many dozens of people.

"Doesn't anyone else live here?" Justin asked curiously as he looked around the long room with its empty tables.

"Yeah, if this is the American embassy, where are all the people?" Jenny added.

Steve grinned as he dished up three bowls of what he informed them was "sancocho"—a Colombian stew thick with unfamiliar ingredients. "The American embassy is in the center of town—with hundreds of people going in and out all day. This is just a guest house where we house VIPs—Very Important People, that is."

"And *we* are Very Important People?" Jenny asked impishly.

"Let's just say we want to keep you out of trouble," he answered. "At the moment, you Parkers are the only ones here. There are two security guards who double as cooks—if you can call what they do 'cooking'! They are probably upstairs watching TV. And, of course, there are the soldiers on duty outside—though they don't sleep here."

Uncle Pete still had not returned by the time Steve showed the twins up two flights of stairs to where their luggage awaited them in adjoining bedrooms. But late that night, Justin awoke to hear Uncle Pete's familiar whistle from the bedroom next door.

▼▼▼

The next morning, Justin and Jenny joined Uncle Pete and Steve for breakfast in one corner of the long dining room. One of the security guards was working in the kitchen, and, contrary to Steve's opinion, the cheese omelets were delicious. The twins had already discovered that the "TV" that so absorbed the security guards was actually a series of television screens that kept a distant eye on every inch of the property.

"How did your meetings go yesterday, Uncle Pete?" Justin asked, wiping his mouth on a napkin.

Uncle Pete set down his coffee cup with a sigh. "Allen Johnson, a young engineer on his first assignment here, was responsible for catching the two men who tried to blow a hole in the pipeline. He deserves a medal for it, but now the guerrilla band these two men belong to are threatening revenge on all our American personnel if we don't release them."

"Are you going to let them go, then?" Jenny asked, her eyes open wide.

"No, we're not. For one thing, the Colombian police have them in custody—not us. Besides, if we gave in to a threat like that, our workers would never be safe again. The terrorists would come back with another threat every time they wanted something."

"What are you going to do, then?" asked Justin.

Uncle Pete leaned back in his chair. "We'll let the Colombian police force take care of the two guerrillas. What happens to them is no business of ours. But as for Triton Oil, the engineers can't keep their minds on their work if they're worrying about their families. We've decided to pull all our married American executives out of Colombia and replace them with single workers. We'll have to step up security around our bases and office as well."

Catching Jenny's puzzled look, Justin whispered, "That means adding more guards and locks!"

Uncle Pete turned a stern eye on his nephew and niece. "As for you two ... I want to get you home as soon as possible. I should be done here in a couple of days."

He stood up. "I'll be meeting with the chief of police and our office staff this morning. Steve tells me he has plans for you, so enjoy yourselves and stay out of trouble."

Steve stood up too. "Yeah, I told the kids I'd take them out to Zipaquirà. It's one of the biggest deposits of rock salt in the world—and a lot more!"

"A lot more what?" Justin and Jenny asked at the same time, but Steve just grinned and refused to explain.

A heavy mist blanketed the street outside, and the twins pulled their jackets tight as they waved good-bye to the soldiers on guard duty. An hour later, they had left the last skyscraper behind. Cultivated fields and green pastures wet with fog made a patchwork against low, rolling hills. Fat holstein and jersey cows munched contentedly behind neat barbwire fences. Brick-red farmhouses and barns reminded Justin of last year's vacation in New England.

Bordering the wide, paved highway were mile after mile of long sheds with peaked roofs of translucent green glass. Jenny cried out in delight as she caught sight of a flower stand in front of one shed. The stand was heaped high with carnations, roses, and strange tropical blooms.

"Those are greenhouses, aren't they!" she said with astonishment. "But why so many? You could grow enough flowers for the whole world in those!"

"Not quite," Steve answered. "But a good portion of the flowers you buy back home in the U.S. are grown in those greenhouses."

Justin had just noticed something more to his liking. A stand at the gate of a prosperous dairy farm announced in large letters, "Fresas con Crema." At the bottom of the sign, someone had scribbled for the benefit of tourists: "Strawberries and Cream."

Steve stopped the minivan. "You can't leave Bogota without trying the local strawberries and cream. They're delicious." A few minutes later, Justin and Jenny were nodding agreement over a bowl of oversized strawberries and cream too thick to pour.

The sun had burnt away the mist by the time they were back on the road, and they could now see the mountain range that ringed the high Andes valley. The cone-shaped snowcaps reminded Justin of the steaming peak they had seen from the plane. He told Steve what Uncle Pete had said about the strange peak.

"Yeah, that was quite a disaster! I wasn't in Colombia yet, but there was plenty about it in the news." Steve looked suddenly interested. "You saw steam, eh? Nevada del Ruiz must be simmering again. I hope she keeps a tighter lid on things this time!"

Jenny looked nervously at the ring of snowy mountains. "It ... it isn't going to erupt again, is it?"

Steve laughed. "There's nothing for you to worry about, Jenny. The Nevada del Ruiz is eighty miles away from Bogota. Besides, the seismologists—those are the scientists who study volcanoes and earthquakes—have been keeping a close eye on that mountain ever since the last eruption. The next time it goes off, everyone will have plenty of warning to get out of the way."

The highway was now winding down out of the vast mountain valley, and they soon left the snowy peaks behind. Palm trees and tropical flowers now mingled with the pine and cypress. Wiping a suddenly damp face, Justin pulled off his jacket. Jenny followed his example.

Noticing their movements without taking his eyes off the road, Steve commented, "Here on the equator, temperatures are pretty much the same all year around. But every time you drop a few hundred feet in elevation, you move into a new climate zone. If we dropped clear to the bottom of these mountains, you'd be in steaming-hot jungle."

Steve himself looked cool and tough in a T-shirt and jeans. Jenny made a face at him. "Do all Marines know as much as you do, Mr. Cardoza?"

"Steve!" he corrected automatically, then grinned. "Well, I do try to read up on all the countries I get stationed in."

A short time later, the winding highway dropped into a small town several centuries removed from the skyscrapers of Bogota. A stone cathedral lifted its weathered spires and arches above low whitewashed homes with the black, wrought-iron balconies and red-tiled roofs the twins had noticed in the colonial sections of Bogota. Modern green traf-

fic signs reading "Zipaquirà—Catedral de Sal" pointed their
way through narrow cobblestone streets.

"What does 'Catedral de Sal' mean?" Justin asked, stumbling over the unfamiliar words. But Steve just shook his
head. "You'll see!"

The road ended in a parking lot at the foot of a narrow
concrete path that wound its way up a steep hill through
cypress groves. As Steve locked the minivan, a long bus with
"Zipaquirà" emblazoned across both sides pulled up beside
them.

Steve and Jenny started up the steep path, but Justin
paused to watch an assortment of foreigners—nearly all clad
in the international tourist costume of shorts, T-shirt, and
camera—pile out of the bus. The few local passengers were
easily marked by their dark hair and solemn clothes.

Falling in behind the group of tourists, Justin stopped not
far up the path to adjust his own camera. He had just focused
the camera on the parking lot, when a car different than any
Justin had ever seen roared into the camera frame. Its red
body was low and short and round, like an overgrown lady-
bug. Snapping a picture, Justin lowered the camera for a better view as the car slammed to a stop at the far end of the
parking lot.

Justin was more interested in the strange car than the
slim, wiry man who jumped out. He was too far away for
Justin to see his face, but his smooth movements and tight
jeans gave the impression of youth. Justin hardly noticed the
car's passenger until the young man hurried to the other side
of the car. Justin caught a glimpse only of a straight back and
a long, dark ponytail, as the young man took his passenger
by the arm and hurried her off in the opposite direction.

"More locals," Justin thought, losing interest. He hurried
to catch up to Steve and Jenny, now far up the path. He
caught up with them near a cluster of long, low cement-block

sheds, and what looked like some sort of mine diggings. Justin guessed that these were the salt mines, but before he could ask, Steve motioned him to move up the path.

The twins had to trot to keep up with Steve's long strides, and both children were out of breath by the time he stopped. They were standing on a wide terrace paved with stone blocks a yard across. To their left was a long, low building. From the brightly covered tables scattered outside, Justin guessed that it was a restaurant. A low wall on their right gave a clear view of the whole valley.

Just ahead, a high wire-mesh gate opened onto a wide, dark opening in the hillside. A loud chatter of different languages echoed like so many tropical parrots as the busload of tourists they had followed up the hill pressed around the ticket stand outside the gate.

Jenny collapsed against the stone wall and wiped her forehead. "Boy, am I out of shape!"

Justin eyed Steve's hard-muscled bare arms respectfully as the Marine lieutenant hurried over to join the line at the ticket stand. "I'll bet they lift weights in the Marines!"

He propped his elbows on the wide stone wall, then suddenly straightened up. Rubbing the heels of his hands against his eyes, he took another look. "Jenny!" he exclaimed in a low voice. "I think I'm being haunted by girls with long, black hair!"

CHAPTER FOUR

Footsteps in the Depths

The low, wide wall on which Justin was leaning ran along the top of the hill they had just climbed. From here he could see the entire valley—the burnt-red roofs and whitewashed walls of the small colonial town, nestled within a surrounding patchwork of green and gold fields. The salt diggings were spread out across the hillside directly below him. Scattered among the mounds of disturbed earth were long, flat ore-cars heaped with what Justin guessed was rock salt.

Leaning further over the wall, Justin rubbed his eyes again. Yes, he was right. In the shade of one of the ore-cars stood a small figure. The heaped-up salt ore cast a shadow across the face, but the long, black ponytail was unmistakable. The girl turned, one arm over her eyes, to study the mountainside above.

"What did you say?" Jenny asked, jumping up to sit on the wall.

"I said I'm being haunted by girls with long, black hair!" Justin repeated.

Jenny sniffed scornfully. "I'd just as soon not be, if they're all as unfriendly as the last one!"

"There she is again. See?"

Dangling her feet over the wall, she followed his pointed finger. "What do you mean? I don't see anyone but tourists!"

Justin looked again. The girl had disappeared. "There *was* a girl standing right there!" he insisted. "She must have ducked behind that cart."

His mind quickly flipped through its memory banks: He saw a young girl petting the white dog that had invaded the guest house; Estrella in the Gold Museum; the girl with a long ponytail who had jumped out of the strange red car. "That's the fourth one!"

"Justin!" Shaking her head with disgust, Jenny said reasonably, "*Most* Colombians have black hair! And at least half of them are girls! And probably a good part of those girls wear their hair long!"

Her explanation was interrupted by a now-familiar whistle, and she jumped off the wall. The rest of the tourists had disappeared. Standing alone outside the wire gate, Steve waved three small pieces of paper in the twins' direction. Jenny hurried across the stone terrace to join him. Still smarting from her sarcasm, Justin followed more slowly, stopping to read the signs warning tourists against rowdy behavior, loudness, and possible cave-ins—printed in English, Spanish, French, and German.

"This is where we go in," Steve informed them as he handed them their tickets. He motioned toward the dark opening in the mountainside. Justin and Jenny followed him out of the bright sunlight to where an impatient guard waited to collect the last tickets. Handing him the slips of paper, both twins looked around in surprise.

Ahead of them, a tunnel wide enough for a dozen people abreast slanted endlessly downward, until it was lost in the inky-black of the mountain depths. Dim lights high above hardly disturbed the darkness, but the rough walls and even the tunnel floor shimmered with a faint light of their own.

The walls were protected by a heavy wire mesh. Justin touched a finger to the grayish-white, quartz-like rock that protruded through the mesh, then cautiously licked the tip of his finger. "Why, it's salt!" he exclaimed.

"That's right," Steve answered. "This whole mountain is made of pure rock salt. Come on! There's plenty more to see."

They hurried after the fast-disappearing group of tourists, their eyes gradually adjusting to the dimness as the sunlight of the entrance dimmed behind them. No one else was in sight now, but once, when their own hollow footsteps paused in front of a statue of a very young angel set into a wire-covered crevice, Justin thought he heard the echo of another pair of feet behind them. But the faint pitter-patter instantly died away, and no one joined them in the bright circle cast by the alcove floodlight.

This place is just plain spooky! Justin told himself as their own footsteps again drowned out any other sound. He stopped again as they came to the first of a series of tunnels that opened up on either side of the main tunnel. Pieces of lumber had been nailed across this opening, but Justin could see it would be easy to crawl over the makeshift barrier.

"Oh, no you don't!" Steve put a hand on Justin's shoulder as he stepped up onto one termite-eaten board to peer into the vast blackness beyond. "Those tunnels are blocked off because they aren't safe anymore. *And* to keep tourists like you from getting lost—maybe forever!"

"I wasn't going in!" Justin answered hastily. "I was ... I was just looking."

Justin didn't know how long he had been walking when the tunnel abruptly ended. All three stood still for a long moment, then Justin found his voice. "It's a church! A church built out of salt!"

Steve looked thoroughly pleased with their surprise. "Quite a sight, isn't it! This is the world-famous 'Catedral de Sal de Zipaquirà'—'Cathedral of Salt' to you. The only one of its kind in the world!"

Opening before them into the sparkling heart of the mountain was a cavern so vast that the scattered busload of tourists seemed lost in its depths. The lights refracted diamond colors off every nodule of salt in the far-flung walls, dazzling their eyes after the dimness of the tunnel. Massive pillars of solid rock salt, gleaming faintly red in the floodlights at their bases, supported a vaulted ceiling so high that it was lost in what looked like star-strewn darkness. Rows of carved wooden benches ran between the pillars.

Above an ornate archway to their right, a trumpeting angel called them to step into his alcove. Grinning at the twins' shouts of wonder, Steve leaned against a salt pillar while Justin and Jenny inspected the shrine inside. Climbing to the top step, Justin suddenly noticed a green glow across the cavern.

"Wait for me!" Jenny ran after him as Justin hurried across the cavern. Reaching the grotto hollowed into the far end of the cavern, Justin was disappointed to discover that it was only a colored floodlight that caused the faint green sparkle of the walls. But he forgot his disappointment in the gentle beauty of the grotto.

A low wooden barrier protected the wide, gleaming steps leading up into the grotto from the dusty shoe marks of countless tourists. Leaning over as far as he dared, Justin saw that the altar, which shimmered the translucent white of pure quartz, was actually carved from one solid block of rock salt. As Jenny took his place at the rail, Justin read the multi-language sign that told how many tons the salt altar weighed.

Sitting down on one of the wooden benches, Justin slowly relaxed in the peaceful quiet of the vast salt cathedral. As he idly watched a flickering light shimmer over the cross that stretched out gold arms above the altar, his mind slipped back to that day at church camp last summer when he first realized how much it had cost Jesus to die on a cross for the sins of the world. That was the day when he and Jenny both had asked Jesus to be their Savior.

Justin didn't know how long he sat there before he realized that the short hairs on the back of his neck were standing straight up. He instantly recognized the prickly sensation. It had always come in useful when Jenny tried to sneak up on him. He turned his head cautiously, but saw no one but Steve standing close by, his neck bent back to study a tiny alcove above his head.

Beside him, lost in her own thoughts, Jenny sat watching the green gleam of the floodlights. Justin stood up quietly, and ambled casually over to the altar. Then he whirled around, quickly scanning the width of the cavern. He saw only a few scattered tourists, but the shadow behind one pillar a few yards to the right didn't seem quite natural.

Dodging quickly behind another pillar, he trotted in that direction. But he caught only a slight movement, and the pitter-patter-pitter of running feet disappearing into the shadows.

Jenny was watching him curiously as he returned. "What's wrong?"

"I think we're being followed!" Justin informed her. Then, as she opened her mouth, he added, "And don't tell me it's just my imagination!"

"I wasn't going to!" Jenny answered indignantly. "But really, Justin…"

"Justin! Jenny! Come on! There's lots more to see." From a dozen yards away, Steve waved an arm toward the still-unexplored areas of the salt cathedral.

The twins followed Steve toward a far-off, yellow-white beacon. A wooden barrier across the front of a small, well-lit cave brought them to a halt. Here they saw the Christmas story, the crystal-white salt figures radiating light in the beam of powerful floodlights. At one side, Joseph guarded watchfully as Mary bent over the sleeping figure of baby Jesus. Angels proclaimed glad tidings from above, and shepherds knelt in worship at the feet of the baby Savior.

The slight scrape of a tennis shoe against stone echoed loudly in the absolute stillness. Justin whirled around—this time fast enough to catch sight of a thin, pale face just outside the circle of light. Jenny's exclamation told him she had seen the girl's face as well.

"Hey! Why are you following us?" he called. There was a startled gasp and the echo of running feet.

"You go that way!" he whispered urgently to Jenny. "I'll go this way!"

"Hey, kids!" Hardly noticing Steve's call, Justin circled at a run through the salt pillars. Ahead, he caught a glimpse of a slim running figure. Jenny caught up to him just as the running girl darted into a dark opening at the far side of the cathedral.

The twins followed at a trot to discover that the darkness led into a poorly lit cave. The only exit was the opening they had just entered. Against the far wall, the pale beam of the cave's only spotlight full on her face, was the girl they had chased.

"Why, it's Estrella!" Jenny said in astonishment. "Why did you run away from us?" The other girl tensed for flight as the twins walked up to her. Her delicate, pale features seemed thinner than ever with her long hair pulled back into a ponytail.

"That's not the right question!" Justin declared as he casually moved to block any escape. "Ask her why she's been following us!"

He looked at the young guerrilla girl. "You *have* been following us, haven't you?"

Estrella shook her head in a quick no, then—catching Jenny's unbelieving stare—she nodded reluctantly.

"I knew it!" Justin said. He added and subtracted a few memories. "I'll bet that was you in that red car then, *and* up there on the hillside."

He looked triumphantly at Jenny, then knit reddish-brown eyebrows together. "But why would you want to follow us? And how did you know we were here?"

Justin wondered if he had imagined the sly look in the blue eyes before Estrella lowered long lashes. "I ... I heard that man you were with at the museum say you would be coming to Zipaquirà today. I ... I don't often get to speak English ... I thought it would be good practice."

When Justin and Jenny only stared at her with suspicion, she went on quickly, "No, that isn't true! I didn't come here to practice English. After you left yesterday, I was sorry I had been so unfriendly. I wanted to tell you how sorry I am, so you would not think badly of me. That is why I came."

Still suspicious, Jenny answered coldly, "Why do you want to be friends all of a sudden? We're still Americans, you know!"

Estrella bit her lip and looked away. "Yes, well ... I was wrong. It is not your fault that you are Americans. And I ... I think I would like to learn more about my father's country."

Justin broke in. "Then why didn't you just come over and talk to us? Why did you run away?"

Estrella looked wary again. "I was frightened ... I didn't know how to speak to you. I was afraid you would be angry."

Her voice dropped so low that they had to strain to hear. "I ... I think I need friends! Will you please forgive me and be my friends?"

Her lower lip quivered, and Justin softened immediately. Holding out his hand, he said gruffly, "That's okay! We all make mistakes!"

Jenny didn't look impressed by the genuine pleading in her voice. "What about your 'family'?" she demanded. "You said they were all the friends you needed!"

Estrella hesitated, then admitted, "They are busy with other things... Often they are gone... There is no one young."

Straightening her back, she tilted her chin with a touch of her former defiance. "But if you do not wish to forgive, I will go! I will not beg for your friendship! Nor will I tell you the news I have come to give you."

"Jenny!" Seeing Jenny's crossed arms and tightened lips, Justin poked her in the ribs—*hard*. "Remember that verse we learned in Sunday school the week before we left?"

When Jenny looked blank, he added impatiently, "You know! Ephesians 4:32: 'Be kind and compassionate to one another, forgiving each other, just as in Christ God forgave you'!"

He emphasized each word, and Jenny joined in reluctantly halfway through the verse. As they finished, Estrella said oddly, "You believe in God?"

Jenny looked sheepish. "We sure do. But I guess you'd never know it—the way I've been acting!"

She put out her hand. "I'm sorry! I *would* like to be your friend."

"What's the big idea running off like that!" Turning, the three children saw Steve's silhouette against the brightness of the cave mouth. His swift strides brought him across the cave to their side. "I've been looking all over for you two!"

Catching sight of Estrella, his eyes narrowed, and he said in the coldest tones Justin had ever heard him use, "You're the girl who was talking to Justin and Jenny yesterday in the museum, aren't you! What are you doing here? Why are you following us?"

"She just wanted to see us again," Justin broke in hastily, surprised by the Marine lieutenant's anger. "She wants to be our friend, and we'd like to be hers!"

"Are you crazy?" Steve exploded. "Have you forgotten who she is?"

He caught Estrella by the shoulder as she started to move away. "So she just happened to show up again today, and she just wants to be your friend! I'll bet she knows a lot more about who you are and what you're doing here than you think! Don't you?"

He addressed the last stern question to Estrella. Twisting away from his grip, she answered defiantly, "Okay, I do know who they are! I have heard on the streets about the two men who were taken by the police, and the man Parker who has come to decide their fate. When they told me of their uncle yesterday, I guessed who they were!"

The young guerrilla girl lifted her chin, wearing what Jenny had called her "princess look" the day before. "I followed them today to say that I was sorry and to be their friend. It was not hard to know where you would be! You speak very loudly in a crowded place."

As red tinged Steve's bronzed cheekbones, she added, "But I also came because I have heard news that is of great importance to them and to their uncle. If they have told you who I am, then you know that I have ways of finding out things."

"Why would someone like you want to help them?"

Estrella straightened her slim back proudly. "Because they are my friends! They have been kind to me, and I will be kind to them!"

Justin broke in feebly as the Marine lieutenant and the guerrilla girl stared at each other with dislike. "Just a minute,

Estrella. What do you mean about Uncle Pete deciding those guys' 'fate'? He doesn't have anything to do with what happens to them! He couldn't free them if he wanted to!"

Ignoring him, Steve demanded coldly. "Okay, what exactly is this helpful news you've got?"

Cutting him off impatiently, Estrella turned to Justin and Jenny. "It does not matter if your uncle can free those men. It is thought that he can, and that is all that matters!"

There was not even the sound of breathing in the small cavern as Estrella added with a dramatic movement of her hand, "I must speak to your uncle! He is in the greatest of danger!"

CHAPTER FIVE

Kidnapped!

Sudden loud footsteps startled the entire group. They whirled around to see who was there. Justin was sure he recognized the young man standing just outside the cave mouth as being the driver of the red car he'd seen earlier. Estrella's eyes widened when she saw him, and she whispered urgently, "I can't talk more! I must go!"

Justin protested, "But you can't just go like that! When will we see you again?"

"I will be at the house of Simon Bolivar tomorrow at three o'clock."

Before either Justin or Jenny could say a word, Steve said firmly, "Fine! I'll be there to receive any information you have."

Estrella shook her head. "No! I will speak only to my friends. Bring your uncle and come alone! I will tell *him* what I know!"

Ducking under Steve's outstretched arm, she darted across the cave floor. By the time Steve and the twins reached the entrance, both Estrella and the young man had disappeared.

There were still parts of the salt caverns that they hadn't explored, but Steve had obviously had enough sightseeing. He hurried the twins out of the salt cathedral and up the steep tunnel so quickly that they had to trot to keep up.

Jenny finally broke into Steve's silence. "Steve, what kind of danger could Uncle Pete possibly be in? He didn't have anything to do with those guys! We just got here!"

"Yeah!" added Justin. "Uncle Pete couldn't do anything about those guys anyway! He isn't government or anything!"

"What he can or can't do doesn't matter!" Steve answered grimly without slowing his stride. "Like your friend said, it's what the guerrillas *think* he can do that counts!"

"Well, what *do* they think he can do?" Justin asked, puzzled.

Steve came to a stop. "By threatening Triton Oil property and personnel," he explained patiently, "the guerrillas are trying to force your uncle and the American government to pressure the Colombian police into letting those men go. I'm sure you realize that your uncle has a lot of influence in government circles."

Justin hadn't known this, and he pricked up his ears as Steve continued. "What they don't realize is that both the American and Colombian governments have a rigid policy that they won't give in to threats. If they did, every American citizen abroad would be in danger. Terrorists would take them hostage to force the American government to give in to their demands. So even if your uncle would agree to use his influence to free those men, it wouldn't do any good."

He started walking again. "But the guerrillas don't seem to have gotten that point yet. That's one reason we've got you and your uncle where you are—to keep you safe!"

The twins followed him in silence, but as they neared the

entrance, Justin said quietly, "I guess I was pretty stupid, then—telling her our names like that yesterday!"

Steve stopped so suddenly that Justin slid into him. "Now just a minute, Justin! Don't blame yourself. If there was fault, it was mine. I should have warned you not to speak to strangers."

A curious smile lit his bronzed face. "It just never occurred to me you'd find anyone to talk to in a foreign city. Anyway, what's done is done!"

He strode on ahead, nodding to the guard at the entrance, and pushed through the wire gate. The twins fell behind as the brightness of the early afternoon sun dazzled eyes now accustomed to the darkness below. Blinking, Justin commented, "Well, at least Estrella has decided to be our friend. With her help, maybe Uncle Pete can get this all cleared up right away."

Jenny frowned. "I don't know. It still seems pretty strange to me! Why should she go to all this trouble when we've only met her once? She sure changed her mind about being friends in a hurry!"

Justin paused, one hand on the gate. "She explained why she changed her mind. *And* she came all the way out here to warn us about Uncle Pete being in danger. I'd call that pretty nice. Anyway, you promised you'd be her friend!"

Glancing sideways at her brother, Jenny teased, "She's awfully pretty, isn't she!"

Red crept up the back of Justin's neck. "You know that's not it! It's just ... oh, I don't know!" He shook his head. "There's just something about her... I think she really does need friends."

He added, "I mean, look at us! We've got a great family *and* lots of friends! I wonder how it would feel to lose it all."

Jenny suddenly looked ashamed. "Yeah, I guess you're right. We did promise to be friends. Anyway, if Uncle Pete really is in danger..." She darted across the terrace to where Steve was leaning over the stone wall, waiting for them to catch up. "Steve, we *are* going to meet Estrella tomorrow, aren't we?"

Following Jenny, Justin caught Steve's sudden frown. "I don't know, kids. It could be risky. If this girl knows all about you, who knows how many others do too? Maybe you'd all better sit tight until we can get you out of the country."

Jenny looked like she wanted to argue, but Steve stood up. "We can't decide anything until we've talked to your uncle and Mr. Bascom, so let's get going!"

As they hurried down the winding path, Justin scanned the parking lot below. There was no sign of the little red car or its occupants. He suddenly realized he hadn't told Steve and Jenny about the car, or the driver he'd recognized later in the caverns.

"It must have been a *peta*," Steve decided when Justin finished describing the ladybug-shaped car. "Good work, Justin. That could be a useful piece of information."

Catching their puzzled expressions, he added, "A *peta* is a little turtle—they're shaped just about like one of those cars. A Volkswagen 'bug' we'd call the car in English. They're one of the most popular cars in South America—cheap and easy to fix."

▼▼▼

Both Uncle Pete and Mr. Bascom, the embassy secretary, were at the guest house when they arrived. Over supper, Steve briefly outlined the events of the last two days. To the twins' surprise, Mr. Bascom seemed very interested in the young guerrilla girl, asking questions until Justin and Jenny had repeated all they could remember of their conversations with Estrella.

When they had finished, Uncle Pete raised his eyebrows at Mr. Bascom. "This whole situation still makes no sense! I can understand this guerrilla band threatening Triton Oil. But how could they possibly know anything about me—or even that I'm in the country?"

Mr. Bascom shrugged. "These groups have ways of getting information. They could have bribed a secretary—or even a janitor—to snoop around the Triton Oil office. Who knows? What matters is that they obviously *do* know about you."

"Yeah, and somehow that information got around to whatever group this girl calls her 'family,' " added Steve. "News travels fast on the street."

He frowned. "Of course, that's assuming this Estrella's telling the truth. I don't trust that girl! Maybe it would be safest just to pretend we never met her..."

Mr. Bascom disagreed. "This girl could be a valuable contact for our intelligence gathering bureau. I would certainly like to know what information she has to pass on." He shook his head. "But I don't know that I want to involve the kids."

Steve said thoughtfully, "I could go alone, but I'm sure she wouldn't show unless she saw the kids. Now, if there was some way we could stake out the place... That way, if it's a trap..."

Uncle Pete slapped a hand against the table. "Now, just a minute! I'm not putting Justin and Jenny in any position where they will run a risk of being hurt!"

The twins had been listening while the adults talked, but Justin couldn't keep quiet any longer. "Uncle Pete, Estrella wouldn't do anything to hurt us! She's our friend! If we don't show up tomorrow, she's going to think we lied when we said we'd be her friend."

Jenny spoke up in support. "I agree with Justin. We did promise to be her friend. Besides, if she does know something, then maybe the police can catch those guys, and Uncle Pete's company can get back to work." She grinned impishly. "Then Steve won't have to baby-sit us anymore!"

"Yeah, if you're in danger, Uncle Pete," Justin added, "we really should find out about it. We don't want anything to happen to you! We just want to talk to her! What could possibly happen?"

Uncle Pete's green eyes twinkled as he looked from one pleading face to the other. "It seems I've heard that from you two before. All right, we'll go. But only if Steve takes the proper security measures."

As Justin and Jenny started to protest, he raised a stern hand. "No, I don't care what this girl said. I'm not taking you anywhere alone!"

"Don't worry!" Steve put in. "I'll hide a couple of guys in the bushes. She won't even know we're there."

The next afternoon, Mr. Bascom brought the minivan around to the front door of the guest house. Steve had left an hour earlier with two other Marines whose duty it was to protect the American embassy. As they pulled away from the curb, Justin noticed a group of children playing soccer at the end of the block. *Looks like the same bunch as before,* he thought idly. But he saw no sign of the little white dog.

"I'll drop you off at the entrance," Mr. Bascom told the Parkers as he turned onto a six-lane avenue lined with business offices. "Anyone watching will think you've come alone. You will then leave here with Steve. He should have his men staked out around the grounds by now."

"Do we really *need* to go through all this spy stuff just to talk to a girl?" Justin muttered to Jenny.

"Don't ask me!" Jenny whispered back. "It seems pretty silly!"

From the driver's seat, Mr. Bascom said sternly, "We've learned the hard way here in Bogota not to take any chances!"

"Exactly what *is* this house of Simon Bolivar?" Uncle Pete put in quickly, as the twins flushed with embarrassment.

With a smile, Mr. Bascom looked back at the two children. "Can either of you tell us who Simon Bolivar was?"

Justin answered hesitantly, "Wasn't he the guy who helped South America get its independence from Spain? Like George Washington back home?"

"That's right!" Mr. Bascom nodded approvingly. "He was also the first president of Colombia. We are going to his family mansion here in Bogota. It's now open to the public."

Leaving the office buildings behind, he drove through a wide intersection, then pulled to a stop halfway through the next block. Jumping out onto a broad cement sidewalk, Justin looked both ways as the embassy minivan drove off. There was little traffic at this hour of the afternoon, and no one else shared the sidewalk as far as he could see.

Above Justin's head, untrimmed cypress trees leaned over a weathered stone wall to run feathery green fingers through his hair. Justin followed Jenny and Uncle Pete to the heavy metal gate that swung between tall stone pillars. As Uncle Pete dug the small entrance fee from his pocket, the usual guard handed tickets through a barred stone window and swung open the gate.

The gentle, green oasis on the other side of the gate was unexpected, and as the click of the heavy latch shut out the bustle of the city, Justin felt that he had stepped back into another, quieter century. Even the roar of distant traffic was cut off by the gentle rush of wind through the evergreens.

The three Parkers walked through a maze of oddly cut yew hedges that bordered a series of spouting fountains, stone statues, and small ponds where goldfish glinted in the afternoon sun. Tucked into odd corners, and blazing from formal, carefully tended beds, were the flowers, their colors splashed across the garden like a child's spilled paint box.

Justin paused to look across the maze of green. It was a warm weekday afternoon. The only visitor in sight was a middle-aged tourist taking pictures of the flowers. If Steve and the other security agents were somewhere in the mass of shrubbery, they were too well hidden to be seen from where Justin stood. The idea of terrorists and danger suddenly seemed ridiculous.

Uncle Pete stopped in front of the square, two-story mansion at the far end of the garden. The usual burnt-red tiles of the roof contrasted with the blinding white of the old adobe walls. Flower pots nodded colorful heads from the black iron balconies overhead. Glancing at his watch, he announced, "Three o'clock on the dot. Do you see any sign of your friend?"

Justin shook his head reluctantly, and Jenny suggested, "Maybe she's inside. Why don't we take a look?"

"Good idea," Uncle Pete agreed. "If she doesn't show, you'll get a history lesson out of the afternoon, at least."

As they filed through the tiled entryway, Justin discovered that the entire house was wrapped around a large courtyard. In the center, a few stunted citrus trees in pots sheltered another fountain. High pillars held up a verandah that circled the courtyard. In its shade, rows of hand-carved doors opened into high-ceilinged, whitewashed rooms. Heavy ropes across the open doors kept visitors from entering.

There was no sign of a guide or Estrella. *Maybe she's just late*, Justin thought as he followed Jenny and Uncle Pete along the verandah. Although a small part of his mind stayed alert for the tell-tale prickle at his neck that would inform him of spying eyes, he decided to enjoy the tour.

He peered over Jenny's shoulder into a room that was once a study. The room looked as though the nineteenth-century liberator had just stepped out for an afternoon stroll.

One corner of the verandah opened into a long room where finely embroidered chairs, imported from France a century before, sat around highly polished tables. Paintings by famous European artists looked down from the walls, and a crystal chandelier hung unlit from the mural-covered ceiling.

In every room, treasures of china and silver peered out of locked glass cases. Justin and Jenny followed Uncle Pete up one of the broad, tiled staircases that curved up to the second floor from each corner of the courtyard. Here too, a row of carved-wood doors opened onto a wide balcony that circled the courtyard.

Justin whistled as he pointed out a four-poster bed with a faded silk canopy in the master bedroom. "Look how small that bed is! People must have been awfully short back then."

Reading a sign printed as usual in several languages, Justin mentally translated the centimeters to inches. "Wow! That guy was only four feet ten inches tall!"

Jenny giggled at a set of the liberator's clothes preserved in a glass case. "I couldn't even get into those."

As the two children followed Uncle Pete down the far staircase, Justin paused again to scan the courtyard. "I wonder what's keeping Estrella!"

"Maybe she never meant to come," Jenny suggested idly, leaning over the rail to watch a pair of bright-yellow birds. "Maybe she was just pulling our leg."

Justin bristled. "Don't be ridiculous! There could be a hundred reasons why she's late."

"Let's get a move on, kids!" Uncle Pete was waving at them from the top of a stairway that led below ground. Forgetting their argument, the twins hurried to catch up and followed Uncle Pete down toward the servants' quarters and kitchen.

They entered a vast underground chamber dimly lit by a few barred windows high on the wall. Copper utensils and ladles hung from its low rafters. Brick ovens built into the earthen walls were still blackened with a century or two of soot, and a rusty, three-legged pot was perched in a fireplace large enough to roast an entire ox. A heavy iron spit showed that it had probably been used for that very purpose.

As they emerged back into the afternoon light, Uncle Pete glanced at his watch. "Well, kids, it doesn't look like your friend is going to show. This has been an interesting outing, but I have work waiting."

"Yeah, let's go home!" Jenny agreed. "She's obviously not coming!"

"Can't we wait just a little longer?" Justin begged, scanning the courtyard one last time. "We might not get another chance to find out what she knows."

Uncle Pete shook his head firmly. "It's already four o'clock. If she planned to show, she would be here by now. Come on. We'll try to locate Steve and get a ride home."

In the tiled entryway, the twins used the last of the savings they had brought along for the trip to buy a covered silver sugar bowl—supposedly a copy of Simon Bolivar's, and incredibly low in price. Silver was plentiful and still quite cheap in Colombia, Uncle Pete explained.

Trailing a few feet behind as they threaded back through the maze of walkways that led to the gate, Justin saw with disappointment that the garden was empty. Even the solitary tourist was gone, and if Steve and the other agents were there, they were well hidden.

"Justin! Jenny!" Justin instantly recognized the cool, precise girl's voice. Pointing, he announced triumphantly, "Look! I told you she'd come."

Dark-shaded blue eyes were peering through the grillwork of the iron gate, then a slim arm waved through the opening. Justin and Jenny hurried to the gate, Uncle Pete close behind. "Estrella, where were you?" Justin demanded. "We were just about to leave!"

What they could see of Estrella's expression looked

uneasy. "I ... I could not buy the ticket to get in. I have been waiting here for you to come out."

Uncle Pete bent down to look through the grillwork. "Kids, would you introduce me to your friend?"

"Oh, yes." Jenny turned hurriedly to Uncle Pete. "Uncle Pete, this is Estrella. Estrella, this is my uncle that you wanted to talk to."

Uncle Pete studied the slim, pale features closely. "If you want to talk to me, come on in. We'll take care of your ticket."

They could see Estrella shake her head, then she stepped out of sight. "No, I can't let you do that," her voice floated stubbornly from the other side of the gate. "If you wish to hear what I have to say, you must come out here and speak with me."

Uncle Pete glanced around the garden, and Justin guessed that he was looking for some sign of Steve. "All right," he said at last, looking exasperated.

Pushing open the gate, the three Parkers stepped out onto the sidewalk. Justin looked up and down the street. It was empty of pedestrians, and the only traffic was a long, black Mercedes Benz limousine moving in their direction a couple of blocks away.

"Hi, Estrella! We thought you weren't coming!" Estrella looked surprised at Jenny's quick hug, but she hugged her back and shook Justin's outstretched hand.

"Estrella, I'm glad to meet you, but we can't stay here long." Uncle Pete looked down kindly at the young guerrilla girl. "Why don't you go ahead and tell me what you have to say—*and* how you learned about us."

Moving away from the twins, Estrella stared up at Uncle Pete. Her speech sounded rehearsed as she answered calmly, "I hear many things in the street. When Justin and Jenny told me their names, I knew who you were. They were kind to me and promised to be my friends, so I decided to help them."

Her voice died away as she glanced up the street. Justin followed her gaze, but saw nothing but the black limousine now only a block away. Uncle Pete's big foot tapped impatiently, but he repeated gently, "Well, what is it that you heard?"

Estrella opened her mouth, but her voice was suddenly drowned out by the loud gunning of an engine. Startled, Justin looked up to see the Mercedes Benz now hurtling down the street toward them. The mirror-like one-way glass of the windows hid any sign of a driver. As it neared the four on the sidewalk, the limousine suddenly braked and a rear window slid down.

Justin glimpsed a black hood and a gloved hand clutching an egg-shaped object. Then, as a black, leather-clad arm reached through the window and made a smooth overhand toss, Estrella shouted, "Run!"

Justin instinctively jerked away as she grabbed at his jacket and caught Jenny by the hand, and she hissed, "Don't be stupid!"

With more strength than they would have guessed possible, the young guerrilla girl shoved Justin and Jenny away from the car. Stumbling back against the stone wall, Justin watched as the egg-shaped object tumbled end over end through the afternoon sun. From the corner of his eye, he saw Estrella cover her head with her arms. Then, with a blast of thunder, his world exploded!

CHAPTER SIX

The Search for Uncle Pete

Justin lay unmoving, one cheek against the cement pavement where the explosion had thrown him. His lungs felt deflated. He vaguely sensed that someone lay beneath him, but he couldn't move. Lifting his head cautiously, he choked as a sharp odor and dust rushed into his lungs.

Several yards beyond the gate, dust and black smoke drifted up from a gaping hole in the stone wall. Chunks of concrete and shattered stone littered the sidewalk. *How could they possibly have missed us?* he wondered numbly. Then, as he blinked the dirt and debris from his eyes, he again felt his breath snatched away.

The rear door of the black limousine stood open, and a tall, hooded figure all in black was shoving Uncle Pete into the back seat. Another slim, black-hooded figure—Justin couldn't tell whether it was a man or a woman—scanned the sidewalk, while balancing a machine gun with an obviously experienced hand.

Justin tried to shout, but his voice came out in a squeak. Before he could even move, the first hooded figure had climbed in beside Uncle Pete. The one with the machine gun slammed the door shut and jerked open the front door. The door was still open when the engine roared and the Mercedes Benz moved smoothly away from the curb.

"Justin, you're squashing me!" a muffled voice gasped from beneath him. "Get off!"

Justin rolled over and struggled to his feet just as the heavy gate in the stone wall clanged open and Steve ran out, followed by the other two Marines. *Nice of you to show up now!* Justin thought savagely, before he realized that no more than a minute had gone by since they first stepped out the gate.

Holding an army-caliber pistol high with both hands, the Marine lieutenant took in the scene with one glance. Dropping into a crouch, he brought the pistol down expertly to bear on the black limousine. But whatever he planned to do, it was too late. Still picking up speed, the Mercedes Benz was already far down the block.

It had all happened so quickly that Justin stood unmoving, staring down the street in frozen dismay. Part of his mind registered Jenny and Estrella struggling to their feet behind him. Grabbing his arm, Jenny cried out, "What happened? Where's Uncle Pete?"

Justin motioned hopelessly after the speeding car, which at that instant turned a corner and disappeared. The other two security agents had dropped their guns. One was shouting into a walkie-talkie while the other scanned the debris. Steve walked back toward them, frustration all over his bronze features.

"Okay, kids!" he snapped. "What happened? Where is Mr. Parker?"

Jenny was looking around in a daze, one hand rubbing sudden tears from her dust-covered cheeks. She choked, "I … I don't know! They took him away!"

Putting an arm around his sister, Justin got out an

answer. "Some men in that big, black car—I saw them throw the bomb. Then they shoved Uncle Pete in the back and took off."

Justin's arm dropped as Jenny moved away to stand in front of Steve. Looking angrily up at the broad-shouldered Marine, she demanded, "Why did you let them get Uncle Pete? You said you were watching us! You said we'd be safe!"

"You *were* safe!" Steve snapped an answer. "Inside that gate! Why did you leave the property? Don't you have any sense?"

"Estrella called us out," Justin explained wearily. "She wouldn't come in. We didn't think a few minutes would hurt anything."

Steve seemed to notice the young guerrilla girl for the first time. He looked down at the dirt-streaked, thin face with cold anger. "I might have known you'd be in on this!"

Estrella looked just as angry as the Marine lieutenant. Turning to Justin, she stormed, "Why is he here? I told you to come alone!"

"I was the one who insisted on coming. I was sure you weren't to be trusted. And I was right, wasn't I?" Steve caught Estrella by the shoulders. "You planned this, didn't you! You're in more trouble than you've ever been in your life."

Justin caught a look of fear in the blue eyes as Estrella protested, "I know nothing of this, I swear! I stayed outside because I had no money for the ticket."

She turned to the twins. "You tell him."

"We'll see!" Steve muttered as Justin and Jenny nodded agreement. Estrella looked faintly triumphant when Steve checked her pockets and found them empty. "You see? It was of this danger that I came to warn you. Those were the men who wanted to harm your uncle."

Steve was still angry. "Didn't you look around, girl? Those men probably followed you all the way here!"

Estrella pulled herself up proudly. "Don't blame me! How do you know they didn't follow you? It wouldn't be hard to find out where you are staying!"

Justin had a sudden mental picture of the band of children outside the embassy guest house. He raised his hands to his still-ringing ears, suddenly exhausted and desperately wishing he could shut out the angry voices. "Who cares whose fault it was! They've got Uncle Pete! We've got to get him back!"

He dropped his hands back to his side and turned to Steve. "Estrella couldn't have anything to do with this. She saved our lives when that guy threw the bomb. If it's anyone's fault, it's ours for going outside the gate."

Steve looked suddenly tired, the anger draining from his face. "I'm sorry, kids. I've no right to yell or to blame anyone. It's just that this was supposed to be such a simple operation."

A siren interrupted him, and moments later the street was crowded with army vehicles and Colombian soldiers. With the ease of much practice, a pair of military police threw up a heavy rope along the sidewalk. One of the Marines hurried over, holding out a few glinting fragments. "Looks like an Army-issue grenade they threw!"

Steve nodded agreement as he glanced over the fragments, then led the three children away from the roped-off area. Justin saw the dark-blue embassy minivan screech to a halt behind a police jeep. Mr. Bascom climbed down, and Steve hurried over to talk to him.

As Justin slumped against the stone wall to wait, he noticed for the first time the painful sting of his face and hands. Wiping the grit from his skinned palms against his jeans, he touched one cheek cautiously. His fingers came away red-stained, and he realized that he must have scraped it against the concrete pavement when the blast sent him flying.

As the two girls came over to stand beside him, he noticed that Estrella was limping and that the knees of her worn jeans were torn and red-stained. Jenny had a long scrape down one arm. Their hair and clothes were as coated with chalky dust as his own.

"Kids!" Justin stood up as Steve waved the children over to the minivan. "Dave and Mac will take care of the local police." He indicated the other two security agents who were talking with a Colombian army officer inside the roped-off area. "Mr. Bascom and I are taking you back to the guest house."

As the twins climbed into the back of the van, Steve looked down at Estrella, who stood alone on the pavement, looking very dirty and a little lost. He added without his former anger, "You too! We'll have a few questions to ask you."

The rest of the day had the unreal quality of a bad dream. Mr. Bascom kindly refrained from asking any questions until the three children had all bathed and changed—Jenny lending Estrella a spare pair of jeans and T-shirt—and Steve had administered basic first aid to their cuts and scrapes.

Only when they were drinking the last of another pot of Colombian "sancocho" did Mr. Bascom take Steve and the three children, step by step, over every detail of what had happened since he had dropped the Parkers off earlier in the afternoon.

When they finished, Mr. Bascom said heavily, "Well, kids, I can't tell you how sorry I am about this. Be sure that we will be doing all we can to get your uncle back."

Running long fingers through his receding tight curls, he eyed Estrella sharply. "So you knew something like this might happen?"

"I heard that there were men who wanted to capture

Justin and Jenny's uncle—to keep him until you let your prisoners go. It was for this reason that I came today." Estrella shrugged. "I am sorry that I was too late."

Justin's mind seemed to clear for the first time since the kidnapping. He said thoughtfully, "Those guys who took Uncle Pete must have been from that guerrilla band who tried to bomb the oil line—the ones who have been threatening Triton Oil. Well, you've got two of their guys in prison. Maybe they'd know where those guerrillas might have taken Uncle Pete!"

Mr. Bascom looked approvingly at Justin. "That's good thinking. You can be sure the Colombian police are going to be questioning those two men pretty thoroughly."

He looked down at the young guerrilla girl. "What about you, Estrella? Can you think of any place they might have taken Mr. Parker—or anyone who might be able to find out?"

Estrella nodded. "I will do all I can to help find my friends' uncle. I have many ways of finding things out."

She added hesitantly, "But there is one thing. I ... my 'family' left the city today. I ... I stayed behind to warn my friends. I don't know where I will stay."

Justin spoke up immediately. "Well, I'm sure you can stay with us. Can't she, Mr. Bascom? ... Steve? ... I mean, she stayed behind just to warn us."

His back to the children, Steve leaned over and spoke quietly to Mr. Bascom. Justin barely caught Mr. Bascom's soft answer. "It might be the best way to keep an eye on her."

Steve nodded to the waiting children. "You're certainly welcome to stay, Estrella. We'll appreciate any help you can give us."

Still pink around the eyelids, Jenny had been staring down at her empty bowl. But at this, she looked up and smiled at the young guerrilla girl. "She can sleep with me. I've got plenty of extra clothes—even an extra toothbrush."

Estrella nodded satisfaction. "That is good. Then I will go out now and see what news I can find. I will be back tonight to sleep."

"Oh, no you don't!" Steve suddenly stood up. "No one is going in or out of this building except myself and Mr. Bascom. We aren't taking any more risks. If Estrella is really anxious to help, she can just tell me what she knows and I'll check it out myself!"

His expression was so discouraging that Estrella didn't argue. She said glumly, "If that is what you wish! But I can't promise that my friends will speak with you."

Mr. Bascom rose to his feet as the security guard Justin had seen in the kitchen that morning came in to collect their empty dishes. "Well, kids, I don't think there is anything more we can do right now. Steve, why don't you write down any contacts or information Estrella can give you and begin working on that. Justin and Jenny…"

As he paused, Justin suddenly realized that what he wanted most in the world right now was to talk to his parents. As usual, Jenny echoed his thoughts. "Mr. Bascom, could we please call Mom and Dad?"

"Just what I was going to suggest." Mr. Bascom again ran his fingers through his tight, black curls and sighed. "I imagine they'll want you on the first plane home."

Leaving Estrella and Steve bent over a notebook, he led the twins to the next room and showed them how to dial the international area code.

"You go first!" Jenny told Justin. "You're better at explaining."

Justin waited impatiently as the dial tone buzzed in his ear, then sighed with relief as he heard his mother's warm voice say, "This is the Parker residence."

But his relief turned to dismay as the voice went on, "We

are unavailable at the moment. Please leave your name and number after the beep."

His father's voice suddenly broke into the taped message, "Pete, Justin, Jenny—if you should call, we'll be back in a few days. I managed to finish that project sooner than expected, and Helen and I decided to get away..."

As his father's voice continued, Justin looked blankly at Mr. Bascom. "They went camping! It ... it's just the answering machine. They won't be home for three more days!"

Mr. Bascom took the phone from Justin and spoke crisply into the receiver, "Mr. and Mrs. Parker, this is Mr. Marvin Bascom from the American embassy in Bogota. Your children are fine, but we would appreciate you getting in contact with us at your earliest convenience. Our phone number is..."

He rattled off a line of numbers, then hung up. Turning to the twins, he explained, "We need to get hold of them as soon as possible, but I didn't want them thinking something has happened to you."

Justin slumped into a chair. He hadn't realized how much he had counted on hearing his parents' reassuring voices. "What do we do now?" he asked.

"We'll keep you here under guard until we hear from your parents," Mr. Bascom answered firmly. "Then you'll be on the first plane home—with or without your uncle!"

Dropping into another chair, Jenny said hesitantly, "But ... but you'll have found him by then, won't you?"

Mr. Bascom faced the two children squarely. "Look, I'm going to be honest with you. We could find your uncle in a couple of days. But Colombia is a big country. We don't even know if your uncle is still in Bogota. Sometimes it takes months to recover a hostage taken by guerrillas. Sometimes..."

He broke off, and Justin finished for him, "Sometimes you never get them back!"

Justin jumped to his feet. "Sometimes they kill them, don't they! They could be hurting Uncle Pete right now!"

Mr. Bascom patted him on the shoulder. "Don't worry, Justin. I'm sure your uncle is just fine. They won't hurt him as long as they hope to trade him for their two men in prison. And by the time they realize the government won't trade…"

He hesitated, then went on, "Well, we'll just have to make sure we've found him by that time."

Estrella came into the room just then, followed by Steve, who seemed very satisfied with the scribbled notes he was reading over. A short time later, the three children climbed the stairs to their rooms. Justin joined the girls in Jenny's room as Jenny showed Estrella the extra twin bed and dug out a spare sweat suit.

It wasn't yet their usual bedtime, but as Justin stretched out on Jenny's bed, he realized how tired and sore he was. Echoing his thoughts, Jenny gave a mouth-splitting yawn. Estrella smiled slightly. "It would be well if we went to sleep. There is nothing more we can do tonight."

At her words, Justin suddenly straightened up. "Oh, yes there is!"

He looked at his sister and knew she'd had the same thought. Estrella paused with one hand on the bathroom door as Jenny scrambled over to sit by Justin. She stood there unmoving as Justin and Jenny bowed their heads and, first one, then the other, prayed that God would protect Uncle Pete, wherever he was, and bring him safely back.

When they had finished, Estrella asked curiously, "Do you really think God is going to hear your prayers?"

The twins looked at each other again and smiled for the first time that evening. Justin answered, "We *know* He does!"

"Carlos says that God is an invention of the rich and powerful to keep the poor under their thumb," Estrella remarked, still with her hand on the doorknob. "If the poor pray to God for help, they will not think to fight those who are oppressing them."

But she spoke thoughtfully rather than with scorn, and as she left the room, she added, "I once knew someone who spoke about God as you do."

Much later, Justin lay still awake, staring into the darkness above his bed. Tiredness pressed on his eyelids, but his mind would not stop going over and over the events of the afternoon. He was envying the two girls sleeping peacefully next door when a light tap at the door startled him into sitting up.

"Justin, are you awake?" he heard his sister whisper. He felt a weight settling on the far end of the bed.

"Yeah, I'm awake!" he whispered back. "You couldn't get to sleep either?"

He felt her shake her head. "No. I've been thinking and thinking!"

Giving up any attempt to sleep, Justin asked, "Yeah? What about?"

"Justin, I've been wondering," Jenny said, still in a whisper, "Do you think it could really have been Estrella who brought those guerrillas to kidnap Uncle Pete?"

"What?" Justin sat up, his exclamation almost a shout.

"Shh!" Jenny hissed, then added, "Well, what if Steve was right! I mean, don't you think it's strange that those guerrillas showed up right after Estrella called us out of the gate?"

"No, I don't!" Justin answered flatly, reaching over to switch on a lamp that stood on a wooden table beside the bed. Jenny blinked at the sudden light as he demanded, "Have you forgotten she saved our lives when that grenade went off?"

A knock at the door startled them into silence. The door opened, and Estrella looked in. "I woke to find Jenny gone. Is there something wrong?"

As Justin and Jenny quickly shook their heads, Estrella joined them on the twin bed. Drawing her knees up to her chin, she wrapped her arms around them and said hesitantly, "I am sorry that you cannot sleep. I too am very sad about your uncle. I wish I had never asked you to meet me..."

Throwing a glance at Jenny, Justin interrupted gruffly, "It wasn't your fault, Estrella! Anyway, we sure appreciate the way you're helping us get him back."

"*If* we ever get him back!" Jenny said, wiping at suddenly overflowing tears. "Oh, Justin, what if we never..."

"Justin! Jenny! Please do not be so sad!" Even Jenny could not mistake the genuine sympathy in Estrella's voice. She jumped off the bed. "Please do not cry, Jenny. You must not worry! Your uncle *will* come back to you soon. I promise you! I, Estrella, will find him myself!"

CHAPTER SEVEN

I Found Him!

Justin and Jenny stared at Estrella in surprise. Jenny demanded, "How are you going to do that? You're not even allowed to leave the building!"

Estrella looked scornful. "Do you really think they can keep me here if I want to leave?"

Justin thought of the locked, heavy metal doors, and the surveillance cameras he had seen in the halls. He said slowly, "I don't see how you can possibly get out. You know they'll just stop you if they see you."

"There are ways," Estrella answered vaguely. She added sharply, "I *must* get out. No matter what Steve says, the people I have told him of will not speak to him as they will to me."

"Well, why don't you tell Steve that," Jenny said reasonably. "Maybe he could take you along with him or something."

"No!" Estrella shook her head sharply. "If they saw that I did not come alone, they would not speak to me, either."

"I still think you should talk to Steve," Jenny argued. "It could be dangerous for you out there."

"No, I will not talk to that man again! You know he doesn't like me. He would just try to stop me. Besides, there is no one trying to kidnap *me!* Why should I be caged up here like a prisoner?"

Estrella looked from one to the other. "If you want your uncle back, you must promise to keep quiet—or I will not be able to help you."

Jenny opened her mouth to argue further, but Justin, wearily rubbing his eyes, interrupted, "Let her try, Jenny! We've got to do anything we can to help Uncle Pete. Anyway, it's time we all get back to bed!"

"Good! Tomorrow I will see what I can find out!" Estrella started toward the door, and Jenny reluctantly followed her. Turning out the light, Justin soon fell into a troubled sleep.

▼▼▼

There was no further news about Uncle Pete the next morning, and the next three days settled into a pattern of waiting. Steve was often gone, and when he was there, he was usually on the phone or sifting through the pile of reports that a Colombian police officer dropped off twice a day.

It was noon on the first day when Mr. Bascom informed the three children that the embassy had received a ransom note. "We were right. It's the same group that threatened your uncle's company. They want to exchange him for their two members in prison."

"What are you going to do?" Justin asked.

"There's nothing we *can* do," Mr. Bascom answered grimly. "You know the government policy about giving in to kidnappers."

As he left the room, Jenny turned to Estrella and said desperately, "Estrella, you've got to find him soon!"

Estrella squeezed her hand sympathetically. "Don't worry! I will find him in time."

Estrella often slipped away, but she was never gone long and managed to be there every time Steve or Mr. Bascom reported any updates on the search for Uncle Pete. As they had promised, the twins said nothing about her occasional disappearances. But Justin couldn't restrain his curiosity.

The afternoon after the kidnapping, Justin decided to try to leave the building for himself. He made his way through darkened hallways down to the basement, but was still yards from the back door when a security guard tapped him on the shoulder.

"You don't want to go out there!" the guard said, kindly but firmly.

"I didn't really want to go out. I just wanted to see if I could do it without being caught," Justin answered with a grin. He gave up trying to figure out how Estrella managed to leave the guest house undetected.

The twins discovered that the security guards' row of surveillance screens weren't the only TV sets in the guest house. They located a large recreation room on the third floor. Here, the security guards relaxed when they were off duty. Occasionally joined by Steve, Mr. Bascom, or one of the guards, the three children spent most of their time there—reading magazines, playing board games, deciphering the Spanish news broadcasts on the big-screen TV, or just talking.

It was after Justin's attempt to defeat the security system, as the three children huddled on the floor over an antique Monopoly game, that Justin suddenly remembered something. Glancing up from a pile of paper money, he asked, "Estrella, who's Carlos?"

When Estrella looked up in surprise, he added, "You know ... you mentioned him last night."

"Yes, I had forgotten I said his name." Estrella hesitated, then went on. "Carlos is the leader of my 'family.' It was he who found me on the streets—he made me a part of his band."

Looking up from the board, Jenny asked curiously, "How old were you when you joined this band?"

Estrella dropped her paper money. To Justin's surprise, she answered readily. "I was nine years old the day Carlos found me on the street. I remember very well... I was looking at a magazine I found in a barrel. I was cold and hungry—I had been hungry for so long! To forget my stomach, I was reading out loud the words I knew on the page. Then Carlos spoke to me. He took me to a *panaderia*—a bakery."

Estrella suddenly smiled, her completely charming smile that the twins had seen so seldom. "I remember that I ate so much I was sick! But he was not angry. He spoke to me other days, and one day he took me to meet his band."

She spread her hands out. "And that is all! I have been part of his 'family' ever since. Perhaps someday you will meet them and see how kind they are."

Jenny had lost interest in the Monopoly game. In a rapid-fire series of questions, she demanded, "Where did you go after Carlos took you to meet his band? Do all your 'family' live together? How many are there? Do you go to school?"

When Estrella seemed reluctant to answer, she pleaded, "Come on, Estrella! We've told you all about us. Now we'd like to hear about you!"

When Justin added his persuasion, Estrella continued. "Well, I told you that my 'family'—Carlos—paid that I might better learn my father's language. Carlos took me to a school. I studied English and all the other things children study in school—writing, arithmetic, science. I lived there for a long time—with many other girls who did not have families close by."

"It sounds lonely," Jenny commented.

"I had food to eat and a place to sleep!" Estrella answered. "That is what matters. And Carlos came often to take me to visit the rest of my 'family.' "

Seeing that the twins still looked interested, she went on. "They have a big house. I do not know how many there are—perhaps a dozen, perhaps twenty. They come, they go. They have important things to do. When I grew bigger, Carlos let me do things for them—carry messages sometimes, translate English words, speak to..."

She broke off suddenly, and Justin added curiously, "Well, I guess that *was* pretty nice of them to do all that for you. But aren't you awfully young to be a guerrilla? You're no older than *we* are. Didn't you say there weren't any other children in your 'family'?"

"Yes, I am the only one," Estrella answered proudly. "Children are not allowed in the freedom fighters. But I am *special* ... their—how do you say it in English?—their mascot."

Jenny looked puzzled. "I still don't understand! Steve says there's thousands of kids who live in the streets. What made them pick *you* for their band?"

"Because she speaks English," Justin commented idly as he put away the Monopoly board. He looked up as Estrella's hand froze in mid-air. "I mean, it must be pretty useful!"

Forgetting the scattered pair of dice she was reaching for, Estrella said in a whisper, "It ... it *was* an English magazine! I remember now. Carlos asked me how I knew the words."

She jumped up. "No, it was not because of that! They are kind ... they *care* about me. I am glad to use my English to help them!"

At that moment the door swung open and Mr. Bascom walked in, ending their conversation. The twins scrambled to their feet, eagerly asking if he had any news for them.

Mr. Bascom looked serious as he shook his head. "And I'm afraid the Colombian police haven't been able to get any information out of those two prisoners. If they do know where this bunch is hiding out, they sure aren't telling!"

Mr. Bascom asked if Justin and Jenny had heard from

their parents yet, and when they glumly admitted they hadn't, he left again abruptly. None of the children felt like playing games or talking after that, so they decided on an early bed-time.

On the second morning, Justin looked up from a battered checkerboard as he caught a familiar name. A shot of a steaming, snowcapped peak filled the TV screen. Estrella wasn't there to translate, so he called over to Steve, who was leafing through that day's newspaper. "Hey, Steve, isn't that the mountain we saw spouting steam? The one that erupted and buried that town?"

"The Nevada del Ruiz," Steve confirmed, lowering the paper. "It sounds like it's going to do more than spout steam! They're warning of another eruption any day."

Studying Jenny's red checkers with care, Justin said idly, "I meant to ask you before—how could that mountain do so much damage? I mean, I can see a volcano burning up a town. But you'd think you could just climb out of the way of melting snow!"

"Justin, I don't think you've got the picture. I remember watching that disaster on the news." Steve folded up the paper before continuing. "Just imagine literally hundreds of tons of snow melting from the heat of that eruption. You've got as much water as the Niagara Falls rushing down the mountain canyons, scraping away dirt and boulders and trees ... carrying it all down into the valleys. It's called *lahar*—that mixture of ice, mud, rock, you name it.

"By the time the lahar reached Armero, it was a river of sticky mud and rock forty feet high ... that's taller than most of the buildings. Most people were sound asleep when that mud slide swept over the town. I saw the pictures—you couldn't even see the church steeple!"

"Oh, that's awful!" Jenny shuddered as she absently

moved a checker piece. "What's going to happen this time? Are they going to move all the people?"

"They won't need to evacuate this time," Steve reassured her, listening closely to the rest of the news clip. "They say this will be a fairly small eruption, and the seismologists can tell exactly how the snowcap will melt. The only thing up that way are uninhabited mountain gullies. Hikers are being warned to stay out of the area. The mud will probably catch a few wild animals and lost cattle, but that's all!"

Just then Justin took advantage of Jenny's lack of concentration to jump her last four checkers. Jenny's cries of indignation quickly drove the news story from their thoughts.

Estrella came in a short time later. After a short talk with her about his scribbled notes, Steve left the guest house as soon as the lunch dishes were cleared away. Estrella showed no signs of going out again, but as one of the security guards had decided to spend the afternoon with them in the lounge, the twins were unable to ask her if she had made any progress.

After supper, Jenny and Estrella were alone again in the lounge—Estrella was translating the international news for Jenny—when Justin walked in and tossed a newspaper onto the coffee table. "Hey, look what the guard gave me!"

Jenny and Estrella quickly joined him around the spread-out newspaper. At the top of the front page was the title, *The Miami Herald*, and Jenny instantly forgot the newscast when she recognized a photo halfway down the page. It was one of Uncle Pete, probably dug out of some old company file.

Justin read aloud, "The United States government is presenting strong protests to the Colombian guerrillas over the kidnapping of a prominent American citizen. FARC, the largest guerrilla group, presently negotiating with the Colombian government to become a recognized political party, has denied all involvement in the kidnapping...."

Looking over his shoulder, Estrella interrupted sarcastically, "Your government is always using its power to lean on those less fortunate. What right do they have to make demands here?"

"Don't you think they have a right to protest when someone kidnaps one of their citizens?" Justin answered in surprise.

"And don't say 'your' government," Jenny added hotly. "If you have an American father, then you are an American citizen too!"

Estrella clenched her fists. "Don't you call me that. I want nothing of my father's! I will never be American!"

Brown and blue sparks clashed as the two girls stared at each other. Justin said mildly, "Lay off, Jenny! She's just repeating what someone told her!"

As the two girls lowered their angry eyes, he dropped into an armchair and said, "Estrella, you never did tell us about your father. Do you still remember him? Who was he? Why did he go away?"

Sitting down on the sofa, Estrella answered slowly, "Yes, I remember him. He ... he was a big man with eyes as blue as mine. I ... I used to run to meet him when he came home each night. He would throw me up to the ceiling and laugh. My mother would laugh, too. That is what I remember best— the laughing, the happiness! His name was ... yes, I do remember ... it was Gary Adams."

She pronounced the name with an odd foreign accent. "But I did not call him that. He taught me the American word ... 'Daddy.' He always spoke to me in English and was proud that I learned his language better than my mother. He went away often, but my mother always told me he had gone to his country on business and that he would be back. And he always did come back. Until one day..."

Estrella stared blindly at the blank wall opposite her, her

eyes focused on long-ago memories. "I remember ... I was going to be eight years old. He hugged me when he left. He told me he loved me ... that he would be back soon ... that he would bring me a present for my birthday!"

Estrella sat stiffly on the edge of the sofa, tears trickling down her face. Jenny moved over and put a sympathetic arm around her as she continued, almost in a whisper. "He never came back! He never even sent a letter! We waited and waited!

"My mother spent the money he had left. Then she got sick. If only I could have brought a doctor ... but there was no money even for medicine. It was his fault she died! And then they said I had to leave. I could pay no rent."

She shrugged Jenny's arm away angrily. "I was on the street for months! Do you know what it is like to live on the streets? To have no one who cares if you live or die?"

Justin tried to imagine life without Mom, who would always drop what she was doing when he dashed in from school to ask in her gentle voice about his day. Or without Dad, squealing into the driveway every night in the old station wagon with some crazy new idea for a family outing. He had a sudden mental picture of a forlorn little boy huddled in a drafty cardboard box. He said slowly, "Yeah, we've seen it. It's awful!"

"I'll never forgive him!" Estrella said fiercely, wiping at her cheeks with the back of her hand. "I'll never forgive my father for what he did to my mother ... and to me!"

There was an uncomfortable silence. As Estrella stared down at her clenched fists, Justin suddenly remembered something his Sunday school teacher had said the Sunday before they left Seattle. "I'm really sorry about your father, Estrella. It's been terrible for you."

He added hesitantly, "But you can't keep hating your father for the rest of your life! God says to forgive other people just like He forgave all the bad things *we've* done."

"God!" Estrella replied scornfully as she jumped off the couch. "You two sound just like Doña Rosa! Always talking about God and telling me to forgive my father!"

"Doña Rosa?" the twins chorused together, trying to pronounce the name as Estrella had: *Do-nee-u Ro-su.* "Who's she?" asked Justin.

Then Jenny demanded, "I thought you said you didn't have any friends ... just your 'family'! Who's this Doña Rosa?"

"Doña Rosa is..." Estrella sat down again, looking shamefaced. "Well, you know how I told you about Carlos finding me on the street?"

They nodded, and she went on. "That was true, but not all the truth. One day soon after Carlos found me, I was at the... What do you call it?—the garbage heap... I was looking for something to eat. This lady ... she had brought her garbage... I knew her and she knew me. She had once lived in our neighborhood—she sewed clothes for me and my mother.

"She was so sorry to see me there. She took me to her home. Her husband was kind to me, too. I was there many weeks. They talked like you ... like those words you said in Zipaquirà... I can't remember them all."

Looking at each other, Justin and Jenny repeated, "Be kind and compassionate to one another, forgiving each other, just as in Christ God forgave you."

"Yes, Doña Rosa was like that ... kind and compassionate. She kept telling me I must forgive my father and forget what he had done ... that I would never be happy until I forgave him."

Her expression softened suddenly. "I wonder sometimes what happened to Doña Rosa. She cried when Carlos took me away. She and her husband had no children of their own. They wanted me to stay forever!"

"Why did you leave, then?" Jenny asked, confused. "It sounds like they were nice people!"

"I didn't like her words," Estrella admitted. "I was very angry. Then Carlos found me. The people on the street told him where I had gone. He told me that God was a lie—that Doña Rosa and her husband were foolish.

"One day Doña Rosa had to move ... her husband had a new job. They wanted me to go with them, but Carlos came and told me that he had a place for me ... that with him I could fight against people who would leave children to starve in the street."

Estrella waved an expressive hand. "So I went with him ... and that is all!"

Jenny sniffed. "Well, it seems to me it would have been smarter to stay with this Doña Rosa."

"Yeah, Doña Rosa was right—about forgiving your father, I mean," Justin added.

Estrella jumped up again. "It is easy for you to say this!" she stormed angrily. "If you were me, you would not forgive either!"

She turned and ran from the lounge, leaving the twins looking blankly at each other. After a long moment, Justin shrugged and said, "Well, I guess she really has had it pretty rough!"

"Yeah, I don't know *what* I'd do if Dad just disappeared someday." Jenny frowned. "No wonder she doesn't trust Americans."

Estrella didn't reappear that evening, but Steve showed up briefly before they went to bed. As he read through his usual stack of reports, Justin asked him, "Steve, how would you find someone who's missing?"

When Steve looked up in surprise, Justin explained, "It's Estrella's dad. Do you think you could find out what happened to him?"

"Well, if you know his name, and when he was last in Bogota, I suppose we could do some checking," Steve answered thoughtfully. He looked suddenly interested. "What did you say his name was?"

Steve promised to look through the embassy passport records for any information about a Gary Adams. Estrella was in bed when the twins went upstairs and was nowhere to be found when they got up the next morning. She didn't appear for breakfast, but neither Steve nor Mr. Bascom were there, and the security guard who dished up scrambled eggs and bacon only made a comment about kids sleeping in while soldiers—meaning him!—had to slave for their country.

When Estrella still hadn't appeared by eleven o'clock, Justin began to feel uneasy. She had never been gone this long, and Justin knew Steve or Mr. Bascom would be certain to ask where she was if she didn't show up soon. As though his thoughts had summoned them, Steve and Mr. Bascom chose that moment to walk into the lounge together.

Steve looked frustrated as he continued whatever conversation he had been having with Mr. Bascom. "It just seems like every lead that girl gives us comes to a dead end!"

He stopped short as he caught sight of the twins. "Don't worry, kids! We're sure to find your uncle any time. We're doing all we can!"

But he didn't sound at all convincing, and the twins exchanged a worried look. Jenny made a slight motion with her head, and Justin followed her out of the lounge and back upstairs. Shutting the door to her room behind them, Jenny said with determination, "Justin, don't you think it's strange that every tip Estrella has given Steve has come up a dead end?"

Justin sat down on the bed. "No, I don't! You know Estrella told us people wouldn't talk to Steve."

"Well, Estrella hasn't come up with anything either, has she!" Jenny answered. "I'm beginning to wonder if she's really trying."

Justin walked over to the barred window and stared down at the dusty alley. "Come off it, Jenny! I'm worried about Uncle Pete too. But you can't blame Estrella!"

"I'm not blaming her!" Jenny slid off the bed and joined him at the window. "I'm just asking questions that need answers. Like why, if Estrella has hated Americans for so many years, did she suddenly decide to talk to us at that museum?"

Reading Justin's thoughts before he could answer, she added, "Yes, I know she was sorry for being so rude and wanted to be our friend. But why did she come over to talk to us in the first place? She must have known we were Americans the minute we opened our mouths!

"And there at Simon Bolivar's house! It just seems too much of a coincidence that those guerrillas showed up right after Estrella called us out."

"Jenny, she saved our lives!" Justin answered impatiently. "Why would she do that if she wasn't doing her best to help us?"

"Oh, come on, Justin! That bomb didn't come anywhere near us, and you know it!" Jenny answered scornfully. She looked suddenly exasperated. "What's got into you, Justin? Usually, you'd be the one asking questions—*and* wondering what Estrella's up to!"

Justin shook his head stubbornly. "This is different. I *know* Estrella was telling the truth when she said she wanted to be our friend. I can tell she really cares about us!"

Before Jenny could argue further, the door slammed open. Both Justin and Jenny were startled into silence as Estrella burst into the room, her pale features ablaze with excitement. Justin cast a glance of triumph at his sister as

Estrella announced, "I've found him! At last I have found your uncle!"

Betrayed!

"**E**strella, that's great! Where is he? Is he okay? How did you find out?" Justin and Jenny's questions tumbled over each other. Jenny—her suspicions swept away—was as excited as Justin.

Justin started for the door. "Well, come on you two! We've got to find Steve right away! Once Estrella tells him where Uncle Pete is, Steve can take his men in there to get him out in no time!"

"Just one moment!" Estrella blocked the doorway. "You do not understand. I cannot tell Steve where your uncle is. I do not even know!"

Bewildered, Justin demanded, "But, Estrella, you said you found him!"

"I have learned where he is, but I don't know exactly how to get there," Estrella explained. She added quickly, "But that does not matter. I have a friend who does know. He will help us find your uncle."

Sitting on the edge of Jenny's bed, she told them how an acquaintance had admitted that he had heard rumors of an American hostage. "I told him that your uncle was a friend of mine, and begged him to tell me what he knew. He was frightened and would tell me nothing at first, but at last he told me that he knew the man who takes supplies to the group that holds your uncle. From this man he learned where your uncle is being held."

"Then your *friend* will help Steve and the soldiers rescue Uncle Pete!" Justin said with satisfaction.

"No!" Surprised at her violent response, the twins stared at Estrella. The young guerrilla girl jumped to her feet. "No! Have you forgotten who I am? Never will I deliver freedom fighters into the hands of the soldiers—not even for you! Nor would my friend ever lead soldiers to the camp."

The excitement drained from Justin and Jenny's faces. Jenny demanded angrily, "Why did you bother finding him if you aren't going to tell us where he is? You promised to help us rescue him!"

"But of course I will help you!" Estrella said with a shrug of her slim shoulders. "It is very simple. *I* will take you to your uncle—and no one else!"

The twins stared at Estrella skeptically. Justin found his voice first. "Are you crazy, Estrella? You don't really think three kids can walk into a guerrilla hideout and just grab Uncle Pete, do you?"

Estrella looked very pleased with herself. "I told you this man I know will help. He has everything planned, and he will be armed. There are no more than two guards where your uncle is. It will not be difficult."

"Well, that's great, Estrella!" Justin said, a little doubtfully. "You've certainly been a great friend!"

Estrella stared at Justin, a strange expression flickering in the black-fringed, blue eyes. She looked away. Turning toward the door, she said in a hard voice, "Well, are you coming with me or not?"

This time it was Jenny who blocked the doorway. "Just a minute! Justin was right. This *is* crazy! You haven't even told us where we're going! Is Uncle Pete still in Bogota? How long will we be gone? What do we need to take with us?"

Planting her feet firmly, she crossed her arms. "I'm not moving from here till I get a few answers!"

Seeing Jenny's determined expression, Justin added his support. "Come on, Estrella! We're your friends! You can at least tell us where we're going!"

Estrella looked sulky, but at last shrugged her shoulders. "I guess it does not really matter. You will find out soon enough!"

She pointed at Jenny's jacket, lying in a heap at the foot of her bed. "We are going into the mountains, so you will need that. It is not far—an hour or two past Armero. We will have your uncle back here before dark."

Justin nodded agreement, but Jenny shook her head with a frown. "I don't know. I think we should at least leave a message for Steve—let him know where we're going. What if something goes wrong? He won't have any idea where we are!"

Estrella's pale cheeks were stained red with anger. "No! If you tell Steve anything, I will leave and so will my friend. You will never see your uncle again!"

Justin looked at his sister, his jaw set with determination. "Jenny, we have to go! If we hadn't talked Uncle Pete into going with us that afternoon, he wouldn't be in this fix. You know Steve said they might never find him. If there's even a chance we can get him back, we've got to try!"

There was a long moment of silence, then Jenny nodded. "Yeah, I guess you're right! We don't really have much choice."

"Then let us go!" Estrella said urgently. "We have already wasted much time!"

"Just a minute! I'll get my jacket." Justin dashed next door and picked up his jacket from the chair where he had tossed it. He was pulling it on when he paused. *Jenny's right,* he thought suddenly. *No matter what Estrella says, we can't just run off without telling anyone. Steve would think we'd been kidnapped too.*

Grabbing the newspaper he had brought up the day before, he tore a strip from the broad margin that edged the paper. Pulling out a pencil, he scribbled rapidly, "Steve, Estrella's taking us to Uncle Pete. The mountains—an hour or two past Armero. Don't worry about us. We should have Uncle Pete back by tonight."

He was looking for a place to put the note when he had a sudden thought. Unfolding it, he hastily added a rough sketch of the turtle-shaped car he had seen at Zipaquirà. Folding the note into a tiny rectangle as he hurried into the connecting bathroom, he stuffed it into the frame of the mirror over the sink.

He had just returned to the other room and was pulling on his jacket when Estrella pushed open the door. She looked around the room so suspiciously that Justin was glad he hadn't left the note on the table as he had at first planned. She asked impatiently, "What is taking so long?"

"Just had to use the bathroom! I'm ready to go now," Justin answered hastily, zipping up his jacket and following her into the hall.

The three children walked casually down the wide stairs. There was no one in sight. Estrella led them down a dark passageway toward the back of the house and into an unlocked room piled high with cardboard boxes and barrels.

Half-used buckets of paint stood in one corner, and remnants of rope and other odds-and-ends hung on the walls. Justin grinned to himself as Estrella paused behind a tall stack of boxes to pry out the screen that covered an air vent. So *this* was how Estrella had been getting out of the house!

The tunnel behind the vent screen was too small to permit the passage of an adult. Estrella and Jenny wormed their way through with ease, but Justin had to force his wider shoulders through the narrow space. He was breathing hard by the time he tumbled out behind the girls into a small, dark room. From the clink of cutlery and the odors filtering through the cracks in a wooden door, Justin guessed they were in one of the kitchen storerooms.

Crouching behind a pair of large, galvanized metal cans that—judging by the smell!—held a month's supply of the guest house kitchen's garbage, Estrella pointed toward a faint red light that indicated one of the surveillance cameras high on the ceiling in the opposite corner of the small room. Then she motioned toward a dark, square opening in the floor, sheltered from the view of the moving camera by the garbage cans.

Estrella disappeared feet first into the opening, and Jenny reluctantly followed her. Then Justin swung his feet into the opening and found himself sliding quickly down some sort of metal chute—obviously meant for the kitchen garbage. His shoulders jammed as the chute leveled out at the bottom, and he felt a momentary panic until the two girls tugged him free.

Justin carefully climbed off the pile of black plastic bags of garbage that lay at the foot of the chute. He was standing in a dusty alley that ran along the back of the guest house. The sun was shining, but a cold breeze whistled down the alley, and Justin pulled his jacket close.

"Wow!" he said with admiration as he peered back up the dark garbage chute. "Estrella, how did you learn about this?"

She shrugged. "Buildings are much alike. There are few from which one cannot escape."

She seemed nervous as she urged the twins quickly down the alley. Justin too looked back frequently as Estrella led them through several small side streets, but no one seemed to have discovered their escape. About three blocks from the guest house, Justin suddenly caught sight of a familiar red Volkswagen "peta." Lounging against the side of the car was the young driver he had seen at the Salt Cathedral.

"Hey, I've seen that guy before! He's your friend, isn't he?" Justin exclaimed. Estrella abruptly stopped and demanded, "How would you know about him?"

"I saw him with you at the Salt Cathedral," Justin explained. "I had a feeling he might be the man you were talking about!"

Estrella looked displeased, but she admitted as they reached the red car, "Yes, this is Alejandro. He will take us to your uncle."

She added something in Spanish, and the young man, who looked only half-a-dozen years older than Justin, straightened up. Pulling off a pair of sunglasses, he stared down at Justin and Jenny, his dark features cold and unfriendly. Then he growled something to Estrella and opened the back door of the car.

Pushing the twins toward the open door, Estrella said impatiently, "Come on! He says we must hurry!"

Justin instinctively disliked the young man. Reluctantly, he followed Jenny into the back seat. Estrella climbed into the front seat beside the driver. Ignoring the twins completely, the young man she had called Alejandro slammed on the accelerator, barely missing an oncoming truck as he zoomed onto a main avenue.

Though fast, the young man was not a good driver. He pushed in and out of the heavy traffic with complete disregard of traffic laws. In the front seat, Estrella and the driver were speaking quietly together in Spanish. Justin leaned over to whisper to his sister, "I don't trust this guy! I hope Estrella knows what she's doing!"

Her knuckles white as the car swerved to miss by inches

what seemed a certain collision with a bus, Jenny whispered back, "You were the one who wanted to come!"

Justin had no answer to that. He watched alertly as they left the city behind, and quickly recognized this as the highway Steve had taken to the Salt Cathedral. But they soon turned onto a two-lane paved road that headed directly toward the great mountain range that surrounded the valley of Bogota.

No one spoke as Alejandro slowed through several small towns with whitewashed buildings. There was little traffic, but occasionally Justin heard the drone of an airplane. And once, he glimpsed a helicopter lazily tracing patterns overhead.

He leaned forward suddenly as he caught sight of a familiar-looking snowcapped peak ahead, its heavy, gray-white plume drifting up to lose itself in the bank of clouds that was closing in over the mountains.

"Hey, Jenny, there's that mountain again—the Nevada del Ruiz! Look at all that smoke! Maybe it's about to erupt!"

"It always looks like that," Estrella answered from the front seat in a bored voice.

Justin was about to tell her what they had seen on the news when, with no slackening of speed, Alejandro turned onto a dirt road that wound up into the foothills of the mountain range. All three children clung to their seats as the dirt road grew narrower and bumpier. The cloud cover seemed to drop to the ground, and fog soon blotted out all but the road directly ahead.

The red Volkswagen hit an extra-large bump that crashed Justin and Jenny against the roof of the car, then Alejandro slammed to a stop. Climbing out, he hurried around to the back of the car. Opening the passenger door, Estrella pulled the seat forward and motioned impatiently to the twins. "Come on! We have to walk from here."

They climbed out. The fog pressed in around them, but Justin could see that the dirt road had ended on a ridge of the mountains. They were above the tree-line here, but in the gullies sweeping downward on either side were stunted cypress, tamarack, and junipers.

A strong, icy wind blew through their jackets. Justin took in a deep breath that stung his lungs with cold, then sniffed at the air again. "What's that smell?" he demanded. "It smells like rotten eggs!"

Estrella looked impatient. "I don't smell anything! Come! We have no time to waste."

Alejandro had opened a door of the little car and yanked out a backpack. He lifted the pack to his back, then pulled out a machine gun of the same type the soldiers had carried in the airport.

Jenny gasped as the young man checked the gun for bullets, and slung an extra belt of bullets over one shoulder. "What does he need that for?"

"Yeah, we wouldn't want to shoot anyone!" Justin said with determination.

"And how did you think we would get your uncle out?" Estrella replied scornfully. "Do you think you can just say 'please' to the guards, and they will let your uncle go?"

She added smoothly, "Of course we will not hurt anyone. If the guards see that Alejandro is armed, they will let your uncle go without any shooting."

Alejandro slammed the car door shut, and his sharp words whirled the children around. Estrella translated his order. "We are leaving the car here. We must go that way."

The three children followed Alejandro up the bank where the road ended and along the top of the mountain ridge. There was no path, but they picked their way across the springy, moss-like grass that cloaked the mountain meadow with green. Justin's tennis shoes were soon soaked through, and he could see that Jenny was shivering. Though she wore only a thin windbreaker, Estrella seemed immune to the cold.

Alejandro came to a halt at the edge of a gully. With his machine gun, he pointed out a faint animal trail that led down into a tangle of evergreens. The same wind that bit through their clothing had carved these evergreens into short, twisted forms not much taller than a man.

No one else seemed to notice the odd smell that still caught at the back of Justin's nostrils, and he wondered if he could be imagining it. As the two girls scrambled down the trail ahead of him, he paused to wipe his fog-wet face with a jacket sleeve. He looked with keen interest at the gray-white streak left on his sleeve.

A sudden blow to his back pushed him down the trail. Justin looked up angrily. Alejandro, his dark eyes cold and watchful, pointed his machine gun impatiently down into the gully. Estrella, already at the bottom, called up to him, "Justin, come! We have not much time!"

Justin scrambled down hastily to join his sister and Estrella. As they threaded their way through the evergreen thickets, Justin glanced back at Alejandro, his machine gun cradled easily across his arms as he brought up the rear.

Pushing a soggy branch out of his face, Justin muttered loudly, "I thought he was supposed to be leading us, not taking us prisoner!"

Estrella, at the front of the single-file line, looked back. "He is making sure no one follows us."

Justin was suddenly reminded of the note he had tucked into the bathroom mirror. He wondered if Steve had found it.

The fog had rolled away by the time Alejandro finally brought them to a stop. They had been climbing up and down one gully after another for more than an hour, scrambling over logs, wading across shallow streams, and occasionally breaking into the welcome short grass of a mountain meadow.

Now they were on flat ground—a small mountain plateau choked with underbrush. Here the evergreens grew tall, in the shelter of the mountain ridges that pressed close overhead. The trail they now followed bore the obvious marks of human feet, but they could see only a few feet ahead, and Justin had lost all sense of direction.

Alejandro pushed them into the partial shelter of a tangled thicket, and the twins squatted down to rest while Estrella and Alejandro held a whispered conference. The growling of his stomach reminded Justin that they had missed lunch.

Estrella walked over and squatted down beside them. "The camp is just ahead—down in a canyon. Alejandro and I will check out the camp—to make sure there have been no changes since our last information. You two will stay here out of sight."

Justin protested. "Why should we stay here? Wouldn't it be safer if we all stuck together?"

"You do not know how to move silently as we do," Estrella answered flatly. "You would bring danger to us. If you stay here out of sight, you will be safe enough. We will be back in just a few minutes. If there are still just two guards, we will take you in to get your uncle."

Estrella jumped to her feet as Alejandro snapped out a Spanish order. At the sight of his scowling face and expertly held machine gun, Justin didn't argue. Alejandro and Estrella disappeared without a sound into the underbrush, and Justin admitted to himself that he could never move that quietly.

The twins huddled further into the thicket. The tangled branches of a pair of junipers trailed to the ground around them, but there was room enough to lean upright against their intertwined trunks. Here, the weak rays of a late-afternoon sun couldn't reach their damp clothing, and without the exercise of walking to warm them, both children were soon shivering.

Justin glanced over at his sister. Her dark curls were plastered to her head, and her lips were blue with cold. She frowned. "I hope they come back soon! At this rate we'll never get back before dark!"

In fact, no more than five minutes had passed when they heard a twig crack on the path just outside the thicket. Justin whispered eagerly to his sister, "There they are! Let's go."

But it was neither Estrella nor Alejandro who poked a head into the thicket where they crouched. Justin's mouth fell open as Steve Cardoza squatted down on his haunches and, holding a branch out of his face, said softly, "Hello, kids!"

"Steve! How did you find us so fast?" Justin exclaimed. The enormous relief he felt made him realize how much he had counted on Steve finding his note. Now everything would be all right!

As Steve dropped the branch behind him and joined them in the thicket, Jenny demanded, "How did you find us at all? Estrella's going to be really mad when she sees you here!"

Justin sheepishly told his sister of the note he had left behind. "I was afraid you wouldn't see it!" he told Steve.

"You couldn't have been gone long when I came up to look for you," Steve explained quickly in a low voice. "I searched your rooms up and down once the security guards confirmed you weren't in the building."

He looked approvingly at Justin. "That sketch of the car—that was good thinking. I remembered what you'd told me about Estrella's acquaintance in the red car, and got on the phone right away to a friend over at the Colombian Air Force. I asked him to call out a couple of helicopters to check out every mountain road leading out past Armero for a red Volkswagen *peta*."

Justin suddenly remembered the helicopter he had seen tracing patterns overhead—what seemed like hours ago. Steve went on, "Of course, I knew there was a good chance you might have taken a different vehicle, but it was the only lead we had. And it paid off!"

He grinned. "I was already at Armero when the helicopter radioed that they'd seen your car heading up this way. I found the *peta* abandoned at the end of the road and followed your tracks. None of you took much care to cover them. I'm sure glad to find you here safe and sound."

His grin suddenly disappeared as he leaned forward. In a stern whisper, he demanded, "Now tell me what ever possessed you to go off like this! This is the most stupid stunt I've ever seen! Don't you know better than to let that little guerrilla friend of yours talk you into something like *this*? You could have been killed!"

Both children squirmed under his sharp words, but Justin defended Estrella. "Estrella didn't want anyone to get hurt. She said you'd bring in soldiers and maybe get some of the guerrillas killed—and Uncle Pete, too! She and her friend have it all planned. There are only two guards, and Alejandro can take care of them. They'll be back in just a few minutes, and we can get Uncle Pete out without any shooting!"

Steve shook his head grimly. "It was still stupid! Anyway, we'd better try to get your uncle and get out of here. This is a very dangerous place to be right now."

"What do you mean?" Justin asked curiously.

"I mean that we're too close to the Nevada del Ruiz. Don't you remember they announced yesterday that they were expecting another blowup?"

"But you said it would just be a little one—that the mud

and snow would just go down the mountain canyons!" Jenny protested. Her voice trailed off as she caught her breath.

"That smell! It was *sulfur!*" Justin exclaimed suddenly. He brushed at the faint powdering of gray-white dust that coated his jacket. "This dust must be ash falling!"

"That's right," Steve added grimly. "And that melt-off will be heading this way. These guerrillas obviously don't pay close enough attention to the news."

He turned to leave the thicket. "By the way, Justin, it's unlikely that you'd find only two guards in a guerrilla camp. Which way did you say Estrella and her friend went?"

Crawling out of the thicket behind him, Justin pointed out the direction. In spite of the tongue-lashing, he had to admit that the presence of the tough Marine lieutenant was enough to send his optimism soaring.

Steve said calmly, "I'll take a look. You two stay here and don't move!"

"Oh, please, can't we go along?" Justin protested. "We'll be quiet!"

Steve nodded curtly, his keen eyes expertly scanning for any movement. "Okay! But you step where I step and do what I do—and don't make a sound!"

Jenny, holding a branch back to look out of the thicket, made no move to follow them. When Justin looked back at her in surprise, she said, "I'll wait for Estrella. Someone has to tell her where you are."

They had only moved a few dozen yards through the thick undergrowth, Justin following Steve's footsteps as quietly as he could, when they heard faint voices. Dropping to his stomach, Steve hissed, "Get down!"

He wriggled forward through a tangle of brush, then stopped. Wriggling up beside him, Justin's heart skipped a beat as he saw what had frozen the Marine lieutenant to this spot.

About thirty feet below them was a wide gully—almost a narrow valley—pierced through the center by a rapidly-moving stream. Two crude thatched huts perched on the bank of the creek and, directly below the brush thicket where Steve and Justin crouched, several small Army-style tents had been erected to form a circle with the huts and the canyon wall. At least half-a-dozen men huddled around a bonfire in the center of the circle.

That's a lot more than two guards! Justin thought angrily. *I never did trust that Alejandro! I hope he didn't lead Estrella into a trap!* But it wasn't Alejandro who walked that moment into the smoky light of the fire, laughing and clinging to the arm of a tall, slim man with a commanding stride who carried a machine gun slung over the other shoulder.

"It can't be Estrella!" Justin whispered blankly. "But ... but it is!"

CHAPTER NINE

The Guerrilla Camp

Justin stared in horror at the scene below, trying to persuade himself that Estrella was a prisoner. But just then, the tall commander bent his head to speak to Estrella and her tinkling laugh rang out in response. He shook his head numbly and whispered, "I don't understand! She's our friend! What's she doing down there?"

Steve reached over and grabbed Justin by the wrist. "Don't you get it? That's Estrella's guerrilla band down there—her 'family'! She led you into a trap!"

Turning his head to catch Steve's grim expression, Justin made a discovery. "You aren't surprised! Did you know?"

"I never did trust that girl!" Steve answered bluntly. "I've been checking around her old neighborhood. This morning one of the neighbors told me they'd heard a couple of men from her band were arrested. I was on my way to ask Estrella about it when I found you gone."

Steve began to slither backward. "Your uncle is probably in one of the tents—or one of those huts. Let's go get Jenny. We'll have to go for help and hope they don't move your uncle before we get some soldiers up here."

Justin watched the scene below a moment longer. He shook his head in amazement as Estrella laughingly greeted the other men around the fire. She had seemed so sincere. He could have sworn she desperately wanted their friendship. There had to be an explanation!

"Justin!" At Steve's urgent command, Justin began to wriggle quietly backward. He was out of the brush and about to stand up when he heard a sudden thud and a grunt of pain.

"Steve?" he called quietly.

There was a rustle in the tangled brush beside him. Justin froze as he heard heavy footsteps, then slowly turned his head. He stared at the combat boots planted firmly inches from his nose. They were dusty and scuffed, and very, very real. His eyes rose slowly upward to focus on a rifle held in rock-steady hands.

Justin slowly rolled over and sat up, raising his arms in the air. The rifle didn't waver, and his gaze moved upward to meet a pair of young, black eyes that burned with hatred. He turned his head cautiously. Steve lay on the ground a few feet away, blood streaming down one side of his face from a cut on his head. Standing over him was an older guerrilla, an M-16 machine gun cradled in one arm.

Steve groaned, then slowly sat up. As soon as the two guerrillas saw that he had regained consciousness, they motioned for their two captives to stand up. Aware of the rifle only inches from his stomach, Justin jumped to his feet, carefully keeping his hands in the air.

Shaking the blood from his eyes, Steve didn't move fast enough for their two captors, and the older guerrilla jabbed him in the stomach with the butt of his machine gun. Wiping a hand across his face, Steve swayed to his feet.

Just then Justin heard his sister's angry voice. "Let go, Alejandro! You're hurting my arm!"

A moment later, Alejandro—smiling for the first time since they'd met him—shoved Jenny into their midst. Catching sight of her brother, Jenny exclaimed breathlessly, "Justin, I don't know what's got into Alejandro! Have you seen Estrella?"

Her voice trailed off in a gasp as she caught sight of the two armed guerrillas. "You mean ... Alejandro's one of them? One of the guerrillas?"

She looked around as the two guerrillas, their guns trained on their three captives, spoke in Spanish with Alejandro. "I suppose they got Estrella, too!" Jenny continued.

Justin shook his head wearily and motioned toward the gully. Estrella was now seated on the edge of a roughly-built picnic table beside the fire. Jenny stiffened as Estrella's voice suddenly rang out in a laugh. Sadly she declared, "I knew it! I never did trust her."

Alejandro suddenly barked out an order, and Justin's captor used his rifle butt to push him toward the edge of the cliff. Stepping around the bushes, Justin caught sight of a very steep trail that cut diagonally across the cliff face, down into the gully.

As he started down the path, he saw that the gully widened into an open valley downstream. But about half a mile upstream, it narrowed into a bottleneck canyon that wound up into the hills. Half-slipping down the steep trail wide enough only for one slim person, he caught a faint glimpse of snowy peaks upstream, stained with the red of sunset.

Two women were clearing a pile of dirty metal plates from the picnic table when their captors shoved Steve and the twins into the circle of tattered tents and huts. Everyone in the camp paused to watch their approach, and Estrella hopped down from the table, waving a slim arm.

"Justin! Jenny! You're all right, aren't you?"

She motioned toward the slim, dark man who leaned unmoving against the picnic table. "I told you that you would meet Carlos one day."

Her welcoming smile turned to a scowl as she noticed Steve. "What is *he* doing here?"

The man she had called Carlos didn't even look at the children as he barked out an order, and the two guerrillas who had captured Justin and Steve shoved the Marine lieutenant toward one of the huts. Carlos followed them, leaving Justin and Jenny standing alone with Estrella. Justin quickly scanned the camp, but any thoughts of dashing into the darkness evaporated at the sight of Alejandro lounging against a nearby tree, machine gun cradled and ready.

Confusion fought with anger as Justin turned to the young guerrilla girl and demanded roughly, "Estrella, what's going on? Where's Uncle Pete?"

A shrill bark rang out. A little dog with tangled, dusty-white hair dashed out from behind a tent, and suddenly everything became horribly clear to Justin. "You were the girl with the dog—the one who sent that message to Uncle Pete! You've been in this all along!"

As Estrella leaned down to pick up the dog, Jenny added scornfully, "Yeah, it was no 'accident' when you met us at the Gold Museum, was it? I'll bet you'd been following us the whole time! You were the one who led the guerrillas to capture Uncle Pete. And you pretended to feel so sorry for us!"

Estrella flushed with embarrassment as Jenny looked her up and down with disgust, and Jenny added impatiently, "What I don't understand is, why this silly play-acting? Why didn't you just take us all at once?"

For the first time since her greeting, Estrella spoke up. "They did not want you—only your uncle. But he will not cooperate. Carlos told me to bring you here so that your uncle will do as he is told."

She lifted her chin defiantly. "You don't understand! Your uncle's people took our friends—Eduardo and Paco. Now they are in prison. It is only fair that we should take your uncle. With his help, we can get them out."

"There is a difference!" Justin answered shortly. "Those men were criminals. Mr. Bascom said two men were killed when they tried to bomb the pipeline. The police had every right to put them in jail."

Estrella's eyes flashed. "No! That is not true. They wouldn't kill anyone! Nor will anyone hurt you. All we want is to get Eduardo and Paco out of jail."

Her expression was half-pleading, half-defiant. "Don't you understand? They are my 'family.' I *had* to help get them out!"

Justin said bitterly, "So you pretended to be our friend. And all the time it was just another of Carlos' orders. I suppose all that time you were out 'looking for Uncle Pete,' you were just going out to get orders from Carlos. How could I have been so stupid!"

Justin didn't often lose his temper, but when he did, all his friends knew to get out of his way. The hot anger and hurt that had been building up since he had first seen Estrella in the guerrilla camp tightened into a hard lump in his chest.

Clenching his fists, he exploded, "You are a liar and a cheat, Estrella! We were your friends! We cared about you. And you were pretending and lying to us all the time!"

"But I *am* your friend! I would not hurt you!" Estrella stepped forward just as Alejandro moved to separate the three angry children.

As the young guerrilla shoved the twins toward one of the tents, Justin glared back at Estrella. "I'll never forgive you for this, Estrella! Never!"

The tent Alejandro took them to lay back under a cluster of tamaracks. A guard stood at attention in front. As Alejandro raised the tent flap and shoved the two children inside, Justin and Jenny caught sight of a bound and gagged figure half-sitting, half-lying at the far side of the tent.

"Uncle Pete!" Jenny cried joyfully, almost knocking him over with her exuberant bear hug. "You really *are* here!"

"At least she told the truth about something!" Justin muttered as he quickly knelt behind his uncle. "Come on, Jenny! Help me get him untied."

Jenny yanked off the dirty strip of cloth that had served as a gag, while Justin struggled with the tight knots that bound Uncle Pete's hands behind his back. Uncle Pete didn't look at all pleased to see his niece and nephew. The instant the gag was off, he said gloomily, "So they got you too. I overheard their planning, but I hoped you wouldn't fall for it."

Justin finally loosened the last knot. As the rope fell to the ground, Uncle Pete rubbed his swollen wrists and looked sternly at his niece and nephew. "How could you fall for that girl's story? Didn't you have more sense than to try to rescue me single-handed?"

Both twins looked shamefaced, and Uncle Pete sighed. "Well, it's done now. Okay, tell me what happened."

They had only a few minutes to recount the happenings of the last few days when the tent flap lifted again and a guerrilla motioned to the three to step outside. He too carried a machine gun—obviously the favorite weapon of the guerrillas—and waved it toward the three Parkers as he led them back to the fire.

It was pitch dark now, and the only light was that of the campfire. The whole group of guerrillas had gathered, and Justin counted eight men and three women. All were dressed in mismatched bits of civilian clothing and Colombian army uniforms.

Steve also was there, a rough bandage now covering the gash on the side of his head. His battered face was expressionless, but his eyes were alert. *He'll do something to get us out of here*, Justin thought hopefully. But Steve's hands were tied tightly behind him, and one guard kept a gun trained on his back.

A brisk wind whistled down the canyon, and Justin was suddenly aware of how cold he was in his still-damp clothing. A branch snapped in the fire, and the flames flared up, casting red shadows across the angry face of the tall leader of the guerrilla band.

"Señor Parker, you have been very uncooperative!" he snapped in strongly accented English. "Our comrades have not been released."

Still clutching her dog, Estrella sat on the edge of the picnic table, intently watching as the guerrilla leader waved a threatening arm. "Now we have your family and this American spy. Surely your government will consider the four of you an adequate exchange for release of our comrades."

Uncle Pete looked regretfully down at his niece and nephew, but he shook his head firmly. "Carlos, I have explained this to you before. There is nothing I can do to secure the release of your men. Neither your government nor ours will give in to your demands. Extra hostages won't make any difference at all!"

Estrella was suddenly at Justin's side. She whispered urgently, "You must convince him to let our friends go! Please!"

Carlos looked furious. "Do you think I am a fool? You are an important man, Señor Parker. Your embassy will do what you command. You and your family will not leave here until our demands are met."

Steve took a sudden step forward. "We can't stay here! Like I told you already, we've *all* got to get out of here—and soon!"

He motioned toward the surrounding mountain peaks, now masked by darkness. "The Nevada del Ruiz is due to erupt again soon, and this place will be right in the path. Have you forgotten Armero?"

The events of the last hour had driven the strange odor in the air out of Justin's mind, but he suddenly realized the smell of sulfur had grown stronger. Carlos' sharp features showed uncertainty, then his expression hardened. "I have already told you that this is nonsense. If this were so, we would have heard about it."

"Only a small eruption is expected. If you'd been listening to the news you would have heard about it. It won't reach any towns, and there aren't supposed to be any people in this area. But you're right in the canyon! You should at least move up to high ground."

Steve looked around impatiently at the rest of the small band. "Haven't you seen the smoke rising from the mountain?"

The rest of the guerrillas stared back blankly, unable to understand Steve's words, but Carlos answered curtly, "There is always smoke above the Nevada del Ruiz."

"But is there always ash falling? Look for yourselves!" Steve pulled off his jacket and held it out. The thin film of gray-white ash was clearly seen against the dark-brown leather.

The guerrilla leader ran a finger down his own sleeve, then spit on the ground. "It is nothing but dust blown by the wind—the same dust we have seen since we camped here."

Before Steve could say anything else, he added sharply, "This is but a trick to escape from here, but it will not work! We will wait no longer. Your embassy will be informed tonight of your capture. They have until morning to announce the release of our comrades. If doesn't happen, ... then you will all be very sorry you ever came to this country!"

Carlos snapped an order, and Alejandro and another guerrilla herded the captives back toward the tent. While the other guerrilla stood guard, Alejandro roughly bound their hands and feet. As they left the tent, Justin slumped against the tent wall next to Jenny, his bound hands on his pulled-up knees.

Wearily resting his forehead against the rough ropes, he said in a voice too low to be heard by anyone but Jenny, "This is all my fault! I was so sure Estrella was our friend... If only I hadn't believed her!"

"She fooled the rest of us, too—even Steve!" Jenny whispered back.

That wasn't quite true, but Justin felt better. Jenny really was a great sister, he thought gratefully. She never rubbed it in when a guy was wrong.

His thoughts were interrupted as Steve whispered urgently into the darkness, "Mr. Parker, we've got to get out of here tonight!"

He added, still in a whisper, "Mr. Parker, I wasn't bluffing about the danger. I figure we don't have more than a day before that melt-off comes shooting down this canyon. We've got to get to high ground!"

Uncle Pete was silent, but Jenny whispered, "How can we escape? We're all tied up!"

"Yeah, and what about the guards?" Justin added quietly.

Steve's low voice suddenly carried a note of amusement. "I picked up a few tricks in the Marines. I can be out of these ropes in ten minutes. As for the guards ... well, it's pitch dark. This band is pretty amateur. It wouldn't be hard to evade them. How about it, Mr. Parker? Are you willing to try?"

There was a moment's silence, then Uncle Pete answered slowly, "Lieutenant Cardoza, I think you do have an excellent chance of getting out of here. But we aren't trained soldiers. We can't move as quietly or as quickly as you can. They'll be checking on us, and once they discovered our escape, they'd be after us in a second. We'd just slow you down."

Steve sighed. "I'm aware of that. But I'm willing to risk it if you are."

"No!" Uncle Pete whispered decisively. "Our chances of escape are too small. And if we failed, we'd never get another chance. You'd better go for help. We'll cover for you here."

Steve sounded relieved. "That's probably the best plan. I'll go as soon as the camp is quiet. It'll take me a few hours to get to a main road, but I should have help here by morning."

He broke off abruptly at the sound of voices approaching the tent. The tent flap opened, the distant glimmer of the campfire making only a slight difference in the darkness. A small figure slipped in. Justin heard a thump, and the sound of a striking match—then the red-yellow flicker of a candle lit Estrella's unhappy face.

"Justin! Jenny!" The candle dripped wax and sent long, wavering shadows across the tent floor as Estrella leaned down to pick up the bundle she had dropped. "I knew you would be cold so I brought you some blankets."

Seeing their bound hands and feet, Estrella set down the candle. Shaking out the pile of heavy wool blankets, she carefully draped a blanket around each of the prisoners.

"Thanks a lot, Estrella," Jenny said gratefully as Estrella tucked her blanket close.

Uncle Pete and Steve, on the side of the tent opposite the twins, nodded their thanks. But Justin, snuggling into his own blanket, just said grudgingly, "While you're in here, why don't you do something useful—like untie our hands!"

"No!" Justin wondered if he had imagined the sudden look of fright on Estrella's face. Then she frowned. "No, I cannot let you go!"

"Yeah, I forgot you're one of them!" Justin answered sarcastically. "Why don't you just go away and leave us alone!"

Instead of leaving, Estrella squatted down in front of

Justin and Jenny. "Please, I know you are angry with me. I ... I don't want you to hate me. I want to explain."

Pushing back the long hair that fell over her slim shoulders, she pleaded, "Carlos did tell me to be your friend. And he told me to bring you here. You see, Carlos and my 'family' have done everything for me. How could I say no when they needed my help?"

"Yeah, so you pretended you needed friends—that you really liked us!" Justin interrupted with a growl. "You sure fooled me!"

"But I was not pretending! ... Well, perhaps at first..." Estrella's low voice shook a little. "When I knew you—how you loved each other even when you quarreled, how you were kind to me when I am not even of your country—then it wasn't pretend anymore. I was glad to be your friend. And when I saw how sad you were about your uncle, I was very sorry."

"You call this being a friend?" Justin growled. He lowered his voice as Uncle Pete and Steve looked in their direction. "Carlos is planning to kill us tomorrow if you don't get your men back!"

Estrella looked surprised. "But I told you already that no one will be hurt. Carlos just talks that way to make the police let Eduardo and Paco go. They promised me they would not hurt you if I brought you here. No matter what happens, you and your uncle will be released unharmed."

She added soothingly, "So you see, there is nothing to worry about. Now you will stop being angry and be my friend, will you not?"

Jenny looked doubtful as Estrella stopped speaking, but Justin was furious. Looking hard at the young guerrilla girl, he whispered sarcastically, "Do you really think we're stupid enough to fall for your lies again? Did Carlos send you in here? Does he think we'll tell you our escape plans or something if you're nice to us?"

Estrella's chin went up proudly. Leaning forward, she hissed, "You talk about God and forgiveness—but do you forgive?"

Justin didn't answer, and she jumped to her feet so fast that she bumped her head on the ridge pole of the tent. They had been talking too softly for the adults to overhear, but now Estrella almost shouted, "I should have known better than to be friends with you! *You* are the liars—like all Americans!"

She grabbed the candlestick and turned to storm out of the tent when Steve called out quietly, "Speaking of Americans, I found out what happened to your father."

Estrella froze, then turned around slowly. Justin exclaimed with sudden interest, "So you did check it out! That's great!" He glanced at Estrella, and his excitement turned into a scowl.

"That's right! I checked the embassy records for a Gary Adams traveling from Bogota to the U.S. that year, and then ran his name through the Interpol computer."

Looking up at Estrella, he said gently, "Your father never did leave you, Estrella. He was in a car accident in Miami and was killed instantly. He didn't have any close relatives in the U.S., and I guess the insurance company that settled everything didn't know he had a wife and daughter in Colombia."

"My father didn't leave me?" Estrella looked dazed. Shaking her head, she whispered, "I ... I have hated him for so long! I went with Carlos because I hated him."

"Yes, I know," Steve said gently. "You joined the guerrillas because they were fighting those so-called rich men like your father who would leave a little girl out in the streets to starve."

"And all the time he was... !" Estrella suddenly whirled

around. The candle dropped unnoticed to the floor and went out as she plunged through the tent flap.

Justin was blinking his eyes in the sudden darkness when Jenny spoke up quietly. "Justin, don't you think you were a little hard on Estrella?"

"I don't want to talk about it!" he muttered. Rolling over on his side, he nestled into his blanket. Faint rustlings told him that the others were also trying to get comfortable. Only the occasional twitter of a bird settling down for the night and the chirping of crickets disturbed the sleeping camp.

Justin stared into the darkness. At least his angry thoughts took his mind from the gnawing hunger pains and growing discomfort in his bound arms and legs.

She lied to us! he told himself fiercely.

That was what really hurt. He had trusted Estrella—given her his friendship—and now they were all in great danger because of her. He didn't believe for one minute that those hard-eyed men and women around the campfire had any intention of letting them go as easily as Estrella claimed.

He tried to get to sleep, but somehow Estrella's angry words echoed in his mind, *"You talk about God and forgiveness! You are the liars … the liars … the liars!"*

"Stop moving around!" Jenny said crossly. "I'm trying to sleep!"

Justin lay still and finally dozed off. It seemed only minutes later that he was disturbed by a movement at the end of the tent. A firm hand touched his shoulder.

"I'm leaving now." Justin could hardly hear Steve's whisper. "I've left my blanket humped up in case the guard looks in before morning. I'm sorry I have to leave you tied up, but it's better they think you don't know anything about my escape."

Soundlessly, he dropped to the floor of the tent. Justin sensed rather than heard Steve lift the canvas wall of the tent just enough to thrust his head and shoulders through. He lay flat on his stomach for a long moment. Justin knew that Steve was scanning the area, checking for guards. Then, without a whisper of a noise, Steve was gone.

CHAPTER TEN

Danger in the Canyon

Justin awoke coughing. Lying on his side, his head pillowed on something hard, he wondered for a moment where he was. He shifted position, and a twinge of pain shot up his numb arms and legs. Instantly, the events of the last few days flooded into his mind. He now realized that a sharp rock under the canvas beneath his head was digging into his ear.

He struggled to a sitting position, noticing that the wool blanket had slipped from his shoulders. Although the mountain dawn usually was bitterly cold, the air seemed strangely warm and thick. He breathed in deeply and almost choked as the biting smell of sulfur burned his lungs. Outside, a rooster—probably destined for the big cooking pot Justin had seen the day before—announced the dawn, and the first light began to replace the darkness inside the tent.

Justin had been awakened twice during the night as a guard briefly flashed a powerful flashlight around the tent. The guard had done no more than glance at the humped-up blanket that marked the spot where Steve had been. Cold fear suddenly struck Justin's empty stomach as he realized that Steve hadn't returned yet. The guard would check again any minute now. In full daylight, he would have to notice that one of his prisoners had escaped.

Beside him, Jenny stirred and sat up. She grimaced, cautiously moving her bound arms and legs, then bent over in a sudden coughing fit. At the sound, Uncle Pete too raised his head from where he leaned in a sitting position against the side of the tent. His keen eyes took in his wide-awake nephew and niece.

"Well, kids," he said softly, "it looks like Steve didn't make it back."

"Yeah, and smell the air!" Justin answered. "We've got to get out of here!"

"What are we going to do, Uncle Pete?" Jenny asked anxiously.

Before Uncle Pete could answer, the tent flap lifted. But instead of the guard they expected, Estrella slipped in, a sharp knife in her hand. Justin turned his head away as she knelt to saw at his bonds.

Estrella explained briefly, "You will not need these during the day. I will take you down to the river to wash. Then there will be something to eat."

As the ropes binding Justin's hands and ankles fell to the ground, she turned to Jenny, who smiled at her in her usual friendly fashion. Estrella didn't smile back. She looked as though she hadn't slept. She cut through the first strand of the rope that bound Jenny's ankles. "We must hurry. It looks like a bad storm is coming."

She glanced over Jenny's shoulder at the other end of the tent, and the black-fringed, blue eyes widened in sudden horror. The knife dropped from her hand as she demanded, "Where is Steve? Where did he go?"

Fear pinched her thin features as she grabbed frantically at the heaped-up blanket that had taken Steve's place. "No, he can't be gone!"

Forgetting her errand, she ran from the tent. Justin grabbed at the knife and finished sawing through the half-cut rope, then freed Uncle Pete. Rubbing at swollen hands, Uncle Pete said soberly, "There's going to be trouble, kids. I wish you were out of this, but it's too late now."

He looked steadily at the two of them. "I don't know how much more time we have, but there's one thing we can do right now. Let's pray."

Bowing his head, Justin nodded in agreement as Uncle Pete prayed for Steve's safety, and that he would bring help soon. But he opened his eyes in shock when Uncle Pete added, "Help us to be Your witness to our captors. They too need Your love."

They don't need love, Justin thought bitterly. *They need punishment—especially Estrella!*

Angry shouts arose outside the tent. Lifting his head, Uncle Pete said quickly in a low voice, "No matter what happens, kids, don't forget that God is in control of every situation—even this one!"

Just then, the tent flap was yanked back. The guerrilla who had stood guard all night thrust his head through the opening. His black eyes narrowed with anger as he caught sight of Steve's empty blanket. Shoving his rifle through the flap, he angrily motioned for the three Parkers to step outside.

The dawn was slowly lightening the steel-gray of the sky as they emerged from the tent, but there would be no sun that morning. The air was not so heavy out here, but a sharp smell of sulfur still burned Justin's nostrils if he breathed in too deeply.

Justin thought at first it was fog that shrouded the camp with ghostly white. But as he scuffed a sneaker against the ground, he realized that the ground, the tents, and even the trees were cloaked with a thick layer of gray-white dust.

Ash! he thought grimly. *It's coming down faster!*

The guerrilla leader was over by the picnic table talking to Estrella, the rapid motions of his hands expressing his anger. Estrella looked upset. Breaking off at the sight of the Parkers, Carlos marched over and struck Uncle Pete hard across the face.

"Where is the American spy? How has he escaped?" he demanded angrily.

Rubbing his bruised face, Uncle Pete answered evenly, "I don't know. I was asleep."

The ring of truth in his voice seemed to convince Carlos, and he turned his hot, angry gaze toward the twins. Justin was afraid that the leader would question him, but after a long, searching glance, Carlos turned to the guard who still stood there, his rifle trained on the small group of hostages.

"Imbecile!" he shouted. The guard backed up, fear on his dark face, as Carlos switched to angry Spanish. The young guerrilla was trembling by the time Carlos stopped shouting, and Justin wondered what threat could have frightened him so.

Ignoring the guard, Carlos turned again to Uncle Pete. "You knew of this escape, did you not?"

Uncle Pete faced the guerrilla leader steadily. "Yes, I knew he would try to escape. He knew this place was dangerous and he didn't want to be caught in this canyon when the eruption hit."

Uncle Pete reached out a hand and rubbed it against the tent. His fingers came away coated silvery white. "Can't you see he was telling the truth? You must at least move to high ground!"

Estrella moved to Carlos' side and whispered urgently. The guerrilla leader glanced at the strange gray cast of the sky, then reached out and fingered the ash. "There is often ash in these mountains, but we will move out."

Justin gave a sigh of relief, then froze as Carlos gave him

a cold, dark stare. "Do not think this will help you escape! If the American spy should now make his way back, we will not be here."

Motioning toward his hostages, he snapped at Estrella, "Tell the others to begin packing up at once. Then take care of these."

Estrella was back within seconds. She led the Parkers to a crude outhouse, then down to the river to wash, the guard—a different one this time—staying a few feet behind, machine gun ready. Justin scowled to see Jenny chatting quietly with Estrella as they completed a quick wash without soap or towels. Jenny might be softening toward Estrella, but he, Justin, wasn't about to let the young guerrilla girl fool him again!

The camp was already swarming with activity by the time they walked back from the river. The tents were now flat on the ground, and the guard motioned for Uncle Pete to sit nearby, with his back against a tree near the edge of the river. Perching on a large boulder, the guard cradled his gun across his knees. His black eyes didn't move for an instant from Uncle Pete's face, but when Estrella said something to him in Spanish, he nodded and allowed her to lead the twins over to the campfire.

A sizzling smell of something frying twisted Justin's stomach with hunger. Several of the guerrillas were still eating, huddled close to the warmth of the fire. Justin's mouth watered as Estrella handed him an enamel plate piled high with cakes made of finely-ground corn about the size of pancakes, but much thicker. Each was sliced and stuffed with a fried egg.

"*Arepas*," Estrella said, putting an enamel mug in his other hand. Justin growled a reluctant thanks as he took a sip of the strong, sweet "cafe con leche" (coffee with milk) he had already learned to enjoy. Estrella handed Jenny her food, then hurried away with a plate and mug for Uncle Pete.

Squatting down by the fire, Justin hurriedly chewed one of the thick corn cakes. Biting into her own arepa, Jenny looked across the clearing to watch Estrella carry a bundle of blankets over to a pack mule.

Swallowing, she demanded, "Justin, do you have to be so mean to Estrella? You're hurting her feelings!"

"So what?" Justin growled, stuffing the rest of the arepa into his mouth. "She's done a lot worse than that to us!"

Jenny looked exasperated. "Justin, you are so stubborn! You make up your mind about something, and nothing can change it! Like Estrella—at first, you decided she was our friend, so you wouldn't listen when I warned you about her."

Suddenly hurt, Justin snapped, "I already said I was sorry! I was wrong! She had me fooled. What more do you want?"

To Justin's surprise, Jenny answered thoughtfully, "I don't think you *were* wrong! I think she's telling the truth. She really did want to be our friend—at least after she got to know us. You *felt* that—that's why you were so sure she wouldn't hurt us."

She made a helpless motion with her coffee mug. "You know what I mean! I can't explain it very well. Anyway, the only mistake you made was thinking she couldn't be our friend and still lie to us about Uncle Pete and all this. She really believes these guys aren't going to hurt us—and maybe she's right!"

She leaned forward, waving an arepa right under his nose. "But that isn't the point! The point is, now you've decided that Estrella is a jerk and our worst enemy, so you've made up your mind to hate her for the rest of your life. And you're not going to let anyone change your mind about that, either! Mom always says you're so 'sensible' and 'determined.' Well, I think you're just plain pig-headed!"

Justin set his jaw stubbornly and refused to answer, but

his sister's words had hit home. He knew that holding grudges was one of his worst faults. For the first time, he began to wonder what he would have done if he'd been in Estrella's shoes—and his anger slowly began to ebb away.

Justin felt much better with a stomach full of "arepas" and "cafe con leche." He couldn't quite smile when Estrella collected their dishes, but he didn't scowl, either.

It was beginning to drizzle as the twins walked back to join Uncle Pete, and a strong wind stung Justin's face with what felt like blowing sand. In spite of the drizzle, the still-falling ash was beginning to give the camp the look of a silvery Christmas card. A tiny pebble struck Justin's back as he ducked under the shelter of the trees. Others followed, hitting the ground like a shower of tiny hailstones.

"It won't be long now!" Uncle Pete commented as Justin and Jenny squatted beside him. His expression was as calm as ever, but Justin knew he was worried as he looked up at the canyon and murmured, "Where could Steve be?"

Carlos shouted angrily, and the guerrillas began to work faster. The tents had been rolled into bundles, and two of the guerrillas were leading pack mules up the steep path to the top of the gully when a shout caught Justin's attention. It was Alejandro, and Justin suddenly realized that he hadn't seen the young guerrilla at all that morning.

Alejandro jumped out of the way of a pack mule and ran into camp. Carlos strode over, asking a sharp question in Spanish. Alejandro shook his head and poured out an answering flood of words. Justin caught his breath at the look on Carlos' face as he snapped a sharp response, then marched over to the three hostages.

Uncle Pete rose to his feet as Carlos announced coldly, "Your embassy has not done as we demanded. Our men have not been released. Now we are out of time. If the

American spy finds his way back, this place will be filled soon with soldiers."

He looked at Uncle Pete thoughtfully. "Do you truly think that your people will not give in to our request? Even if you write and demand it?"

Uncle Pete's gaze was steady as he answered firmly, "My embassy will not give in to terrorist demands, no matter how long you wait. And I wouldn't want them to give in to threats for my sake."

The guerrilla leader turned somber eyes on the twins. "And what about your family? Would you risk their lives just to keep two of my men in jail?"

Uncle Pete sighed heavily as he too glanced down at the listening children. "You know I would do anything to protect Justin and Jenny. But it doesn't make any difference. Even if I could persuade my embassy to deal with you, your own government would refuse to release the prisoners. Why don't you just let us go and be done with it all!"

Carlos didn't answer. Justin held his breath as the guerrilla leader stared at them for a long moment. Then, shrugging his shoulders as though he had made a decision, he walked away and shouted an order.

The last of the guerrillas, backpacks over their shoulders, began to move up the narrow trail to the top of the gully. Within moments, the campsite was abandoned, except for the Parkers and their guard. The shower of stones and ash was growing heavier, and Justin and Jenny followed Uncle Pete further into the shelter of the cluster of trees.

Carlos walked over, his own machine gun slung across his back and a pistol in a holster at his side. Alejandro came behind him, carrying a coil of nylon rope. He motioned to their guard, and he too headed toward the cliff.

Justin jumped to his feet, relieved that they were at last moving out. When Alejandro began roping his hands together in front of him, he wasn't surprised. The guerrillas were obviously making sure that they wouldn't escape along the way. Alejandro moved along to Jenny and Uncle Pete, quickly looping the same rope around their wrists and pulling it tightly.

Carlos stopped in front of Uncle Pete. "I thought you would wish to know that the American spy was right. We have just heard on the radio that the volcano is again melting the snow on the Nevada del Ruiz. They were careful to announce that no towns or haciendas are in danger."

He gave a sign to Alejandro. Then, to Justin's shock, Alejandro looped the remainder of the long rope around a low limb of the tree. He yanked it so hard that their hands were pulled overhead.

"What are you doing?" Uncle Pete demanded sternly. "If you've heard that the snow is melting, then you know there will be floods through these canyons. Tie us up and leave us at the top of the gully if you aren't taking us with you. But don't leave us here!"

Carlos just turned and walked away. Alejandro gave them a nasty grin and made a taunting remark in Spanish, then began knotting the rope tightly to the branch. Realizing with horror just what Carlos had in mind, Justin kicked Alejandro sharply in the shins. Alejandro kicked back, knocking Justin's feet out from under him. The ropes cut deeply into his wrists as he struggled to regain his footing. Alejandro tied a final knot, then walked away.

Justin glanced up at the cliff face. Estrella was halfway up, a heavy bundle on her back. He shouted bitterly, "So your friends won't hurt anyone, Estrella? So much for your promises!"

Justin's shout brought Estrella to a halt. Even at that distance, he could see the horror on her face as she took in the situation. A moment later, she had dropped her bundle and was flying down the path. Carlos had stooped to pick up a last small bundle of personal items. Estrella rushed at him, screaming, "What are you doing? You cannot leave them here!"

Carlos only paused to swing his pack to his shoulders as he answered loud enough for the Parkers to hear clearly, "Why should we leave witnesses?"

"But you promised not to hurt them!" Estrella pounded him on the chest with her small fists as she shouted, "You cannot leave them here! They will die!"

The guerrilla leader grabbed her wrists, raising his voice. "Do not be stupid! The government will not exchange our men even for three of them. They are no good to us now. They would just slow us down."

Estrella broke away. She flew at the knots, trying to untie them as she cried, "They did promise not to hurt you! They did! Please believe me! I did not know they would do this! Please forgive me!"

As Carlos pulled her away, Jenny answered softly, "We do believe you, Estrella. Don't worry. We'll be all right! Maybe the eruption won't even come here."

Uncle Pete said quietly, "You'd better go, Estrella. Your friends are waiting for you."

"No, I won't go! Not until Carlos lets you go!"

Carlos grabbed Estrella by the arm. "You will do as you are told! You, at least, are still of some use to us!"

He lapsed into Spanish as he forced her across the clearing. Estrella looked back pleadingly, and Justin suddenly knew that he had something to do before it was too late.

"Estrella!" he called. Estrella stopped in spite of Carlos' scowl and iron grip, and Justin added, "I'm sorry I was so mad at you, Estrella. I *do* forgive you!"

Estrella didn't answer. She stood for a moment with her head bowed, and Justin realized with shock that she was crying. With a Spanish curse, Carlos pulled her away. She didn't look back again as he pushed her up the trail. Moments later, the path and the cliff top above were empty, and the Parkers were alone.

"Okay, kids," Uncle Pete said. "Let's figure out a way to get out of this mess."

Fifteen minutes later, Justin admitted to himself that there might not be a way out. They had tried to loosen the rope, but Alejandro had tied the knots too well, and the branch over which he had hung the rope was well out of reach of even Uncle Pete's outstretched arms. Uncle Pete encouraged the two children, even making jokes as they stumbled over each other in an attempt to free their upstretched hands, but Justin saw that the cheerful smile that split the red-gold beard didn't reach his somber eyes.

Justin couldn't see his watch, but he guessed that it was about mid-morning. The shower of rocks had slowly dwindled away, and even the ash-fall was lessening. The sky grew a shade less gray. Relaxing a moment against his burning wrists, Justin caught the faint roar of a distant waterfall. His spirits began to lift.

"Maybe the eruption is over," he declared with relief. "Nothing has happened after all. Maybe we can just wait for Steve to show up. He should be here any minute." He didn't let himself even wonder if something might have happened to Steve.

Uncle Pete shook his head. "It isn't the volcano we have to worry about—it's the runoff. Whether the eruption is over or not, that water and mud will still be heading down these canyons."

He looked down. "See if you can find something we can use to cut us loose."

As Justin scanned the ground at his feet, Jenny cried triumphantly, "Look! There's a broken pop bottle!"

The shard of glass lay against the side of the tree trunk. Jenny was closest. "Try to kick it over here!" Uncle Pete said urgently.

But Jenny couldn't quite reach it. "Just a minute! I'll take my shoes off." In seconds, she had kicked off one sneaker and wriggled out of a sock.

"You'll cut yourself," Justin protested as Jenny tried to grab the broken bottle between two toes.

"I don't think that really matters right now," she panted. Finally successful, Jenny began pulling the piece of broken bottle slowly toward her.

Justin's eyes were glued on the shard of glass slowly moving toward them, when he suddenly realized that the waterfall sound he had heard earlier had grown much louder and seemed to be closer. Justin raised his head. He stared upstream in disbelief, and a desperate fear wrapped around his lungs.

Still far up the gully, its gray-brown mass squeezed almost to the top of the sheer cliff tops by the narrow stone sides of the canyon, was a solid, moving wall of rock and mud. Justin watched in helpless horror as the "lahar" spawned by the Nevada del Ruiz swept relentlessly down toward the camp.

CHAPTER ELEVEN

Unexpected Help

The far-off mass of mud and ice was still hardly visible against the dirt-brown color of the canyon walls. It seemed to move so slowly that Justin wondered momentarily if he was mistaken. He glanced over at his sister, who had just managed to grab the piece of broken bottle between both feet. When he looked back up, he was shocked to see how much the wall of mud had grown in just that split-second of time.

A gasp beside him as Jenny dropped the piece of glass told Justin that she too had noticed the swelling wave of mud. Panicking, Justin yanked hopelessly at the ropes that stretched his arms upward, ignoring the sharp pain as the twisted strands cut into his wrists. He heard the frightened sobs of his sister, but there was no time for words.

The rush of a waterfall rose to the rumble of a mountain-sized cement mixer as the churning mass of boulders and mud grew with every breath. Justin caught sight of the massive roots of an uprooted evergreen giant tossed onto the crest of the wave like a broken twig.

He sagged against the ropes, not bothering to struggle further. He was past feeling any fear. He spared a brief thought for his parents—they would be so sad when they heard the news. Then he bowed his head and whispered quietly, "Dear God, I guess it'd take a miracle to get us out of this one!"

Then it happened—so suddenly he was sure he had imagined it. A soft voice spoke in his ear, "Come! We must leave here!"

He lifted his head to see Estrella standing on tiptoes in front of him. Her face was tense with fear, but she was already reaching up to saw at the ropes that twisted around his wrists.

"Estrella!" he cried, his shout jerking Uncle Pete and Jenny around. "You came back!"

Estrella didn't stop sawing for a second, but she gasped, "I could not leave you here. I ran away from the others."

The knife she held was an old—and dull—kitchen knife. She had sawed only part way through the knotted strands, and sweat already beaded on her forehead. Justin glanced at the approaching wave of "lahar." It was much closer now, and no longer looked solid. His sharp eyes could pick out the boulders, branches, even dead animals that dotted the heaving, slick surface of the mud.

"Estrella!" he cried urgently. "It's too late! Save yourself!"

"No!" Estrella cried, sawing harder. "I will not leave you again!"

"Then just cut this rope up here!" Uncle Pete shouted over the churning rumble of the advancing mud. He motioned with his head toward the single strand that stretched their arms up toward the branch just above his hands. "If you cut this, the rest of the ropes will fall off."

Estrella rushed to Uncle Pete's side, but the rope was well over her head and out of reach. In an instant, she managed to roll a small boulder up beside him. Perching on it, she began to saw frantically, still straining to reach the rope. The towering, gray-brown wall had now reached a thick belt of cypress and tamarack trees that lined the riverbed only half a mile upstream. Justin held his breath as they were broken off and smashed under the relentless movement of the lahar. Within seconds they were gone, and thousands of tons of mud, ice, and debris pushed through the bottleneck of the narrow canyon into the wider valley which spread on down the mountainside.

It was this that gave them hope. The mad rush of the oncoming river of mud slowed a little as it spread out to fill every nook and cranny of the now broader gully. And at that moment, Estrella's knife broke through the rope. The strands that had been so tight instantly loosened, and the Parkers quickly shook off the ropes.

"Come on!" Estrella cried, her voice tight with fear. She began sprinting toward the cliff, the others close behind. Jenny paused long enough to snatch up shoes and socks, but her long legs shot her past both Justin and Estrella.

Running faster than he ever had in his life, Justin glanced upstream. The wave of lahar had dropped in height as it spread out sideways into the valley and spilled over the lower far bank of the gully. But it was now so close that it loomed high over the small, running figures, blotting out the skyline. Justin reached the bottom of the cliff right behind his uncle and Jenny. Estrella, still out of breath from her run to save them, had fallen slightly behind.

The path which they had been herded down the day before was nothing more than a narrow trail carved out of the cliff face by generations of wild animals. Steep enough that climbers occasionally had to use hands to pull themselves up, it was hardly wide enough for one person. Uncle Pete was already climbing rapidly, his powerful hand yanking Jenny up behind him.

The river of mud was still dropping in height. It was now

a race to see if they could climb far enough up the path to escape the reach of the thundering wave as it swept past.

Justin scrambled faster. He kicked his foot loose from a tangled root system that, washed free by mountain rains, was spread out across the path. He grabbed at a clump of grass as he lost his balance. He sure didn't remember this trail having so many obstacles on the way down! Uncle Pete and Jenny were now yards above him.

A sudden scream rose above the deafening roar of the oncoming torrent. Justin glanced backward. Right behind him, Estrella lay flat on her stomach, her foot caught in the root system that had just tripped him. He saw her tug frantically at the root that trapped her, sobbing with fear, but she couldn't pull free. He hesitated only a split second.

"No!" Estrella cried as she saw him turn back "Don't stop!"

The lahar had almost reached them, and the heaving, churning gray-brown mass still reared yards above their heads. Already Justin felt the moisture that splashed ahead of the wave. There was no time to think.

Reaching down, Justin tugged at the root with all the force he could manage, allowing Estrella to pull her foot free. Then, with a single motion, he pulled the still-sobbing girl to her feet and pushed her ahead of him up the trail.

There was only time to take three steps. They had almost made it. It was the very crest of the wave that Justin saw sweeping over them. He gave Estrella a powerful shove up the path, then grabbed for an overhanging branch. He managed to gulp a lung-full of air, then the lahar passed over his head.

It was much colder than Justin had imagined. He had forgotten that the river of mud fed from the melted snow and ice of the Andean glaciers. He was so cold that he hardly felt the branches, rocks, and other debris that battered his body.

Holding his breath and keeping his eyes squeezed shut, he clung to the branch with all his strength, fighting the relentless pressure that tried to pull him downstream.

Long seconds passed before the level of the lahar dropped enough that he could pull his head out of the mud. Shaking his head hard to clear the mud from his eyes, he glimpsed Estrella just beyond him, clinging to an overhanging tree as the mud flow washed her up to the waist.

He had just raised his head to search for his sister and uncle when he felt a movement under his hands. A heavy branch had slammed into the stunted juniper he clung to, tearing it away from the cliff side. Before he could grab for another hold, Justin was swept out into the icy, sticky, racing river of lahar.

Justin's eyes were still filmed over with mud, but he caught a brief, misty glimpse of three figures on the part of the path that was still visible. At least the other three had made it! The screams of the two girls rose above the roaring in his ears as he was carried helplessly down the valley.

Justin kicked to stay afloat, struggling wildly to keep his head out of the mud. Something nudged at his legs, then he caught sight of a branching set of antlers as a dead dear swept by him.

He no longer felt so cold. In fact, he didn't really feel *anything* anymore—not even his arms and legs. The mud oozed up over his mouth. His head felt as heavy as lead, and it seemed it would be so easy just to let himself slip down into the mud. He was so tired!

He hardly felt the bump. Lifting his head with an effort, he saw a log as long as his body floating beside him. Moving along at the same speed as he was, it seemed to be lying still. The broken branches that still extended from the log kept it from rolling. Bunching up numb, exhausted muscles, Justin grabbed for the log just as a sudden wave crashed over his head.

The wave receded, leaving Justin choking. Blinking the mud once more from his eyes, Justin gratefully draped his arms across a couple of branches and rested his weary head against the log. As long as he could hold on, he still had a chance of getting out of this.

A jolt brought his head up. The log had bumped into something large and bulky. Under the coat of sticky gray-brown, Justin made out faint black and white markings, then a long head. It was a Holstein cow that probably had wandered away from some highland farm and was taking a drink at the river's edge when the lahar struck.

Justin thought it too was dead until a low moo protested helplessly. He caught a glimpse of pleading, large brown eyes, then a sudden undertow pulled the cow below the surface of the mud. Justin held tightly to the log, fighting the pull of the undertow. The next time he looked up, the cow was gone.

As the mud flow spread down into the widening gully, the cliff top dropped until now it was no more than a high bank running along one edge of the valley. The other side of the valley now stretched out flat into a heavily forested plateau. As the lahar spread out across the plateau, the river slowed even further.

There seemed to be currents in the mud flow, because the log Justin clung to had begun to drift toward the high bank. Justin heard a shout and eased his head to one side. Three distant figures were racing along the edge of the gully.

He heard a deep call. "Justin! Are you all right?"

Justin raised a leaden arm in answer to the call, and heard a glad shout in response. He could now make out his uncle running along the edge. With new strength, he tried to kick himself closer to the shore. There were branches and trees growing there, and he might still be able to pull himself out.

But just at that moment a new force grabbed at him with an iron grip. He felt himself being carried away from the bank as some undercurrent swung him around in a vast circle. He clung desperately to the log as it whirled around, faster and faster.

A whirlpool! he thought faintly. *I'll never get out of this!*

He had just enough time to take a deep breath before the whirlpool sucked him under the heaving, rolling surface. Clutching frantically at the broken branches of the log, he felt himself pulled down, down. He couldn't even kick against the immense weight of the icy mud that pressed him from all sides.

He couldn't feel whether his numb fingers still clung to the log. He was desperately fighting the urge to breathe when a blinding pain struck across the side of his head. A burst of fireworks exploded somewhere behind his eyelids, then everything went black.

CHAPTER TWELVE

Rescued
or...?

From far away down a long, dark tunnel, Justin heard the murmur of voices. He knew something had happened, but he couldn't remember what. He knew he should get up … find the voices … but he was too tired to move.

The voices came nearer. This time he caught the words.

"Will he be all right, Uncle Pete?" It was the tearful voice of his sister. "He's so cold!"

"He's breathing, anyway," answered Uncle Pete heavily. Justin could hear the worry underlying the steady voice. "He needs blankets and a warm bed."

He tried to open his eyes, to tell them he was fine, but his tongue felt heavy and his eyes were glued shut. He felt something wet against his face. The weight lifted from his eyes, and he opened them slowly.

A somewhat-blurry Estrella bent over him, holding a handkerchief that still dripped muddy water. As his vision slowly focused, she leaned closer. Seeing his open eyes, she cried out joyfully, "He is awake!"

Uncle Pete's face swam into view. His hazel eyes were

full of concern, but the red-brown beard smiled as he asked calmly, "Justin, are you all right?"

Justin attempted a nod, but a sharp pain shot through his head as he moved, and he shut his eyes again. He tried to speak, but he couldn't seem to pry his mouth open. He felt Estrella's handkerchief again and realized it was mud that choked him.

"Don't try to get up!" Uncle Pete ordered firmly. Justin felt his uncle's big hands moving expertly over his arms and legs. He winced as Uncle Pete touched a sore spot on the side of his head.

"Doesn't look like anything is broken," Uncle Pete said at last in a relieved voice. "He'll have a good collection of scrapes and bruises, and he's got a nasty bump on the side of his head. He must have banged it against something."

Justin opened his eyes again. This time, everything stayed in focus. He turned his head slowly. He was lying on a grassy bank. The numbness was leaving his body, and he began to shiver violently.

Uncle Pete moved to tuck a jacket closer around him. Looking up, he saw that neither Uncle Pete nor the girls wore their jackets. Uncle Pete was without a shirt as well. Cautiously turning his head again, he saw his own mud-soaked jeans, shirt, and jacket stretched over a branch. Uncle Pete's mud-streaked, once-white shirt was tossed over a bush. He had obviously used it to towel Justin dry.

Estrella knelt beside Justin, her face tear-streaked. "You should not have come back for me! You could have been killed!"

The drying mud crackled on Justin's cheeks as he grinned weakly. "Look who's talking!"

A thin, smoky haze still hid the sun, but it was no longer cold. Gradually, Justin stopped shivering and began to feel warm under the blanket of jackets. He tried to sit up, and this time Uncle Pete didn't stop him. Uncle Pete helped him prop himself against a tree trunk, and he sat quietly until the world stopped turning circles around him.

He looked out over the bank. A gray-brown lake now filled the entire valley as far as he could see. He suddenly remembered the whirlpool pulling him down into darkness. "What happened?" he asked faintly, one hand on his still-aching head. "How ... how did I get here?"

Uncle Pete picked up the jacket that had tumbled from his shoulders, and tucked it back around him. "Well, as soon as you were swept away, we got up to the top of the cliff and started running downstream. We finally saw you holding onto that log. When you waved, we knew you were alive. Then, when your log started swinging toward the bank, I climbed down, hoping to cut you off."

His expression was suddenly bleak. "I almost had you, but you swung away again and then ... you just disappeared! We thought you were gone."

"It was a whirlpool," Justin murmured, suddenly shivering again. "But how did I get out?"

"You were under for quite some time," Uncle Pete continued. "At least it seemed like it. Then, all of a sudden you popped up again—still holding on to that log. The whirlpool must have tossed you to the surface. We couldn't tell if you were alive or not. You swung around in a wide circle. On the second time around, you came close enough for me to grab you."

Justin suddenly noticed that Uncle Pete too was covered with the gray, slimy mud from the waist down. "You were unconscious, but I managed to grab you before you were dragged away again. The current was so strong, I was afraid both of us would be swept downstream. But Jenny and Estrella here helped me get you up on the bank."

Jenny dropped down onto the grass beside her brother. She too was tear-streaked, but she was grinning as she gave him a hard hug. "You sure scared us, Justin. I can't believe we're all alive! And we've got Uncle Pete back, too!"

Uncle Pete's calm voice broke into her jubilation. "God certainly had His mighty hand around us today, kids! Let's stop and thank Him now."

The sudden snap of a breaking branch brought Justin's bowed head up with a jerk. His heart sank as three armed men quickly surrounded the little group under the tree.

CHAPTER THIRTEEN

Homeward Bound

Unlike the band of guerrillas that had held them hostage, these men were neatly dressed in complete camouflage uniforms. But their machine guns looked as well-kept as those of the guerrillas, and they obviously knew how to use them.

Their dark eyes were cold and watchful as Uncle Pete and the girls slowly rose to their feet, their arms in the air. Justin, covered up by three jackets but dressed only in his boxer shorts, decided to stay where he was.

One of the men barked a question in Spanish, and Justin saw that Estrella looked both angry and afraid as she reluctantly answered. *Here we go again!* he thought wearily.

But just at that moment an impatient, familiar voice snapped an order in Spanish, and the three soldiers' cold frowns turned to smiles. Justin dropped his arms with a sigh of relief as Marine Lieutenant Steve Cardoza, looking as tough and competent as ever, stepped into the clearing.

"Steve!" Jenny was already running toward the broad-shouldered Marine. Glancing sharply around the group, Steve looked relieved to see that they were all there. He eyed Estrella with surprise, but made no comment.

Jenny threw her arms around him with her usual enthusiasm. "We thought something had happened to you!"

Uncle Pete too stepped forward, drying mud crinkling on his bare chest and pants as he said, "Glad to see you made it through safely."

"And am I ever glad to see *you* all made it!" Steve said with a grin as he rumpled Jenny's hair. A small bandage ran across one side of his forehead where the guerrilla had struck him, but he was looking very fit again, and not at all as though he had hiked most of the night.

His expression was suddenly serious as he turned to stare out over the steep bank. "At first, I thought we were too late!"

"What *took* you so long?" Jenny demanded. "You should have been back *hours* ago!"

Steve dropped to the grass beside Justin and asked, "Are you okay, kid?"

When Justin nodded, he turned back to Jenny. "Well, it wasn't as easy to get help as I'd hoped. It took me several hours to find my way out to the main road in the dark. I finally located my jeep and started for Bogota. I stopped in the nearest village and managed to wake up a store owner long enough to use his telephone. I called Mr. Bascom and asked him to get the chief of police out of bed."

He looked disgusted as he continued, "The chief of police wasn't very happy about being yanked out of bed in the middle of the night. It was dawn by the time I got to Bogota, and the men I'd asked for still hadn't shown up."

He motioned to the soldiers, who now stood at ease, looking friendly and pleased. "I finally managed to get together a troop from the Colombian army and started back here, but when I reached the campsite and saw..."

He looked grim for a moment, then cleared his throat. "Well, for a moment, I didn't think I'd need any of them.

Then I saw the tracks leading into the woods and realized that the guerrillas, at least, had escaped. I sent most of my men after them, hoping they'd taken you with them.

"I sent this party to check downstream. Then I saw fresh footprints running down this way along the cliff top—two sets of them fairly small."

He grinned at the two girls. "I figured that at least you two must be alive, so I headed down this way as fast as I could. And of course, you know the rest." After a pause, he added, "Okay, now tell me *your* story."

The three children let Uncle Pete explain what had happened since Steve escaped. Steve looked with respect at Estrella as Uncle Pete told of how she had rescued them. When Uncle Pete finished, Steve stood up.

"Well, now that we have you all safe and sound, let's get back to town. I imagine you could all use a good meal and some warm clothes, and some of you could sure use a bath!" He smiled at Justin and Uncle Pete.

Estrella and Jenny politely turned away as Justin stood up and awkwardly pulled on his mud-encrusted jeans and tennis shoes. He was stiff and sore all over and very thirsty, but the scenery no longer whirled around him when he moved. The mud that still caked his hair and face crackled with every movement, and large pieces of dry mud flaked off his jeans.

As the two girls turned around, Jenny giggled. Justin scowled at her. "What's so funny?"

Jenny's gold-brown eyes danced. "You should see yourself, Justin!" She broke into giggles. "You look like ... like the Abominable Mudman!"

The sudden relief from the tension of the last two days was too much. Estrella started giggling, too, and Jenny was now holding her sides with helpless laughter. Uncle Pete's hearty "Ha, ha!" rang out from behind Justin, and even Steve and the soldiers were grinning broadly.

Justin looked down at the heavy, gray crust that covered even where Uncle Pete had tried to wipe him dry. He *did* look funny, he thought. The girl's giggles were contagious, and the dried mud crinkled around his mouth as he broke into a grin.

Steve interrupted the relieved laughter. "If you can walk, Justin, let's get started. It's a long walk back to the road, even if we cut across from here."

Justin cautiously took a few steps, wincing as his bruised body protested. He was sore, but he could walk. As he followed Steve away from the bank, Justin turned for one last look.

There was no sign now of the bubbling stream, nor of the evergreen forest that had carpeted the mountain valley an hour ago. A tranquil, gray-brown lake now stretched from bank to bank. Only the drift of an occasional piece of debris, and the whistling pop of an enormous air bubble coming to the surface, showed that the "lahar" was still settling.

They took the hike back to the road very slowly. Once there, Steve left the three soldiers with the army transport truck, to wait for the rest of the soldiers. It was late afternoon before Justin joined the others in the lounge of the embassy guest house. A long, hot shower had washed away much of the stiffness, and with a very large meal under his belt, he felt much better.

The twins had just attempted another call to their parents when Steve walked in. To Justin's disappointment, there was still no answer at his home—not even the answering machine. His parents should be back from their camping trip by now!

Steve sat down and stretched out his legs. He too looked refreshed, his hair still wet from a recent shower. "That troop of soldiers just reported in. There's no sign of the guerrillas—they got completely away!"

"Good!" Estrella suddenly spoke up. Steve looked at her in surprise, and she said simply, "Well, they *were* kind to me. They were the only family I had."

Walking over to stare out the window, she added sadly, "Even if it *was* only because I could be of use to them."

"Well, I don't think it will make much difference," Uncle Pete put in. "With all our American families pulled out of the country and security tripled at the office, I don't think they'll bother Triton again."

He shook his head. "I'm afraid it may be a long time before we'll be sending married engineers and families back to Colombia. Perhaps one day there will be a true peace with the guerrillas."

"Well, it's all over for you three, anyway," Steve commented. "You are free to fly home anytime."

Jenny, curled up on the sofa beside Uncle Pete, looked over at Estrella, who still stood at the window. The long, shining curtain of hair hid her expression, but the slim shoulders drooped.

Jenny asked softly, "What about Estrella? What's going to happen to her?"

"Yeah, they can't put her in prison like those other guerrillas, can they?" Justin added anxiously. "She saved our lives!"

"No, of course they won't put her in prison," Steve assured them "For one thing, she is only a child. And as you said, she is responsible for freeing the three of you."

"But where will she live?" Jenny asked. "Her 'family' is gone."

"I think I may have a solution to that," Uncle Pete said. "I've got a missionary friend here in Bogota…"

Justin grinned at his sister. He was beginning to think

Uncle Pete had friends tucked away in every corner of the world.

"I called him," Uncle Pete continued, "and he thinks he may know of a home for her."

The sharp *ding-dong!* of the front doorbell rang through the building. Uncle Pete stood up. "That may be him now."

He hurried out of the room, and Steve went with him to unlock the door. The twins walked over to join Estrella at the window. Like all windows they had seen in Colombia, this one was heavily barred. The window looked down onto the street that ran in front of the guest house. Through the slats of the venetian blinds, they could see a car pulled up at the front steps.

Estrella turned from the window, and the three children looked shyly at each other. So much had happened since the last time they had sat there that they didn't know what to say.

Justin broke the silence. "We haven't thanked you for saving our lives, Estrella. I was wrong about you. You really were our friend all the time. You could have been killed coming back for us like that."

"I had to do it," Estrella answered simply. "It was my fault that you were in danger."

Looking at Justin, she added, "You were right about Carlos. He never did really care about me. None of them did! They just thought I'd be useful to them."

Her head drooped. "At least they gave me schooling and a place to sleep. I don't know what I will do now."

Justin and Jenny were saved from answering by their uncle's booming call. "Kids, come on down here! I've got some folks here for you to meet."

The twins started for the door. Estrella hung back until Jenny grabbed her by the hand and pulled her after them. "Come on, Estrella! He means you, too!"

Justin and Jenny hurried down the wide staircase,

Estrella following reluctantly behind. Justin heard his uncle's deep voice above a chatter of voices in the receiving room. Pausing in the doorway, he saw his uncle talking among a lively group of people. There was a short, bearded man, whom Justin guessed was Uncle Pete's missionary friend, and a Colombian couple perhaps a few years older than the twins' parents.

Silence fell abruptly as the four adults caught sight of the children. Justin eyed the visitors as they rose to their feet. The Colombian man was tall and thin, with curly, dark hair and a kind face. His wife was slightly plump. Something in her expression reminded Justin of his mother, and he liked her at once.

Uncle Pete stepped forward. "Kids, this is my friend, George Elinger. He is a missionary here in Bogota. These are his friends—"

But he never got to finish his introduction. Justin suddenly realized that Estrella hadn't followed the twins into the room. She stood frozen in the doorway, her blue eyes wide and unbelieving as she stared at the Colombian couple.

"Doña Rosa?" Her voice was hardly above a whisper.

The Colombian lady turned toward the doorway with a jerk, astonishment on her plump face. Her dark eyes widened as she exclaimed, "Estrellita (Es-tray-yee-tu)!"

Estrella was moving now. Uncle Pete and Mr. Elinger looked at each other in bewilderment as she ran across the room and threw herself into the plump lady's arms. The tall, thin man moved close, and the room erupted into a babble of laughing and crying and Spanish chatter.

As Mr. Elinger moved away to join the excited group, Uncle Pete continued his introduction to the only two who were listening. "This is Mr. and Mrs. Gutierrez, friends of Mr. Elinger. They work with the street children here in Bogota.

They have no children of their own, but have a house full of teenage girls they have adopted."

He eyed his grinning niece and nephew sharply. "Why do I get the impression you know more about our visitors than I do?"

Just then, Estrella pulled the plump, dark-haired lady across the room to where the three Parkers were standing.

"This is Doña Rosa," she said unnecessarily. "Don Eduardo is her husband... You remember them, the ones I told you about? They took me in and wanted me to be their own daughter. They didn't know it was *me* they had been asked to come here to visit. But they want me to be their daughter—even though I once ran away from them!"

She shook her head in amazement. "How ever did you find them? *I* didn't even know where they had gone!"

Justin shrugged, still hardly able to believe this new surprise himself. "We didn't! I guess God must have found them for you."

Doña Rosa obviously didn't understand a word of what was being said, but she was smiling broadly. Before Justin could move, she stepped forward and kissed him heartily on both cheeks. Then she kissed Jenny, bursting into a chatter of Spanish.

Estrella laughed at their astonished expressions. "She is thanking you for finding me—the Colombian way!"

It was a long time before all the chatter died away. But at last, Mr. Elinger and the Gutierrezes stepped out into the big entryway. Estrella hesitated as Doña Rosa waved a hand and called to her in Spanish.

Turning to the twins, she explained, "They want me to go with them tonight."

She added uncertainly, "I would like to see my new home, but I do not wish to leave you, my friends. Do you mind?"

"Of course not!" Justin assured.

Jenny added, "You go ahead, Estrella. You've probably got lots to talk about... We *will* see you again, won't we?"

"I will not let you go without saying good-bye," Estrella promised. After a quick hug, she was gone.

The guest house seemed strangely quiet with Estrella gone. "I sure wish Mom and Dad would answer the phone!" Justin told Jenny for the third time as he looked with little interest through an outdated *Popular Mechanics* magazine.

Neither paid any attention to the sound of footsteps in the hall outside the lounge. A moment later, Steve poked his head around the door and announced, "Some people here to see you, kids!"

The door swung open, and the twins jumped to their feet, the magazine falling unnoticed to the floor. "Mom! Dad!" they yelled together.

It was several minutes before Justin or Jenny even noticed Mr. Bascom standing patiently by the door. Mr. Parker was finally able to explain. "We got home from our camping trip last night and called the embassy here right away. We were ... well, to put it mildly, we were upset when we heard you were missing. We caught the first flight to Bogota."

He paused, and Mrs. Parker went on. "Mr. Bascom had given us his number to call when we arrived. By the time we got here, he had heard from Steve that you were all safe. We called him from the airport, and he picked us up and brought us here."

A short time later, Justin and Jenny were squeezed in between their parents on the sofa. Mrs. Parker gasped in horror as they poured out the adventures of the last two weeks; Uncle Pete occasionally added a comment in his deep voice. Already, the fear and anger and hurt of the last hours were fading into exciting memories.

▼▼▼

It was very late before any of the Parkers got to sleep that night, but they were all up and at the airport early the next morning. Mr. Bascom had booked them on the first flight back to Seattle, with a brief stop at Miami. This time, Justin appreciated the feeling of security as he watched the soldiers make their rounds of the airport and search through every inch of their bags.

Estrella and her new parents arrived at the airport just in time to see them off. Her delicate features were alive with happiness as she told the twins, "I love my new home and Mama Rosa and Papa Eduardo. Remember that I told you they were moving to find a new job? It was then that they met this man, George Elinger. He was helping the 'gamines,' the street children. Now they work with him."

She added with a smile, "There are four other girls living with us. They are very nice. Now I have sisters! But I will not forget that you two were my first true friends. You have taught me much. This time I will listen when Doña Rosa talks to me about God and forgiveness."

Turning to Justin, she said shyly, "Thank you for finding out about my father. Steve told me that it was your idea. Now I can remember him with love."

"Justin! Jenny!" the twins' father called out, motioning impatiently. The loudspeaker had ordered the passengers to pass through the final checkpoint. Estrella threw her arms around Justin and Jenny and hugged them fiercely.

"I'll never forget you—*never!*" she said passionately. She turned without another word and was gone.

The final call came to board Flight 908 for Miami. Picking up his briefcase as the line of passengers began filing down the long, narrow corridor that connected the waiting area to the Avianca 747, Uncle Pete looked down at the twins.

"Well, kids, our trip is about over. I guess the rest of this summer is going to seem pretty quiet."

"I'm not so sure about that," Mr. Parker interrupted as he handed over their tickets. "I've got some plans of my own!"

He grinned down at his son and daughter. "Remember that I told you we'd finished that Boeing project earlier than I expected? Well, I think it's time for a real family vacation. I've had an invitation to visit a friend of mine on an Indian reservation in Montana. Are you interested?"

The sudden excitement on their faces was all the answer he needed. He turned to his brother as they filed onto the big plane.

"Speaking of that friend of mine, do you think you'd have time for a brief stop in Montana too? There are some strange things going on out there with that mineral prospecting operation I told you about..."

Justin's ears pricked up immediately. As he slung his handbag into the overhead rack and found a seat beside his father, he had a sudden feeling that his summer adventures weren't yet over.

Jenny was sandwiched between Uncle Pete and Mrs. Parker across the aisle. She was busily chattering to her mother as though she hadn't seen her in months. As the big jet lifted from the runway, Mr. Parker looked down at his son.

"You've gone through some frightening times in the last couple of weeks, Justin," he commented. His blue-green eyes that were so like Justin's twinkled as he continued. "I'll bet you kind of wish now that you'd settled for that dull summer vacation you were expecting."

"It *was* pretty scary sometimes," Justin admitted. "But I'm glad I came."

Justin's mind filled with sudden memories. Pedro, their little Quechua Indian friend from the Bolivian highlands, open-mouthed as he saw the power of God rescue the twins

from the cursed Cave of the Inca Re. Mike, the young narcotics agent, his bitterness gone as he watched God answer
prayer and bring the drug dealers to justice.

And then there was Estrella, the unhappy young guerrilla girl who had become such a special friend. She was unhappy no longer! He'd never forget her—or any of them!

He shook his head vigorously. "Yeah, I'm glad I came. I
wouldn't have missed these last two weeks for anything!"